Praise for Jenifer l ... es

Cold Coast

"Brie is so likable and the plot so involving, it's not surprising this series has won several awards."

—Mary Ann Grossmann
St. Paul Pioneer Press

"This engaging police procedural vividly captures the Maine background. . . . The eccentric Mainers add depth to a fabulous step by step investigation."

—*Midwest Book Review*

"*Cold Coast* is superbly written. The characters are easy to follow and well-developed. . . . Brie is a strong female protagonist but in an endearing way, not the stereotypical hard-nosed female law enforcement officer. The descriptions of the harbor and the coast are exceptionally vivid . . . 5 Stars—excellent read!"

—*Reader Views*

"Tense . . . keeps the reader guessing until the final outcome . . . full of wonderful descriptions of life on a sailing vessel."

—Patricia Reid

Danger Sector

"Intelligent and well-written. . . . The strong, smart protagonist is Minneapolis homicide detective Brie Beaumont . . . Sailors will enjoy LeClair's vivid depictions of navigation and sailing, and those who don't know a jib from a halyard get help from a glossary of sailing terms at the end of the book, [but] LeClair never lets the nautical stuff get in the way of her exciting story."

—*St. Paul Pioneer Press*

"If you love sailing, grab this title and prepare to be immersed. . . . A strong sense of place and a fine little closed-room drama make this seafaring read a real pleasure."

—*Library Journal*

"Recommend this agreeable mixture of adventure and crime."

—*Booklist*

"There is something compelling about the sea, particularly when it claims a murder victim. LeClair weaves a yarn that draws in the reader from the first page."

—*Midwest Book Review*

"LeClair combines police procedure, finely-honed investigative skills, psychological insights, and suspense . . . in this haunting story of unrequited love, deceit, and murder [that] involves all five senses. A creative imagination, a love for sailing, and gifted communication skills combine to make Jenifer LeClair a top-notch storyteller."

—*Reader Views*

Rigged for Murder

"A winning combination of psychological thriller, police procedural, and action adventure. It's a five-star launch for [LeClair's] aptly named sea-going series. . . . Tightly written and intricately constructed, LeClair's *Rigged for Murder* is first-class storytelling in a setting so authentic you can hear the ocean's roar and taste the salt from the sea."

—*Mysterious Reviews*

"An engaging New England whodunit. . . . With a strong support cast including the capable crew, the battling passengers, and the eccentric islanders to add depth, fans will enjoy *Rigged for Murder*."

—*Midwest Book Review*

"Brie [Beaumont] is smart and competent, and she uses her brain and not her gun . . . Jenifer LeClair offers another appealing main character in *Rigged for Murder*, first in her Windjammer Series."

—*St. Paul Pioneer Press*

"A strong plot, non-stop action, and first-class character development combine to make this an exciting, page-turning adventure novel. Adding to the tension, intrigue and mystery is the meticulous care in researching the details and terminology of sailing, lobstering, and the Maine coastal islands and communities . . . I have added Jenifer LeClair to my list of 'must read' authors."

—*Reader Views*

"A debut mystery that is so well written you'll hunger for more . . . well-developed characters, and superbly good writing."

—Once Upon a Crime Mystery Bookstore

"The story develops logically, with interesting twists . . . The setting and the weather are well-handled and provide strong context without obtrusiveness. The characters have depth and movement . . . LeClair gets the sea and the sailing just right."

—*Books 'n' Bytes*

"*Rigged for Murder* is a fast-paced story which rings true both aboard and ashore on island communities. The characters are real, the situations are downright scary, the tension is palpable."

—John Foss, Master/owner,
Schooner *American Eagle*, Rockland, Maine

ALSO BY JENIFER LECLAIR

Death in the Blood Moon

Dead Astern

Cold Coast

Danger Sector

Rigged for Murder

APPARITION ISLAND

JENIFER LECLAIR

FOG HARBOR PRESS
St. Paul, Minnesota

Fog Harbor Press
4411 Wood Duck Drive
St. Paul, Minnesota 55127

Cover Design: Linda Boulanger; Telltale Cover Designs

Library of Congress Control Number: 2014958528

LeClair, Jenifer.
Apparition Island: a novel / by Jenifer LeClair – 2nd edition

ISBN: 978-1-7336084-2-8

10 9 8 7 6 5 4 3

Printed in the United States of America

For my dear friend Jeanette Brown.

What a journey we've had!

For your reference, the author has included a glossary of sailing terms in the back of the book.

"So do we pass the ghosts that haunt us later in our lives; they sit undramatically by the roadside like poor beggars, and we see them only from the corners of our eyes, if we see them at all. The idea that they have been waiting there for us rarely crosses our minds. Yet they do wait, and when we have passed, they gather up their bundles of memory and fall in behind, treading in our footsteps and catching up, little by little."

—Stephen King, *The Dark Tower*

APPARITION ISLAND

Prologue

Apparition Island, Maine
August 31, 1958

Blythe Danes sat at the Art Deco dressing table wearing a black silk slip. Behind her, sheer white curtains moved like ghosts on the warm breeze blowing through the open French doors. The air carried the sweet tang of the sea on its breath. Her bedroom suite at the back of the summer house faced the ocean, and from the balcony she could hear the calls of seabirds and the crack of waves on the face of the cliffs. But twilight had given way to night with its forest sounds of owl and cricket. She heard a muffled scrape outside; the long, dry fingers of a dead branch reaching for the back of the house. The thought of a ladder placed there never occurred to her.

She turned back to the large round mirror. It showed the reflection of a woman she little understood—a woman whose beauty far outstripped any sense of certitude, self-confidence, or happiness. She studied the dark hair and eyes, the wide mouth, the long graceful neck, and for a fleeting moment she wondered if either of them—her husband or Douglas—would love her without all those fair attributes. She wondered if either of them really loved *her*.

She had worked one silk stocking up and hooked the garters. The other lay across her thigh, and as she picked it up and bent forward, she saw him in the mirror, standing just beyond the French doors. It gave her heart a jolt. She hadn't expected such an entrance. He was like a god standing there just then, and he took her breath away. But something was different tonight—a confidence, an aura of danger. She shivered, feeling a current of visceral pleasure run through her. She was suddenly glad she was only half dressed—that he had taken her by surprise—caught her unawares. It heightened the excitement. If this was to be their last night together, it should begin like this.

He came across the room and took the silk stocking from her and draped it over his shoulder. He picked her up as though she weighed nothing and carried her to the four-poster bed where they'd made love so often that summer. She studied his profile, knowing he must be deeply hurt. He had asked her to stay on the island, become his wife and a mother to his children. She had said, "No."

He laid her on a silk Chinese quilt of vibrant red that bristled with gold dragons—a memento of her honeymoon trip to Europe and the Far East. He knelt on the bed before her and spread her legs and, sitting back on his heels, took the knife from his belt and slid the cold steel up the inside of her thigh and under the black lace of her panties and slit them in one smooth movement. She shivered in anticipation of what was to come. He dragged the blade across her stomach, slit the other side, and pulled the panties from under her. He slipped them in his shirt pocket and then brought the hard rounded hilt of the knife down between her legs, feeling for her special spot. Blythe gasped when he found it. This was a different man tonight. A man who knew what he wanted and was taking it, and the thought of what was happening thrilled her to her core.

He worked the knife hilt in a slow, almost ritualistic way as her breathing became more ragged. Finally she reached up under his shirt, dug her fingers into his back and whispered, "Harder. Please. Please."

Douglas sat back on his heels and looked down at her in the moonlight. The expression on his face was unreadable, and something in it made her slightly nervous. But he started with the knife hilt again. Harder this time. He watched as she arched and writhed with pleasure. Then he was inside her, and she thought she would lose her mind. He'd never been like this before. Always the polite lover.

He took the silk stocking off his shoulder and, brushing it across the swell of her breasts, coiled it around her neck. He must have seen the alarm in her eyes because he whispered, "Trust me, it will increase the pleasure."

Blythe's eyes widened with wonder and desire. Waves of pleasure rippled through her as he slowly tightened the stocking. She had to struggle to breathe, but she didn't care. She'd never experienced anything like this. She decided in that moment that she couldn't leave him—that she would stay here on the island, that she would be a mother to his children. But then she was really struggling to breathe. She gripped his hand to tell him to stop. But he didn't stop. He tightened the stocking, and now she saw the terrible truth in his eyes. She struggled as he pumped harder, and just before she lost consciousness, she heard him say "Goodbye, Blythe." But it was not the voice of the man she had known.

Douglas lifted her body over his shoulder and carried it to the balcony. A lobsterman by trade, he was powerfully built, and strength and balance were byproducts of his life on the sea. He swung a leg over the railing and onto the ladder and, with his arm around Blythe's body, climbed to the ground. Once he thought he felt a faint heartbeat—heard a faint breath, but he knew that was his mind playing tricks on him. She was gone, and already the first cold fingers of regret had wrapped themselves around his heart.

He started down a trail behind the summer house that would bring him to the shore. He and Blythe had used the trail often that summer to bring a picnic down to the water's edge. At the base of the cliff he slid her scantily-clad body face down into the ocean. The water was deep here, and the tide was going out. The sea would take her now.

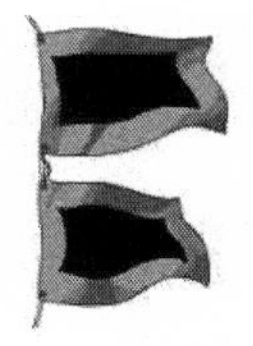

Storm Warning

The Gulf of Maine
Friday, September 13th
Present Day

Hurricane Ivan rampaged toward the coast of Maine with all the vengeance of a pillaging Visigoth. Weather forecasters had already dubbed the storm Ivan the Terrible.

Born off the coast of Africa, the tropical depression had wheeled across the southern Atlantic, morphing into a Category 3 hurricane, fortuitously named Ivan. Ivan had ramped up to Cat 4 as it turned and steamed for the Caribbean. Greater in size than the state of Texas, the massive weather system took no prisoners as it waged war over the islands of Jamaica, Haiti, and Cuba, flattening towns and destroying plantations, before it tracked across the Bahamas.

Ivan shunned the Florida coast, headed north, and savaged South Carolina's Lowcountry. Then, weakened to a Category 2, the storm retreated back to sea and battled its way over Bermuda. Finally, Hurricane Ivan set its sights on New England. But when it ricocheted off Cape Cod, everyone thought they'd seen the last of Ivan's terrible destructive power.

But the weather gods weren't done. Out in the Atlantic, Ivan was regrouping and intensifying. The coast of Maine was now in its crosshairs.

Chapter 1

The *Maine Wind* fought its way upwind in a race to outrun Hurricane Ivan. There was no actual escape, just the need to find a hurricane hole, drop the biggest anchor possible, and ride it out. Ahead of schedule and whirling in from the Atlantic like an insane dervish, Ivan's long arms reached greedily for the Maine coast and its islands. Hurricane flags stood out straight, blood red against a coal dark sky. The hurricane warning flag with its black square on a field of red—like death at the center of chaos—was an apt symbol for Ivan's malignant fury.

Aboard the *Maine Wind,* dories had been taken down from the davits and secured on deck. The hatches and companionways were battened down, and anything that could take flight had been stowed. With the danger of breaking seas, it was crew only on deck.

Brie Beaumont took up the slack in the line as First Mate Scott Hogan sheeted in the jib. She ran the line around the belaying pin in a figure eight and made it off with a slipped hitch. She kept her back to windward, protecting her face from the sting of salt spray and bite of the wind. They were flying a storm jib and deeply reefed main and foresails, and they were on a heading due east, making for Apparition Island, whose harbor, they hoped, would keep them safe from the direct force of the hurricane. She turned and looked aft. The captain was signaling for one of the mates.

"You go, Brie," Scott said. "I need to check the reefing."

Brie tightened the hood on her foul-weather suit and headed aft to see what the captain needed. The whistle bungeed to her inflatable PFD, or personal flotation device, whipped wildly about, letting out shrill little peeps as it caught the wind. As she made her way along the lee deck, seas exploded through the scuppers and washed over her boots. She leaned at an acute angle to the pitch of the deck to steady herself.

Captain John DuLac stood at the helm, feet spread for balance, steering the ship. His foul-weather gear was rust orange, and the bill of a blue ball cap stuck out from under his hood and helped keep the rain from his eyes.

The wind hummed through the rigging and roared along the canvas sails, and when Brie got to the helm, she leaned in close to get the captain's orders.

"We need to change the chart. Go below to my cabin. The charts are on my table. Grab the one nearest to the rail."

"Aye, Cap'n." Brie headed down the companionway across from the wheel and, at the foot of the ladder, stepped into the captain's cabin. She closed the door and stood for a moment out of the roar of the wind. "What's that wonderful noise?" she said to herself. "Ah, yes, silence." But while the wind was silenced below decks, the ship itself hummed with a symphony of creaks and groans, as every wood surface flexed under the pressure of the surrounding ocean. The *Maine Wind* was a sea-kindly vessel—comfortable in rough weather—and as the big schooner reshaped the seas around her hull, in a game of give and take, she was shaped by them as well.

Brie stepped over to the chart table. The captain's cabin was a part of the ship that held a special fondness for her. She didn't linger, though, but collected the chart and headed topside. She'd been aboard the *Maine Wind* for four months now, and just when she thought she'd seen the worst of conditions, some new agglomeration of weather came along and claimed the title.

A homicide detective with the Minneapolis Police Department, Brie had taken a leave from her job after a year of battling a particularly crippling case of Post-traumatic Stress Disorder that had followed her own shooting and the death of her partner Phil. Her dad's folks were Mainers, and her grandma, Nellie Beaumont, still lived in Cherryfield, Maine, so Maine had seemed like the right place to heal. And Brie loved the sea and sailing. If she had believed in past lives, as her friend Ariel did, she would have guessed she'd been a mariner in another time, so great was her affinity for the sea—so deep the spell it cast over her heart. And so it was not much of a surprise when, through a series of unexpected events in May, she had ended up as second mate aboard the *Maine Wind*. She'd been a Great Lakes sailor and had the skill set to do the job. And the simplicity and anonymity of life aboard had been a panacea for the flashbacks and nightmares that plagued her.

John's brown eyes shifted from the horizon to her as she came topside. She felt a warmth in her chest that his gaze always ignited. She held up the chart and crossed in front of the helm. She unlatched the Plexiglas holder on top of the cuddy, slipped the old chart out, rolled it up, and placed it in the cuddy that held the radio and navigation equipment. Then she slid the new chart under the glass and latched it down, swept an arm across the wet Plexiglas, and studied the chart.

Apparition Island lay northeast of their position. A second smaller island—Shadow Island—lay just west of Apparition, separated from it by a narrow gut of water. Brie judged the distance across the chart, knowing that each inch equaled approximately one nautical mile. She looked at the GPS display and noted they were sailing at 10 knots.

She stepped close to John. "Looks like we're about an hour out," she shouted over the wind.

"We should get the hook down before the worst of it hits."

"How's the bottom where we're anchoring?"

"Nice and soft. We'll drop both anchors. We should stick just fine. It's as good a hurricane hole as we're going to find. Ghost Cove is on the west side of the island."

"If Ivan continues its track, that'll put us in the lee of the island," Brie said.

"That's right. But we'll keep a weather eye, and we'll be on anchor watch overnight. We should ride it out."

The radio came to life with the Coast Guard issuing hurricane warnings for the coast and giving the height of the seas.

"I should get back to the bow," Brie said. "Would you like some hot coffee, Captain?"

"I'm fine," John said.

Brie reached in the cuddy for a set of binoculars and hung them around her neck. She pulled a pair of waterproof gloves from the pocket of her foul-weather jacket and put them on, snugged her hood down over the ball cap she had on, and headed forward to stand watch with Scott.

As she approached the galley companionway, a wonderful aroma wafted from the stovepipe atop the cabin. George Dupopolis, the ship's cook, was down in his galley, braving the rise and fall of the seas. He had told Brie that by this point in the season he was so acclimated to the motion that it never bothered him. In seas like these, he did wear motion sickness bracelets that were available to everyone aboard, but other than that, he soldiered on during rough weather days, turning out his usual amazing meals.

She knew most of the passengers would be lying in their berths, staying horizontal to the motion of the seas. It was the only way to keep from feeling seasick below deck. Sailing back from a cup race in Gloucester, Massachusetts, they had planned to make homeport before the storm hit, but bad weather and high seas on their way up the coast had delayed them.

The rain started down again. It had come and gone over the past couple of hours, but Brie knew it would only get heavier as Ivan advanced. She worked her way forward and took up her post next to Scott. They were taking spray over the bow, along with the occasional boarding sea, but conditions were deteriorating. The gale force wind whistled and sang through the rigging, working its way up and down the scale, looking for that one baleful note that would best announce Hurricane Ivan's deadly arrival.

Chapter 2

Brie stood in the starboard bow opposite Scott. In this kind of weather, these seas, the captain had limited visibility from the helm, eighty-some feet aft of them. Hence the need for crew standing watch.

The seas were piling up, and Coast Guard storm warnings had them running four to six meters. When the sea is really rolling, it makes for quite a ride up in the bow of the ship, and Brie could see Scott was feeling it too. Occasionally he turned to look at her—a look that was half concern, half exhilaration. His green eyes were the color of ripe limes, and Brie momentarily contemplated the pleasures of a margarita in hand and a sunny deck chair somewhere in the Caribbean. But her daydream was fleeting. Truth be told, Brie wouldn't have swapped this deck for any other. There was a part of her that liked life on the edge, and Maine was a place of many moods—sun, rain, fog, wind, cold, hot. Heartbreaking, mind-bending sunsets, and frenzied sunrises that often forewarned of trouble in the wind.

She reached under her hood and scratched the base of her neck. She'd worked her long blonde hair into a braid that morning, and some little patch of hair was too tight. She tugged at the base of the braid, brought it over her shoulder, and had just zipped her rain jacket back up when a strong gust blew the foamy top off a wave and sent it over the bow. She turned to look at Scott. His neatly trimmed red beard glistened with spray. He'd grown the beard during the current sailing season, and today, Brie envied him that cozy face covering.

She leaned over and Scott leaned in. "I studied the chart when I went aft. Looks like we're about an hour out."

"If Ivan continues its current track and speed, we should be able to get on the hook and hunker down before he plows over us."

"I hope you're right," Brie said. "Ivan's been the poster boy for unpredictable. Two days ago all the weather gurus had it heading out to sea."

Brie heard a sound behind them, and they both turned to see what it was. George had just slid the forward hatch closed and was making his way toward them with surprising sure-footedness. Working below deck made for good sea legs. He had a small basket tucked under his left arm, leaving one hand for the ship—every sailor's mantra and imperative in these conditions.

George edged around the large windlass that held the anchor chain and came up behind them. "Thought you might like some hot soup. Wind's a cold-edged knife today. Cuts right through you."

George had put the soup in coffee mugs—his clever delivery system for all hot liquids on an unsteady deck.

"George, you're a true blue friend," Brie said. She and Scott steadied him as he fished out the mugs.

George spoke over the wind. "Actually, blue was the color I was worried I'd see if I didn't get some hot liquids into you folks up here on deck."

"Thanks, George."

"When do we make our anchorage? Either of you know?"

"About an hour," Brie said.

"Good. It'll be nice to finish the dinner on a level deck. I'll see you two later. I need to get this last mug back to the captain."

"Later, George," Scott said.

Brie balanced on the sloping deck and dug into her soup. It was chicken noodle with nice chunks of carrot, celery, and onion, and it had a hint of lemon. There was always a secret ingredient in George's cooking—something that made it stand out from the crowd. Brie hadn't realized how cold she was till the hot soup hit her stomach and sent a wave of warmth through her body. She'd been so focused on the watch and keeping her balance on an unsteady deck that she hadn't noticed the cold insidiously creeping through her foul-weather gear and layers of clothing. She'd had a close call with hypothermia a month ago while working a case with the Maine State Police and had acquired a healthy respect for how stealthily the cold can creep up on one and how quickly hypothermia can become fatal.

She turned and looked aft. George stood next to the captain at the helm, his body listing forward as if his shoes might be nailed to the deck. After the last four months of living together aboard the *Maine Wind*, George and Scott felt like brothers to her. And Captain John DuLac? Well, that was another story entirely. In this high-adventure setting, it sometimes felt a bit like a romance novel playing out, except for the fact that, from a relationship standpoint, John was the most real thing that had ever happened to her.

George came back to collect their mugs before going below to the galley, and Brie noticed the captain had turned down the soup.

"I guess the helmsman doesn't get to eat," she said over the wind.

George leaned in. "You know the captain. It's strictly business in these seas."

George headed for the companionway, and Brie and Scott maintained their watch. The top of Apparition Island had been just visible through the gloom when she had changed out the chart, but as they steered their course, it gradually loomed larger on the horizon. It was a tall island with high sheer cliffs to the east. With Ivan's current track, that side of the island would be hit first. By then, they planned to be anchored on the opposite side in Ghost Cove.

They held their course for another thirty-five minutes, and by then the wind had dropped and the seas had grown a bit calmer—effects of the large island lying upwind of them in the distance. Brie leaned toward Scott. "What's the plan for approach?"

"I think the captain will steer the ship into the lee of the island, lower sail and the yawl boat, and we'll bring her in under power."

Brie could just make out a few houses along the shoreline. A couple of them looked imposing. Summer cottages of the well-heeled. She brought the binoculars up for a closer look at the terrain and scanned along the shore. The glasses caught something floating in the water quite a ways off the island. She moved them back and forth, looking for what she'd just seen, scanning the waters southeast of the island.

All of a sudden she froze. "Man overboard!" she shouted to Scott. Her arm shot out straight to mark the bearing. "Forty degrees to starboard."

Scott whipped his glasses up and focused in. He turned and hollered aft. "Man overboard. Man overboard. Zero-four-zero off the starboard bow."

The captain was already correcting course, bringing the bow onto the heading Brie's extended arm indicated. Brie brought the glasses up again for several long seconds. "He's floating facedown," she said. "Not a good sign."

She heard the captain transmitting a message to the Coast Guard.

"Mayday Mayday Mayday. This is *Maine Wind, Maine Wind, Maine Wind*. Apparition Island bears zero-one-five degrees magnetic. Distance two miles. We have sighted a man overboard, floating facedown. We are bearing off course to attempt recovery. *Maine Wind,* over."

The captain waited a moment and repeated the transmission. "I say again Mayday Mayday Mayday . . ."

"Brie, you keep watch and direct the captain. I'm going below to get on my wetsuit," Scott said.

She turned and saw the captain step to the aft companionway. "All able hands on deck," he shouted. "Step lively, now."

Brie heard the same order given by Scott to the forward compartment. The Coast Guard came over the radio now, but from her position in the bow she couldn't make out the message.

In moments George appeared on deck in his foul-weather gear and reported to the captain. George headed forward and got the Lifesling at the ready on the starboard side. He also got a tarp out of one of the lockers on deck.

Brie continued her man overboard watch from the bow, and when she glanced aft, she could see the captain had his binoculars on the body intermittently as he steered the ship on an intersecting course. She lifted her glasses again, and now she could see a fan of dark hair around the head. She guessed the victim was a woman.

George made his way to the bow. "The captain wants you to report back to him, and I'll take over here."

Brie gave him her binoculars and made sure he had a bead on the body before she headed aft, then made her way to the stern to talk to the captain. He had steered the ship from a beam reach onto a starboard tack, and the deck pitched steeply now.

When she got to the helm, she leaned in. "What's the plan, Captain?" she shouted.

"The Coast Guard doesn't have any boats nearby. They're all responding to distress calls. They advised us to attempt recovery if we can do so without endangering our vessel. We're to report back to them."

"So what's our plan for approach?" Brie asked.

"I'm going to try to steer the ship up near the body and then turn upwind. If I can't get close enough, I'll use the quick stop method to circle around and come up near the body. I need to stay at the helm. Scott will go in the water with the Lifesling to recover the victim. You need to organize the passengers to haul the victim and Scott in when the time comes."

"Aye, Captain," Brie said.

"It's George's job to keep eyes on the body from the bow, but as soon as Scott is in the water, George will come back and help you on the lines."

Several able-bodied male and female passengers had come on deck in their rain gear. The captain directed them to the port side of the ship so he'd have a clear view to starboard. Scott came back on deck wearing his wet suit and PFD and carrying goggles and a pair of swim fins that would help propel him through the water if he had to swim very far to the body.

Brie relayed the plan to Scott, and they headed forward to get the equipment together. She got out the boarding ladder and attached it under the starboard gunwale so it was ready to be put outboard. It would get Scott a little closer to the water so he didn't have to jump from the windward gunwale.

George continued spotting and using his arm signals from the bow. The captain would have to leave enough leeway to make the turn upwind, and Brie knew he would have to judge the distances and drift of the body carefully, because once he turned the ship upwind, it would stop dead in the water. Maneuvering a large schooner was quite different from bringing about a smaller sailboat, and in this wind and these seas, any maneuver became more difficult, more dangerous. But over the past four months, Brie had seen the captain do some amazing things at the helm.

She tied a long buoyant retrieving line to the rings on Scott's PFD and secured the other end of it to the ship, then did the same with the line attached to the Lifesling. She headed aft, brought the passengers forward and gave them their directions, dividing them into two groups—one assigned to haul in the body and the other to haul in Scott. She positioned them far enough to port so they didn't obstruct the captain's sightline. Rain started down hard, and she could feel the tension on deck, thick as the atmosphere overhead.

They were close now—within 50 yards of the body. The captain spun the wheel, and the *Maine Wind* started to move upwind. He corrected the wheel at just the right moment so the ship would stop dead into the wind. The big sails began to luff, and Brie and Scott lowered the peak on the foresail to de-power the sail and then got the boarding ladder over the side. Scott went over the gunwale and down the rungs and hung onto the ladder. When the *Maine Wind* stalled, he jumped, feet first, legs open like a pair of scissors. He hit the water and started swimming through the heavy seas toward the body. Brie picked up the Lifesling and coiled line and heaved them over the side. The sling dropped to the water a few feet ahead of Scott, and he towed it with him as he swam the last twenty or thirty feet.

When he reached the body, he laid the sling across the back of the victim, rolled the body over and brought the two sides of the sling under the arms and back up toward the face, so she would be pulled in head first, on her back. Scott gave the signal and the two lines of shipmates on deck started hauling, trying to keep pace so Scott and the body were towed in at the same rate. Out in the water, Scott gripped the bowline knot at the top of the Lifesling to keep himself next to the body as it was towed in.

Once they had them up to the ship, Brie told George's team to keep tension on the line attached to the sling. Scott got hold of the boarding ladder and pulled himself up and soon climbed back aboard. Brie leaned over the starboard gunwale and looked at the victim below. It was hard to tell from that angle, but she didn't think the body was very bloated. She guessed the woman hadn't been in the water very long.

They rigged the hauling line up to one of the blocks on the davits and pulled the victim up with relative ease. Brie and Scott guided the body over the gunwale and down onto a tarp that George had spread out on the deck.

Scott thanked everyone but asked them to step away from the area so the crew could work. Most of the shipmates were happy to head back below decks or back to the stern near the captain. One or two stayed around to rubberneck but kept a respectful distance. George got the boarding ladder back aboard, and Scott sent him back to let the captain know they could get underway. From the time the captain had brought the ship to a stop upwind, the whole recovery operation had taken only twenty minutes.

As soon as the captain got the word, he had the crew reset the foresail. He spun the wheel, and the *Maine Wind* began to fall off to port and pick up the wind. He put the ship on course toward the west side of the island. Brie heard him pick up the radio handset and hail the Coast Guard.

"Pan Pan, Pan Pan, Pan Pan. This is *Maine Wind, Maine Wind, Maine Wind*. We have recovered the body of an adult female that was adrift southeast of Apparition Island. We are proceeding to Ghost Cove, where we plan to anchor. Can you send a boat to Apparition Island to pick up the victim? Over."

Brie, Scott, and George slid the tarp with the body back to a slightly sheltered spot next to the forward cabin. Brie knelt down on the deck to examine the victim. She noted the time on her watch was 4:25 p.m. The victim was a woman—late 20s to early 30s; height approximately five-foot-four; weight about 120 pounds. Her dark hair, tangled with bits of sea wrack, hung in wet strings to just below her shoulders. Her face and hands were blue from the temperature of the sea and the grip of death. From the small degree of bloating, Brie guessed she had been in the water less than twenty-four hours. She was dressed in a turtleneck shirt, denim jacket, jeans, and hiking boots.

There were no outward signs of any kind of attack. No knife or gunshot wounds. No damage to the clothing, which was completely intact, and no apparent signs of trauma, such as broken bones. But until the body dried completely, she knew certain marks could be invisible. Brie continued her inspection of the body. She checked the woman's pockets for a cell phone or something that might identify her but came up empty. She looked toward Apparition Island, wondering if the woman had come from there—wondering if they would be able to identify her. If all else failed, the medical examiner would have to attempt to identify her through dental records. He would also have to establish cause of death. The most likely cause was drowning. In their eagerness to experience the high drama of storm surges, people sometimes get too close to the sea. In 2009 a group of people had been sucked off a ledge at Acadia National Park by an unusually large wave following Hurricane Bill. One of them did not survive.

Brie knew that being near sea level during a storm is truly tempting fate. People think they can outrun the waves, but they forget that not all waves are the same size. While the ocean may appear to be coming just so far up a beach, it only takes one oversized wave to catch the observer off guard and suck that person out with it. Hence the saying *Never turn your back on the sea.*

Brie continued to kneel next to the woman. While her first instincts in such a situation were those of a homicide detective, her secondary response was always a human one. As she knelt there, she felt the same sadness she always experienced at a life ended suddenly and violently and too soon. It was this humanity that always drove Brie to want to know the why of such a death.

"Who are you, and what happened to you?" she asked quietly. "And where did you come from?" She looked off to starboard and studied the rain-cloaked shores of the island, wondering if the answer lay there. If they were able, the Coast Guard would come to collect the body and bring it back to the mainland, where it would be turned over to the Maine State Police for autopsy and identification. Once they were anchored, she planned to put in a call to Joe Wolf, the medical examiner she'd worked with in August when she had joined the Maine State Police on a homicide case in Tucker Harbor, Maine. She also planned to talk to Lieutenant Dent Fenton to see if he wanted her to do any follow-up after the body was turned over.

Brie had been deputized by the Maine State Police when she had worked the case in Tucker Harbor, and Lieutenant Fenton had been eager for her to maintain her deputy status in the event that they wanted her help on a case in the future. She was beginning to realize that it was a little harder to escape her background than she had expected. But truth be told, she had lived and breathed law enforcement for too many years to turn away when she sensed something was wrong. For Brie, the call of duty was not easily ignored, so when it came to getting involved in such situations, she was her own worst enemy.

She folded the tarp over the young woman and tucked it underneath her so the wind couldn't take it. She laid a hand on the tarp. *We'll find your people,* she thought. *And we'll find out what happened, so you can rest in peace.* She stood up and went to talk to the captain. He was steering the ship around the southern end of the island, and she could already feel the wind dropping as they made their way into the lee of the island. It was a deceptive calm, though, and it remained to be seen how they would fare once they were in Ivan's grip.

Chapter 3

Captain DuLac set the ship on a northeasterly heading, and when they reached the waters behind the island, the wind dropped considerably. With the wind out of the equation, the rain was a bit more tolerable. There were actually two islands here, lying in very close proximity, which created a small, deep harbor in between known as Ghost Cove. It was one of the best hurricane holes in the Gulf of Maine, and as he surveyed the terrain, DuLac hoped he'd made the right choice.

Apparition Island took its name from an interesting granite formation on the high cliffs that faced the open sea on the east side of the island. He planned to tell the passengers the story over dinner. It was a good one for a stormy night.

His eyes travelled forward and rested on the body under the tarp. He wondered how its presence might change the complexion of things. Brie was already involved, and if the past were any guide, she'd be more involved soon—a situation he had come to accept over the past four months. And the fact that he'd lost his heart to this sometimes quirky, sometimes overly serious, but ever-fascinating woman delighted and haunted him in equal parts. The delight was easy to deal with, but not so much the haunting. Brie was here in Maine in the most tenuous of ways. She was on leave from her work with the Minneapolis Police Department—a leave that would end in October, one month from now. Her involvement with a missing person's case in July had put her in contact with the Maine State Police and had earned her their respect. Since then she'd been asked to work another case with them—a case that very nearly cost her her life. This was some more of what haunted him. He wasn't used to caring about someone who had regular close calls with the Grim Reaper.

He saw her stand up from where she'd been surveying the victim and head aft. Even with the pitch of the deck, she moved her five-foot-seven-inch frame with a kind of athletic ease. He told himself to keep his cool no matter what was about to unfold.

"Hey, you," he said as she approached.

"Tough situation, considering the looming hurricane," Brie said. "That was a fine piece of helmsmanship, John."

"I do my best," John said. "A trait I've noted in you as well."

"Thanks," Brie said.

"Did you find any ID on the body?" He watched her blue eyes deepen with concern. They were the color of the Atlantic in September when the sun was on it.

"There's nothing on her—no phone or wallet," Brie said. "We sure didn't need this situation when we're in a race to get the anchor down. What's the word from the Coast Guard?" She had heard the static-filled call come over the radio but, from her position forward, hadn't been able to make it out.

"They expect to have a response boat headed back this way within the next hour or so. They'll have the crew divert and pick up the body."

"Good," Brie said unequivocally. "With the hurricane bearing down, we sure don't want to have to go looking for a spot on shore to bring the body."

"You think it's a drowning?" John asked.

"Maybe," Brie said. "People just don't have enough respect for the power of the sea. Thing is, there's no sign the body was submerged, so we'll have to wait for the medical examiner's findings."

John shook his head. "It's too bad."

Brie could see he had his eyes on the tarp that covered the victim.

"We lowering the yawl?" she asked, trying to draw him back from the grim reality that existed under the tarp.

"That's the plan as soon as we get a little farther north."

Just then Scott came up from below. "Should I call people on deck for lowering the yawl boat, Captain?"

"Would you, Scott? We'll need most everyone up here to work the lines."

"Aye, Captain." Scott called down the aft companionway to put the shipmates on notice and then headed forward to roust some more folks from the forward cabin. A number of the passengers who'd helped with the retrieval of the body were still on deck.

The wind was more manageable in the lee of the island, and the captain brought the ship upwind so the crew and passengers could get the sails down and lashed off to the booms. After the sails were furled, all the shipmates reported aft to man the yawl boat lines. The yawl, with its oversized diesel engine, was a beast to lower. But with all hands on deck plus the captain, they got it down to the water. Scott climbed down to the yawl and fired it up, butted it up to the stern of the *Maine Wind,* and started pushing her toward the cove where they would anchor. Brie and George went forward and unlashed the anchor. When they neared the cove, Scott cut the engine on the yawl, and as they drifted to a stop, the captain gave the order and they let go the quarter-ton starboard anchor. They laid out plenty of anchor chain so they'd stick even if it got wild, and they dropped the port anchor off the other side as a backup.

After the anchors were set, Brie went aft to report to the captain, and George went back down to his galley. Most of the passengers beat a speedy retreat back below decks.

"Should we remain topside till the Coast Guard gets here?" Brie asked.

"I think we could all stand to get out of this rain. When Scott comes back aboard, why don't you two report down to my cabin? We'll discuss the situation and the plan for this evening. The Coast Guard shouldn't be too far out. I'm sure we'll hear them when they come into the harbor."

"Sounds good," Brie said. The captain headed down to his cabin, and Brie went to the stern to see if Scott needed any help with the yawl boat. She looked down and saw that he was running extra spring lines to secure the yawl to the stern of the *Maine Wind*. "Need any help down there?" she asked.

"I'm just about done," he called up to her.

"The captain said to report to his cabin when you come back aboard. He wants to brief us on a couple things while we're waiting for the Coast Guard."

"Sounds good. Tell him I'll be there in a few minutes."

Brie headed down the aft companionway. She took off the jacket to her foul-weather gear but kept on her bib overalls, sea boots, and cap. She hung her jacket on a peg outside the captain's cabin and knocked lightly on the door.

"Come," he said.

Brie stepped into his cabin and closed the door. The ship was still now, but her equilibrium hadn't adjusted, and she could still feel the rolling motion of the seas they'd been bucking all day.

"Nice to make port," she said.

"I'll say." John turned from where he was sitting at the chart table. He was wearing the exact same gear as she was, but he'd removed his hat. His dark hair—usually thick and unruly—was plastered to his head. Under his bibs, he wore a red plaid flannel shirt that set off his brown eyes.

"The NOAA weather forecast has Ivan making landfall here around nineteen-thirty hours."

Brie looked at the ship's clock mounted above the captain's chart table in the corner. It was just past five-thirty. In a couple hours, give or take, they'd know if their decision to anchor here had been a good one or not.

He studied her for a moment from where he sat, and Brie could pretty much read his thoughts. He was trying to discern what she was feeling about the body on deck.

"Do you think she got pulled out by the storm surge?"

"Most likely scenario," Brie said. "There are no signs of trauma on the body."

John stood and walked over to her. He reached out and took hold of her braid of hair so his hand rested next to her neck. They stared into each other's eyes for a moment, and a whole silent dialogue was exchanged in those few seconds.

"The ME will have to dry the body before they know if there are any telling marks on it," Brie said.

"What do you mean by 'dry the body'?" John asked.

"At the medical examiner's office they actually have a drying room for bodies that have been in the water. Sometimes, as the water evaporates from the tissues, marks show up on the body that weren't visible at the time of recovery."

"Interesting," John said. "And after that they'll have to do an autopsy. Right?"

"That's right. I thought I'd give Joe Wolf a call. He's the medical examiner I met working with the Maine State Police on the Tucker Harbor case."

"I remember," John said. "I think you said he's Native American."

"That's right. He's of the Penobscot Nation."

"Do you think the dead woman is from the island here?"

"Considering where we found her, that would be the logical conclusion, but with the seas running the way they are and the tidal drift, who knows? If she's not from Apparition Island, it becomes harder to ID her. The ME may have to search dental records if all else fails."

Just then there was a knock on the door.

"Come," the captain said.

Scott stepped inside, and now they were the three suspendered, sea-booted musketeers.

"Is the yawl boat secured off the stern?" John asked.

"I think she'll hold," Scott said. "I ran some extra spring lines."

"Well, we're as battened down as we can get, and you two put in a long, cold day on deck. You might want to grab a little sack time. I suspect we'll be in for a long night, even as sheltered as this anchorage is."

"I thought maybe I should help George with the dinner prep," Brie said.

"George will make out fine. You go crawl in your berth and get some shut-eye," the captain said. "You too, Scott."

Just then they heard a boat motoring into the cove. "That sounds like the Coasties," John said. "Let's go topside." They headed out of the captain's cabin and donned their rain jackets.

"Ahoy, *Maine Wind*, this is the Coast Guard." They heard the hail just as they started up the ladder, single file.

The 45-foot Response Boat-Medium motored up to their starboard side. Two seamen, fore and aft, heaved their lines, and Brie and Scott caught them and made them fast.

The helmsman stepped out of the house. "Petty Officer Williams at your service," he said. All three men wore the dark blue ODU—operational dress uniform—under their PFDs, and on their heads were blue ball caps bearing the Coast Guard insignia.

"Captain John DuLac," John said, "and these are two of my crew, Scott Hogan and Brie Beaumont."

"We got a call that you recovered a body from the ocean."

"About an hour ago, southeast of the island. We spotted the victim as we were making for our anchorage here."

Williams nodded. "My two seamen will come aboard and collect the body. As soon as we have it secured, we'll radio our base, give them our ETA and ask them to contact the Maine State Police. The medical examiner will come to the base and collect the body."

DuLac lowered the boarding ladder, and the two seamen came aboard with a litter—a specially designed stretcher with basket-like sides. They loaded the woman's body onto the litter, zipped the body bag closed around her, and secured the litter's straps across the body. They helped John and Scott lift the litter up to the gunwale, and then the two men went back down the ladder to the deck of the response boat. Petty Officer Williams and the two seamen got hold of the bottom of the litter as John, Scott, and Brie worked it carefully over the side of the *Maine Wind*. The whole operation went off without a hitch. Brie and Scott heaved the lines to the seamen, and the Coast Guard pulled slowly away from their starboard side. Brie could see Petty Officer Williams on the radio, hailing their base, as the response boat motored slowly out of the harbor. They watched as the boat cleared the mouth of the harbor and began to pick up speed.

"I think I'll go find my cell phone and see if I can put that call in to Doc Wolf," Brie said. She headed forward and descended the ladder to the galley.

Her berth was tucked into a space off the back of the galley and along the portside hull of the ship. She greeted George as she came down the companionway but didn't stop to chat. She stepped through a curtain at the back of the galley and another curtain a few feet aft of there. Her sea bag was on the foot of her berth. She flipped on the small reading light over the berth, pulled her bag forward, and reached into the bottom left corner where she kept her phone. She was glad she had charged it when she'd gone ashore a couple days ago. She seldom used the phone, but when she had the opportunity, she charged it up. Occasionally, she got a call from her mom or her friend Ariel back home, but most of the time the phone sat unused in her sea bag. After working with the Maine State Police in August, though, she had upgraded to a smart phone so she'd have access to the internet should she be assigned to another case.

Brie made her way back out to the galley where George was standing in front of Old Faithful—the black cast-iron woodstove—stirring a huge pot of what smelled like some kind of rich beef stew. As she breathed in the wonderful aroma, her stomach suddenly came to life.

"That smells amazing, George," she said.

"It's got another hour or so to go, Brie. It'll smell even better by dinner."

"I don't know how that's possible," she said, and her stomach grumbled at having to wait.

George opened the feeding door on the woodstove and shoved in a couple of split logs. The stove was an Atlantic Fisherman, used by large sailing vessels in the eighteen and early nineteen hundreds. George closed the feeding door. "Gotta get the temperature up for baking the bread," he said.

"George, you're killing me. The air down here smells good enough to eat."

"Gives everyone something to look forward to on a stormy night," he said. He went back to his work, and Brie headed up the ladder. She paused below the hatch that covered the companionway, pulled up her hood, slid the hatch back, and continued up onto the deck.

The rain was misting down. Anchored as they were behind the island, there was little wind at the moment. *Calm before the storm,* she thought. She turned on her phone and waited for it to fire up. She was a bit surprised to see that she had several bars despite Ivan's bearing down on them. She brought up her call log, found Joe Wolf's number, and sent the call. On the third ring a familiar voice came across the connection.

"Joe Wolf here."

"Hi, Joe. It's Brie Beaumont."

"Brie. To what do I owe this pleasure? Are you safe ashore, I hope?"

"We're hunkered down in a hurricane hole," she said. "We just made our anchorage in Ghost Cove at Apparition Island." She pictured Wolf in her mind—the raven black hair worn in a braid that hung to his shoulder blades, and the dark, intense eyes that seemed to look right into a person and read his soul.

"So, what can I do for you? And that's not to imply that you shouldn't just call for a friendly chat occasionally."

"Well, thanks, Joe. But sadly, this is something else."

"Go ahead," he said.

"As we were making our approach to the island, we spotted a body in the water. We were able to recover it with some expert helmsmanship from the captain."

"Tell me about the victim," Joe said.

"It's a woman," Brie said. "Somewhere in her twenties or thirties. There was no ID on the body and no cell phone. And while one might assume she came from Apparition Island because she was floating near the island, with the wind and tidal flow, there's no way to be sure of that."

"Could you tell if she drowned?" Wolf asked.

"No, but the body does not appear to have been submerged, nor did it look like she'd been in the water very long."

She paused but Joe didn't say anything, so she went on. "The Coast Guard was able to send a response boat. They just collected the body and are headed back to their base at Rockland. I wanted to put you on notice in case you might be available to do the autopsy."

"As a matter of fact, I just finished with an arson/murder case I've been helping out with in Knox County."

"The Coast Guard was going to have the base get hold of the Maine State Police. I'm sure the call has gone out by now."

"I'll contact headquarters, Brie, and if the case hasn't been assigned yet, I'll head down there to pick up the body."

Brie was silent for a few seconds.

"So, do you have reason to think this is something other than a drowning?" Wolf asked.

"None whatsoever, but let me know if you find anything unexpected."

"Will do, Brie."

"Thanks, Joe. We'll be anchored here for at least twenty-four hours."

"I hope you guys picked a safe spot. Ivan looks like a force to be reckoned with."

"We should be good here. When it comes to the ship and the safety of his passengers and crew, John is cautious in the extreme."

"That's good to hear. You be safe."

"You too, Joe. And good talking to you."

Brie looked around the deck. It was completely abandoned. She guessed Scott had gone to take a nap, as the captain had urged. She headed below to her berth to do the same.

At the foot of the ladder, she pulled off her sea boots and removed the jacket and overalls to her foul-weather suit. She hung the gear on a peg at the back of the galley where it would dry, stashed her boots underneath, and headed for her berth. Back in her little cubbyhole along the hull, Brie flipped on her reading lamp, took off her ball cap, unzipped her sleeping bag, and crawled in. The heat from the galley nearby made this an extra cozy spot on cold nights. She reached up and turned off the light and snuggled down in her bag.

She could hear the rain on the deck overhead and George humming to himself out in the galley. Both nice sounds. She thought for a moment about the woman they had pulled from the sea. There'd be no cozy bed for her tonight—just the cold, sterile table of the medical examiner's autopsy suite. Brie shivered involuntarily. How terrifying it would be to be snatched away by the ocean and carried out, knowing you'd never make it back to land. Brie loved the sea, but she never made the mistake of turning her back on it. Like most everything in the physical world, duality was part of its nature. The sea could be beautiful and seductive, but in the wrong mood, it was a killer.

She turned onto her side and stretched in her bag. She felt completely drained from their long day of battling the elements. Sleep came easily.

Chapter 4

Brie awoke to the ship's bell being rung to call everyone to dinner. She kicked her way out of her bag and hopped off her berth. There was a small mirror on the partition that abutted her berth. Brie flipped on her reading light and looked at herself. She rubbed her face and eyes, trying to wake herself up. Her hair was still in a braid, sort of, but strands of it had escaped all over. It looked like a crazy mess. She grabbed her *Maine Wind* ball cap, pulled it on to cover up the situation, and headed out to the galley. When she got to the foot of the ladder, she could hear the wind up on deck—not at a roar yet, but ramping up to one.

Some passengers had already slid onto the benches behind the heavy wood table that fit the shape of the bow. The tabletop glowed gold from the hurricane lantern hung on the side of the foremast. The mast passed through the table and down through the galley sole beneath their feet, to where it was anchored to the hull of the ship. The ship's masts had each been carved from a single Sitka spruce, one hundred feet in height, harvested from the Pacific Northwest.

A few more shipmates climbed down the ladder, removed their wet raincoats and hung them at the back of the galley. Each time the hatch was slid back, a gust of wind and rain rushed down the ladder. The captain and Scott were the last to arrive.

There was room for all twelve shipmates around the table, plus the crew. John had told her that once fall arrived, the passenger manifest was always lighter since most folks favored the summer cruises. But fall and spring were the best times for great sailing and adventure, so those trips attracted a different crowd—people who were fine with the unexpected or those who were outright seeking adventure. Well, they'd gotten it on this cruise. Riding out a hurricane, even in the best of spots, was bound to warm the hearts of any thrill seekers that were aboard.

As soon as Brie arrived in the galley, there were lots of questions about the woman's body they had recovered. She wasn't sure how, but word had gone round that she was a homicide detective, and that led to more questions about where the body would be taken; did Brie know who the victim was; had she lived on the island here; and what role would the Coast Guard play, since they had picked up the body? Brie tried to answer all their questions, but she told them it would be up to the Maine State Police to identify the victim and, based on the findings of the medical examiner, to investigate the case or not.

That seemed to satisfy them. Plus they were distracted by George, who just then was dishing his amazing beef concoction into serving bowls. Brie saw lots of mushrooms, vegetables, and barley in a thick brown gravy. At the rich aroma, her stomach struck up the band. George went to the cooler and took out a large bowl of salad greens and asked Brie to put on the dressing. He went back to the stove and pulled out three loaves of homemade bread. Brie and Scott helped get the food on the table, and then they and the captain sat down with the rest of the shipmates. George sliced the crusty sourdough bread into generous portions and nestled the loaves into a cloth-lined basket, which he brought to the table with him.

It would be hard to describe the level of enthusiasm George's meals generated. For many who came aboard, his cooking was the best part of the whole experience. There's nothing like sailing all day on the North Atlantic to stir up an appetite, and what George stirred up to quell that appetite was, simply put, the best cooking in the windjammer fleet.

The stew went down the table to comments of, "This smells amazing."

"Look at that beef."

"Look at those mushrooms."

And of course, "I can't wait to taste this."

The salad went down the other side of the table, and the bread came around last. Then everyone got serious about doing their civic duty with that stew.

"What do you call this, George?" Scott asked.

"Beef, barley, mushroom stew," George said. "Seems like the right name, don't you think?"

"Savory pot of heaven would be better," one woman remarked from the far end of the table. She wore a black watch cap and red wool sweater and looked perfectly attired for a hurricane hole in the Gulf of Maine.

"Yup, that's definitely better," another hardy sailor added from his spot in the middle of the table. Bill Bacon was a burly fellow with a name that fit his physique.

Topside the wind was building, whistling around the masts and the rooftops in the village. Somewhere in the harbor or village, a hatch or door had come unglued, and Brie could hear it banging in the wind.

George's stew made a second and, in some cases, a third round. The salad was mostly consumed, and all that remained in the bread basket were a few crumbs.

"That's good work, folks," George said. "Now, time to get serious."

Brie had been smelling a wonderful lemony aroma issuing from Old Faithful.

George got up and went to the oven and pulled out two of the highest lemon meringue pies Brie had ever seen in her life.

Her heart skipped a beat, and she wasn't even sitting next to John.

"We need to fortify ourselves for Ivan, and I decided this would be the best way," George joked.

A spontaneous round of applause broke out, and George turned and did a funny little stage bow. Then he set to making the coffee while everyone sat back and talked about the storm. Brie got up to help with the coffee prep.

"So, Captain, do you know how this island got its name?" It was the woman in the red sweater. Her name was Libby Robbins, and she was a retired math teacher from upstate New York. She was also an astronomy buff, and Brie'd had a lively discussion with her about her thoughts on dark matter, or as they'd started calling it lately, dark energy.

Libby continued. "I mean . . . Apparition Island . . . Did somebody see a ghost or what?" she asked.

"I'm glad you asked, Libby," John said. "I was planning to tell the story over dinner. And with the storm bearing down, it seems like the perfect night."

George and Brie had the coffee brewing, and Brie sat back down as John started the story.

"So, how did this place get its otherworldly name?" John asked rhetorically. "Since the 1500s, ships from Europe have been fishing these waters in what is now the Gulf of Maine. And there have been settlements on some of the larger islands since those times. But not on this island. Early mariners sailing west from Europe into these waters always gave this place a wide berth. From out at sea, on foggy or stormy days, the gray granite of the island would disappear—simply melt into the surrounding atmosphere of sea and sky—and the image of a woman in a flowing white dress would appear to float in the air where the island should have been. Now, as you may or may not know, mariners are a superstitious lot by nature. Those early sailors named the place Apparition Island and simply steered clear. For over a hundred years, no one would settle here, even though there was a fine natural harbor—the one we're anchored in right now."

"So, is that how the village got the name of Ghost Cove?" Brie asked.

"It's a good possibility," John said.

"But what was the explanation for the apparition the mariners saw?" Libby Robbins asked.

Brie could see that, being a person of science, Libby needed a rational explanation.

"Well, as it turned out, there was a very unique formation of white granite on the eastern side of the island that, under certain conditions, stood out and looked exactly like what the early mariners saw—a woman in a long dress and veil. The cliffs on that side of the island are quite high, and so the figure could be seen from a long ways out at sea."

"What an interesting story," Brie said. "Let's hope Ivan sees the apparition and gives *us* a wide berth."

That got a laugh from the passengers, and John used it as a springboard for his next comments.

"So we need to talk about the hurricane that's bearing down on us. There are some protocols I'd like to go over. Then we'll eat George's wonderful pies and head for our cabins before the weather gets super crazy topside.

"First of all, if it's too windy for people to go topside and get to the galley for breakfast, the crew will bring breakfast to your cabins. I'll send Brie and Scott around to your cabins in the morning to let you know if you should stay put. All of you seem like self-sufficient folks, so hunker down with your books, knitting, and journals and enjoy the coziness of your cabins. And if anyone thinks they want extra blankets, let us know before you leave here.

"The hatches will be battened down tight overnight, so no going topside under any circumstances." John looked around to be sure everyone got the message. "This is a hurricane. Any manner of objects can potentially be airborne during such a storm, so please stay below decks. Shipmates in the forward compartment, I have a set of walkie talkies here. I'll place one of them in the passageway outside your cabins. If you have a problem in the night, call Brie. She and George sleep up here, and she'll have the other handset with her. Scott and I sleep aft, and passengers in that compartment can just knock on my cabin door if there's a problem." The captain looked around at the shipmates. "Any questions?"

Everyone seemed clear on the protocols, and there were no questions.

"How long is the storm expected to last?" Bill Bacon asked, sitting back and slipping his hands into the front pockets of his hoodie, thereby increasing his girth considerably.

"The worst of it should blow through overnight, but I'll have the crew give you the weather forecast when they come around to your cabins in the morning."

George walked over from the stove and set two carafes of coffee on the table.

"Any other questions?" the captain asked. He looked around the table. "Then let's have some of that wonderful pie, George."

George and Brie served up the pie, the coffee made the rounds, and Scott took out his guitar and played some blues as everyone ate their dessert.

Brie could hear the wind whipping itself into a frenzy. Ivan was starting to roar like the king of storms that it was. Apparently, the shipmates heard it too, because they all looked a bit anxious.

Scott must have picked up on the vibe because he put his guitar aside and said, "Well, folks, we should probably be moseying along to our cabins before the top comes off this box of Cracker Jack and we get a big, unpleasant surprise."

That was all the encouragement the passengers needed. They slid out from behind the table and bundled into their raingear, and everyone thanked George for the fantastic meal.

Scott pulled his foul-weather coat on over his bibs and lit a second hurricane lantern. He told everyone he'd go up first and open the hatch and escort the group to their companionways.

"You want any help topside?" Brie asked.

"No, you stay here and help George. I'll check the anchors and the lashings on the sails."

"I'll come topside and help with that," the captain said. He stood and put on his raincoat, and he and Scott led the way up the companionway.

When John slid back the hatch, the cold wind and cutting rain barreled down the companionway like the Furies. He and Scott climbed up on deck, followed by the shipmates. Scott battened down the hatch, and sanity was restored to the galley.

Brie got busy helping George clean up. They washed and dried the dishes, put them away, and checked to be sure there was plenty of wood for the stove. They had decided they should make a trip to the lazarette for more wood when John and Scott came back down from securing the deck. One of them must have read George's mind, because they were both carrying armloads of wood.

"Everything shipshape up there?" Brie asked.

"For now," John said, "but we'll need to keep checking on the status of things every hour to be sure the sails stay lashed down and we're not dragging our anchor. We'll work in pairs. If anyone got hurt up there, no one would know for an hour." He looked at Scott and Brie. "You two can take the first watch."

"I'd be glad to help tonight," George said. Normally the cook has no part of any nighttime watch because he's on duty nonstop from five a.m. till after dinner.

The captain considered his offer for a moment. "Well, okay, George, if you're game. Why don't you grab some sleep now? Set your clock so you're ready to stand watch with me at 2330. We'll make it a three-hour watch, and then Brie and Scott are back on."

With that settled, George looked around to be sure all his duties were done and headed for his berth, which was just forward of the galley in the bow of the ship.

John sat down with Brie and Scott and had another piece of pie before heading for his cabin in the aft compartment. When he left, Brie and Scott were just getting out the cribbage board to pass the time till they had to go topside again.

They cut the deck of cards for low card to see who would deal. Brie won the cut, and she shuffled and dealt out six cards to each of them. While she waited for Scott to discard two cards into her crib, she thought about how nice it would be to curl up with John tonight. Stormy nights aboard were always the best. People claimed all those negative ions worked like an aphrodisiac. She wasn't so sure about that, but what she did know was that, aboard a ship like the *Maine Wind,* one was much more a part of the elements, so storms were felt, not just heard.

Scott tossed two cards across the table and the round started. After they counted their hands and pegged their points, it was Scott's deal and Brie went back to her thoughts. John had wanted her to bunk in with him now that they had coupled up, but Brie had resisted, feeling that it muddied the waters too much, what with her being a member of the crew.

"You back in Minnesota?" Scott asked, seeing how distracted she was.

"No, somewhere a lot closer."

"Ahh. I get it," Scott said.

And Brie knew he did. Scott was as discerning a human being as she'd ever met. He didn't miss much. *When you live with people day to day, they get very good at reading you,* she thought. That went double for Scott and George. Plus she'd had a couple of close calls this summer, which had really brought out their male protectiveness. What was more, she knew that Scott had something of a crush on her, which he hadn't tried very hard to hide.

He fixed his green eyes on her for a few seconds, which Brie found mildly unsettling. "So, whatcha gonna do come next month, Brie?"

"I don't know, Scott. I really don't." She gave him what she knew must be a pleading look.

"Maybe you're one of those people who just doesn't like to plan ahead."

"Actually, you're right. I'm more of a one-day-at-a-time kind of person. Even more so since I was shot. For a long time after that, I saw no point in planning ahead. In fact, I found the future a pretty questionable proposition."

"That would make sense after what you went through. And you've been through more stuff this summer."

"And now here we are, facing a hurricane. Like I said, a questionable proposition. So in the words of a wise person, 'Life is uncertain; eat dessert first.'"

Scott let out a guffaw. "A philosophy made for George."

They played the next hand, and all of a sudden the wind, which had been somewhat muted, buttoned up as they were below decks, mounted to an audible roar. The huge masts shuddered, sending a physical vibration through the *Maine Wind,* and the anchor chain let out a loud metallic screech of protest as the hurricane-force winds rocked the ship and the heavy chain went taut.

"I think Ivan has just made his official entrance," Scott said.

They stopped their game and just listened, eyes cast upwards, imagining the scene unfolding above their heads. It sounded like all the hounds of hell had been let loose as the hurricane howled over the island and through the ship's standing rigging. Ivan had strengthened to a strong Category 3, which meant wind speeds topping out near 130 miles per hour.

The flames in the lanterns flickered as the wind carved its way through every crack and swirled around the galley. George's pots and pans, hung above the stove, started to vibrate and swing gently on their hooks. The ship's skin and bones—all the wood planking above, below, and around them—started to creak and groan, telling the tale of what was unfolding topside.

"Well, we're in it now," Scott said. "Good thing we were just up there and got everything secured."

"Think we'll hear if anything cuts loose?" Brie asked.

"I think we'll be the first to know."

Brie and Scott listened to the maelstrom, spellbound by the strange and haunting chorus of sounds Ivan had scored. The music of chaos. Ivan's low-pitched roar was accompanied by loud bangs and pops, dull thuds, and metallic squeals as the storm tore over the island, stripping off wood and shingles, downing trees and power lines and turning legions of innocuous objects into deadly projectiles.

Once they had decided the masts were staying up and the cabin top was staying on, Brie and Scott went back to their game of cribbage. They knew they'd have to go topside several times to make sure the sails were securely lashed and they weren't dragging their anchors. But right now they waited for the fierce leading edge of the storm to pass over.

A half hour passed, and Brie sensed a slight lessening of the wind velocity.

"You hear that, Scott?"

"I do. Let's go topside right now and do our check. I'll go up the ladder first. You stay behind me, and when we get on deck, stay close."

They pulled on their foul-weather gear and sea boots and snugged down their hoods. Brie picked up the battery-operated floodlight and followed Scott up the companionway. He paused a moment, then slid back the hatch. A deluge of water hit them, and they hurried up the last few rungs of the ladder onto the deck, and Brie slid the hatch closed. Topside, it was black as the bottom of the Mariana Trench. She stayed behind Scott as they staggered against the wind to the bow of the ship to make sure they weren't dragging the anchors. They shined the floodlight to port and starboard to check their position in relation to the lobsterboats around them. The anchors had held fast, and they headed aft to check the lashings on the sails.

The mad roar of the wind precluded any communication. The rain felt like a thousand needles on Brie's face. Tight as she had made her hood, the water still got in and ran down her neck. They weren't topside for more than five minutes, but by the time they regained the companionway and headed below, she felt completely drained. Even protected as they were on this side of the island, the mere act of standing upright against Ivan's vicious winds had sapped her energy.

"Well, that was a trip to hell," Scott said as he shook the water off his foul-weather jacket and hung it up.

"And back," Brie said. "Don't forget we made it back."

Scott walked over to the woodstove, opened the feeding door, and shoved in a couple logs. Under normal circumstances the stove was never kept burning overnight. But these were not normal circumstances. John had decided they'd stoke the stove tonight to keep the crew warm while they battled the elements.

And so it went throughout the night as they clung to their anchorage in Ghost Cove. The watch rotated and the crewmates remained vigilant of the storm, making regular pilgrimages topside to be sure everything stayed battened down. It was still dark when Brie finished her last watch and crawled into her berth. *The Maine Wind* had weathered Ivan's wrath, but she wondered how the islanders had fared and what kind of scene might greet them as the day dawned. Her last thoughts before sleep were of the young woman, her hair laced with sea wrack, nameless, blue, and cold as the Atlantic, the question of what had happened to her heavy as the atmosphere on Brie's mind.

Chapter 5

Brie woke to the sound of George moving about in the galley. It was her usual wake-up call and better than any alarm. She heard the creak of the feeding door on Old Faithful, and her nose caught the sharp tang of wood smoke in the air as George stirred the embers and stoked the stove. Brie climbed out of her berth and dressed quickly in a pair of cargo khakis and a snug-fitting, long-sleeved black tee shirt. She pulled on a pair of wool socks, stuffed her feet into her sea boots, grabbed her small toiletries bag and her rain jacket, and made for the head in the forward compartment.

"Morning, George," she mumbled as she started up the ladder.

"Morning, Brie."

It was too early for idle banter.

Up on deck the air felt unctuous and smelled of low tide. Light rain was falling, and heavy fog gripped the cove. Even the lobsterboats to port and starboard had been erased by the gray-cloaked invader, and the island was but a memory. What she could see of the deck was strewn with litter, compliments of Ivan. Pieces of debris, both natural and manmade, had sailed off the island and come to roost aboard the *Maine Wind*. She hurried below to take care of her ablutions, knowing Scott would be on deck soon to start the morning chores.

After washing up, Brie went below to drop off her toiletries and grab her *Maine Wind* ball cap. She brushed her hair into a ponytail, which she pulled through the hole in the back of the cap, and headed out into the galley.

"Been up on deck yet, George?"

"Not yet. Why?"

"Lots of debris from the storm. I'll help Scott get things shipshape up there and then come down and help with breakfast."

"No worries, Brie. I've got things in hand. Could you and Scott make the rounds and tell the shipmates that breakfast will be in the galley at the usual time?"

"Sure thing."

Brie headed up the ladder and walked aft to get the buckets and mops out of the amidships storage box that doubled as a bench for passengers to sit on. She saw Scott emerge from the aft companionway carrying a couple of small push brooms.

"Morning, Brie. Although it could be just about any time, any place." He gestured toward the fog with a hand that held one of the brooms.

"You have just entered the Twilight Zone," Brie joked.

"And it seems to be a messy place." He opened the storage box and tore two large plastic bags off a roll. "Well, let's sweep up all this debris first, and then we'll get the decks swabbed."

Brie went forward and Scott went aft, and they swept everything toward the middle of the starboard deck, where they bagged it. They moved over to the port deck and repeated the process. There was all manner of flotsam and jetsam—lots of twigs, leaves, and small branches, pieces of Styrofoam and plastic. You name it, they had it.

Brie found a couple pieces of paper plastered against the side of the forward cabin. She picked them up and studied them. One looked like a page from some kind of legal document, but there was no name on it. The other was a birth certificate for one William Abbott. She brought them back to show to Scott.

"How do you suppose these got out here?" she asked.

Scott looked toward the island, which was still invisible. "I wonder if someone lost their roof during the hurricane."

"I'll take them down to the galley where they can dry."

"We'll see about going ashore later. Maybe we can find their owner," Scott said.

Brie took the documents below, laid them on one of the tables, and headed back topside. She and Scott bagged up the rest of the trash and then lowered their buckets over the side to bring up salt water for swabbing the decks. Each bucket had a long piece of line attached—as long as the *Maine Wind's* hull was high. They traded their brooms for string mops and got busy. Twice a day, the deck got swabbed with salt water to keep the planks nice and tight.

By 0630 they had finished most of their deck chores and went below to inform the passengers that breakfast would be in the galley at the usual time—eight o'clock, or 0800.

George came topside and rang the ship's bell at exactly 0800. Nine of the twelve passengers were already on deck visiting with one another and having a first cup of coffee. At the sound of the bell, the last three shipmates soon appeared. Everyone filed down to the galley, with the crew bringing up the rear. Brie was just about to start down the ladder when her cell phone rang. She had stuck it in her pocket when she got dressed, knowing that Joe Wolf, the medical examiner, might be calling her with news on the woman they'd recovered from the ocean.

Brie stepped out of the line as she pulled the phone from the back pocket of her khakis. She walked aft, where she'd be out of earshot of the passengers. She saw John just emerging from the aft companionway and nodded to him as she took the call.

"Hey, Joe. Weather the storm?" she asked.

"Just fine. And you, Brie?"

"Yup. Our anchors held, and aside from a lot of debris blown aboard when Ivan passed over, the ship is just fine."

"Good to hear. I wanted to inform you that I collected the body of the Jane Doe yesterday and brought it to the ME's office. I've had it in the drying room since then to evaporate the water from the tissues."

"Did anything unusual show up?" Brie asked.

"I'm afraid so. It appears the victim was strangled. There are distinct finger markings on the neck that were invisible until the body dried."

"I see," Brie said. She remembered the turtleneck shirt the victim had been wearing. Even if the marks had been visible, Brie wouldn't have seen them. "So, we've probably got a homicide on our hands."

"I'm performing the autopsy this morning, and then I'll have a ruling on cause of death."

"Have you notified Lieutenant Fenton?" Brie asked.

"Just called him before calling you. I'd talked to him yesterday when I went to collect the body from the Coast Guard, so he's up to speed on your involvement in the situation. You should be getting a call from him this morning, Brie. Sounds like he wants you to do some inquiries on the island—see if we can get an ID on the vic. With the high seas from Ivan, it may be hard to get anyone out there for a couple of days."

"Well, thanks for the heads-up, Joe."

"I'm sending a picture of the victim to your cell phone. Now that the body has dried, she'll be more recognizable."

"Any idea how long she was in the water?"

"I'd say less than twenty-four hours."

"All right then. I'll wait to hear from Dent—Lieutenant Fenton—and to get your ruling on COD. And let me know if you find anything unusual, Joe."

"Will do, Brie."

They signed off, and she wondered whether she should stay topside and wait for Dent's call. With a loud growl, her stomach advised against it. She set her phone to vibrate, stuffed it in her pocket, and headed below for some breakfast.

She slid onto the bench next to Scott, and George brought her a plate of blueberry buckwheat pancakes with a side of thick cut bacon. She poured on some Maine maple syrup the color of pale amber.

The pancakes were delightfully thin, like Swedish-style pancakes, and bursting with wild Maine blueberries. The result was a pancake so moist it nearly melted in her mouth. Brie downed two cups of rich dark coffee with her pancakes and finished off breakfast by peeling and eating a large orange from the basket of fruit on the table.

John was giving the weather forecast to the passengers as she ate. "The worst of Ivan has passed over," he said. "But we may see some residual rain, wind, and fog over the next day or so. More if the storm stalls—less if it continues its track inland. We'll stay at our anchorage here today and possibly tomorrow, as the seas will be high."

"Can we go onto the island?" Bill Bacon asked.

"That will depend on the condition of things ashore," John said. "The islanders won't want us underfoot if they're dealing with a lot of storm damage. When the fog lifts, I'll row ashore and see how the village has fared."

"If anyone needs help, I'm sure some of us would be happy to lend a hand," Harry McCarthy said.

Harry was an architect from Cleveland who ran marathons. He was in his late thirties and undoubtedly the most physically fit of the passengers on this trip.

"That's a nice offer, Harry, but the folks on this island tend to be kind of insular. It's an artist's colony and a year-round lobstering community. They may not welcome even well-intended intrusion."

"Well, that's fine too." Harry shrugged noncommittally.

"Let's just play it by ear," John said. "If it looks like things are in chaos on the island, I'll let them know we're willing to help."

The breakfast gathering broke up, and several of the shipmates stayed to help George with the dishes. Brie finished the last of her coffee and headed topside.

Scott had the idea to do some knots and rope work with passengers who might be interested. Usually there was no need to come up with ways to entertain the passengers. People who sailed on the Maine windjammers were a self-sufficient lot. But Brie offered to help if he got any takers. Just then her phone vibrated. She pulled it out of her pocket and saw it was Dent Fenton from the Maine State Police. She walked aft as she answered the call.

"Hey, Lieutenant."

"Morning, Brie. Good to talk to you. We haven't spoken since the case in Tucker Harbor wrapped up."

"We sure don't want any more like that one," Brie said. "I talked to Joe Wolf this morning. He said to expect your call."

"This case of the woman you recovered yesterday—the Jane Doe—looks like it may be a homicide."

"Doc Wolf told me about the marks on her neck that appeared after he had dried the body."

"He's completing the autopsy this morning, and then we should have cause of death. Do you think she's from the island there, Brie?"

"There's a good possibility," she said. "Although with the high winds and tidal flow, it's not a given. But the island's the logical place to start."

"Will you be anchored there for a while?"

"Today for sure, and possibly tomorrow."

"Good. I want you to dust off your badge and go ashore, Brie. See what you can learn. Joe said he'd send you a picture of the dead girl you can use to make inquiries."

"I should have that by now," Brie said.

"With the high seas, we may not be able to get anyone out there for a couple of days. By then the trail can go mighty cold, as you know."

"I'm on it, Dent. I mean Lieutenant." She pictured his heavy brow bone, penetrating blue eyes, and thick thatch of brown hair, and she thought about the calm and measured way he dealt with things.

"Dent's fine, Brie. Remember, we're not all that formal. Anyway, until a couple months ago, we held the same rank—detective."

"Yeah, but that was a couple months ago. Now you're the boss."

"Don't remind me."

Brie chuckled at that. It was a position she had never wanted. She liked the nuts and bolts of investigating too much. Being the boss led to myriad other duties and a world of bureaucratic responsibilities.

"Well, I'll let you know what I find out after I go ashore and do some asking around."

"Thanks, Brie. Homicide or not, we still have to ID her, and with those marks on her neck, it's a good bet there's a killer out there."

"My thinking too, Dent."

"Watch your back, as always."

"Roger that."

She ended the call and checked to see if Joe had sent the picture. He had, and Brie studied it for a few minutes. The bloating was gone, and for the first time Brie could see exactly what the victim looked like. The sea wrack had been washed out of her dark hair, which fell away from her face. It was a lovely face. The young woman had fine symmetrical features and high cheekbones. Her mouth was a little wider than normal, but not quite Julia Roberts. Her eyes were closed, but Brie had the feeling they were blue.

The victim had a long, graceful neck, which made the presence of the red finger markings there even more shocking. Brie could tell from the position of the bruises on the neck that the woman had been attacked from the front, which might suggest that she knew the killer. Brie would have to wait for the ME's ruling, but she guessed death by strangulation was a good bet.

She closed the phone and fought to control the feelings of anger that rose up in her. One might have thought those feelings had to do with the age and gender of the victim, but that wasn't the case. Brie just simply hated the baseness and cruelty that was all too present in human nature. Whether it was one child bullying another, a man beating his wife, or a psychopath stalking his next victim, to her it was all rooted in the same dark force—man's inhumanity to man.

Over the years, plenty of cops had told her she shouldn't care so much, but Brie had never found lack of caring an effective tool in crime solving. While she was quick to admit that too much emotional involvement could cloud one's judgment, she also knew that, in the homicide business, too little caring often led to cold cases. And nothing troubled Brie more than a case gone cold.

She turned as she put the phone back in her pocket and nearly ran into John.

"Sheez, you scared me, John."

"Sorry, Brie, you seemed to be deep in thought. I didn't want to interrupt. Is there any word on the woman's body we retrieved?"

"I've just talked to Dent Fenton, and Joe Wolf sent me a picture of the body. Now that it's been dried, she'll be much more recognizable. The lieutenant wants me to ask around the island—see if I can ID her. And one more thing, John. The death is now a potential homicide." She showed him the picture with the marks on the neck.

John shook his head. "It's horrible." He stared at the image on the phone for a few more seconds. "The fog's starting to lift a bit, so we should be able to row ashore soon. We'll see what kind of havoc Ivan's visited on Ghost Cove."

"I suppose most of the island's inhabitants live in and around the village."

"More than likely. This island has a year-round lobstering community, and those guys are gonna want to live close to the harbor where their boats are."

Brie nodded. "Well, Dent told me to dust off my badge and see what I can learn. Hope you don't mind, John." She knew her involvement with a couple of cases over the summer had sometimes strained relations between them. Understandable, since she was a member of his crew, and her first responsibility was to him.

John shrugged. "Well, we're not going anywhere today. And to tell you the truth, I'm troubled by that girl's lack of ID. Her people need to know what's happened to her."

"I'm not sure flashing a badge will go over great out here."

"You're right about that, Brie. Folks on these islands don't like a lot of intrusion from the mainland—especially from the police."

"I can't very well pretend I'm not with the police."

"True." John thought for a minute. "It may not be a bad thing. At least you won't run up against the *who are you and what makes you think you can ask questions on our island* treatment."

"Yeah, we'll see about that." Brie smiled to herself. "Well, I think I'll go below and collect my badge and notebook."

"I'll have Scott help me get the dory back up on the davits so we can lower it for going ashore."

Brie walked forward and headed down the companionway. She made her way through the galley and back to her berth along the port hull. She flipped on her small reading light. Her sea bag lived at the foot of her berth. She pulled the bag forward, unzipped it, and took out her gun, shield, and ID for the Maine State Police. She was attached to the criminal investigation division of the Maine State Police and worked as a homicide detective on a case-by-case basis. She used her own weapon—a Glock 9mm that she had obtained and registered with the department after the case in Tucker Harbor last month. Her previous off-duty weapon had been lost on Granite Island in May in a bizarre turn of events.

She decided to leave her gun on board and just take her shield and ID since she was only making preliminary inquiries. Until she got the ruling on cause of death, there was nothing to investigate, and no point in alienating the natives by wearing a gun. She found her small notebook and pen and put them in her back pocket, grabbed her daypack off a peg at the foot of her berth, and started to leave, but then stopped. She picked up a box from the corner next to her berth. It contained a few supplies Dent Fenton had given her in the event she was assigned to a case. Inside were evidence envelopes, a box of latex gloves, and what cops call a bootie box that contained shoe covers. She folded a few of the envelopes in half and put them in her daypack along with a pair of booties. She pulled out a couple gloves and stuck them in the pocket of her rain jacket. *In circumstances like these, one never knows when one might come upon a crime scene,* she thought to herself. She turned off her light and headed topside.

John and Scott were in the process of lowering *Tango,* the small three-man dory they carried aboard the *Maine Wind.* John climbed down the boarding ladder, took the center thwart, and put the oarlocks in place. Brie was about to start down the ladder when she remembered the documents she had found on deck that morning when they were cleaning up.

"Hang on, John," she called down. "I forgot something."

She ran back down to the galley. George had set the papers aside, and he gave them to her. Brie rolled them up, slipped them into her daypack, and headed back up the ladder. She climbed over the port gunwale and down the ladder to the dory, where she sat in the stern.

John pulled for shore. The fog spun a gray gauze-like veil over the harbor, docks, and village so that Brie had only the vaguest idea of what was happening ashore. She could just make out the outline of the large historic inn that loomed out of the mist on the hill above the harbor. And she was aware of a number of people moving about near the shore but couldn't tell what they were doing.

"We'll stay clear of the ferry dock," John said, "although I'm sure the ferry won't be running today with the current sea conditions."

"What size ferry is it?"

"Just a small passenger ferry."

They were close enough now for Brie to spot a small stretch of beach down the shore from the ferry dock.

"How about there?" She pointed, and John paused at the oars and looked over his shoulder.

"That'll do nicely, Brie."

He headed for the small strand, and before long the dory struck the beach. John moved to the bow and jumped ashore. He pulled the dory up a bit, and Brie came forward and jumped out. They were nearly at high tide, so it was easy for John to get the dory far enough ashore to be safe from the tide.

They climbed a small embankment and made their way along a dirt road toward the village of Ghost Cove. The road ran behind shake-sided houses that lined the harbor at this end of the village. When they reached the crossroad that ran down to the ferry dock, they were greeted by a frenzy of activity. The fog in the village was still quite thick, which leant a surreal aspect to the scene. Villagers, young and old, male and female, scurried about picking up sheets of paper that were scattered everywhere. The pages were plastered to the ground and stuck in bushes. They clung to the sides of houses and buildings and to piles of lobster traps that were stacked here and there throughout the village.

"Something definitely came unglued around here," John said.

Brie now had a pretty good idea where the documents she'd found aboard the *Maine Wind* had come from.

They spotted a short, round man who seemed to be in charge of the chaos. He wore a dark green windbreaker and a pair of tan khakis. Brie grabbed John's arm and nodded in the man's direction.

"Let's go talk to him."

They made their way up to him and waited while he dealt with two people holding handfuls of soggy papers.

"Thank you for helping, Dorothy and Bob. Take everything you find to the inn. They've opened their ballroom and set up tables to dry the documents."

"Excuse me," Brie said when it was their turn. "I'm Brie Beaumont, and this is Captain John DuLac. We're from the schooner *Maine Wind*. We anchored in your harbor last night."

Something registered on the man's face—a combination of respect and excitement.

"Such a beautiful ship. I'd love to know her history, but as you can see, we're in a bit of trouble here."

"What happened?" John asked.

"The roof blew off the island archives." He nodded toward a small gray-frame building perched partway up the hill behind them. "All our records, historical documents, and newspapers have scattered to the four winds. The islanders are trying to recover as much as possible, but . . ." The man held his arms out in a helpless gesture of supplication. He looked like he wanted to cry.

"I found these aboard ship this morning when we were cleaning up." Brie handed him the documents she'd brought with her.

"Thank you, Miss. I'm sorry I forgot to give you my name. I'm Gilford Doubtwater, town manager. I'm in charge of all this." He made a desperate wave of his arm.

"Pleased to meet you, Mr. Doubtwater, and sorry for the circumstances," John said.

"You can call me Gil. Everyone does. At least the rest of the village stayed standing—that's a blessing."

Gilford Doubtwater had the girth, face, and gentle disposition of a manatee. Brie could see he was overwhelmed by the situation, and she thought his last name somehow fit the unfolding drama.

"Mr. Doubtwater—Gil. I hate to cause you any more concerns," Brie said, "but as we approached the island yesterday, we spotted a body floating in the water."

As she spoke, she could see concern rise to a fever pitch in Gil, and two bright red spots formed on his previously sallow cheeks.

"How terrible." He stopped scanning the village chaos and riveted his eyes on her.

"We were able to recover the woman's body and brought it with us to our anchorage here. The Coast Guard sent a response boat to collect the victim and take her to the mainland."

"Somebody told me they'd seen the Coast Guard in the harbor and thought they'd taken someone off your ship on a litter."

"Yes, well, now you know the sad details." Brie took out her phone, brought up the picture of the victim, and showed it to Doubtwater. "Do you recognize this woman?" she asked.

He took the phone and studied the picture carefully. "She doesn't look like anyone I know on the island. But she could easily be a tourist. We still get some of them at this time of year."

Brie nodded and put the phone away. "She had no ID on her and no cell phone."

"I may not be the best one to ask," Gil said. "I've been off island for a few weeks, visiting my children in New York and Massachusetts. I just got back to the island yesterday. And now all this . . ." He made a sweeping movement with his arm to indicate the chaos.

"You may be wondering what authority I have to be asking about the victim." Brie took out her ID and told him she was a deputy detective who worked with the Maine State Police on a case-by-case basis.

Gil's eyes moved to the shield on her belt that had become visible when she pulled out her ID.

"I'm on leave from the Minneapolis Police Department and in Maine for the season. I'm a member of the crew on the *Maine Wind,* but I've had call to work with the Maine State Police on a couple of cases."

Gil nodded like that made sense, but to Brie it sounded completely absurd. She hadn't gotten used to the strange duality her life had taken on over the summer.

She decided she'd said enough by way of explanation.

Gil Doubtwater's eyes moved to the pocket where Brie had placed her phone, and his look of concern deepened. "I'm worried the woman might have been staying on the island or be related to someone who lives here. You might ask at the Windward Inn." He nodded toward the large inn on the hill. "Or maybe the ferry dock or the general store down the way here." He gestured along the road to his left. "If she was staying on the island, someone will surely recognize her."

"Thank you, Mr. Doubtwater," Brie said, deciding she should keep a degree of formality.

"I'm sorry I can't be of more help. It's most troubling. And those marks on her neck . . . It looks like she was attacked."

Brie could read between the lines, and she realized a part of his concern must extend to the island's reputation and solidarity. But she chose not to comment on the marks—she simply didn't have enough information yet to do so.

"Thank you again, Mr. Doubtwater," she said. "I'll let you get back to the situation at hand."

"Please, call me Gil," he said again. "I hope you find out who this young woman is."

Brie nodded, and she and John stepped away from Doubtwater.

Then John seemed to remember something and turned back to the man.

"Mr. Doubtwater—Gil—do you need any extra help collecting your documents here? I'm sure some of my passengers would be happy to help."

"That's most kind of you, Captain, but I think we'll be okay."

"Well, we won't be going anywhere for a couple of days. If you change your mind, just let us know."

Brie noticed that John didn't push the issue. Like he'd told the passengers, the islanders preferred to keep to themselves, even at a time when outside help was available.

She and John walked back down the road a ways out of the fray, toward the spot where they had landed the dory.

"Do you need me, Brie? Or would you rather proceed on your own?"

"I've got this, John. You go on back to the ship. I'm gonna nose around a bit and make some inquires. Doubtwater gave me a couple places to start."

"Kind of an odd duck, don't you think?"

"Yeah, I guess. But I think it goes with the territory." Brie looked at the scene around them. "Nice enough, though. Seemed genuinely concerned about the girl."

John nodded. "I'll turn on my phone when I get back aboard. Give me a buzz when you're done. I'll row over and get you."

"Okay, pardner. You mosey along."

John planted a kiss on the side of her head and moseyed down the hill to the dory.

Chapter 6

Brie headed back in the direction of the Windward Inn and the ferry dock. Its modest name aside, the inn, high on its hill above the harbor, had the look of a grand period hotel. If the dead woman was a tourist, maybe she'd been staying there.

Brie's long blonde ponytail swung in rhythm behind her as she strode back toward the ferry dock. The fog lent an air of mystery to her surroundings, giving everything soft, nondescript edges. But even with the overcast sky and shroud of fog, the village had charm and the island itself natural beauty.

Tall hills, folded in an amphitheater-like curve, cradled the village of Ghost Cove that sat at their base. Brie guessed, this far out from the mainland, fog would be an almost daily presence, and she wondered if that was how the village had gotten its name, or if the name was connected to the story John had told the night before. A small cemetery, whose granite headstones poked their shoulders above the mist, huddled halfway up the hill that rose behind the village. On the ridge of the same hill, a white stone lighthouse stood guard, flanked by a small keeper's house with a red roof.

Brie rounded a bend in the road and came upon a *plein aire* painter at his easel, capturing the events of the day. In the scene, the villagers darted about in the fog gathering up the island's historical documents. Probably a once-in-a-lifetime occurrence, so the artist had been wise to capture the drama as it unfolded.

Gardening was obviously a preoccupation with the islanders. Flowers bloomed everywhere—from carefully terraced gardens tucked among the granite outcrops to sturdy clumps of bushes covered in showy pink and yellow blooms. The entire village had the look of an English cottage garden. Brie guessed that the maritime climate was especially conducive to the pastime.

When she got to the road that intersected hers, she went left and down the hill toward the ferry dock. She saw a building just off the dock that housed a small deli and café. As she got closer, she could make out the name on the sign above the windows—Ferry Good Deli. Brie smiled—*so clever, these Mainers,* she thought. When she got to the place, she walked up four weathered, open steps to a small deck. Right away she noticed the sign on the door of the establishment was turned to "Closed." With the ferry out of service, maybe the owner had taken a day off. Odd, considering all the villagers buzzing around, cleaning up from the storm. The potential for the coffee and sandwich business today seemed great.

She peered in the window and saw a large glass case that looked like it might usually hold pastries and sandwiches. Across from that, there were tables with heavy wood tops along a wall with windows that looked toward the sea. There was a pop cooler along the back wall. Of course, the Mainers would call it soda, but to Brie it would always be pop. Next to the cooler was a shelf unit that held tee-shirts, books, and postcards.

She turned from the door and walked back down the steps and up the road to where it branched off toward the Windward Inn. The road climbed a short, steep hill and, at the top, dead-ended in a small parking area behind the inn. There was a door with a sign over it that said "Guests Register Here." Brie walked up the granite stairs and entered the inn.

A large foyer ran toward the front of the inn and opened into a dining room that looked out over the harbor and the sea.

Brie noticed, even from where she stood next to the tall registration desk, that the dining room had a five-star view. Down the hall to her left, she heard a buzz of activity and assumed that was where the villagers were bringing the documents they had found around the island. Her suspicions were confirmed as an older man came in the door, clutching a handful of papers, and headed down that way.

As she stood staring after him, she heard someone come through a door behind the reception desk. Brie turned and saw a woman with voluminous red hair that fell in waves to well below her shoulders. She wore a long green cotton dress that showed off her slender figure and complemented her red hair. A small name tag below her left shoulder said "Mary."

"Do you have a reservation?" the woman asked. She seemed quite surprised to see Brie. With the ferry out of service, they wouldn't be expecting any new guests.

"No," Brie said. "I don't." She took out her badge and ID and explained how a detective with the Maine State Police had blown ashore on their island.

The woman listened and nodded, and Brie explained further how they had recovered the body. Then she took out her phone and showed the picture of the dead woman to Mary, watching her carefully to see if she had any immediate response —any sign of recognition, no matter how subtle.

The woman studied the image for quite a while and then handed the phone back. Brie noticed her hand was shaking as she took the phone.

"I'm sorry I don't know her," Mary said. "What happened to her . . . ?" The words seemed to catch in her throat, and she brought her hand up to her neck—a gesture that Brie found interesting, but not too surprising, considering the marks on the victim's throat.

"We're not sure yet," Brie said. "We're just trying to identify her right now."

Mary nodded. "I'm sorry I can't be of more help."

"That's all right. If she was somehow connected with the island here, we'll find the truth."

Mary nodded again and then seemed at a loss for words.

Brie thanked her and left by the back door, the way she had come.

She walked along the back of the structure and around the far corner toward the front of the inn. She stood on the hill, high above the harbor. It was a beautiful vantage point, even though a light rain had started to fall. As she stood looking out, the image of the young woman floating in the ocean—sea wrack tangled in her hair—came back to her. It was such a stark and lonely image, and in this land of fog and sea, Brie suddenly had a moment of homesickness. Oddly enough, she longed for the sub-zero crunch of snow under her boots. A sound only ever heard when the mercury plunged well below zero. Then the sky took on that signature Minnesota blue—an arctic blue, hung above a silent white world. *Did the sky in Maine ever get that exact shade of blue,* she wondered, *when this state is locked in winter's chilly embrace?*

That was the moment she knew she had to go back. If she didn't go back, she'd never know for sure if this were the right place for her or not. Some things are only seen clearly from a distance, after reflection, glimpsed in the mirror of one's heart.

She thought about her affairs back home—job, apartment, possessions. She had to take care of things—make decisions.

And it wasn't about John. Nothing had ever felt so right as John. It was about roots and geography and career. It was about pulling up stakes and starting over. Well, not completely, she had to admit. Clearly there was an opening for her here with the Maine State Police.

Still, she thought it might take a kind of pioneer courage. And yet, she'd come here when she was most at loose ends—

her back to the wall, psychologically. Hadn't that taken courage? Up till now, she'd thought of it as a lack of courage—a kind of running away. Now, she wondered.

Some things only seen clearly from a distance, in the mirror of one's heart.

"Huh," she said to herself. "Well, what do you know?" It was one of those moments of clarity—like she could see forever —accompanied by a large dose of hope.

Brie turned and walked down toward the village along the foggy dirt road, and there was a lightness in her step. *Nice to know that maybe you're not a coward,* she thought. She headed back toward the ferry dock where the road looped around toward the main street of the village and the general store that Gil Doubtwater had mentioned.

A short ways along the road she came to what seemed like the center of the village. The village folk were busy unboarding windows and collecting debris. The buildings were gray frame structures that looked as if they'd stood for many decades. The hurricane seemed to have left them no worse for wear. Brie guessed they'd faced down dozens of storms and would survive many more.

There were a couple of small shops, a tiny post office, and an unassuming inn—much smaller than the one she had just visited. She spotted the general store down on the end of the row of buildings. If the victim had been staying on the island, she'd have to have procured food, so the general store seemed the logical next stop. Brie headed toward it and stepped up onto a wood frame porch that ran along in front of the buildings, kind of like one might see in an old Wild West movie.

She paused at the door of the store and peered inside. The interior was brightly lit. There didn't appear to be anyone in the store, but then she heard noises, so she wandered in and down one of the aisles toward where the sounds were coming from.

The bread and produce were right up front, with dry goods and canned goods along the back wall and on shelves along a couple of short aisles. At the end of one aisle, Brie found a woman kneeling on the floor, stocking cans of tomatoes. She looked up as soon as Brie appeared.

"Can I help you?" she asked, stopping in midstream, a twenty-eight-ounce can of tomatoes grasped firmly in each hand. The woman had short, dove-gray hair and a devil-may-care twinkle in her blue eyes. Brie guessed she was in her fifties.

"I hope so," Brie said.

The woman put the cans on the shelf and sat back on her heels.

Brie introduced herself and showed her ID, at which the woman decided to stand up. She brushed off her jeans even though there was nothing on them.

"I'm Edie Hanover, the store owner. What's this about?" she asked. She was taller than Brie and had a low voice—not husky like a smoker's, but richly resonant, and she spoke with a slow Yankee cadence that, coupled with the soothing voice, had a calming effect.

Brie told her about the body they'd retrieved on their approach to the island yesterday. She took out her phone, brought up the picture, and handed it to Edie.

"We're trying to ID the woman. Since she was near this island, we're starting our search here."

Edie took the phone and looked at it silently. "I know her," she said. "Her name's Claire. Been on the island a few weeks, I think. Nice gal. Used to stop in most days for something. Was renting the Westburgs' camp on the south shore of the island."

Brie pulled out her notebook and started jotting down notes. "Was she vacationing here?"

"Don't know," Edie said. "Didn't ask, and she didn't say."

Brie had been around the Maine coast and its islands enough to know that this was standard operating procedure for the Mainers. They just didn't ask a lot of questions. They figured if you wanted them to know, you'd tell them.

"Do you happen to know what Claire's last name was?"

"Why, yes. It's Whitehall. Not an easy name to forget."

"Why's that?" Brie asked.

Edie shrugged. "I don't know, it's got kind of a grand sound to it, don't you think?"

Brie thought about it for a second. "Well, actually, yes it does, now that you mention it." She looked up from her notes. "So, did Ms. Whitehall seem happy, carefree, like one on vacation?"

"She was friendly. Don't know about carefree." Edie handed the phone back to Brie. "It looks like someone attacked her—those marks on her neck." Her gaze traveled to the front door of the store as if she might be wondering who in their peaceful little hamlet could have done such a thing.

"So was Ms. Whitehall here on the island alone?"

"Seemed to be," Edie said. "Never came in the store with anyone else." She dusted off her jeans again and put her hands in her back pockets, elbows akimbo.

"You said she was renting the Westburgs' camp. Any idea how I might get hold of them?"

"Well, that's easy." Edie's blue eyes twinkled. "The Westburgs own the house right next door to the camp. Just follow the trail south of the village. It'll take you out to their place."

"I suppose you grew up here—probably know everyone on the island," Brie said.

"Well, I didn't grow up here, but I've been here for five years, so I guess I know everyone by now."

"What made you move here?" Brie asked, always curious about why people choose such remote places.

"Don't know, really. When I saw the sale ad for this store, I jumped on it. It just felt like the right move."

Brie nodded, thinking about her own sudden move to Maine this summer. "I get it," she said. She pocketed her notebook. "Thank you for your help, Edie."

"Sure." She said it "shu-ah," Yankee style.

"I'd like to grab an apple and a candy bar before I go." It was strictly a goodwill gesture, since one never needed to obtain food while in George's care aboard the *Maine Wind*.

"Let me just take these to the back room, and then I'll check you out." Edie picked up what was left of the case of tomatoes. There was another case of smaller cans on the floor as well.

"Let me help you," Brie said. She picked up the other case and followed Edie to the back room.

They put the cases on a shelving unit filled with canned goods, and just then, the phone rang. Edie went to answer it, and Brie waited next to her desk, which was covered with inventory lists, adding machine tapes, and invoices from vendors. Edie greeted the person on the other end of the line and jotted down a list of groceries on a tablet with a small crest in the corner. She tore the list off, laid it with a couple others on the far side of her desk, and said "Goodbye" to her customer.

"Looks like you do deliveries," Brie said.

"For some of the older folks who can't get down to the store so easily."

"That's nice," Brie said.

"Gotta take care of our own here," Edie said.

They walked out to the front of the store, and Edie rang up an apple and a Snickers bar for Brie.

Brie tucked the goodies into her pack, thanked Edie, and headed out the door. She walked to the edge of the porch and looked south toward the end of the village. There was no reason she needed to be back at the ship, and her bloodhound detective gene was activated now that she had some kind of scent. She stepped off the porch and headed for the end of the village, hoping this trail out to the Westburgs' would be easy to find.

Chapter 7

On the outskirts of the village, Brie pulled out her phone and brought up the number for Lieutenant Dent Fenton at the Maine State Police.

He answered on the second ring. "Hello, Brie. Anything to report?"

"As a matter of fact, yes," she said. "I've got a bead on our Jane Doe."

"Was she from the island there?"

"She wasn't a permanent resident, but she'd been here for a few weeks. Her name is Claire Whitehall. I'm following up now on some info about where she was staying."

"That's good work, Brie. You've got booties and gloves with you just in case?"

"Roger that, Dent. Any sign of a crime scene, I'll step back and notify you."

"Good. Let me know what you turn up."

"Will do, Lieutenant. Any word from Doc Wolf on the death verdict yet?"

"Nothing yet, but I'll keep you posted."

With that, they ended the call.

She followed the road south of the village for a short ways, past a number of houses, and sure enough, it soon petered down to nothing more than a grassy trail. She'd forgotten to ask Edie how far it was, but it didn't really matter. When she got to the southern end of the island, she guessed she'd be near the camp Claire had been renting. Back in Minnesota it would have been called a cabin, but these small summer homes were often referred to as camps in New England.

Brie felt relieved to have some kind of handle on the young woman's identity. Maybe the camp she'd been renting would yield some clues. She hoped to learn more from the Westburgs about what Claire Whitehall was doing on the island. Brie assumed she had been vacationing, but that needed to be clarified.

No matter what the autopsy showed, they had to assume Claire had died under suspicious circumstances. Someone had attacked her, and recently. That fact alone would warrant an investigation.

The trail had narrowed some more, and the farther Brie progressed, the more she felt like a traveler in a strange and distant land. The fog grew thicker as she went, lending that air of mystery that only fog can. She passed several small houses but saw no sign of life and suspected the residents were in the village or possibly out lobstering, though the seas would be rough today.

John had told her this was a year-round lobstering community, unlike many along the coast or on the islands closer to the mainland. It required a certain kind of intrepidness, an extra degree of grit, to lobster year round. The winter brought higher seas and brutal temperatures. The lobstermen out here were a breed apart.

Brie figured she'd gone a quarter of a mile or so when she caught a glimpse of a dark green, two-story cottage, whose roof and gables would appear and disappear as the fog cast its gauzy net around them. *So far, the island is living up to its name,* she thought. She stopped on the path and could hear the sea breaking on the shore, and she wondered if the house she was glimpsing belonged to the Westburgs. As she stood looking toward it, a particularly thick patch of fog swirled around the roof, obliterating it from view. At that moment her phone vibrated. She pulled it from her back pocket and saw it was Joe Wolf, the medical examiner. She answered the call.

"Hey, Joe."

"Hi, Brie. Are you on the ship? It's hard to hear you."

"I'm on the island, Joe, following up a lead. I'll keep walking and you tell me if the reception improves."

"I'm calling with the ruling on manner and cause of death on our Jane Doe."

"I've learned her name. It's Claire Whitehall. She was staying on Apparition Island, where we're anchored."

"I can hear you better now," Wolf said.

"Good. I'll stay put till we're done talking. So what's your ruling on cause of death?"

"Well, it wasn't asphyxia from strangulation as the marks on her neck might have indicated. Nor was this a drowning."

"Really? That's a surprise. My money would have been on one or the other of those. So, what did she die from?" Brie asked.

"Massive trauma to the internal organs."

"Consistent with . . . ?" Brie waited for Doc Wolf to fill in the blanks.

"Consistent with a fall from a pretty good height," Joe said. "She had a ruptured spleen, and one of her ribs had punctured the heart. She bled to death internally."

"Huh. Well, that certainly raises some questions."

"It does, indeed."

"And the bruising on her neck? Was it recent?" Brie asked.

"I'd say she sustained those bruises no more than a few hours before she died," Wolf said.

"So, they could relate to her death?"

"They very easily could. And it's tempting to assume the marks on her neck are related to her death, but we have no proof of that since she did not die from asphyxiation. Claire Whitehall's death could be a homicide, a suicide, or even an accident, and because of that, I'll be ruling the manner of death as 'undetermined.'"

"So we're left with a quandary. She could have jumped from a cliff overlooking the ocean, she could have slipped and fallen, or she could have been pushed."

"That's right, Brie. A verdict of undetermined death creates a lot of ambiguity."

"It's not a homicide detective's favorite ruling—I'll give you that. But, in this case, it does at least eliminate some possibilities."

"Such as . . . ?"

"Well, there are only certain places on the island where she could have fallen from that kind of a height. So that at least narrows the possibilities as to the site of the death. If we can discover the location where she took the fall, it may hold some significance. Could you identify any defensive wounds?" Brie asked.

"Sadly, no. Nothing that couldn't be explained by the fall and contact with terrain on the way down."

"Any signs of sexual assault?"

"Other than the marks on the neck, there was no bruising or other signs of trauma to the body. We did a rape kit, even though she'd been in the water. We'll see what comes back on that, but most likely, her time in the salt water would have eradicated any DNA that was there. My guess is she wasn't raped, but again, there's no proof one way or the other."

"Okay, Joe. I guess we'll just have to figure this out the old fashioned way."

"What's that, Brie?"

"Hard work and clever deduction."

"Well, you're the girl for that."

"Thanks, Joe."

"Call me if I can help in any way."

"Will do."

"Walk safely."

"Thanks, Joe."

They ended the call.

Brie stood on the path for a few minutes thinking about her conversation with Joe. Her gut told her this young woman had been murdered, but she set those thoughts aside—objectivity required that she set them aside. It was way too early to speculate at all. Her first job was to find out who Claire Whitehall was and what she was doing on Apparition Island. Was she simply vacationing, or was she here for some other reason? Did she know someone on the island, or had she come to an anonymous place to end her life? Had she simply met with an untimely accident, or had she met up with the wrong person—someone bent on her destruction?

Brie stuck her phone in her back pocket and continued along the trail toward the cottage with the gabled roof. Within about fifty yards, another path intersected the one she was on. The new path veered off to the left, or southeast, and she took it, knowing the house she'd glimpsed lay in that direction. The sounds of the ocean were getting louder, and within a few minutes, the trail bent right and came out into a clearing before a dark green house, so much the color of its surroundings it looked like it had sprouted from the forest.

Off to the left side of the house stood a small barn covered in the same cedar shakes as the house and stained the same forest green color. Brie heard the sound of a power saw coming from the open door and headed in that direction.

As she approached the barn, a woman rushed from the house with such vigor that the screen door flew back and smacked the wall. She was of Julia Child stature, and Brie wondered if there was something in the water here that the females ran to such Amazonian proportions. The woman was wearing a long, multi-colored skirt, ankle boots, and a gypsy-style blouse. Her hair was mostly gray and cut in a bob that did nothing for her square face. As she came down the steps and steamed toward Brie, she was waving a rust-colored scarf and calling, "Here I am," as if the possibility that a visitor would be there to see anyone but her simply didn't exist.

Brie waited as the woman took bold strides toward her. When she was within a few feet, Brie said, "I'm looking for the Westburgs' house."

"I'm Muriel Westburg," the woman said.

Brie took out her ID and held it up. "I'm Detective Brie Beaumont with the Maine State Police." She noted Muriel had glanced down at the shield clipped to her pants when she went for her ID.

"What's this about?" Muriel asked. She crossed her arms on her chest.

Brie noted some of the color had drained from her face. "I've been told a young woman named Claire Whitehall was renting a camp from you."

"That's right. There's a small camp on our property, just a little east of our house here, that Claire is renting. Is something wrong?"

Muriel had an odd way of tipping her head back and looking down her nose at Brie as if her superior height made her somehow all-around superior.

"I'm afraid something *is* wrong." Brie took out her phone as she spoke. "A young woman was found floating off the island yesterday, before the hurricane hit. Edie Hanover, at the general store in the village, identified her as Claire Whitehall and told me Ms. Whitehall was renting your camp." Brie brought up the picture and showed the phone to Muriel.

Muriel sucked in her breath in a silent gasp. "Oh my God . . . Walter," she screamed and pushed past Brie. "Walter, get out here. Walter, do you hear me?"

Brie followed her toward the barn, curious about Walter. She assumed Walter was Muriel's husband, and that

Muriel simply needed his support. But, as a detective, another possibility flashed through her mind as well. *Could Walter be responsible?* In the early stages of a case such as this, there's no reason to be suspicious of anyone in particular, which means there *is* reason to be suspicious of everyone in general.

Muriel stopped at the open barn door and yelled Walter's name again, but the saw kept buzzing. She huffed her shoulders and marched in, waving her scarf.

Brie followed her into the barn, which was redolent of sawdust. As Muriel got closer, Walter looked up and shut off his saw. He appeared both surprised by her presence and a bit sheepish.

"Muriel, what's the matter?" His voice was surprisingly calm considering Muriel's theatrics.

"Walter, it's terrible. Simply terrible." Muriel burst into tears, and Walter hurried over and put his arm around her as he regarded Brie with some confusion.

It was an odd little tableau, as Walter was slightly shorter than Brie and considerably shorter than Muriel.

"What's this about?" he asked Brie. "And who are you?"

Brie introduced herself, then showed Walter her ID and the picture of Claire while observing his reaction carefully. There were no histrionics, but Brie noted that as he looked at the image his hand shook a little, as Mary's had at the Windward Inn. She explained where Claire had been found and that she had learned the woman's identity from Edie Hanover at the general store in the village.

Walter nodded and handed the phone back to her. Muriel sobbed and put her head down on top of Walter's.

"What can we tell you?" Walter asked.

Brie noted that neither of them had asked about the marks on Claire's neck, and she found that curious. She pulled out her small notebook and pen.

"Let's start at the beginning. You rented the camp on your property to one Claire Whitehall. Is that right?"

"That's right," Walter said.

"And the picture I just showed you is the same woman?"

"That's right," Walter said again.

"How long had she been staying here in your camp?"

"A little over a month. She came out here the second week of August."

"And how did she happen to rent from you? Did you know her?"

"Not at all. We have our camp listed with an agency that takes care of renting out properties. They do the advertising and take care of prospective clients—help them to find a rental that suits their needs."

"I understand," Brie said. "So where was Ms. Whitehall from?"

"She lived in Portsmouth, New Hampshire," Walter said.

"And do you know what she was doing on the island? Was she just vacationing here?"

"Miss Whitehall told us she was a freelance journalist." It was Muriel speaking now. She had straightened up from her huddled position over Walter and seemed to have regained her composure. Brie had the feeling that Walter was probably done talking.

"I don't suppose you know what she was working on?"

"Why, yes," Muriel said. "We had a nice talk with her about it when she first got here. Isn't that right, Walter?"

Walter started to say something but Muriel powered on. "She told us she was writing an article on the lobster wars on some of the outer islands."

Brie was familiar with the term. It referred to families who got into disputes over their lobstering territories. Outcomes of these conflicts ranged from feuding lobstermen who didn't speak to the farthest extreme—those who ended up shooting each other over their disputes. And there were a host of other possibilities for vengeful behavior in between those extremes. John had told her some of the crazy stories. She reminded herself to ask him what he knew about the goings-on out here.

She looked directly at Walter when she asked her next question, hoping to get him talking again.

"Do you know which lobstermen or families Claire might have talked to on the island?"

"Well, it's no secret that the Lancasters and the Beloits have been feuding over their territories for decades. I think that war is on its third generation. They keep passing it down, just like near-sightedness."

Brie smiled, thinking it was a pretty good analogy. She asked Walter for the full names of the lobstermen and jotted them down in her notebook.

"Do you know if she had talked to anyone from those families?" Brie asked.

"I would assume so," Walter said. "I told her they'd had a war going since God was a boy."

Brie nodded. "Any other names you can give me? Folks she might have interviewed?"

"Well, on a lesser front, there are the Flambeaus and the Herringtons. I've heard they mostly shout insults at each other. It's been going on for a long time now. No one can really tell if they seriously dislike one another or are just carrying on tradition."

Walter supplied their full names and the general location of where the four families lived on the island. Brie wrote the information down in her notebook. Walter seemed to know the island folk pretty well, which led to her next question.

"Do you and Muriel live here year round?" she asked.

"We have for the past few years, since we retired," Muriel said. "Before that we just came here for a month every summer."

Brie thought about asking them for their opinion of the lobstermen Walter had named but decided she'd prefer to form her own impressions of them when she interviewed them.

"I'd like to see the camp where Claire was staying," Brie said.

"Certainly," Walter said.

"Walter, go get the key and we'll show Detective . . ."

"Beaumont," Walter filled in. "Her last name is Beaumont, dear."

"Oh, for heaven sakes, Walter. I know that. Now go get the key," Muriel ordered.

Walter colored a bit and stalked off toward the house to retrieve the key. By the time he got back he seemed to have calmed down. Brie decided right away that this marriage never would have survived if Walter hadn't learned to take Muriel with a grain of salt.

Muriel snatched the key from his hand and power walked toward a trail that originated between the house and the barn and ran east. Walter trailed in Muriel's wake like a tugboat following a freighter—seemingly insignificant, but responsible for the heavy lifting nonetheless. Brie followed behind Walter. She couldn't help reflecting on marriage and feeling a bit gun-shy about the convention at the moment.

A few minutes along the trail, they came out into a clearing, and there sat one of the most picturesque log cabins Brie had ever seen. And she'd seen more than a few in the north woods of Minnesota. The cabin or camp sat back about twenty-five or thirty yards from the rocky shore and had a screen porch that ran all the way across the front. There was a green carpet of forest grass around the cabin, and six or eight large spruce trees stood sentry-like.

"We'll show you the inside," Muriel said, striding across the lawn toward the cabin.

"Muriel," Brie called, putting plenty of authority into her voice. "You need to hold up there. Do not go near the cabin."

"Excuse me?" Muriel said, wheeling around.

"Until we determine what happened to Claire Whitehall, we need to treat this as a potential crime scene."

Muriel stopped in her tracks and her mouth literally dropped open. But nothing came out.

"Surely you noticed the marks on Claire's neck. While the cause of her death has been ruled 'undetermined' at this point, we need to take great care here so as not to contaminate a potential crime scene."

"Crime scene? This is our home, our property," Muriel bleated.

"Nonetheless, you are not to set foot in this cabin until further notice."

Muriel huffed her shoulders again. "Walter, do something."

"There's nothing to be done, dear, but to follow the detective's directions."

"Hmmph." Muriel turned and slapped the key into Walter's hand and stormed off down the path toward the house.

"You'll have to excuse my wife," Walter said in his calm-after-the-storm demeanor. "She takes great pride in our property here. I'm sure she was looking forward to showing you the camp."

"I understand," Brie said. Now that she had Walter alone, it seemed like a golden opportunity to pump him for a little information.

"I noted when you looked at the picture of Claire that you didn't comment on the bruising on her neck. Neither did Muriel. Frankly, I find that strange."

"My wife gets upset easily. Sometimes even borderline hysterical. I felt it was better not to dwell on the gruesome image you showed us."

Better for you, Brie thought, deciding it was Walter's self-protective device for avoiding Muriel's behavior.

"I'm not blind, Detective. And I'm not stupid. I know those marks indicate that someone attacked Claire. And I also know, whether the cause of death is undetermined or not, that you're looking at this as a potential homicide. Am I right?"

"That's very good, Mr. Westburg. And yes, you are right." It occurred to Brie that, free of Muriel's orbit, Walter was a very different person.

Before she could continue, he said, "You see, Detective Beaumont, I was a defense attorney. And while I now construct furniture instead of cases, I'm very privy to what you are dealing with in this kind of an investigation."

"That's good to know, Mr. Westburg. It gives me a much better sense of you. Something a detective is always looking to acquire."

"I understand, Detective. Now, you'd probably like to proceed with your inspection of the premises."

"Before I do, can you tell me if Claire talked to you about any of her interviews with the lobstermen?"

"She didn't discuss her work, except to say that she wanted to give her article a human interest angle. Profile the families fairly and show what motivated them to keep up the wars."

"I see," Brie said.

"She was rather a no-nonsense young woman. Kept to herself. I could see she was consumed by what she was working on."

Brie found that an interesting phrase to use for her demeanor. *Consumed by what she was working on.* She didn't question the truth of it, but something about the word "consumed" didn't seem like a fit for the topic she was investigating. Unless she somehow had a personal stake in the story.

Brie turned and studied the camp for a moment before turning back to Walter.

"Well, I'll take it from here, Walter." She held out her hand for the key. "Thank you for the information. It's very helpful—gives me a place to start."

"If I can help you with anything else, Detective, I'm at your service. Just lock the door when you're done. You'll find me working in the barn if you want to return the key to me."

Walter was a mind reader. Brie had no desire to go any more rounds with Muriel right now. "Thanks. I'll check in with you when I'm done."

They parted ways, and Brie headed for the cabin and climbed the three open wood steps to the porch. She paused, pulled the pair of booties from her pack and the latex gloves from her pocket, and put them on. She opened the screen door, stepped onto the porch and looked around. It had that homey feel typical of a Maine front porch. There were a couple of rocking chairs and some interesting bentwood willow furniture. At the far end of the porch was a weathered table and four ladder-back chairs. She walked over to the table. On top was a basket with some rocks and shells. The porch was enclosed by screens only, and in a bad storm the rain would come in. Brie noted the floor and furniture were still damp from the hurricane that had passed through, but the structure itself didn't seem to have been damaged.

Brie walked to the front door and tried the knob. It was locked. Her eyebrows went up. *Finally, someone on a Maine island who locks her door.* But then she remembered that Claire wasn't a native. Brie turned the key, pushed the door open, and peered inside before entering. Nothing seemed disturbed, and there were no outward signs of a struggle. She stepped through the door and stood on the small entry rug and continued to look around for a few moments before proceeding.

The cabin had a vaulted log ceiling and log walls, golden as the color of honey. About ten feet from the door, a half-log stairway went up to a small loft that overlooked the living room. The downstairs had an open floor plan, which gave the cabin a feeling of spaciousness. To Brie's right, on the far wall, stood a large stone fireplace with a raised hearth. The kitchen and dining area were at the back of the cabin under the loft. A bank of windows flooded those spaces with light.

To Brie's left was an open door. She walked over to it and looked in. It was a small bedroom, simply furnished with a double bed, small bedside table, and antique dresser. The bed was made with a dark green chenille bedspread pulled up over the pillows to form a bolster. The room was empty except for the furniture, and Brie walked to the room behind it and looked in that door.

This was obviously the room Claire had been sleeping in. The covers were thrown back as if someone had just gotten up. The room was a bit larger than the first bedroom and nicely appointed. The bed had rose-colored sheets and a lightweight down comforter. A set of cottage pane windows on the side wall let in plenty of light. There was a comfortable looking lady's chair in the corner by the window. Several pieces of clothing were draped over the chair, and a pair of athletic shoes sat next to it on the floor. Brie recalled that Claire had had on hiking boots when they had pulled her body out of the ocean the day before.

She checked the dresser drawers. They held items of Claire's clothing but nothing else. The small closet was empty except for a good-sized backpack that Claire had most likely carried all her stuff in, and a couple pairs of jeans and a pull-over hoodie hanging on hangers. There were several paper-back novels on the bedside table, but nothing that seemed to relate to Claire's work—no notes or notebooks.

Brie headed back out to the living area and walked around to the kitchen. There was a laptop computer on the dining table and next to it, a small stack of lined paper, a note-book, and a couple of pens. Brie flipped open the notebook, but it was blank, as was the stack of paper. She looked around the kitchen. There were no other papers or notes in evidence. *Odd,* she thought. *Where are all her notes? She was supposedly working on an article and interviewing people.*

The laptop was open, and Brie hit a key to see if it was turned on. The computer came to life and opened a screen for a password. Brie ran a finger over the touch pad, moved the arrow to the icon, and clicked on it, hoping the computer wouldn't need a password. But it did, and she realized that was as far as she'd be going. She'd have to take the laptop with her and get it to the Maine State Police to someone in computer forensics. She shut down the system and closed the top on the computer, took an evidence envelope out of her pack, and slid the laptop into it. She sealed the envelope, marked the date and time on the front, and put it into her pack.

Brie spent a few more minutes looking around the cabin and checking the loft for any work materials Claire might have left up there. She came up empty. Wherever Claire had been attacked, Brie's instincts told her it hadn't been here. There was no evidence that this was any kind of a crime scene. And as to Claire's notes pertaining to what she was working on, there were only a couple of possibilities. Either she had no notes and was here on the island for some reason other than work, or she had taken her notes with her the day she died, which somehow didn't make a lot of sense.

Brie did find Claire's handbag on the kitchen counter, but there was no sign of her cell phone, which would have contained all of her contacts. People carried their whole lives on their phones, and personally, Brie didn't like relying on any single device to that degree. She believed in backup systems. She'd seen, with her colleagues at the department, the kind of havoc that losing a cell phone created.

Claire's handbag did yield one item of importance—her wallet with her driver's license. From it Brie learned that Claire

Whitehall was thirty years old and that she had indeed lived in Portsmouth, New Hampshire—information that hopefully would help the state police locate the victim's next of kin. Brie took the handbag and wallet into evidence and added them to her pack.

She checked to be sure the back door was locked before leaving the cabin and locked the front door on her way out. She crossed the porch and stepped outside, took off her gloves and booties, and stuffed them in her pack. As she straightened up, she thought she heard a rustling from the edge of the woods. She looked to her left and was sure she saw movement there. Her hand went to her belt for her gun, and then she remembered she hadn't worn it and silently reprimanded herself. She jumped off the steps and ran in the direction she thought she'd seen the movement. She made her way cautiously into the woods at the edge of the clearing and moved forward, watching for any sign of a presence. Finally, she decided it must have been an animal rustling around. She backtracked to the clearing where the cabin stood and headed along the trail that ran back to the main house. She wanted to find Walter and ask him a couple more questions, and also reiterate her instructions that no one was to enter the cabin until further notice.

When she got near the end of the trail, she heard hammering coming from the barn and headed in that direction. She knocked on the open door, but Walter didn't hear her, and she walked into the barn and over to where he was working on what looked like a mantelpiece. When he saw her, he set down his hammer.

"Did you find anything out of order at the camp?" he asked.

"Nothing at all," Brie said. "I did find Claire's handbag and her driver's license, but no cell phone. I assume she must have had one."

"She did," Walter said. "I saw her talking on it one day."

"Good to know," Brie said. "Did you see Claire at all yesterday, before the storm hit?"

"Just once. We were shuttering the windows on the house, and I happened to look up and see her on the path heading toward the village. I came down the ladder and called after her, but she was already out of earshot."

"And what time was that?"

Walter thought for a moment. "Maybe around eleven to eleven-thirty. I can't say for sure, but it was before I had lunch."

"What did you want to talk to her about?" Brie asked.

"I just wanted to make sure she knew the hurricane was coming, and that it was going to be bad. I didn't want her to get caught out in it."

"Do you remember if she had anything with her?"

"She had a small daypack on her back, like she might be going for a hike. That's why I was concerned."

"But you didn't go after her?"

"No," Walter said. "I figured she'd talk to someone in the village. I also thought maybe she was just going to get a few supplies from the store before the storm hit."

"I see," Brie said. "Well, that's all for now, Walter." She handed him the key. "I must caution you and your wife again not to go into the camp until further notice."

"I understand, and I'll make sure no one does," Walter said.

With that, Brie headed back along the trail toward the village. In her mind was a picture of Claire Whitehall, happy and alive, along with a host of questions about what had led to her death.

Chapter 8

Brie followed the trail that led away from the Westburgs' house. She was thinking about Muriel and Walter Westburg, the camp where Claire had stayed, and the rustling in the forest as she had exited the camp. While she told herself it was nothing, her gut was busy telling her it *was* something.

When she came to the intersection with the main trail that ran to the village, she pulled out her phone to see if she had reception. She had talked to Joe Wolf along this part of the path, and pretty soon the bars appeared on her phone. She stopped and brought up Dent Fenton's number and put the call through.

"Fenton here. What's up, Brie?"

"I found out that Claire Whitehall was renting a camp from some people named Westburg on the south shore of the island."

"That's good work."

"There's more. Ms. Whitehall had a New Hampshire driver's license that shows her address in Portsmouth." Brie read off the address and gave Dent the license number.

"That should help us locate someone who knows her," Dent said.

"The people she was renting from—one Walter and Muriel Westburg—live on the property. They said she was an independent investigative reporter out here doing research for an article on the lobster wars on the outer islands."

"That could be a hot button issue for some of the locals."

"Just what I was thinking. I got the names of some local lobstermen who've had some notorious feuding going on time out of mind. I plan to question them—see if Claire Whitehall interviewed any of them. See what kind of a vibe I get from these guys."

"We'll work on locating next of kin," Dent said.

"You might try some of the media outlets in Portsmouth. Maybe the newspaper and local TV station. She may have worked for one of them in the past or submitted work to them."

"Good idea. We'll work that angle, Brie. Anything else?"

"I took her laptop into evidence. It's password protected, but it may hold some clues. We're gonna need to get one of your computer forensic guys on it. See if he can access what she was working on."

"How about her notes? Any clues there?" Dent asked.

"That's the weird part, Dent. There were no notes that I could find at the cabin where she was staying."

"Huh . . . what do you make of that?"

As a cop, Brie had dealt with too many reporters over the years not to know that, as a group, they were heavy on note taking. Like most writers, their world was one of notebooks, notepads, thoughts and questions written on napkins, scraps of paper, around the margins of magazines. When a writer has an idea, nothing is sacred.

"I think there are only two possibilities," Brie said. "Either someone got to the cabin before me and cleaned out all of Claire's notes, or else she took them with her the day she died. Makes me think there was something in those notes that was never supposed to see the light of day."

"You think she was going to meet someone the day she died?"

"I think it's a good possibility," Brie said.

"It's looking more and more like we may have a murder on our hands, despite the ME's ruling of 'undetermined death.'"

"My thought exactly," Brie said.

"I'm sending Marty Dupuis out there to help with questioning. He can stay on the island if necessary until we get some answers."

"Roger that, Dent. I'll fill him in on any new details when he gets here. Tell him to call my cell phone when he arrives, and I'll meet up with him."

"Will do. You watch your step, Brie."

"I will, don't worry."

They ended the call, and Brie pocketed her phone. She knew Detective Marty Dupuis from two previous cases she had been involved in and had worked closely with him during the Tucker Harbor case in August. He was a nice guy and a good detective. She'd be glad to have him on scene to lend a hand.

She continued along the trail to the village. The Westburgs' property was so isolated she wondered how they got things in and out. The trail didn't seem wide enough for a pickup. She guessed they could carry their groceries from the village, but even if Walter made all of their furniture—which she suspected was his plan for staying clear of Muriel most of the time—what did they do if they needed a new refrigerator or mattress? After thinking about it for a while, Brie decided such large items must be delivered by boat.

As she made her way along the trail, the wind picked up and sent a shower of droplets off the spruce trees onto her head. She wondered if John was planning to sail back to port later today and decided she should stop back out to the ship and check in with him before she tackled the interview with the lobstermen whose names Walter Westburg had given her.

In a few more minutes she reached the outskirts of the village. She noted again that, other than a lot of debris blown around, Ivan had been merciful to this side of the island. The one exception was the island's archive building, which had lost its entire roof. It was an odd casualty, she thought. But then she remembered the small building that housed the island's records was perched up on the side of the hill above the village. A freak downdraft of wind into the valley during the hurricane could have caught the roof from an odd angle. And who knew how many decades had passed since that little structure had seen any repairs?

The small beach where John had landed the dory was a ways down the shore from the ferry dock and the Windward Inn. Brie cut across the village and found the dirt road that ran down there. She pulled out her phone and called John to ask him to send someone over to pick her up.

As she came down the embankment to the beach, she saw *Tango*'s cheerful red bow headed in her direction. Scott was at the oars, and the early afternoon light reflected off his russet-colored hair.

"Hey, Scott," she said when the dory hit the beach. She handed him her pack, and he stowed it under his thwart. Then she gave the dory a shove, hopped aboard, and sat in the bow, and Scott pulled for the ship.

"You missed lunch, but George kept some soup on the stove for you and one of the grilled sandwiches he made for the passengers."

"Mmmm. That sounds delicious. I've worked up an appetite tramping around the island. And there's more tramping to do after lunch."

"Any luck on the girl's ID?"

Brie filled him in as they rowed to the *Maine Wind*.

Scott brought the dory up to the starboard side of the ship, and Brie climbed up the boarding ladder. He tied off the dory and followed her. She thanked him for picking her up and headed down to the galley.

George was doing some prep work for the dinner. "Hey, Brie. Want some lunch?"

"I'm starving, George. Whataya got?"

"I saved a grilled sandwich for you. It's on the back of the stove along with some hot soup."

"That sounds perfect. Mind if I take it topside and find John? I need to talk to him."

"Be my guest. Can I help you carry anything?"

"No worries. I got this, George." Brie went and put her daypack on her berth. Back out in the galley, she got a plate for the sandwich and ladled out a mug of black bean soup, rich with tomatoes and vegetables.

"This smells delicious, George. Thanks."

"No problem, Brie."

She put the mug on the plate and headed up the ladder to the deck, balancing her plate and soup with the skill of an acrobat. She looked around the deck but didn't see the captain, so she headed aft and down the companionway to his cabin. She knocked lightly on the door, hoping she wasn't waking him from a nap.

"Come," she heard immediately. She opened the door and stepped into his cabin.

"Brie, you're back. Any news?"

"There is. Mind if I eat while we talk?"

"Be my guest." He started to get up from his chair at the chart table.

"I'll just sit on the berth." Brie crossed the cabin, climbed onto John's berth and folded her legs Indian style. She set the plate next to her and picked up the mug of soup.

"George saved lunch for me." She smelled the soup and then took a spoonful. "Umm, that's so good." She picked up half of the grilled ham and cheese, took a couple of bites, and set the sandwich back down.

"I got a positive ID on the victim," she said.

"Who is she?" John asked. "Did she live on the island?"

"Her name was Claire Whitehall." Between bites of sandwich, Brie filled him in on who Claire was, what she was doing on the island, and on the camp she had rented from the Westburgs.

"Did you find any evidence of foul play at the camp she was renting?"

Brie smiled. Over the summer, John had picked up some of her cop-speak phraseology.

"There was no evidence of anything out of place at her camp. The only odd thing is that I found no notes for the article she was working on."

"That's weird. You'd think a journalist would have lots of notes scattered around."

"I know. It's really odd. Unless she took them with her the day she died for some reason. The other possibility is that she wasn't working on what she claimed to be. But that doesn't make a lot of sense, since she had talked to the Westburgs about her research on the lobster wars."

"Did you find a laptop there?"

"I did, but it was password protected. I'll have to get it to computer forensics at the Maine State Police—see what they can find."

"So what's your next move?" John asked.

"Well, Walter Westburg gave me four names of families on the island who have been involved in lobster wars over time. He told me he gave Claire those names, too, when she asked him about possible leads for her article. I figure I'll start by interviewing those lobstermen and see if she contacted them."

"I can't get that picture of her out of my mind," John said. "Those marks on her neck . . ." His voice trailed off.

"I know. It's disturbing."

"Any word from Doc Wolf yet?"

"Yes. I forgot to tell you. He called me while I was on the island. Claire Whitehall died from massive internal trauma consistent with a fall from a significant height. There was no water in her lungs, so she was dead before the sea took her out."

"Wow. What does that mean?"

"It's hard to say. It means she fell from a high place, but it's impossible to determine from her injuries if it was a homicide, a suicide, or an accident. Doc Wolf has ruled the manner of death as 'undetermined.'"

"So what happens now?"

"The investigation will go on. We don't know if someone killed her, but we also don't know otherwise. And there are those marks on her neck. Very troubling. Joe Wolf thinks she sustained them within a few hours of her death."

"Well, we're here today for sure," John said. "I'm planning to head for port tomorrow, seas allowing. If you have to stay, it's no big deal. I think Scott, George, and I can get the *Maine Wind* docked and tell the passengers farewell."

"I hate to create extra work for Scott and George," Brie said.

"Hey, those two guys are the last ones who'd ever make a stink. They're both way too fond of you."

"And how about you, Captain?"

"I'm a little bit fond of you, too," he said. He lifted his eyes and held hers for a moment, and she noticed a devilish little twinkle there. "I know you'll find some way to thank me."

Brie ignored his last remark. "Listen, John, before I shove off, can I ask you a couple questions about these lobster wars that go on between some of the fishermen?"

"Well, I'm no authority, but being a Mainer, I've heard and read plenty over the years about the problem."

"So from what you've told me in the past, it sounds like someone gets their traps into someone else's territory, and then all hell breaks loose."

"That's most of it. The territories, as they're known, are carefully guarded and usually handed down generation after generation. So it's kind of a turf war, you might say."

"But it's the ocean. It's not like land that you can survey and say 'Yours ends here or mine starts there.'"

"They're called 'imaginary lines,' and by the way, the state doesn't recognize them, but to the lobstermen, it's deadly serious business. Also, the lobstermen from each coastal area or island hang tightly together. Rivalries erupt sometimes where their turf meets—their turf being the seabed where they place their traps."

"Jeez, you make it sound like gang warfare," Brie said.

"When things get ugly, it's a little like that. Only it's lobsters instead of drugs."

"So retaliation consists of cutting the other guy's gear free of its buoy?"

"Usually, although there are cases where things have escalated to destruction of a guy's lobsterboat, or even stabbing or shooting."

"You're kidding."

"Nope. A few years ago an incident on Matinicus Island led to a guy getting shot. He survived, but he was partially paralyzed."

"My God. It sounds like the Wild West. So, do you think it was safe for this Claire Whitehall to be approaching these guys and prying into their conflicts?"

"It's hard to imagine that could have led to her death, but you never know. Some of these guys have a short fuse. Still, I think she'd have to have really touched a nerve and rubbed it raw to put her life in jeopardy. With most of these guys, it's just a lot of bravado."

Brie didn't say anything. As a homicide detective, she had always been amazed at how quickly people could escalate a situation into one that became life threatening.

"Well, that's good info, John. It helps me know what I'm likely to encounter when I start interviewing these guys."

"You want me to come with you?"

"No. I think I can handle a few lobstermen. When you've been up against the real deal, like the gangs we dealt with in

Minneapolis as I came up through the ranks, you learn how to watch your back."

"Sounds scary," John said.

"I won't lie to you; there were times it was."

Brie climbed off John's berth. "Mind if I take the dory? I need to go ashore and do these interviews."

"Go ahead." John stood up from where he sat.

"I'll try to be back before dinner so I can help out down in the galley."

"Roger that," John said.

Brie headed for the door but then stopped and turned back to face him. "You're a good man, John. Probably better than I deserve. You make so many allowances for me, and what do I do in return? Leave you short on crew."

"You're the one who was shot, Brie, and went through a year of hell. I think I can make a few allowances. What's more, you've made a good connection with the Maine State Police. I think it's an important connection. It's helping you find your footing again. So how could I take issue with that?"

"Thanks, John." She stepped close to him and placed the backs of her fingers against his neck. "I'll catch you later, okay?"

He kissed her lightly. "We'll see who does the catching," he said softly.

Brie knew it was time to make her exit before she lost her resolve. She stepped away from him and out the cabin door with her dishes. She headed forward and brought them down to the galley, where she washed them and put them away. She was still wearing her rain jacket against the chill of the day and still had her badge and ID on her. But she headed back to her berth to clip on her gun and holster. After the rustling in the forest near the camp and her pursuit of whatever or whoever was there, she knew it was time to start wearing her weapon.

She headed topside and climbed down the boarding ladder to the dory. She untied the painter, pushed off from the side of the *Maine Wind,* and set the oars in the locks. She took her seat in the center of *Tango* and pulled for shore. She was thinking about Claire Whitehall. She knew the young woman had been murdered. She knew it with the kind of gut knowing she'd learned not to question. And she wondered how long it would take before she crossed paths with a killer.

Chapter 9

Brie headed for the spot where she and John had beached the dory that morning. Walter Westburg had told her roughly where to find the homes of the Lancasters and Beloits. She figured she wouldn't have too much trouble locating them, and with all the villagers out and about after the hurricane, she could easily ask someone for directions if she needed to. She beached the dory and walked up the hill toward the village. Walter had told her the Lancasters' house lay north of Ghost Cove, along the shore road.

The fog that had cloaked the village earlier had mostly lifted. As she got near the ferry dock, she noticed that the frantic tenor of the morning had subsided. The villagers still prowled about, searching yards for the town's scattered records, but the pace had slowed considerably.

Brie stopped and looked about, hoping to spot Gil Doubtwater, the town manager. She was going to ask him the whereabouts of the Lancasters' place, but he was nowhere to be seen. As she scanned the area, she saw a man standing on the deck outside the deli. He seemed to have her fixed in his sights, but as soon as her gaze fell on him, he looked away. He obviously had her sized up as an off-islander, which made her an automatic interloper and rubbernecker on a day when there were problems here. She carried on toward the road that ran north of the village.

What roads existed on the island were gravel and in varying degrees of repair. There were few vehicles here, and anyone visiting via the ferry came on foot—a fact that lent a kind of old-world charm to the village and to the island.

Brie continued north along the road and, when she encountered a woman coming the other way, asked where the Lancasters lived. The woman told her to keep going till she came to a house just around the first bend in the road. Brie kept walking and just past that bend, she found the Lancaster house and headed up the drive. She soon noticed a man sitting on an old straight-backed chair behind the gray Cape Cod. He was repairing a lobster trap that sat on the ground in front of him.

He looked up as she approached and sat back in the chair, sizing her up.

"Logan Lancaster?" Brie asked as she got closer.

"A-yah," he said, standing up.

Lancaster wore old baggy jeans, work boots, and a tee shirt with the sleeves cut off. He was not overly tall, but broad in the chest—built strong from hauling lobster pots. Brie placed him at late thirties. He was so ruddy from life at sea, he almost reminded her of a boiled lobster.

"My name's Brie Beaumont, Mr. Lancaster." She showed him her ID. "I'm with the Maine State Police." She didn't waste any time telling him the how or why of it, but took out her phone and showed him the picture of Claire Whitehall, watching his reaction closely. His brows knit together, and a troubled look darkened his face.

"We're investigating the death of this young woman who was found floating off the island yesterday. Her name was Claire Whitehall. I've been told you may have talked to her."

"Told by who?" he asked, his tone guarded.

"Walter Westburg, who owns the camp where Ms. Whitehall was staying. According to him, she was a freelance journalist out here researching a piece on the lobster wars. Westburg says he gave her your name along with several others'—families who've been known to carry on feuds over their lobstering territories."

Lancaster crossed his arms on his chest and stared at her for a moment, undoubtedly deciding what he did and did not want to say.

"Is that true, Mr. Lancaster?" Brie prodded.

Finally he dropped his arms and stuffed his big hands in the pockets of his grimy jeans.

"A-yah. She come out here a couple times, asking me about lobsterin', the wars and such, and my family's history on the island."

"And did you talk to her? Give her the information she was looking for?"

"I guess," he said noncommittally, and Brie sensed something unsaid.

"But . . . ?" she asked.

Lancaster shrugged. "I dunno."

Brie waited, hoping he'd go on.

Finally he said, "I got the feelin' she was fishin' for something other than lobster." He said it "othah" and "lobstah," Yankee-style.

"Like what?" Brie asked.

"Dunno," he said. "Just a feelin'."

At that moment a boisterous voice from the road below them bellowed, "Yo! Log!"

"Sinkah!" Lancaster yelled back.

Brie figured that translated to "Sinker" and wondered how he'd gotten the name. But it wasn't the first odd nickname she'd encountered on these islands since May. "Log" seemed more obvious—short for Logan, she guessed.

"Any bugs today?" Log shouted.

Brie knew "bugs" meant lobsters.

"Thick o' fog out they-ah today. And a chop to make a strong man puke," came the report from Sinker.

"I warned ya to let it ride today, Sinkah." Warned came out "wahned."

"Can't make a livin' hidin' out he-ah, Log."

"Yeah, well, ya can't make a livin' if ya washes overboard either." It came out "ovabahd" and "eithah."

Sinker carried on his way, and Brie marveled at the fact that she seemed to have been invisible during this entire exchange. After a moment she continued her interview.

"So, Mr. Lancaster, when Ms. Whitehall came to visit you, did she write down any notes?"

"Nah, she didn't write nothin' down. She had some kind of small recorder. There was no tape or anything. Must o' been digital. The thing wasn't much bigger than a pack o' gum."

"So, she never actually wrote anything down any of the times she visited you?"

"That's right," Lancaster said.

"And when did you last talk to her?"

"Maybe a week or a week and a half." He paused for a moment and looked troubled. "It's too bad what happened to her," he said.

"Yes," Brie said. "Very sad." She weighed his words, trying to decide if they were sincere. "One more thing, Mr. Lancaster. Can you tell me where Henry Beloit lives?"

"Buzz Beloit?" Logan Lancaster turned and spat on the ground—an act Brie translated as disgust at his even having to hear the name of his sworn enemy.

"Keep goin' up the road he-ah," he said. "You'll come to his place, God help ya."

Brie nodded and put her notebook away and headed down to the road.

She turned left at the road and continued along it, watching for the Beloits' place and thinking about her encounter with Lancaster. It hadn't revealed much, but the information about the recorder was important. She planned to go back to the Westburgs' place and have another look around Claire's camp—see if she had somehow missed seeing the recorder.

The road bent to her right, and the next driveway she came to bore a rough board sign with the name Beloit. She started up the overgrown drive, and a small light blue house with black shutters came into view. It had seen better days, but she doubted its state of disrepair was due to a lack of money. The lobstermen on these outer islands plied their trade year-round and were among the wealthiest of their ilk.

As Brie approached, the back door opened and a man stepped out and headed toward her. Brie sized him up. He had a multi-day scruff going and a mean set to his jaw. *Probably has a chip on his shoulder the size of a lobster trap,* she thought. In his right hand a lit cigarette had burned down most of the way.

"What's your business?" he asked in a tone that said whatever it was, it had better be good.

"Henry Beloit?" Brie asked as she came up to him.

"That's right. Who wants to know?" He took a drag from the heater and blew the smoke directly in her face.

Brie didn't even flinch at this act of aggression. She knew that to do so would give him the upper hand.

"Detective Brie Beaumont, Maine Sate Police," she said, producing her ID and shield.

Beloit had just brought the cigarette to his mouth for another go at her, but when he saw her badge, he sucked in so hard, a coughing fit ensued.

Brie smiled to herself. *Instant karmic backlash,* she thought. She wasted no time producing her phone.

"Mr. Beloit, do you know this woman?" She held the photo of Claire Whitehall up for him to see and watched him carefully.

His eyes were watering now, but despite that, they became hooded. He took a step back. "What happened to her?" he asked.

"She was found floating off the island yesterday. Do you know her, Mr. Beloit?"

His eyes turned mean. "Since you're here, you obviously think I do. Why?" He dropped the cigarette butt and ground it out under his heel.

"I'll ask the questions, Mr. Beloit, and yes, I have information that she may have contacted you. Is that correct?"

Although they were standing in the great outdoors, he moved like a big man trapped in a small cage, casting his glance down at the ground and shifting from side to side. Body language that said he might be guilty, but guilty of what? Brie wondered. She spread her feet to parade rest—a signal that she wasn't going anywhere—and waited for a response.

Finally Beloit cleared his throat. "I met her," he said in a controlled tone. "She came out here to ask some questions about the feud between me and Lancaster, down the way." He nodded his head to the right, indicating the general direction of Logan Lancaster's house.

"And how did that go?" Brie asked.

"I don't like people prying into my business, so it didn't go very well."

"Meaning you were rude to her? Or maybe just downright mean," Brie said.

"What happens on this island, that's island business. Not for anyone else. We keep to ourselves, and we expect others to do the same."

"So you were angry that she was writing an article on the lobster wars."

"Damn straight. And I wouldn't call them wars. Maybe more like conflicts."

Brie smiled to herself. *A man of discernment. Who would have guessed*?

"Did you threaten Ms. Whitehall in any way?"

Again, his eyes became hooded, which gave Brie the answer before he even spoke.

"Why would I threaten her? She reminded me of a fly. I just shooed her away."

Brie noted that he hadn't answered the question. She also reflected on the fact that flies were often swatted, not shooed away.

"I'll ask you again, Mr. Beloit. Did you threaten Claire Whitehall?"

Before Beloit could respond, the back door of the house swung open with a bang, and a woman wearing a nightgown and smoking a stogie stepped out on the stoop and bellowed for Beloit to get in the "f-ing" house because the toilet was backing up.

Beloit turned and headed for the door. "The answer is 'no,'" he called over his shoulder.

Brie decided not to pursue the interview any further. She had a lot more digging to do, and certain things were clear to her as related to Buzz Beloit. She turned and headed down the driveway.

While Beloit landed at the bottom of her list for charm and deportment, she hadn't gotten much sense of him beyond that. Yes, he had acted guilty, but guilty of what, was the question. The appearance of a police officer often has the effect of eliciting a guilty response from individuals being questioned. Who knew? Maybe Buzz beat his wife, although, having seen her, Brie decided that gate might swing the other way, too. Clearly, the woman was a force to be reckoned with. And there were other possibilities. Maybe Beloit had a stash of weed or crack just behind the door of his homey abode—after all, his nickname was "Buzz." Or maybe he knew more about what had happened to Claire Whitehall than he was admitting. Brie knew the solution was to keep working the case. *Things have a way of turning up when you just keep working the case.*

She headed back toward the village. Walter Westburg had told her that the other two families—the Herringtons and the Flambeaus—lived south of the village. She planned to visit them and then head back to the Westburgs' to have another look around the camp where Claire had been staying. If she could locate the pocket recorder Claire had used, it might hold a wealth of clues.

Past the ferry dock, Brie took the shore road that ran down toward where she had beached the dory. A ways beyond that spot, she came to a sign for the Flambeau residence and turned up the driveway. The place was better kept than Buzz Beloit's digs, and like the other lobstermen's houses she had visited, there was an ample supply of spare buoys and square metal lobster traps piled up behind the house. Brie climbed the steps to the back door and rang the bell. She waited a respectful amount of time and rang again, but no one answered. This was the first house where she'd struck out. She retraced her steps back down to the road and continued on.

Walter Westburg had told her that there were two Herringtons—father and son—that lived along this road, so Brie kept her eyes peeled for two different residences with the name Herrington. When she came to the first one, she turned in and headed toward the residence. The Cape Cod-style house stood up on the knoll of a hill, looking out to sea. Even without the sun shining on it, the cape was pretty as a picture, painted white with deep blue shutters. The lawn was freshly mowed, and out front, a wooden swing hung from a large log frame and overlooked the sea. She sensed that whoever lived here was cut from a different cloth than the last two lobstermen she'd interviewed.

As she moved toward the back door of the house, a tall, extremely handsome man stepped out the door. He was holding a bottle of beer, which he set down on the granite stoop. He came down the steps and moved toward her with an easy grace, and for the briefest moment Brie wondered if her hair looked completely crazy. The man was six-foot-one or two with brown hair and eyes. He wore clean, dark blue jeans that accentuated his manly assets and a white polo shirt that showed off tanned, muscular arms. Despite herself, Brie couldn't help feeling a little star struck. As she was assessing him, she could see him doing the same, but in a curious, not a hostile way.

"Can I help you?" he asked as they closed the distance between them.

"Are you Paul Herrington?" Brie asked.

"Junior," he said. "Paul Herrington Junior." And somehow his voice matched the rest of him perfectly.

"Ah, I was told you and your father both lived down this way. I'm Detective Brie Beaumont with the Maine State Police. I wonder if I could ask you a few questions."

By the time she had showed her badge and ID, she noticed an odd look had clouded Herrington's handsome face—a look of confusion mixed with alarm. Brie almost hated to open her phone, but knew she had to.

"Mr. Herrington, do you know this woman?" She handed him the phone, watching his reaction.

Paul Herrington stood perfectly still, but his eyes filled with tears, and after a moment, Brie saw him swallow a lump in his throat. His stunning looks somehow lent an air of tragedy to the scene. Brie read between the lines. You put a pretty new girl on an island, someone's going to come calling. She guessed that someone had been Paul Herrington Jr.

"It's Claire," he said, his voice little more than a whisper. "What happened?" He looked up at Brie, and his eyes flashed with pain and anger.

"We don't know yet," Brie said. "Ms. Whitehall was spotted floating off the island yesterday by a schooner that was heading here to take shelter from the hurricane." Brie didn't mention her own connection with the ship, as it was superfluous to the case. "The crew was able to retrieve Ms. Whitehall's body," she said. "The police have just begun to investigate her death."

Brie paused for a moment before continuing. "Do you know anything about the marks on her neck, Mr. Herrington?"

"Of course not." He looked shocked that Brie would ask that. "Was that the cause of her death? Did someone strangle her?"

"We're not prepared to divulge that information just yet, Mr. Herrington."

"Where is Claire now? Where have they taken her?"

"She was taken by the Coast Guard to the mainland. Her body is at the medical examiner's office."

Brie noted that Herrington looked increasingly distraught.

"I knew something was wrong. I couldn't find her anywhere yesterday. I've been really worried about her, what with the storm passing over the island."

Brie suddenly remembered something. "Were you watching her camp this morning from the woods nearby?"

"No, I was out on my boat this morning, pulling my traps. Why?"

"When I came out of her camp this morning, I got the feeling someone was watching her place from the woods nearby."

Herrington knit his eyebrows together at that, and Brie could see the information troubled him.

"Did you go out to pull your traps yesterday, Mr. Herrington?"

"No, I was ashore all day boarding things up here and at my dad's."

Brie took out her notebook and jotted that down. "Did you inquire at the Westburgs' yesterday as to Claire's whereabouts?" Brie asked.

"No, but I went to her camp several times." He shifted his weight and dropped his glance to the ground. "I suppose you think it's odd I didn't ask them if they knew where she was."

"Why didn't you?" Brie asked, deciding not to pass judgment till she had the facts.

"It's just that Muriel Westburg is a nosy piece of work. We didn't want her prying into our business."

"But wouldn't the Westburgs have seen you coming and going from her camp?"

"There's a secondary trail that swings around the back of their property and comes close to the camp. I took that route."

"Mr. Herrington, what was your relationship to Ms. Whitehall?"

"We were friends."

Brie waited a couple of ticks for him to elaborate, but he remained silent.

"Just friends, or was it more? Maybe friends with benefits?"

"I'm not like that," he said strongly.

It was clear to Brie that he was taken aback by her comment. *The noble lobsterman*, she thought a bit cynically. And yet, there was something about his demeanor that seemed trustworthy.

"So, you were just friends," Brie stated.

"Right," he said.

But his eyes shifted to the side as he said it, which told Brie there might be more to it than that. Maybe he was aware that significant others always go straight to the top of the suspect list. But for whatever reason, he remained steadfast in his declaration that he and Claire were just friends.

"And when did you meet her?"

"The first day she was on the island. I was at the general store picking up some groceries when she came in. She said 'hi' and we got to talking. I liked her right away. She was lovely and refined. Smart too."

"I sense there's more to you than just lobster traps and buoys, Mr. Herrington. So what's your story?"

He smiled in his easy way. "Are you saying I don't fit the mold?"

Now it was Brie's turn to smile. "Just curious about your pedigree, Mr. Herrington."

"Not a lot to tell. Local lobsterman—that would be my dad—dreams big for his son. Son makes good—really good—and goes to a fancy Eastern college. But that's not why I'm different from your run-of-the-mill lobstermen, if that's what you're thinking."

"Not thinking anything for now, Mr. Herrington. Just listening to your story. So, why are you different?" she asked.

"Not to diminish the effect a fine education has on one, but the man I am came straight from my parents. I think in a different life they would have both been academics—teachers maybe. Dad lobstered for a living, and it provided a good living. But he and Mom loved books. They were always reading. And we took vacations. Dad made sure we got off the island and saw a bit of the world. And Mom, well, she was just a fine woman in every way. Gentle, insightful, wise." Herrington paused and glanced up at Brie.

She studied him for a moment, feeling pretty certain about what had attracted him to Claire.

"So, if I seem like a square peg in a round hole, now you know why."

"So, what made you come back here and take up the life of a lobsterman?" Brie asked. "Seems like you were bound for something different."

"I'm sure that's what Dad thought, and to this day, I pray I didn't disappoint him. But, you know, I love the sea, always have. I worked with my dad on his boat from the time I was fourteen. I caught the bug, no pun intended."

Brie smiled.

"There's a freedom to it that just doesn't exist anywhere else. And I'm kind of a loner by nature. The work suits me. And when I met Claire, well, truthfully, I started to think maybe I'd found the missing piece in my life. She loved her independence, and I think she might not have been immune to living out here. Although I never got the chance to ask her."

"So you must have known what Claire was working on."

"Sure. She was doing an article on the lobster wars that take place on some of the islands out here. Of course, we've got no monopoly on them. The same shenanigans go on over on the mainland, too."

"Speaking of which, I've been told there's a history between your family and the Flambeaus," Brie said.

Paul Herrington smiled an easy smile. "That hatchet was buried long ago, thanks to my dad's working to establish good relations with Gus Flambeau. But I guess the stories still persist as part of island lore. You don't have to take my word for it, though. You can ask Gus if you want. He'll tell you the same thing."

"I'll do that," Brie said. "Do you, by chance, have any information about Claire's parents? We're trying to locate her next of kin."

Herrington shook his head. "I don't really know much about them, except that Claire said they live in Boston."

"I guess that's all for now, Mr. Herrington. We'll be in touch if we need anything else from you." Brie closed her notebook and put it in her pocket.

Paul said goodbye and turned to leave, but not before Brie noticed the sadness that had seeped back into his face, like a storm cloud passing over the sun. She watched as he climbed the hill next to his house and stood looking out to sea. She turned and walked back toward the road, feeling the weight of her work heavy upon her as she always did at moments like these.

Chapter 10

Brie looped back to the south end of the village and caught the grassy road that ran through the center of the island and out to the Westburgs' place. She wanted to take another look around Claire's camp—see if maybe she could locate the pocket recorder Logan Lancaster had mentioned. She also had a few more questions for Walter Westburg.

She wasn't sure when Marty would be arriving on the island. He may have had other work to finish, and he'd have to find transport out to the island since the ferry wasn't running today. She knew the Maine State Police cooperated with the Maine Marine Patrol, so maybe that was how he would get out here.

As she walked, she thought about the facts of the case so far. There weren't many. She knew she would need a lot more information before she could firm up any kind of a suspect list. Any attempt at it now would be nothing more than conjecture. There was one possibility, though, that interested her. If Claire Whitehall hadn't died—if she had continued with the interviews for her article on the lobster wars—might she have unearthed something that someone here hoped would never see the light of day? Say someone had actually died as a result of one of these conflicts. Say the death was ruled an accident, but maybe there was more to it—something that a savvy investigative reporter might have uncovered. Such a scenario could have put the reporter at great risk.

The outlying islands of Maine were, for all intents and purposes, self-policing places, where what happened on an island stayed on that island. So the islands became little worlds unto themselves, which made them breeding grounds for secrets. And if a secret were big enough, well, in Brie's book that could make for a powerful motive for murder. Again, it was all just conjecture, but such speculation is the detective's *raison d'être.*

She thought about Buzz Beloit—the second of the lobstermen she had interviewed. He seemed like he could be a mean guy. And he certainly was aggressive—she remembered the cigarette smoke blown in her face. She could imagine something flipping his switch pretty easily.

And then there was Paul Herrington. He certainly seemed honest and trustworthy, yet there was something he'd chosen not to reveal. Brie was sure of it. That was why she wanted to talk to Walter Westburg again. Maybe he had seen something that might confirm that Claire Whitehall and Herrington had been lovers—a situation Brie was pretty sure had existed, but she wanted to know for sure. It seemed a real long shot that Paul Herrington had killed Claire Whitehall, but she knew enough not to rule him out completely. If he and Claire had been lovers, it would certainly place him on the suspect list.

She thought about the tears that had come to his eyes when she showed him the picture of Claire. But those tears wouldn't be enough to expunge him from the suspect list if it turned out he had been her lover. After all, the tears could have been ones of grief, but also ones of guilt. Brie smiled. "Pretty cynical, aren't we?" she said to herself and took it as a sign that she had switched into full detective mode.

She could hear the sea now, making noise, intent on its long-term project of reshaping the island. Up in the atmosphere, clouds had been playing tug-of-war with the sun, vying for supremacy. At the moment they were winning, and a misty rain began to fall just as she reached the trail that led to the

Westburgs' place. She pulled up her hood and kept walking. A little farther along, she took note when another trail forked off to her left. Paul Herrington had told her he got to Claire's camp by an alternate route. She reminded herself to check the other trail later and see where it came out.

She soon picked up another sound. It was the buzz of one of Walter Westburg's saws, chewing away on whatever project he was engrossed in out in his barn. Brie smiled, wondering if Walter ever went to bed at night or just holed up in his barn like an owl.

As she reached the clearing and approached Walter's workshop, the pungent smell of sawdust hung in the air, heavy as perfume. She stepped through the barn door and walked toward Walter, who was splitting a long board on his table saw. He nodded when he saw her but finished his run of board before shutting the saw off.

"Hello, Detective. Any progress? Did you find the lobstermen whose names I gave you?"

"I did and I've talked to most of them," Brie said. "I'm just beginning to gather information, so it's hard to say yet if it can be classified as progress."

She took out her small notebook. "Mr. Westburg, were you aware of any relationship between Paul Herrington Jr. and Claire Whitehall?"

Walter Westburg looked down at his feet and slowly moved one back and forth, making a track through the sawdust on the barn floor.

"There was something going on," he said.

"Could you elaborate?"

"I was headed out to Claire's camp one night just after dark. She had asked for an extra blanket, and I was bringing one out to her. Just as I approached the cabin, I saw a man open the porch door and step inside. I was too far away to tell who it was, so I moved in closer, feeling concerned about the situation. When Claire opened the door and light poured out from inside, I recognized the man as Paul Herrington Jr."

Westburg paused in his narrative, and Brie noted that he looked uncomfortable.

"What happened next?" she asked.

Walter stroked his chin. "It was clear from the moment she opened the door that they were lovers. She kissed him on the mouth, and he was already unbuttoning her shirt as she pulled him inside."

"How long before her death did you witness this?"

"About two weeks ago," Walter said.

"Mr. Westburg, why didn't you tell me about this when you learned Claire was dead?" There was an edge to her voice, one that was not there by accident. This was her I-expect-an-explanation cop inflection.

Walter shrugged as if it were nothing. "It was clear they were crazy about each other. Paul's a nice guy. I didn't want to implicate him unnecessarily."

"That judgment is mine to make, Mr. Westburg. You're not his attorney, are you?"

"Of course not."

"Then you must know that withholding information is obstruction."

"I figured it would all come out when you talked to him about Claire's piece she was doing on the lobster wars."

Brie studied him for a moment. As a former defense attorney, Westburg would certainly know that any lover of Claire's would go straight to the top of the suspect list. She also thought she knew why he hadn't divulged the information. Her guess was Walter Westburg did not intend on making any enemies on this island. Now she wondered what else he might not have told her, and unbeknownst to Walter, he slid effortlessly onto her list of suspects. And though he made the bottom of the list, it had always been her policy as a detective that anyone who lied to her during an investigation became a person of interest.

Walter may have read her mind, because now he was looking uneasy.

"I wonder if you would mind not mentioning the tryst between Claire and Paul Herrington to Muriel," he said.

"Why's that?" Brie asked, raising an eyebrow.

"It just wouldn't sit well with her," he said. "She has a certain sense of propriety about things, if you know what I mean."

"What you mean is she wouldn't have approved."

"That's right," Walter said.

"What makes you think Muriel didn't already know about them?" Brie asked.

"Because, if she had, I'd have heard about it. And not long after that, so would everyone else on the island."

Brie wasn't so sure. She knew little about the Westburgs, but Muriel struck her as a woman who liked to be in control. And that kind of need for control can lead to confrontation. So Muriel slipped into place on her list of persons of interest as well.

"Mr. Westburg, this is not some kind of a game. Do I need to remind you that this is a death investigation?"

"No, of course not. You're quite right. Whatever you have to do, I will cooperate."

Except he wasn't, Brie thought. He had already withheld information pertaining to Claire. *What else hadn't he told her*?

At that moment her phone rang. She pulled it out and answered, seeing it was Marty Dupuis.

"Hey, Marty. What's up?"

"I just arrived on the island, Brie. Where are you at?"

"I'm south of the village, Marty. If you walk down the main road, past the general store, and keep going, a grassy road continues south beyond the village. Why don't you head down that way, and I'll meet up with you?"

"Will do, Brie. See you in a bit."

They ended the call, and Brie turned back to Walter Westburg.

"That was Detective Dupuis with the Maine State Police. He's come out to the island to help with the case. I'm going to go meet up with him, and then we're coming back here." She paused and fixed her eyes on him, giving him her best cop stare. "And from here on out, Mr. Westburg, I need your complete cooperation."

"Of course," Walter said, looking chagrined. "Whatever you need."

Brie turned and left the barn without commenting.

She headed along the trail that ran from the Westburgs' barn toward the road that Marty would be taking. This was good timing. She still had to search Claire's camp for the pocket recorder Logan Lancaster mentioned Claire had used in her interviews. With Marty's help, the process would go more quickly. In a few minutes she reached the intersecting trail—the one she had a hard time thinking of as a road—and turned north toward the village.

A few more minutes' walk and Brie saw a man up a ways, heading her direction. He seemed vaguely familiar, but she wasn't able to get a good look at him, because at that moment he turned into the driveway of one of the houses that lay along the road. By the time she got to the spot and looked toward the house, there was no sign of him.

"Brie!"

She turned at the hail and saw Detective Marty Dupuis about a hundred yards up the road, waving at her. She waved back, and they closed the gap toward one another. It seemed like a while since she'd seen Marty. But in reality it was just a little over a month. The Tucker Harbor case in August had been a tough one, and over the intervening time, she had tried to distance herself from it psychologically. But a warm feeling filled her at the sight of Detective Dupuis. He was a good guy —a solid guy—one she could always depend on. Physically, he reminded her of a small bulldozer. Powerfully built, he moved with a kind of steady determination that said, "Just try to stop me." Today he was wearing khakis and a Maine State Police windbreaker. The jacket was unzipped, and she could see his shield clipped to his belt and his holstered gun on his right side.

"It's good to see you again, Brie," Marty said as they came up to each other. He surveyed her for a second. "How are you doing?"

"I'm doing, Marty. How about you? Those kids keeping you hopping?" She knew Marty and his wife had three young and very active boys.

"Hopping is putting it mildly. I don't have to worry about eating a donut here and there with those three in my life."

"They're your live-in diet plan," Brie said, and that got a laugh from Marty.

They started back along the road the way Brie had come. She told him she wanted to go back to Claire's camp and look for a digital recorder Claire was supposed to have been using for her interviews with the lobstermen.

"So, any luck yet locating the vic's next of kin?" she asked.

"We struck out on any Whitehalls living in the Portsmouth area, but your suggestion to contact some of the media outlets paid off. It turns out Claire worked for the *Portsmouth Herald* for a few years. Her best friend, Michelle York, still works there and was able to give us contact information for Claire's parents, who live in Boston. We're also getting a search warrant sworn out in New Hampshire for Claire's apartment.

"Here's something odd, though," Marty continued. "Apparently Claire Whitehall wrote down her parents' phone number and address and gave it to Michelle York just before she left for the island here. She told Ms. York that if anything ever happened to her, no one would know how to get ahold of her parents."

"Huh, strange," Brie said. "The synchronicity of it, I mean."

"It's almost as if she had some kind of premonition," Marty said.

"Or knew what she was doing was dangerous."

"So, what does that suggest?" Marty asked.

"It suggests there may be something here we're not privy to," Brie said.

"Or maybe Claire Whitehall just liked a bit of drama."

"I don't know, Marty, that's not quite the read I have on her. But I could be wrong."

"Well, there's only one way to find out." Marty raised an eyebrow.

"Work the case," Brie said.

"You got it."

They continued on in silence toward the Westburg property. The wind was picking up a bit and starting to whisper through the spruce in a ghostly susurrus—a sound that always took Brie back to her time spent hiking in the deep pine forests of northern Minnesota. She drew a long, slow breath, as if to breathe in the sound around her and internalize that memory of home.

When they arrived at the Westburgs' cottage, Brie half expected Muriel to burst forth and accost them. If she saw Marty, she would want to know what was up and who he was. But nothing happened as they entered the clearing and made their way toward the barn.

As soon as the two of them stepped inside, Walter stopped what he was doing and came over.

"This is Detective Marty Dupuis," Brie said in way of introduction. "He'll be helping me with the case."

Walter extended his hand and Marty shook it. "Pleased to meet you, Detective Dupuis."

Brie thought of something she wanted to ask Walter. She pulled out her small notebook and consulted one of the pages.

"Mr. Westburg, you said that yesterday, when the hurricane was moving in, you saw Claire heading toward the village with a daypack on her back and dressed as if she might be going hiking."

"That's right," Walter said.

"Had you seen her go off like that before? What I mean is, did she seem interested in exploring the island? And if so, did she usually carry a daypack on such junkets?"

"She had asked me about trails on the island, and a few times she'd mentioned she was going for a hike. But she always just carried a round canteen with a long strap that she wore crisscross over one shoulder. I think the only time I saw her with the pack is when she was going to the store in the village for some supplies."

Brie wrote notes as Walter talked. When he finished, she nodded and closed her notebook. "Do you have any questions for Mr. Westburg?" she asked Marty.

"Nothing right now," Marty said.

"In that case, we need to have another look around Claire's camp. Do you happen to have the key out here with you, Walter?"

"Yes, I do." He reached in the front pocket of his jeans, fished out the key, and handed it to Brie.

"I'll stop back with it when we're done," she said, taking the key.

They took their leave of Walter, and Marty followed Brie as she headed east along the trail that led to the camp.

They passed through the woods that separated the camp from the rest of the Westburg property. Renters of the camp had a nice degree of separation from the main house, which would have appealed to anyone wanting a vacation spot with some privacy.

As they approached the camp, Brie got the odd sense that something was amiss. It was her sixth sense kicking in—one she always heeded. She stopped in her tracks.

"What's up?" Marty asked.

"Not sure," said Brie. "Just a vibe."

Marty drew his gun and took the lead, and Brie followed—gun held two-fisted next to her shoulder. They swung off to the left so as not to be seen approaching the cabin from the front. When they got to the porch, they crept along the front, opened the screen door, and stepped silently onto the porch.

Brie nodded toward the front door, where one of the small mullioned panes had been broken to let an intruder into the camp.

They took up positions on either side of the door, and Brie took a quick peek inside. "Clear," she mouthed to Marty, letting him know she didn't see anyone in the main room.

She turned the knob silently and Marty slipped through the door, gun pointed. Brie followed him in.

At that moment a man walked out of one of the bedrooms to their left—the one where Claire had slept.

"Freeze," Marty said, leveling the gun on the man.

"Dude!" the guy exclaimed. "Don't shoot."

Brie recognized the man. He was the guy who'd been watching her from near the ferry dock earlier that day, and she also thought he was the same one she'd just seen along the road when she went to meet Marty. He must have been on the way here then and had turned into that house to avoid passing her.

While Marty waited, she went and patted him down to be sure he didn't have any weapons. "Clean," she said and directed him into the main room so they could question him.

"What's your name?" Brie asked.

The man glared at her for a few moments before answering. "James Levy," he said, giving them a put-off look. He was around five-foot-ten and had medium brown hair spiked up with too much gel. He might have been considered good-looking except that his arrogant attitude was an instant turn-off.

"What are you doing here?" Brie asked, deciding for the moment to hold off on the breaking and entering charge.

"Looking for someone," he said.

Brie took out her phone and showed Levy the picture of Claire. "Is this who you are looking for?"

The man shifted his eyes from the phone to Brie for just a second and bolted for the door. He blasted across the porch and out the door, jumped off the steps and ran flat out.

Marty and Brie charged after him and, bulldozer or not, Marty was fast. Brie took a tangential course, arcing to the right on a route that would take her behind the barn and back to the connecting trail, where she could cut the guy off in the event Marty didn't catch him.

Just as she came back in view of them, she saw Marty go to the air and knock the guy flat from behind. By the time Brie got there, Marty had pulled the guy to his feet, grabbed the cuffs off his belt, and handcuffed him. He proceeded to pat him down again to be sure he had no weapons and had not taken anything from the camp.

"Why did you run?" Marty asked him.

"I've got nothing to say," Levy spat out.

"In that case, James Levy, you are under arrest." Marty read him his rights and then turned to Brie.

"Call Lieutenant Fenton and tell him to send the Marine Patrol back out—that I've got a suspect I'm bringing in for questioning."

"Roger that."

Walter Westburg had come out of the barn when he heard the fracas, and now Muriel Westburg flew out the front door of the house and barreled toward them, calling out, "Walter, what's happening? Who is this man?" as if Walter were somehow the guilty party.

Walter intercepted her before she got to them and corralled her at a good distance from the unfolding drama—an act for which Brie was supremely grateful.

Marty turned Levy around to face the Westburgs. "Do you know this guy, Mr. Westburg?"

"I've never seen him before," Westburg said.

Muriel placed her hands on her hips. "What's he doing on our property? Walter, do something. This is an outrage."

"There's nothing to be done, dear. The detectives have it in hand."

"Humph." Muriel drew herself up to her considerable height and glared at Brie.

Brie drew Walter aside. "You need to go to the camp. There's a small window pane broken in the door. I'd like you to board that up and lock up the camp." She handed him the key. "Nobody goes near there until I get back to do a more thorough inspection. Is that clear, Mr. Westburg?"

"Crystal," he said.

She and Marty marched the suspect toward the trail that led back to the village. As they left the Westburgs' property, Brie could hear Muriel exclaiming, "I demand to know what's going on here, Walter." She didn't envy Walter Westburg the evening that was in store for him.

Chapter 11

Brie and Marty headed back toward the village with their suspect in tow. As soon as she got to a spot where she had phone reception, she put in the call to Lieutenant Dent Fenton and filled him in on the situation. He told her that he'd call the Marine Patrol to pick up Marty and the suspect.

"Do you know where this Levy character lives?" Dent asked.

"No. He's chosen to remain silent. But if he knows Claire Whitehall, it's a good bet he's either from Portsmouth or the island here."

"I'll do a little digging. See if I can unearth anything."

"Any luck on reaching Claire's parents yet?" Brie asked.

"Negative," Dent said. "That phone number is a landline, so we can only reach them if they're at home. Ms. York, Claire's friend, didn't have their cell phone numbers. But we've notified the Boston PD that we need to reach William and Marian Whitehall about their daughter's death. So I'll keep you posted."

"Let me know what transpires with this Levy character."

"Don't worry, Brie, I'll keep you in the loop."

"Thanks, Dent." She ended the call.

Brie told Marty she had to go back to the ship to get Claire Whitehall's laptop.

"The laptop is password protected, so I need you to take it with you—get it to the guys in computer forensics."

"I'll deliver it after I bring Mr. Levy in to be charged."

"Great. I'll row back out to the ship and get it and meet you down by the ferry dock in a little bit."

"Roger that, Brie."

Marty Dupuis continued along the road with James Levy, and Brie cut through the village and down to the small beach where she'd landed the dory. She pushed off, jumped aboard, got her oars into the locks, and started pulling for the ship.

Scott saw her coming and lowered the boarding ladder so she could come aboard. She tied off the dory, climbed to the deck, and immediately went below to get her pack that contained the laptop and Claire's handbag and ID. On the way back through the galley, Brie told George she had to return to shore briefly, but hoped to be back aboard in a little while and that she could help him with the dinner prep.

"No worries, Brie. I've got things under control. The captain's filled me in on what's going on, so if you don't get back, no biggie. I've got this."

"Thanks, George. You're a peach."

"Maybe more of a pomegranate," he joked.

"I don't know, George. I think you're sweeter than that."

"Ah, get out of here," he said, but a smile crept onto his face.

Brie headed up to the deck with the daypack slung over her shoulder. Scott held on to it while she climbed back down to the dory and then handed it down to her. She told him she should be back soon and pushed off from the side of the *Maine Wind*.

She rowed ashore to the same spot she'd just left and beached the dory. Slipping the pack onto her back, she headed up through the village toward the ferry dock. When she got close to the dock, she spotted Marty sitting at a table on the deck outside the Ferry Good Deli. James Levy was slouched down in his chair, staring out at the ocean. They were the only ones seated there. With no ferry running to or from the island, there were no tourists waiting to return to the mainland. She walked toward them and climbed the wooden stairs to the deck.

Brie signed the articles over to Marty. Then she thought of something.

"Marty, do you happen to have the contact info with you for Michelle York?"

"Right here," Marty said. He pulled his small notebook out of his pocket and found the page.

Brie copied down the address and phone number she found there and handed the notebook back to Marty. "Just in case something comes up and I have to contact her."

"If you find you need anything else, just call me," Marty said. "And I'll be in touch as we know more."

"Great," Brie said. "I'll finish up with my last interview out here, and tomorrow I'm headed back to the mainland with the ship."

"Check in when you get back, and I'll let you know where we're at with this new development." He nodded toward James Levy when he said it, and Levy turned and gave him a sneer.

Brie raised an eyebrow and made momentary eye contact with Marty. "Will do. Thanks." She turned and walked down the steps and back up through the village. She wanted to stop back at the Flambeau residence and see if she could find anyone home this time. He was the last of the lobstermen she had on her list, and she wanted to find out if Claire Whitehall had talked to him or not.

When she got to the Flambeau place, she headed up to the house as she had before and rang the doorbell. Again, she waited and, after a time, knocked on the door, but there was no one home. She retraced her steps back to the road and was standing there debating what she wanted to do when she noticed Paul Herrington Jr. heading in her direction. She waited as he closed the gap, knowing she had a few more questions for him.

"Hello again, Detective," he said when he came within speaking distance.

"Mr. Herrington. I've been trying to find someone home at the Flambeau house but without any luck."

"Oh, I guess I should have told you. Gus Flambeau and his wife have gone off island. They went to visit their daughter up in Vermont, who just had a baby. Gus has got a friend tending his traps while they're gone."

"Any idea when they left the island?"

"I think it was Wednesday," Herrington said. "His buddy Bob Foster has been working Gus's traps the past few days."

Brie took out her notebook and jotted down the information. Claire Whitehall had died yesterday—Friday. If this Bob Foster character could confirm that the Flambeaus had left the island on Wednesday, then that put Gus Flambeau out of the running as a suspect.

"Can you tell me where Foster lives?" she asked Herrington.

"Up north of the village next to the Lancaster property."

"I know where that is," she said. "Mr. Herrington, did Claire ever mention a man by the name of James Levy to you?"

Herrington's brows knit together. "I don't think so. Why?"

During an investigation, Brie liked to keep the facts of the case under wraps, so she said, "I'm sorry, but I can't discuss that right now." She leafed through her notebook to her first interview with him. "I have a couple more questions for you."

"Okay," Herrington said a bit hesitantly.

Brie heard the guarded tone in his voice, which told her he knew he hadn't been completely honest with her in their first interview.

"I have it on good authority that you and Claire Whitehall were more than just friends, Mr. Herrington. That you were most likely lovers." She fixed him with her cop stare. "Is that true?"

Paul Herrington dropped his eyes to the ground. "Yes, it's true."

"Why did you lie to me when I questioned you before?"

"I don't know. I guess I'm kind of a private person."

"That's fine, Mr. Herrington, but this is a death investigation, and you must know that having been Ms. Whitehall's lover automatically makes you a person of interest in this investigation. And frankly, your lying about it also makes it look like you might have something to hide."

"Well, I don't. I was crazy about Claire. I'd never have hurt her."

"That may well be, Mr. Herrington, but once I know that someone I'm questioning has lied to me, it makes believing what they say in the future far more difficult."

"I can understand that," Herrington said.

"In fact, it makes me think there may be other things they are hiding." Brie wasn't sure if she believed any such thing regarding Herrington, but she put it out there just to rattle his cage a little.

"Well, I'll try hard to earn your trust from here on out," he said quietly.

"You do that, Mr. Herrington." But when she met his eyes this time, they were filled with a mix of intense sadness and desperation, almost as if a part of him were on fire, burning, and he was powerless to extinguish the flames—powerless to help himself. Seeing it shook Brie to her core; she knew firsthand what that kind of powerlessness felt like. She wanted to offer some words of comfort, but as a detective investigating Claire's death, she knew she couldn't—it wouldn't be appropriate.

"Mr. Herrington, I'm going to go speak to this Bob Foster you mentioned. I'll leave you to continue on your way." She put her notebook away.

Paul Herrington nodded, but as she walked off, she knew he was just standing there. She glanced back once and saw him riveted to the spot, staring off into space with blind eyes—eyes that couldn't see a way to go on or any reason to do so.

Brie made her way back north of the village to the Foster residence just one property beyond Logan Lancaster's place, where she'd been earlier in the afternoon. As she approached the house, she saw a man and woman bent over an engine. Husband and wife were both in coveralls, and the wife appeared to handle a wrench with the ease of a professional mechanic. Up on blocks in front of them was a Ford engine that Brie guessed had come out of a lobsterboat.

"Bob Foster?" Brie asked as she approached.

"A-yah," Foster said, pausing to wipe his hands on a rag. Bob Foster was somewhere in his forties, wiry and bald, with a brown mustache that matched his fringe of hair.

"And is this your wife, Bob?"

"A-yah. That's Bonnie. My better half." He said it "bettah."

Brie was fairly sure he meant it literally, considering Bonnie's skill with the wrench. Bonnie was also surprisingly pretty, with strawberry blond hair and an upturned nose reminiscent of Scarlett Johansson.

Brie introduced herself and told them her business—that she was looking into the death of a young woman, an investigative reporter who'd been staying on the island.

"I have reason to believe that Claire Whitehall may have interviewed Gus Flambeau. I've also been told that Mr. and Mrs. Flambeau left the island this week and that you are tending to his lobster pots in his absence."

"A-yah. That's right," Foster said. He put his hands in the pockets of his coveralls and rocked back and forth on his heels.

Brie could see that he was a man of few words, like many native Mainers. She smiled to herself. *I'll take a laconic person any day over a gabber,* she thought. She took it as a sign she fit in pretty well in Maine.

"Can you tell me what day the Flambeaus left the island?" Brie asked.

"That'd be Wednesday," Foster said. "That was the day I starting tending traps for Gus."

Brie nodded. It was really the only piece of information she was after, and it took Gus Flambeau off the suspect list. But since she was here . . .

"Did you by chance talk to Claire Whitehall while she was on the island?" she asked Bob Foster.

"Can't say as I did," Foster responded.

"How about you, Bonnie?"

"I saw her here and there around the island but never really talked to her, except to say 'hi' in passing."

Brie closed her notebook and thanked them. She retraced her steps down to the road and back toward the village. She'd gone a short way when her phone rang. She fished it out and saw it was Dent Fenton calling.

"Hello, Lieutenant. Anything new?"

"Yes, as a matter of fact. We did a search of the records under the name of James Levy—the guy you and Marty apprehended out there on Apparition Island. We also contacted the police department in Portsmouth, New Hampshire, where Claire Whitehall lived. They were the ones who turned up something."

"What did they find?" Brie asked.

"Apparently Ms. Whitehall had taken out a restraining order against a man named James Levy."

"Really? Well, that's pretty interesting."

"There's more. This same guy, James Levy, has been arrested for domestic assault for choking his former girlfriend. I've sent you a picture of the guy so you can confirm that it's the same man you and Marty arrested."

Brie checked for the picture and saw she had received it. She opened it and immediately recognized Levy as the same man who had broken into Claire's camp.

"That's him, all right," she said. "Looks like we may have our man."

"It's a good possibility, but we'll have to see what comes out when we question him," Dent said. "The main problem I can see is that Claire Whitehall did not die from asphyxia. She died from a fall, and so far the manner of death is 'undetermined.' Any decent attorney will have a field day with that."

"Still, it's mighty damning that Levy has a prior for the exact same kind of assault on his former girlfriend."

"No doubt about that," Dent said. "Do you know if Marty has left the island yet with the suspect?"

"Affirmative," Brie said. "The Marine Patrol picked them up within the last hour."

"Good. I'm driving to headquarters in Augusta. I'll meet up with Marty there, and we'll see what transpires."

"I'm heading back to the mainland tomorrow morning with the *Maine Wind.* We plan to haul anchor around oh-five-hundred."

"Good to know, Brie. I'll be in touch as things develop."

Brie and Dent ended the call. She had been walking as they talked and had stopped on the outskirts of Ghost Cove. She put her phone away and stood there for a few minutes, thinking about the case as she surveyed the village.

More than likely, James Levy was responsible for the death of Claire Whitehall. As a cop, Brie knew that in 70-80 percent of intimate partner homicides, the man had previously physically abused the woman. A staggering statistic. But in this case, with an ambiguous cause of death, they would need further evidence—say someone who had seen Levy with Claire within hours of her death. Without a stronger case, they might get him on breaking and entering, but that was like a slap on the hand if in actuality he had killed her.

As far as her part in the case went, she fully expected it was about at an end. As of tomorrow she'd be sailing back to Camden with John and the crew, and Dent Fenton and his team would deal with James Levy. But she noted she had mixed feelings about the situation. The cop in her was used to seeing a case through to the end, and it was strange to think of not doing so.

As she stood on the edge of the village mulling on all of this, she noticed Gil Doubtwater heading up the hill toward the inn, where the wet and damaged village documents had been taken in the aftermath of Hurricane Ivan's huffing and puffing the roof off the island's archive building. All of a sudden she had a thought. There was something she wanted to ask him, but he was too far off for her to call out to him, so she headed toward the inn where he was going.

When she got up to the inn, she entered through the same door she had earlier—the one that faced a small parking area at the back of the building. Mary, the woman she had talked to earlier, was not at the reception desk. Brie turned to her left and walked down a long hallway where she had seen villagers going with the soggy documents. Near the end of the hall, she came to a set of ornate double doors, above which an engraved brass nameplate read "Ballroom."

One door was ajar, and Brie stepped through it. The ballroom had rich wood paneling and ornate chandeliers. French windows and doors stretched the length of the far wall, filling the room with light and a spectacular view of the sea. She imagined the space had hosted some grand balls in its day, and more recently, some fine weddings. But today the polished parquet floor was lined with rows of tables covered with all manner of documents. She walked along the first row, seeing everything from birth, death, and burial records to old island newspapers and property records. There were documents from the island school going back many decades and what looked like budget statistics and minutes from town meetings.

There were probably twenty or so people in the room organizing the documents, regrouping them and turning them over so they could dry on their opposite sides. Brie spotted Gil Doubtwater on the far side of the room. He was gesturing to a table where two or three volunteers were listening. Brie made her way in his direction and waited at a polite distance until he was done instructing the group with what he wanted them to do.

"Hello, Detective . . . it's Beaumont, isn't it?"

"That's right, Mr. Doubtwater."

"Oh, it's fine to call me Gil. Everyone here does. Have you had any luck discovering that young woman's identity?"

"As a matter of fact, we have, and we know she was renting the Westburgs' camp here on the island."

"Do you have any idea what happened to her?"

"There've been a couple of developments, but I'm really not at liberty to talk about them."

"Of course not. I understand. So how can I help you?" Doubtwater asked, obviously deciding she wasn't there to volunteer her services.

"Well, Gil, I know you've been off the island for a few weeks and that you didn't know Ms. Whitehall, but I'm wondering if you could help me with something?"

"I will if I can," Doubtwater answered.

"Is there anyone on the island that Claire Whitehall might have talked with to learn about the history of any of the families here? Especially those who may have been involved in lobster wars over the past decades?"

"Well, we have a small history center on the island. It's housed in the former keeper's quarters up at the lighthouse. Belle Westgate is our devoted island historian. She oversees the place. But I'm afraid the history center is closed for the season, and Belle has gone off island as she does every year at this time."

"I see," Brie said, filing away the information.

She felt no urgency about locating Belle Westgate right now. She had interviewed the lobstermen and knew why Claire had been on the island. Until Dent Fenton and Marty Dupuis had finished questioning James Levy at police headquarters in Augusta, she saw no reason to dig any deeper here. Plus she needed to get back to the ship and take up her duties there.

But she had one more question for Gil.

"Mr. Doubtwater, can you tell me where the highest spot on the island is that would be accessible to the public?"

"Why, yes. That would be on the far side of the island—the east side. The village here lies on the west side of the island. The high cliffs are directly on the opposite side. And they are spectacular—several hundred feet high. But the trail that leads to them is rough hiking and steep in places. It might be a little late in the day to start over there."

"Oh, no worries. Just gathering information," Brie said.

Doubtwater nodded and then looked a bit awkward, like he didn't know what to say next.

That was Brie's cue. She thanked him for his time and turned to go. When she looked back, he was already at the far end of the line of tables, instructing another set of people about what they were to do there.

Brie asked herself whether she should try to hike up to the other side of the island today. It was the most likely spot from which Claire Whitehall would have fallen. But she knew it would probably take a couple hours to get there and back, and the chances of finding any evidence were slim. Hurricane Ivan had hit that side of the island first and would have hit it hard. What was more, the trail might be obstructed with blow-downs and could well be impassable. She decided she would wait to hear from Dent about further developments with James Levy before digging any deeper here.

She had wandered down one of the rows of drying tables as she was processing her thoughts. She looked left and right at the array of documents spread out there, thinking what a job it was going to be to put this all right again. Near the end of the row, she glanced down at a very old copy of the *Island Gazette* newspaper that was spread out there. But what she saw stopped her dead in her tracks.

She read the headline and actually squeezed her eyes shut for an instant and looked down at the paper again to be sure she wasn't hallucinating. But no, there it was, the same disturbing headline.

Dead Woman Found Floating Off Island

The date on the newspaper was September 8, 1958. Brie felt as if she'd just passed through a time warp. She bent to read the yellowed text of the news story, her heart pounding in her ears as if she were deep underwater.

> On Sunday, September 7, the body of a woman was found floating off Apparition Island. The 33-year-old woman has been identified as Boston socialite and actress Blythe Danes Whitehall.

Brie drew in a silent gasp, her eyes riveted on the name as if the ink with which the letters were imprinted might suddenly dissolve. She continued reading:

> Mrs. Whitehall had been vacationing on the island for two and a half months, enjoying a rest cure, while staying at the family's summer cottage, *Cliffside*, on the northeast side of the island. Her husband is Boston industrialist

> Harrison Whitehall. The cause of death was drowning, but the Maine State Police are investigating the case. Mrs. Whitehall is survived by a son, age three, and a daughter, age one.

Brie scanned through the rest of the news story, haunted by what lay before her. It was like a harbinger from the distant past, calling to her, telling her she wasn't done—that there was a mystery unfolding here—that more than ever, this case needed her attention. She felt a chill run down her spine as she realized how easily this connection might have gone unnoticed, and she wondered if the death of this woman so long ago—a woman with the same last name—could relate to Claire Whitehall's death. But this chapter of the island's history was so long ago that the likelihood of someone here remembering Blythe Whitehall's fate, or her name, and connecting that memory to Claire Whitehall seemed almost nil.

But then, like an electric shock, another thought hit Brie. Maybe someone on this island had remembered—had connected the names. And when Claire Whitehall came here investigating not the lobster wars but rather, Brie suspected, the death of a relative of hers—possibly her grandmother—that person had acted. Maybe to protect an island secret—to keep the ghosts of the past in the past. But for Brie, this was no longer a case of "undetermined death." She knew in her gut that Claire Whitehall had been murdered, and she believed there was a strong chance that someone on this island meant to keep a part of the past forever buried.

She straightened up and looked around the room for Gil Doubtwater. She spotted him a couple of rows away and walked over to him. When he was available, she asked if she could show him something. She took him back to where she'd found the newspaper and pointed out the article.

"That's most strange," Doubtwater said, and Brie could tell that he'd made the connection with the names and that he was deeply troubled by what he saw there.

"I need to take this newspaper into evidence, Mr. Doubtwater. We'll handle it with the greatest of care."

"Of course, Detective. By all means. This is most alarming." He pushed his glasses up his nose, and Brie noticed he'd gone pale as a cod.

She reached into her pack and took out the last evidence envelope she'd placed there and carefully slipped the copy of the *Island Gazette* into the envelope. She wrote the date and time on the envelope and where the evidence had been collected and tucked the envelope inside her pack. Then she thanked Gil Doubtwater, left the ballroom, and headed for the back door of the inn.

The sky had turned a freshly minted shade of blue, as if the hurricane had wrung any murkiness out of it—as if Ivan had cleaned house atmospherically. And something in that newly rendered sky seemed to reflect a sudden clarity Brie felt about the case. She stood for a few moments, considering this turn of events and feeling amazed by it. Her friend Ariel, back in Minnesota, had always talked to her about synchronicities—about how often they occur in life. Brie had considered the topic just another chapter in what she thought of as Ariel's weird mumbo-jumbo. But she had to admit that stumbling on this old newspaper would probably qualify as a world-class synchronicity, and as she had so many times in the past few months, Brie thought about her friend Ariel with both affection and a growing respect for ideas she had previously brushed aside.

She started back down the road toward where she had beached the dory. She needed to get back to the ship and, tomorrow, back to the mainland. She needed to meet with Dent Fenton and Marty Dupuis and locate the old case file on Blythe Whitehall's death—see where the investigation had led all those years ago—see if the clues she needed to solve the mystery of Claire Whitehall's death lay in the dust of that distant past.

Chapter 12

When Brie got back to the dory, she stepped aboard, sat on the center thwart, and took out her phone. She wanted to talk to Dent about this new development in the case, and she wanted a degree of privacy while doing so—something she wouldn't have aboard ship.

Fenton answered on the third ring. "Hello, Brie."

"Lieutenant."

"No news yet on Levy," he said. "Marty just got to headquarters with the suspect about fifteen minutes ago. So we're still processing him."

"That's not why I'm calling, Lieutenant. There's been another development in the case."

"Oh? Fill me in."

Brie heard the sudden interest in his voice and knew she had piqued his curiosity. She told him about happening on the old newspaper story from September of 1958 and being stunned to see that the dead woman's name was Blythe Whitehall.

"That's pretty interesting, I have to say."

Dent was silent for a moment, and Brie thought she could read between the lines.

"You're thinking it might be a coincidence, aren't you, Lieutenant? That Claire Whitehall's family once owned a summer cottage here and that's all there is to it."

"Well, you have to admit, it could be coincidence," Fenton said. "It looks like we have a motive, means, and opportunity in the case of James Levy. And he's nervous as a cat on a hot tin roof, which doesn't make things look good for him."

"That may well be, Dent, but you know I don't believe in coincidences. At least not ones that crop up during a death investigation."

"Well, I have to admit, it's a mighty odd development," Fenton said.

"We're sailing back to port early tomorrow. I'd like to head up to Augusta and take a look at the old case file on the Blythe Whitehall investigation from 1958."

"You know what, I'm at headquarters now. I'll locate that case file and sign it out. We can meet up tomorrow and go over it. We're also waiting for the warrant to come through for Claire Whitehall's apartment in Portsmouth. I was just going to call the Portsmouth PD and see where we're at with that. If the warrant is sworn out by tomorrow, I'd like to send you and Marty over to New Hampshire to search the victim's premises."

"I'm good with that," Brie said. "How about if I call you tomorrow once we've docked the ship and I'm free to head out?"

"Do that, Brie. In the meantime, we'll be interrogating James Levy and see what we get on that front."

"Sounds like a plan," she said. "I'll talk to you tomorrow, Lieutenant."

They ended the call, and Brie climbed out of the dory, pushed it down to the water, and hopped aboard. She set the oars in the locks and pulled for the ship.

John saw her heading toward the *Maine Wind* and lowered the boarding ladder. She tied off the dory and climbed up to the deck.

"Hey, Brie," he said when she came aboard. "I saw the Marine Patrol leaving with Marty Dupuis and another guy."

John had met Marty Dupuis back in May when he had driven Brie to headquarters to file a report on the case that had unfolded on Granite Island, when the ship was marooned there during a nor'easter.

"Looks like there are some new developments," John said.

"That there are, Captain. But I'm thinking I should get back to my duties here as chief swabbie and bottle washer, and maybe I can fill you in on everything later tonight."

"I like the sound of later tonight."

As he said it, John stepped close to her, and his voice sent a vibration along her heart strings. She placed a hand briefly on his chest, wishing this were an abandoned island and they'd washed up here together with nothing better to do than collect coconuts and make love. She let out a sigh.

John smiled down at her. "It's been too long, Brie."

"I know," was all she said. She stepped back from him reluctantly. "But I should go below and help George. I'm not really holding up my end today."

At that moment they heard one of the passengers, Bill Bacon, calling, "Captain DuLac," and heading in their direction.

Brie turned and walked toward the galley companionway.

John called after her, "Later, Brie."

After the moment they'd just shared, those two words were imbued with a new and thrilling meaning.

At the bottom of the companionway ladder Brie found George humming away, deep in dinner prep mode.

"Hey, George. I've come to earn my keep," she said, feeling suddenly lighthearted beyond all reason. After all, the case hadn't gone away. But her brief encounter with John had allowed her to shift realities momentarily. And truth be told, Brie was never happier than when aboard the *Maine Wind*. If ever there had been a safe haven for her, this was it.

"So, how can I help down here?" she asked.

"Give me just a second," George said.

George Dupopolis was busy butterflying a pork loin roast and stuffing it with a concoction of syrupy apples and raisins that smelled like cinnamon and sugar.

"That looks amazing," Brie said. "How do you come up with these things?"

George looked a little flustered at the praise and repeated one of his favorite lines. "Just doing my job."

"Oh, George, you're way too humble."

A smile lit his dark eyes. "Yeah, but humble never seems to get you in trouble."

"Ah, saith the wise windjammer cook."

George chuckled and shook his head. "Okay, that's enough flattery. I was born with kind of a big head, so you need to be careful about making it any bigger." He walked over to the feeding door on Old Faithful and shoved three split logs into the stove to bring up the temperature.

"So, what do you have planned for sides? Can I help with that?"

"Sure. There's a big bag of fingerling potatoes over there by the sink." He nodded across the galley. "Why don't you wash those and put them in that large flat pan on top of the stove so the heat will dry them. When they're dry, we'll toss them with olive oil and season them, and they can roast in the oven along with the meat."

So while George rolled and tied the pork roast, Brie got busy processing the potatoes. As they worked, they carried on a discussion about what George had in mind for meals for the next cruise and what Brie thought about the menu plans. Brie said what she always did—that it all sounded delicious.

Before coming to Maine, cooking and food prep were as foreign to her as mountain climbing. She was the original cereal-in-the-morning, sandwich-at-noon, and take-out-on-the-way-home-from-work kind of girl. But often the last meal of the day came so late that, once home, she was too tired to eat, and most of it would end up as leftovers.

So, in the first month or two aboard the *Maine Wind,* when George had encouraged her to help in the galley, she had done so with the greatest trepidation—always afraid she might set fire to the ship or cut off a much-needed finger. But over time, she had found that working with George, prepping food, had a wonderfully calming effect on her. To this day she wasn't sure what was responsible for the phenomenon—the work itself or the steady presence of George. But she suspected it was the latter.

They worked on in silence, George starting on dessert, which was blueberry pie, and Brie finishing up the potatoes for the oven.

"Should we eat on deck tonight, George?"

"I think we should. It's nice topside."

"Great. I'll get things set up in a while."

There didn't seem to be anything else she could do in the galley, so she went topside and found Scott.

"Are you going ashore anymore today?" he asked.

"I don't think so. I'm at a stopping point with the case until I can meet with the Maine State Police and see how a couple of things are playing out."

Scott nodded. "Then we may as well haul the dory up and get it secured."

Brie climbed over the starboard gunwale and down to the dory. She rowed it around to the port side of the ship, and Scott lowered the boarding ladder for her to climb aboard. Together they hauled the dory up onto the davits and secured the lines. Then they worked at tidying up the deck and generally making things ready for an early morning departure.

At 6:30 p.m., or 1830 hours, Brie rolled out the rubber mats on the cabin top for the dinner buffet. She went below and helped George finish up the salad, and then crew and passengers lined up to pass dishes and food up the galley companionway and down the deck to the cabin top.

The wind had died down and the temperature hovered around 70 degrees—a perfect evening. Shipmates and crew plated up their food and found their favorite spot on deck to eat. George's roast with its apple stuffing was a big hit, and after dinner the crew brought up the pie and coffee. As the sun went down, the passengers ate dessert and visited on deck, and Brie and Scott went below to help George clean up.

Scott set the first watch for 10:00 – 1:00, or in maritime parlance, 2200 – 0100 hours. That was Brie's watch, and he would take the longer watch from 1:00 – 5:00 a.m. Brie and Scott switched on and off from day to day, and the cook and the captain did not stand watch except under special circumstances.

After finishing in the galley, Brie went to her berth to grab a short nap before her watch. She lay there for a few minutes, in her mind's eye seeing the news story in the *Island Gazette* about Blythe Whitehall. After a few minutes she fell into a fitful sleep.

Twenty-five minutes later, she woke with a start, hearing her name called. She must have fallen into a deep sleep, because she had been having a dream. In the dream she was floating face up on the surface of the ocean, and she was unable to move —paralyzed. She sat up and swung her legs over the edge of the berth, trying to clear her head, which felt as fuzzy as a bag of cotton candy. To boot, she had a mild headache. She rubbed her face, trying to dispel the remnants of the dream that she guessed had been brought on by the motion of the ship at anchor.

"You awake, Brie?" Scott said softly. His head was sticking through the curtain at the end of her berth.

"Yup," Brie said. "I'll be topside in a minute."

"Take your time. I know how it is when you doze off like that."

"I'm not a napper, Scott, and this is why. It never works out well for me. But today has been an unusually long day."

"Well, at least you've got the short watch tonight," he said.

"That's something, I guess." She hopped off her berth, ran a brush through her hair, put it back in a ponytail, and pulled on her *Maine Wind* ball cap, her windbreaker, and her PFD. Coast Guard regulations mandated that any crew or passengers on deck after dark when the ship was underway were required to wear their personal flotation devices. Captain DuLac had extended the rule to include use of PFDs after dark when they were anchored away from shore, as they were tonight.

Brie stepped out into the galley, poured herself a mug of coffee, and climbed the ladder to the deck. The night was already turning cool, and she was glad for the extra layer of warmth her PFD provided. She took a turn around the deck. There were still a couple of passengers amidships talking quietly. She said hello to them and carried on her way up toward the bow, where she swung a leg over the trunk of the bowsprit and sat for a few minutes, drinking her coffee and thinking about the next day—wondering if Dent Fenton had found the case file from 1958 on Blythe Whitehall. Wondering what it contained and if any of the players were still alive, so many years later.

After a little while, she heard Libby Robbins and Harry McCarthy—the two passengers still on deck—say goodnight to each other and go below. Brie got up and brought her mug down to the galley and returned to the deck. Now she was alone with the ship and its night sounds—a creak from the anchor chain, the slap of a halyard on a mast, or the whisper of a small wave kissing the hull.

After being shot a year and a half ago, it was often hard for Brie to still her thoughts, especially when she was involved with a case. All the names and facts and evidence would run through her mind like the ticker tape at the stock exchange. But on the ocean at night, during watch, the ship seemed to cast a spell over her, releasing her from all her earthly bonds. Tonight she welcomed that respite, and as she kept her watch over the next two and a half hours, the *Maine Wind* spoke softly to her in creaks and groans.

Fifteen minutes before the end of her watch, John came on deck. She was surprised to see him until she remembered their encounter earlier that evening.

"Still game for a little down time together?" he asked, and in the light from the lantern, she saw in his eyes a look at once quizzical, warm, and mischievous.

A slow smile crept onto Brie's face, much as she tried to control herself.

When John saw it, he said, "I think I'll take that as a 'yes.' Anyway, you promised to tell me what's up with the case." And before she could respond, he said, "Why don't you go below to my cabin. There's something I want to touch base with Scott about. I'll be below as soon as he comes on watch."

Brie nodded, feeling a little thrum of excitement inside. "I'll see you below, then."

She headed down the aft companionway and at the foot of the ladder stepped into John's cabin to her left. She knew John was trying to bridge any awkwardness she might feel, heading below to his cabin after Scott came on watch. She and John both tried hard to maintain a degree of discretion in any meetings aboard ship. Not that Scott and George didn't know about their relationship. They did, and both of them seemed happy for her and John, even though they would occasionally rib her about it, as her brothers might have during her teen dating years. But the fact was that the four of them spent so much time together aboard ship—were so much like family—that there was great acceptance among them and great support for one another.

Brie shed her PFD and jacket, pulled off her deck shoes and socks, and slipped out of her khakis. The night was cool below deck, so she left her tee shirt on, climbed onto John's berth, and wriggled under the bedding. In a few minutes she heard him come in, but it was black as the bottom of an inkwell in the cabin, so until he climbed in beside her, she had no sense of where he was.

If they had intended to talk, that plan was quickly foiled by Brie rolling into John's arms and their pretty much devouring one another with kisses. For the next hour that hunger consumed them, and while they were careful to be very quiet, the *Maine Wind* creaked and moaned in rhythm with the sea. To Brie, these were happy sounds, as if the ship were somehow voicing her approval—as if she knew that both John and Brie had been lonely in their separate lives for too long.

Afterward, they lay in each other's arms, and Brie told John about the case and the old newspaper article she had found at the inn.

"I need to go to Augusta tomorrow after the ship docks and we disembark the passengers. Dent Fenton is going to locate the old case file on Blythe Whitehall's death. We're also hoping to go to Portsmouth and search Claire Whitehall's premises—see if we turn up anything of interest there."

"You can take my truck if you need to get to Augusta."

"That'd be great, John, but what are you going to do for a car?"

"Remember, I've got that old Honda Civic back at my place. Scott or George can drop me at home after we finish up at the *Maine Wind*."

"This is an unexpected turn of events. I'm not sure what will transpire over the next couple of days."

"That's okay, Brie. We'll just play it by ear. I've gotten used to sharing you with the Maine State Police. What's more, now that it's getting late in the season, the cruises are shorter and there are fewer passengers."

"Thanks, John. I should know better where things are at by the end of tomorrow."

He kissed her forehead. "If Dent and Marty need you on this case, I can always improvise. Ed Browning works for himself. He told me he's always happy to fill in aboard ship."

John was talking about his former first mate, Ed Browning, who had moved back to Maine this summer and worked building furniture in the barn on his dad's property near Liberty, Maine. Brie had met him in August when he came aboard the *Maine Wind* as an extra deckhand on their trip to New Brunswick.

"I forgot about Ed. That takes the pressure off a bit. Thanks, John."

They slept in each other's arms for another hour, and then Brie got up and dressed and made her way back to her berth at the other end of the ship. She wanted to get up early and grab a shower before she had to be on deck for their early departure from Ghost Cove.

Chapter 13

At 5:30 a.m., or 0530, the heavy chain rumbled up through the starboard hull and clattered onto the windlass as the crew of the *Maine Wind* hauled her anchor. The captain needed to get the ship back to port by noon, and with the prevailing winds out of the southeast, they would make it easily, with time left over for docking—always a painstaking process with a ship as big as the *Maine Wind*.

One of the local lobstermen had offered to push them out of the harbor, but the yawl boat was still in the water, so there was no need for that. John joked to Brie that the offer was probably more about getting them out of Ghost Cove quickly, thereby allowing the harbor to return to its status quo as a lobstering only, working waterfront.

Once free of the harbor, all available hands hauled the yawl boat and hoisted sail.

The wind blew east by south, and within a half hour of getting under way, it freshened up to 18 knots. Captain DuLac put their starboard beam to windward and set a heading on a fast point of sail for their berth in Camden. The sea, so troubled the past two days, had transformed itself into a brilliant azure canvas across which the *Maine Wind* painted itself, leaning into the wind, her canvas aroar, spindrift frothing off the surface of the water, exploding against her bow, and fracturing into a million prismatic droplets.

Brie took up her watch in the bow, feeling tired but happy, the wind on her face an invigorating force. She zipped her windbreaker all the way up and tightened the strap at the back of her ball cap to keep it from sailing off her head. Her long hair, which she'd put in a braid after her shower, had been pulled through the hole in her cap, and it swung pendulum-like in the wind gusts.

She felt the deck rise and fall beneath her feet as the ship sliced through the seas. It was a ride she could never get enough of, and she worried momentarily that the Whitehall case might keep her from crewing on the upcoming cruise. There were so few voyages left before the end of the season, before the ship was hauled out for the year, before she'd have to leave Maine and return to Minnesota, either to take up her life there or settle her affairs for the move here. But she put those thoughts aside. It was too beautiful a day to worry about the future—too beautiful a day not to be in the moment. And so, for the next hour, she stood her watch at the bow in deep communion with the elements.

The spell was only broken when George came forward with a steaming mug of coffee for her. They chatted for a few minutes and, after he left, Brie focused on what the afternoon had in store. It promised to be a long day, what with having to meet Dent Fenton and Marty Dupuis at headquarters in Augusta and possibly having to drive to Portsmouth, New Hampshire, if the warrant came through. That was okay, though. Brie could deal with a lack of sleep for one day, as long as she caught up the following night.

She ventured not a guess about what would unfold with the case over the next twelve hours. All she knew was that things had reached a turning point—something all detectives like to see this early in the game. Not even 48 hours had elapsed since they'd spotted Claire's body in the water, and already there had been two significant developments—the arrest of James Levy and the newspaper article about the death in 1958. In her detective's mind, Brie knew these developments boded well for the case. However, she worried about Claire

Whitehall's death possibly being tied to a case from so long ago —over 50 years ago. Such a case could prove extremely problematic. And if by chance the original case had gone cold, well, that could present another challenging set of circumstances.

There was nothing Brie hated more than a case gone cold. Such a case was like a ghost that haunted you—that would never let go. She'd only dealt with a few of them in her career, but those were the victims, the cases, that occasionally woke her in the middle of the night—that had the power to rob her of her peace of mind and her certitude about her investigative skills, for which she had so often been praised. So she worried about the possibility that Claire Whitehall's death might be tied to such an enigma.

You're getting ahead of yourself, Brie, she thought and remembered Marty Dupuis' mantra—*Just work the case.*

She didn't realize how long she'd been lost in her thoughts until Scott arrived in the bow to enlist her assistance in prepping the halyards for lowering sail. Just before 1100 hours, Captain DuLac brought the *Maine Wind* up into the wind for lowering and furling sail. The crew took their places on the halyards and slowly brought the mainsail down the mast as the passengers—lined up on either side of the boom—worked the canvas into large folds atop the boom and lashed it off.

Next all hands went to the stern of the ship to lower the yawl boat that would push the ship into the harbor and up to the dock. Camden was one of Maine's most beloved seaside villages, often called the jewel of the Maine coast, and its busy recreational harbor was home to a good chunk of Maine's windjammer fleet. After the peace of being at sea for any length of time, Brie always had to adjust herself to the hustle and bustle of this popular tourist spot, which was one of Maine's most picturesque but busiest coastal locales.

The passengers were always encouraged to have their belongings packed before the ship made port. So once they had docked, the shipmates said their farewells and immediately began to disembark, and it was surprising how quickly the *Maine Wind* emptied out. Some of them had long drives ahead, and others had flights to catch. Brie, Scott, and George did their best to help everyone disembark as efficiently as possible. Then the crew cleaned the deck and loaded the sheets and towels from the cruise into Scott's car so he could take them to the laundromat that processed them.

Brie had packed a small duffel with the belongings she would need in the event she didn't get back to the ship tonight or tomorrow. There was no way to guess where the Claire Whitehall case might lead over the next twenty-four hours, so in addition to her gun and badge, she had packed a change of clothes, a sweater, pajamas, and toiletries—enough to weather today and possibly tomorrow.

She and John walked along the wharf to where he had parked his truck. He opened the driver's door and pulled out a map and, being a man of charts, spread the map out on the hood of the truck.

"The best way to get to Augusta from here is to take Route 105, also called Washington Street, here in Camden." John tapped his finger on the map to show where Route 105 intersected US Route 1—the Coastal Route. "You'll turn right on Washington, just a couple blocks west of here, and head north across the Megunticook River."

Brie ran her finger along the map, tracing the route all the way to Augusta.

"How far is it to Augusta?"

"Just about fifty miles, but plan for it to take more than an hour, because you travel through a number of small villages. There's very little traffic on One-oh-five, though, and some gorgeous views of Appleton Ridge as you drive along. At this time of year, with the fall foliage just coming on, it should be beautiful."

"Thanks, John. I wish we could drive it together, but I know you've got your hands full back at the ship. Plus, this trip is strictly about business for me."

Brie folded the map in half so she could see the route and was just about to climb into the truck when her phone rang. She pulled it out.

"It's Dent Fenton," she said to John. "Hello, Lieutenant. I was just leaving for Augusta."

"Change of plans, Brie. The warrant came through for Claire Whitehall's premises. I'm sending you and Marty over there to pick it up and carry out the search."

"Where should I meet up with Marty?" she asked.

"Head toward Portland and you can meet him at Troop G headquarters on Congress Street, just off I-95. The address is 2360. Marty will be waiting for you there, and you can leave your vehicle in the parking lot."

"Any luck on the old case file on Blythe Whitehall?" Brie asked.

"Yup. I signed it over to Marty. Only had a chance to peruse it briefly. Nothing jumped out. The COD was drowning. Case went cold and most of the players have passed away, including one of the two investigating detectives."

"I see," Brie said, feeling bummed by what she was hearing.

"Here's something, though. I called Joe Wolf to see if he knew anything about the coroner who had done the autopsy on Blythe Whitehall back in 1958. His name is Ezra Appleton. He's quite elderly, but Joe says he still lives on Apparition Island."

"Well, it's a thread at least," Brie said.

"Oh, and one other thing that will interest you. Apparently Claire Whitehall visited headquarters and viewed the Blythe Whitehall case file back in June."

"That's interesting," Brie said.

"But I still believe Levy's our guy. Marty will fill you in about the interrogation."

"Thanks, Dent."

"Call me later and let me know if the search reveals anything."

"Will do."

Brie and Dent ended the call, and she filled John in on what she'd learned.

"I should get going. Marty will be waiting for me in Portland," she said.

"Take the Ninety cut-off around Rockland. It'll save you a little time. Use the GPS."

"I'll do that, John." She gave him a quick kiss on the lips and hopped in the truck. "I'll probably know a little more by the end of the day."

"Call me then and fill me in. You can use the truck as long as you need to."

"Thanks, John." She started the truck and steered carefully through the village and turned left onto Route 1.

Just beyond Camden she took a right onto Highway 90 so she could bypass the town of Rockland, which was sometimes congested. Highway 90 intersected with Coastal Route 1 again just beyond the town of Warren.

Brie used the drive time to think back over the people she'd met on Apparition Island. She mentally relegated them to two lists—*Persons of Interest* and *Others*. Under Persons of Interest she placed James Levy—recently arrested; the three lobstermen: Logan Lancaster, Buzz Beloit—the rude guy, and Paul Herrington—Claire's lover. Also making this list were Walter and Muriel Westburg, mainly because of their access to Claire's comings and goings. On the list titled *Others,* she placed a miscellany of islanders she had encountered. Gilford Doubtwater, the town manager; Edie Hanover, the general store owner; Mary, who worked at the Windward Inn; Gus

Flambeau, lobsterman—supposedly off island at present; Bob and Bonnie Foster, lobsterman and his wife, who were tending Gus Flambeau's traps in his absence. Added to this list were a couple people who'd been mentioned but whom she'd not met —Ezra Appleton, the elderly coroner who had done the autopsy on Blythe Danes Whitehall decades ago, and Belle Westgate, who ran the island's History Center, according to Gil Doubtwater. When she was done, Brie thought back over the two lists, calling up a mental picture of each person and noting the feeling each face evoked. She guessed the next step—her next course of action—would be revealed by either the case file on Blythe Whitehall or the search of Claire Whitehall's premises in Portsmouth, New Hampshire.

Traffic moved well until she reached the bridge over the Sheepscot River going into the village of Wiscasset. Tourists heading to and from Red's Eats scurried back and forth across Route 1, or Main Street, stopping traffic just west of the bridge. The iconic little lobster shack had stood at the corner of Water Street and Main Street in Wiscasset since 1954. Brie sat patiently on the bridge, knowing that Red's stopped traffic for a very good reason—they served up some of the best lobster rolls that could be had anywhere. She'd first gone to Red's with George back in June, when they had a day off from the ship and were hitting tag sales and flea markets along the mid-coast. That was the first lobster roll she'd had in years—since her childhood visits to Maine—and her mouth started to water just thinking about it.

She craned her neck as she came off the bridge and up into the village, wishing she could stop at Red's, but predictably the line looked to be at least a half-hour long. She promised herself she'd treat herself to at least one more of Red's lobster rolls before she left Maine in October. She noted that the thought of leaving this place and John put an odd ache in her chest.

The final delay along the road came as Brie crawled through several traffic lights on the east side of Bath. But just beyond that, she picked up the four-lane and cruised toward Portland without further delays.

Just below Freeport, she took the I-295 Falmouth Spur toward I-95—the Maine Turnpike—and about 18 miles later exited on Skyway Drive, just west of the Portland Jetport. She followed the directions John's nav system spit out to 2360 Congress Street, where she spotted Troop G headquarters for the Maine State Police. She saw Marty waiting for her. He was leaning against his unmarked Chevy Impala cruiser, drinking from a paper coffee cup. She parked John's truck a couple spots away, got out with her duffel, and headed toward him.

"Hope I didn't keep you waiting too long, Marty."

"Nope. Just got here about fifteen minutes ago. I picked up a coffee for you in case you're dragging your anchor."

Brie smiled. "Very clever, Marty. And thanks. I could use a cuppa joe." She stretched her arms over her head and leaned to right and left, getting the kinks out. Then she walked around the front of the car and climbed into the passenger seat for the drive down to Portsmouth.

Chapter 14

Before they got under way, Marty reached in the back seat and handed her the envelope that contained the case file on Blythe Whitehall. Brie buckled her belt, took a sip of her coffee, and pulled out the file. Marty navigated back to the Maine Turnpike, and they headed south toward Portsmouth, New Hampshire.

She was about to open the file when she remembered that Dent had told her Marty would fill her in on the James Levy interrogation. She picked up her coffee and turned toward Marty.

"Dent said to ask you about the James Levy interrogation."

"Oh, right. Well, we questioned him for a few hours. At first he denied having any contact at all with Claire Whitehall while she was on the island. But he was nervous, and all the 'tells' said he was lying."

"Did he say how he even knew she was out on the island?" Brie asked.

"He claimed he got that information from one of her friends."

"Yeah, not likely, considering Claire had taken out a restraining order against him."

"Exactly what we thought," Marty said. "Personally, what with his penchant for breaking and entering, I wouldn't be surprised if we find evidence that he broke into Claire's place in Portsmouth and somehow found the information there."

"Not an unlikely scenario, I'd say. Something else to look for when we get to her place."

"Anyway, we told Levy we knew he'd been arrested for assault for choking a previous girlfriend. That's when his behavior changed. He got skittish and confrontational. He swore up one side and down the other that he hadn't killed Claire Whitehall—that she had been alive the last time he saw her."

"So he walked into that one," Brie said.

"Right. Once we knew he'd been with her at some point on the island, we bored in on that."

"Interesting wording of his comment—that she was alive the last time he saw her. Why would he mention that she was alive if he hadn't attacked or injured her in some way?" Brie drank some more of her coffee, waiting to see what Marty would say.

"That's a very good point, Brie. He knew the deck was stacked against him once we brought up the prior arrest. He finally broke down and admitted to choking Claire. Said he'd gone to her cabin and when she saw it was him, she tried to slam the door. He admitted to forcing his way into her camp and trying to tell her how he felt about her."

"Just what every girl dreams of," Brie said.

"Really. Anyway, Levy said things escalated to a heated argument and that's when he choked her."

"Wow, so he admitted to it."

"Yup, but that's all. He swears he realized suddenly what he was doing and stopped. Claims he left the camp immediately without saying anything. Claims he was ashamed and admitted to us that he needed to get help. But he also swore she was alive and that he never saw her again after that."

"And what day was this?" Brie asked.

"The day before yesterday. Friday the thirteenth—the day the hurricane hit the coast. Levy swears that, until you showed him Claire's picture on your phone, he had no idea she had died." Marty reached for his coffee and took a swallow and set the cup back down. "We asked him how she had died. He said he had no idea and why were we asking him? And then he started asking us what had happened to her—if she had died in the hurricane. If she had drowned."

"A good tactic to use if you're the killer."

"It's true. But I'll tell you one thing, he sure was agitated. Like he really wanted to know what happened to her. Could be an act, of course, and he refused to take a polygraph, which makes him look guilty as sin."

"Did you ask him what he was doing in Claire's camp yesterday?"

"We did. He said he was trying to find her—that he wanted to apologize."

"Yeah, that sounds a little fishy, but here's the thing. If Levy killed Claire on Friday, would he really have been hanging around her camp yesterday, just waiting for us to catch him?"

"Good point," Marty said.

"The problem is that Claire Whitehall died from a fall, not by strangulation, so even though Levy's admitted to choking her—thereby explaining how the marks got on her neck—there's no evidence of him pushing her off that cliff. Unless, of course, we can find someone on the island that saw him with her that afternoon when she headed out for a hike."

"We're holding him for forty-eight hours until the DA makes a decision about the case."

"What's your gut tell you, Marty?"

"Tells me he's a dangerous dude. But the cause of death is so ambiguous, I think it'll be hard to make the charge stick."

"Did Dent tell you what I found on the island—the newspaper?"

"He sure did. It's freaky. And I'm with you, I don't like odd coincidences in a case where the water's already pretty muddy."

"We'll see what we find at Claire's premises. Maybe we'll get some kind of a lead. Did you get a chance to look through this case file on the Blythe Whitehall death in 1958?"

"Just briefly."

"I'm not convinced that Claire Whitehall was on the island researching the local lobster wars. Not after finding that newspaper clipping. I'm hoping there's something in this file that'll give me some kind of a clue. Personally, I think it's much more likely that this is why Claire went to Apparition Island." Brie tapped her finger on the case file as she said it.

"Well, it's an odd turn of events. Maybe we'll get some clarity when we search her place."

"I'd also like to follow up with that friend of Claire's you spoke to. What was her name again?"

"Michelle York. It might be worth talking to her again, considering what you found on the island yesterday."

"For now, though, I think I'll delve into this file and see what's what. How long till we get to Portsmouth?"

"A little less than an hour with the current traffic," Marty said. "Can you really read that without getting carsick?"

"I can," Brie said. "But I'm not going to do any in-depth reading. Just familiarize myself with what's in here—who the players were in the Blythe Whitehall case. Dent said that one of the detectives who worked the case is still alive."

"That would be Jack Le Beau. He's quite elderly but still has all his marbles. Lives in the village of Wiscasset, I believe."

"Huh. Do you think he'd mind talking to me about the case?"

"I think he'd love to talk to you, Brie. You know what they say—once a cop, always a cop. Plus it's been a lonely time for him. His wife died last year."

"How old would he have been in 1958?" Brie asked.

"He would have been a young guy—maybe thirty? Jack developed a reputation for having good instincts and was the lead investigator on a number of really tough cases down through the years."

"How well do you know him?"

"Not well, but I've had a chance to talk to him at a few Maine State Police functions over the years. He's a good man."

"And the other detective?"

"Tom Stratton," Marty said.

"When did he pass?"

"About three years ago. Died of a heart attack while shoveling snow."

"Curses on that," Brie said. "We lose a lot of good people in Minnesota the same way. Every year they put out the warnings, and every year there are more deaths from snow shoveling. Mostly men."

"It's hard for us to admit we can't do something we've been doing our whole lives."

"I know, but it's sad nonetheless." That said, Brie opened the file in her lap and started looking through what was there.

Several sheets down, she came to a photograph of Blythe Whitehall. She had been a remarkably beautiful woman, but what struck Brie most was the strong resemblance she bore to Claire Whitehall. The same wide mouth, the same fine bone structure and high cheekbones. The resemblance between the two women was haunting. The photograph dispelled any doubts Brie may have had about Claire Whitehall being related to Blythe Danes Whitehall. The photo in her hands was most certainly that of Claire's grandmother.

Brie looked over some of the reports of the interviews Detective Le Beau had conducted. He had been meticulous in his recording of the events and interviews that followed the discovery of Blythe Whitehall's body. The fact that Mrs. Whitehall had resided in another state and that her husband was wealthy would have put great pressure on the police in Maine to discover the truth of what had happened. From the number of interviews Jack Le Beau had conducted on Apparition Island, Brie guessed he had left few stones unturned. But as she glanced over the reports, one thing became clear—Detective Le

Beau had hit a dead end at almost every turn. What she found in the file made her even more eager to meet with the elderly detective and see what his recollections of the case were.

There was one point of interest that she noted in a report Le Beau had written. Apparently several of the islanders who had gotten off the ferry around the time Blythe had gone missing from the island had claimed to have seen a man get off the ferry who seemed suspicious, who didn't seem like a tourist. In reading deeper, Brie found that these allegations had led to a theory that Blythe's husband, Harrison Whitehall, had hired this man to kill his wife. That speculation really piqued Brie's interest and made her even more eager to talk to Jack Le Beau. She pulled out her phone and put a call in to Dent Fenton.

"Hi, Lieutenant," she said when he answered.

"What's up, Brie?"

"I've just been looking over the case file you gave me, and I'm wondering if you could get me a phone number and address for Jack Le Beau. I'd like to talk to him about his recollections of this case."

"No problem. I'll look that up and get back to you." He ended the call.

Brie saw the exits for Portsmouth coming up. She closed the file, slipped it back into the envelope, and set it on the back seat. Just then her phone rang. It was Dent calling back. She answered it and reached in the pocket of her jacket for her small notebook. Dent read off the phone number and address he'd found for Jack Le Beau in Wiscasset, and Brie jotted them down.

"Thanks, Dent. We're just coming into Portsmouth now. I'll call you if the search turns up anything of interest."

"Roger that, Brie."

They ended the call, and Brie stared out her window as they passed through the historic district of Portsmouth. There were lots of people on foot, and she could see why. A charming mix of shops, restaurants, and gardens lined the cobblestone streets of historic downtown Portsmouth. As they drove toward police headquarters, Marty told her that Portsmouth had been named one of the best walking cities in the US.

At the sight of all the local eateries, Brie's stomach started to rumble, and she realized she hadn't eaten anything since breakfast aboard the *Maine Wind* that morning.

As if reading her mind, Marty asked, "Do you want to stop for a bite after we pick up the warrant? I know a great little spot here for burgers."

"That'd be good, Marty. I'm actually starving."

"Not on my watch," Marty said.

In a few minutes they pulled into the headquarters for the Portsmouth PD. "I'll just run in and grab the warrant. Then we'll eat lunch before we head over to Ms. Whitehall's place." Marty opened the door and stepped out of the car.

He was out within ten minutes. He backed the car up, turned left out of the parking lot, and made a right on Junkins Avenue, where they crossed South Mill Pond.

"You up for a great burger?" he asked.

"I'd kill for a great burger," Brie said.

Marty laughed. "Dangerous words from a homicide detective."

"Okay, how about I'm dying for a great burger?"

"We can't have any of that. I'm taking you to Lexie's Joint. It's less than a mile away, and they have these amazing burgers and fries."

"You're my hero, Marty."

"Well, that was easy," he joked.

They wound their way west for a few more blocks till Marty pointed to his left. Lexie's Joint was a little corner restaurant on Islington Street next to an auto repair shop. Marty parked and they headed inside, and the aroma of beef and onions grilling made Brie feel almost euphorically happy. She knew it was a lucky thing that she had good genes and a job that kept her hopping, because food was one of the great comforts in her life—period. And she never apologized for seeking out the next great meal. She had long thought that people would have fewer problems with food if they stopped feeling guilty about liking it and simply upped their activity levels.

They sat at a table near the bank of windows that ran along the front of Lexie's, and Marty told her about all his favorites on the menu. Brie decided to go with the Bistro burger that came with tomato confit, braised onions, bacon, and herbed aioli. Marty ordered the Burning Down the House burger loaded up with jalapenos, pepper jack cheese, and chipotle aioli, and he added a side of their Herbed Parm fries and a cola. There was only one other couple in Lexie's. They were sitting on high stools at a table by the far wall beneath a poster of the peace sign. Brie checked her watch—just past two-thirty, well beyond the lunch rush.

The burgers came out quickly, and while they waited for them to cool, they shared some of Marty's fries. Then they dove into the burgers and all talking ceased. The mixture of condiments perfectly complemented Brie's juicy Bistro burger, and when she asked about the wonderfully soft bun, Marty told her Lexie's used potato rolls. Brie polished off her iced tea as Marty downed the rest of his fries. They paid their tab, praising the food again, and headed for their cruiser. The lunch break had taken just slightly over a half hour.

"Thanks for recommending Lexie's, Marty. That may be the best burger I've ever eaten."

"Don't tell George that," Marty said.

"I've never known George to cook burgers on the ship, so not to worry."

Following the directions Marty had written down at the police department, they headed south through Portsmouth to the Elwyn Park neighborhood, where Claire Whitehall had lived. About three miles from the downtown, they located the apartment complex in an appealing woodsy setting. The apartments were set up more like small townhomes or condos, and each unit had its own entry door to the outside. They parked and found the caretaker's office.

The caretaker was a tall, rangy, mostly bald man who wore scuffed workmen's boots and painters' coveralls with the name Zach stitched on the pocket. They showed him the warrant, and he took them to apartment number eight and unlocked the door, asking if everything was all right with Miss Whitehall. They stepped inside, and Marty told the caretaker that Claire had died two days ago. Zach's eyes clouded over, and he pulled an old rag out of his back pocket and dabbed at them. He asked what had happened, and Marty told him that they were not at liberty to say much about the case.

"She was a very nice young woman—always with a kind word." Just then Zach seemed to notice something. "What the . . ." He headed toward the kitchen, and Brie and Marty followed.

When they stepped through the door, Brie saw what had caught the caretaker's attention. There was glass on the floor from a window that had been broken. The window was still ajar, and Brie was about one hundred percent sure who had climbed through—James Levy. Zach said he was going to get a broom to clean up the glass, but Marty told him they would have to call the Portsmouth PD and get a team out here to process the scene of the break-in. Zach nodded and stuffed his hands in his coveralls as if he didn't know what to do next. Marty told him he could go and that they would check in with him before they left and leave him a list of anything they took from the apartment.

Marty called the Portsmouth PD to let them know about the break-in. Then he and Brie gloved up and walked back to the living room to look around. It was a newer apartment, and Claire's tastes had run to Scandinavian furniture with its light finishes and clean lines. There was little art on the walls except for some framed photographs hung above the sofa. But the apartment had a good exposure and was filled with natural light.

They went first to a large computer desk that stood against the side wall of the living room. It contained some pigeonholes filled with mail. There were several stacks of notes on the desk that looked like they might pertain to projects Claire was working on. There was no computer, but Brie knew Claire had taken it with her to the island and that it was now in the hands of the Maine State Police.

Spread out on the desktop was a map of the Maine coast and notes on ferry departure times to Apparition Island.

"Levy wouldn't have had to look far to learn where Claire had gone," Marty said.

"That's for sure. It's all right here for the taking."

"So that's one mystery solved. We now know exactly how he tracked her to the island."

"He's got a penchant for breaking and entering, doesn't he?" Brie said.

"Works in our favor," Marty said. "Gives us a reason to put him in jail."

"Should we work our way through the desk together?" Brie asked.

"Sounds like a plan," Marty said. "Do you want to look through her notes, and I'll search through the bills?"

"Sure," Brie said. She went and got an extra chair from the dining room table, sat down at the desk next to Marty, and collected several stacks of notes—both typed and longhand—that Claire had made.

As Marty searched through the bills and correspondence in the pigeonholes, Brie started reading through Claire's notes to see what projects the journalist had been considering or was working on, and whether any of the notes pertained to either the topic of lobster wars or to the unsolved case of Blythe Whitehall's death in 1958.

There were several groups of notes covering topics that ranged from the reasons for snowy owl sightings to the legalization of medical marijuana to controversy surrounding degradation of the cement at the Seabrook Nuclear Plant. Among the myriad notes, Brie found several articles that Claire had printed off about the lobster wars on Matinicus Island, Maine. She also found printouts of articles about Apparition Island, Maine, that had more of a tourism spin to them. She put all the notes into an evidence envelope and marked the date, the location from which they were taken, and her shield number.

Marty had found the phone bills and was studying two or three of the most recent ones.

"It looks like after Claire left for the island in August, there was a rash of calls from the same number. They went on until about a week ago and then stopped."

"I'm surprised that bill is even here. You'd think her mail would have been on hold," Brie said.

"Maybe she had someone picking it up and leaving it in the apartment here."

Brie looked around and realized the place was full of plants. "Let's ask Zach," she said. "Maybe he was coming in watering the plants for her and dropping off the mail."

"Or he might know who was," Marty said.

"But back to the phone bill. Any ideas on the number that's showing up there?"

"I recognize it," Marty said. "The calls were placed from James Levy's cell phone."

"Looks like he got tired of calling and decided to take the direct approach," Brie said.

"I'd guess he watched her place for a couple days and when he determined she wasn't at home, he went ahead and broke in."

"What a psycho," Brie said.

"It definitely dials him up into the scary range," Marty said. "So far we've got this guy on a number of counts."

"Do you think he killed her, Marty? I mean, what's your gut telling you?"

"Dent's sure he's our guy," Marty said. "I'm just not one hundred percent there yet. Don't know why."

"Nor do you need to be," Brie said. "That's what the gut is for. And beyond that, we just keep working the evidence."

"Levy's a lock for motive, means, and opportunity. Claire Whitehall had rejected him and filed a restraining order. Guy like Levy—that'd make him even more determined. So that's motive. Means and opportunity—he was there on the island. We caught him red-handed right in her camp, and he admits to choking her."

"The only question is, did that happen before Walter Westburg saw Claire heading out for a hike the day the hurricane hit? Or did he attack and choke her up on the cliffs? After which, Levy might have figured he'd be going to jail and so decided to push or throw Claire Whitehall off the cliff."

"What's *your* gut saying, Brie?"

"If it weren't for Claire's connection to this case from the past, I wouldn't doubt Levy's guilt for an instant. I'm curious to talk to Jack Le Beau—the detective who worked the Blythe Whitehall case back in fifty-eight. I don't know what it will prove, but . . ." Brie let her thoughts trail off.

"Did you find anything in those stacks of notes about Blythe Whitehall or her death in 1958?" Marty asked.

"Nothing," Brie said, feeling a little deflated. "While you finish up here, I'm going to search Claire's bedroom."

"Go ahead," said Marty. "Then we'll find the caretaker and wrap things up here."

Brie headed up the stairs to the master bedroom. The walls were painted a soft green, and the queen-sized mattress sat on a simple wooden bed frame and was covered with a lightweight, cream-colored down comforter. The only other pieces of furniture in the room were two Scandinavian-style bedside tables and a dresser with a wood-framed mirror above it.

On the far side of the bed the covers had been hastily pulled up, and the pillow still held an indentation left by Claire's head. It made Brie a little sad, seeing that evidence of life, knowing that Claire Whitehall had had a good life, a nice place to rest her head, and a job she obviously was passionate about. She had been an investigative reporter. She would have wanted someone to take up the mantle of her case—to discover the truth of what had happened that last day on Apparition Island.

Brie had felt the weight of that responsibility in every case she had investigated down through the years. There was a vast gulf into which any case gone cold was likely to flow. It was often a bottomless gulf from which that case would never emerge—from which justice would never be meted out for that victim. Brie often felt like a fisherman who must cast the net wide to catch all the intricacies that could so easily flow past investigators—connections, clues, nuances of the case that could so easily be missed, so easily get by them and be lost forever in the ocean of unrecognized but crucial information.

As the early hours and days ticked by in a case, Brie inwardly experienced something akin to panic that she would miss some crucial bit of information. And while she worked each case with a methodical steadfastness, that other feeling was always there, just below the surface, driving her forward. Her first homicide commander, old Jed Waters, had told Brie never to lose that discomfort—that sense of something about to be lost, because it was what drove the best detectives, what kept them turning over rocks when everyone else had given up.

Brie felt that panic tug at her now as she walked around the far side of the bed. Several stacks of books sat on the floor. They were neatly arranged according to size and pushed up against the wall. She smiled, thinking about the stacks of books in her apartment back in Minnesota and how she never got around to purchasing bookshelves. She knelt down on the floor to read the spines on the books, and out of the corner of her eye, something between the mattress and the box spring caught her attention. It was just a slight gap between the mattress and its foundation—one she never would have noticed had she been standing up. Brie slid her hand in under the mattress and felt the spine of a book.

Carefully, she drew the book out, feeling the leather cover and spine against her hand. When it came into view, she immediately knew the book was a diary, and she felt a little thrum of excitement run through her—a vibrating string of anticipation. The book was old. The leather, once soft and buttery, had dried, and cracks like the lines of an aged hand etched its surface.

Brie opened the cover and read the inscription on the first page.

Blythe Danes Whitehall
June 15, 1958 –

There was no ending date marked on the page because Blythe Whitehall had been suddenly ripped from her own life as violently and definitively as a page torn from this treasured volume.

Brie turned to the last entry in the diary. It was dated August 31st, a number that set Brie's heart pounding. She pulled her small notebook from her pocket and flipped to the page where she'd recorded the date Blythe Whitehall's body had been found in the ocean. The date was September 7, 1958, a little more than a week after this entry had been made. Brie knew that, after drowning, the victim can stay submerged for days or even a couple of weeks. *Could this last entry in the diary have been made the day Blythe Whitehall died?* she wondered.

The sound of Marty's voice came to her from what seemed a great distance, so lost was she in the echoes of the past. She stood just as he entered the room.

"You ready to go, Brie? I'm finished downstairs." He must have caught the sense of something unfolding, because he said, "You found something."

Brie nodded and held out the book for him to inspect. "It's Blythe Whitehall's diary," she said. "The last entry is dated August thirty-first, 1958—one week before her body was found in the sea off Apparition Island."

Marty whistled slowly. "I guess now we know for sure what Claire was doing out on that island."

"Yes, and I believe she may have unearthed more than a ghost from the past—I think she discovered something, something that had never come to light, something that led her to the same watery grave that claimed her grandmother so many years before."

"And we know for sure that Blythe Whitehall was Claire's grandmother?" Marty asked.

"Yes, and I can show you the photograph in the cold case file that lays any doubt of that to rest."

Marty nodded.

"I'd like to keep the diary and read through it. Along with the cold case file, it will give me a jumping off spot when I meet with Jack Le Beau and Ezra Appleton, the elderly coroner who did the autopsy on Blythe Whitehall back in 1958."

"It's really quite amazing that they're both still alive," Marty said. "And Jack is still very sharp. I have no doubt that he'll remember this case. There's something in the mind of the detective that never really lets go of a cold case."

"I agree, Marty, and I believe those impressions will be worth their weight in gold."

"I'll enter the diary into the evidence log for the Claire Whitehall case and note that the book is in your possession," Marty said.

They headed back downstairs. Marty had made a list of everything they had taken into evidence. He added the diary to the list and stapled the list to a copy of the warrant. They were just about to lock the front door when the crime lab team arrived to process the break-in. Brie and Marty left them to their work and went to find Zach.

The caretaker was in his office, entering figures onto a spreadsheet on his computer. Marty gave him the papers and told him the crime lab team was at Claire's apartment. Zach said he'd sent them over there and would lock up when they were done. Brie asked him about the mail, and he said Claire's friend Michelle had stopped by once a week to pick up the mail and water Claire's plants. Brie nodded, and they thanked him for his help. Then she and Marty headed for the cruiser and made their way back through Portsmouth to I-95 and across the Piscataqua River into Maine.

Chapter 15

As soon as they were back on the turnpike, Brie brought up Dent Fenton's number and put through a call. She told him about the break-in at Claire Whitehall's residence and also about the diary she'd found that dated back to the summer Blythe Whitehall had died on Apparition Island.

"We're heading back to Portland now," she said. "I'm planning to read the diary tonight and see if there are any clues in it that might shed light on the cold case. I'm also hoping to meet with Jack Le Beau this evening."

"That's good, Brie. We'll question James Levy about the break-in."

"Any luck reaching Claire Whitehall's parents?"

"Not yet," Dent said. "We're checking the mobile phone carriers to see if we can locate a cell phone number for William Whitehall that keys into the address we have in Boston."

"That's good. Terrible as it is, we need to get the news of their daughter to them." It had only been a little over twenty-four hours since they'd identified Claire's body, but that's an eternity to the parent.

"We'll find them, Brie."

"I'm curious to know how Claire Whitehall came by her grandmother's diary."

"I'll ask the parents that when we reach them," Dent said.

"Thanks, Lieutenant."

They ended the call, and Brie took out her pocket notebook and punched in Jack Le Beau's number. A sense of urgency, like a physical weight, was strong upon her, as if the elderly detective might suddenly vanish from the face of the earth, and along with him, her chance to relive the Blythe Whitehall case through his eyes. After four rings Le Beau answered, and Brie almost let out a sigh of relief. She had done the math and knew he had to be around eighty-six years old. But there was no frailty in his voice. It was strong and clear, as if maybe he'd spent his waning years singing for all he was worth. She made a mental note to ask him if he was a member of a choir.

Brie introduced herself and gave Jack Le Beau a brief summary of who she was, her background as a homicide detective, and her connection with the Maine State Police. Except for a few verbal nods, there was silence at the other end as she talked, but it was an active silence, as if everything she said was being framed into a detailed picture of her.

She gave Le Beau a brief rundown of their recovery of Claire Whitehall's body and the autopsy results, at which point he interrupted her.

"Did you say her name was Whitehall?"

Brie heard a combination of recognition, curiosity, and excitement, as if this were something he might have been waiting to hear for fifty-some years.

"That's right, Detective Le Beau. Our victim has the same last name as Blythe Whitehall—a victim whose case you investigated many years ago."

"I remember it well," Jack said.

"I thought you might," she said. "I was wondering if I might come visit you tonight to talk with you about the case."

"Of course," Le Beau said. "Where are you coming from?"

Brie told him they were on their way back to Portland and that she'd be heading up the coast immediately from there. "I should be in Wiscasset by about six," she said. "Could I bring some food and maybe we could talk over dinner?"

"That would be very nice, Detective. I don't want you to put yourself out, though."

Brie already felt at home with Jack Le Beau, even though they'd only spoken for a few minutes. "It's no trouble at all, Detective. I passed the Sea Basket on the way down the coast. It's right there in Wiscasset, and it looked busy."

"First of all, you call me Jack, and second of all, the Sea Basket has great food. I'm partial to the fried shrimp and scallops."

"That sounds great. I'll get two of those and see you between six and six-thirty. Oh, and I'll be happy to call you Jack if you call me Brie."

"It's a deal, young lady. I'll see you this evening, and I hope I can be of help in your case."

"Thanks, Jack, I know you will be. Oh, before we go, could you recommend a place to stay in Wiscasset?"

"You can't go wrong with the Wiscasset Motor Lodge. The folks that own it are very nice, and they run a tight ship. Their place is clean, cozy, and comfortable, and the price is right. They're just a short ways west of the Sea Basket. It'll be on your right."

"Thanks. That sounds perfect." They ended the call, and Brie turned to Marty. "I like him already," she said.

"Told you so," he replied.

"I'm going to catch a nap until we get back, if that's okay with you. Today started before the crack of dawn, and there's no end in sight yet."

"Go ahead, Brie. You've got about forty minutes till we're back at troop headquarters."

Brie reclined her seat, laid her head back against the rest, and fell quickly into a deep sleep.

She awoke some forty minutes later when Marty shut off the car in the parking lot of Troop G headquarters. Her brain felt fuzzy, and she had a dull headache creeping up on her.

"Come on inside," Marty said. "We'll get you some coffee for the rest of the trip."

Brie grabbed the cup that Marty had given her at the beginning of the trip. It held a good sixteen ounces—enough to get her up the coast in one piece, she hoped. Inside, Marty led her to the coffee machine and filled her cup. A couple of the officers greeted him, but he didn't stop to talk. Brie guessed he was eager to get home to dinner and his family.

Outside, they walked to Brie's truck. "I'm going to see what I can learn from Jack tonight, and tomorrow I think I'm heading back to the island to interview Ezra Appleton—the coroner from the Blythe Whitehall case. I also plan to read the diary we found tonight and see if it reveals anything that might connect the two cases or give us a different view of what happened in 1958."

"I'll talk to Dent and see what he wants me on tomorrow. We're also working a homicide case up in Lewiston."

"I'll keep you up to speed on any new developments, and I'll check in with the lieutenant tonight."

"Great. Drive safe, Brie. See you soon."

Brie climbed into John's truck and made her way back to 95 and headed out of Portland and up the coast. Just before Freeport she got back on coastal Route 1. The traffic was flowing well, and she knew from the trip down that she should make the outskirts of Wiscasset in about a half hour.

She mentally went over some thoughts she wanted to share with Jack Le Beau as well as some questions she wanted to ask him. Before long she started seeing the outskirts of Wiscasset and watched carefully for the Wiscasset Motor Lodge. When she saw the sign coming up on her right, she slowed to a near stop, turned in, and parked next to the office. Dotted around the grounds were towering white pines, and Brie took it as a sign that this was the place for her. After all, the white pine was the official state tree of Minnesota.

Inside she told Bill, the proprietor, that Jack Le Beau from Wiscasset had recommended their place and that she just needed a simple room with a comfortable bed.

"I know Jack," he said with delight, and the smile that already warmed his face traveled to his eyes. "Well, let's see what we've got for you, Ms. . . ."

"Oh, it's Beaumont."

He handed her the registration card. She filled it out and traded it for the room key. "You're right along the front here."

"Thanks, Bill. I'll just drop my things in the room and then I'm going to meet Jack for dinner."

"Well, say hello to him for me."

"I will."

Brie went back to the truck and grabbed her duffel and headed along the wood porch that fronted the rooms. When she got to her number, she opened the door and stepped into an extremely cozy space. The room reminded her of a small north woods cabin. The interior was finished in white pine planking and the ceiling was vaulted, giving the small room a feeling of spaciousness

"Nice," Brie said to herself. "This is really nice." She dropped her bag on the bed and pulled out her toiletries pouch and hairbrush, which she set in the little sink alcove outside the bathroom. After she used the facilities she brushed her teeth, splashed some water on her face, and ran a brush through her bangs. The braid in her hair was holding up pretty well, so she let it be and headed out the door and back to the truck.

Chapter 16

Jack Le Beau lived in a small shingled cottage with green trim and a screened porch off the side. It was down one of the side streets in Wiscasset, on a hill not far from the public landing. Brie circled around several blocks looking for the address and, on finding it, parked the truck out front, grabbed the bags of food, and headed up the walk. As she waited at the door, she turned and looked south. The cottage had a nice view out over the Sheepscot River. On the far side of the Sheepscot, the leaves were taking on color, and the calm evening waters reflected these harbingers of winter as the river flowed toward the Gulf of Maine.

Jack opened the door as Brie stood gazing out over the river. She turned and smiled at him.

He wore baggy dungarees and a blue tee shirt tucked neatly into the pants. He looked surprisingly strong and fit for his age.

"Pretty as a picture, isn't it?" He opened the screen door for her.

"Hi, Jack. Nice to meet you. I'm Brie." She juggled the bags of food so she could shake hands with him. "You've got a nice spot here."

"Well, we used to live in Bangor, but my wife just loved this village. So, when I retired, we came down here and found this little place."

They walked into the living room, which was painted a soft shell color that glowed in the late day light. A comfortable old sofa sat before the fireplace, and on it lay a big black Newfoundland dog. As they entered the room he lifted his giant head, lolled it over the arm of the sofa, and said "woof" in a deep voice.

"That's Angus, my better half since my lovely Annie passed away last year."

Brie went over and squatted down next to the dog. Angus put his big nose right up to Brie's, and it was love at first nuzzle. "Hey there, you," she said as she stroked the giant head. "What a nice name you have, Angus Le Beau."

Angus stretched out his neck to nudge the bags of food Brie held in the crook of her left arm.

"I thought we'd eat out on the porch," Jack said. "You can see the river from out there. It was Annie's favorite spot."

Brie stood up. "I'm sorry about your wife, Jack."

"Leaves a hole in life that's hard to fill. But I'm really glad I have this place. Annie loved it here so much, and that happiness still fills this home."

Brie reached out and squeezed his arm.

"Let me take those bags from you," Jack said, coming back to the present.

Brie handed over the bags. "I have to run back to the truck to get the file. I thought we could go over it after we eat."

"You go, and I'll take these out to the porch."

Brie headed out the door and down to the truck, where she snagged the envelopes that contained the cold case file and Blythe Whitehall's diary. By the time she got back in the door, Angus had lumbered off the sofa and was waiting for her. He led the way to the porch and Brie followed, already thoroughly enamored with the giant creature. Angus deposited himself on the floor on his stomach and heaved out a contented guttural sigh—the loudest Brie had ever heard issue from a dog. His hips were splayed out to either side, and his back legs extended out behind.

"I don't think I've ever seen a dog lie like that," Brie said.

"Well, the Newfies are built for the water. They don't doggie paddle, either, but swim in a breast stroke like a polar bear. Feet are webbed, too," Jack said.

"Really? I know some of the Coast Guards—I think maybe the Canadians or the French—use them for water rescue."

"They train them to jump right out of the helicopters." Jack nodded toward Angus. "He's staked out next to you 'cause he knows I won't feed him from the table."

"And here I thought it's because you like me," Brie said to the big fellow, at which he lifted his head and sniffed the air like a bear.

"Oh, he's taken a shine to you, no mistake. Did you see how he waited for you at the door when you went out?"

"Well, I like you too, Angus." She stroked his silky black head. "But I won't be feeding you from the table either."

Jack had set the bags of food on a round tray in the center of the table. Brie took out the baskets of shrimp and scallops, French fries, and two containers of coleslaw. Jack had made a pitcher of ice tea. He poured out glasses for them, and Brie noticed that his right hand, which would have held his gun back in his cop days, was still perfectly steady, despite the weight of the pitcher.

They sat down and dug in hungrily, and for a few minutes conversation slipped away.

"This is wonderful, Jack."

"The Sea Basket knows what they're doing," he said.

Over the delightfully sweet and tender shrimp and scallops, Brie filled him in on the case—the retrieval of Claire Whitehall's body from the sea and her subsequent identification and connection to Apparition Island. She told Jack about Claire's work as an investigative reporter and that she had supposedly gone to the island to do research and interviews related to the topic of lobster wars.

Jack had a piece of paper next to him and occasionally jotted something down. But mostly he listened with an intensity that Brie could almost feel. She smiled to herself—*Once a detective, always a detective,* she thought, remembering Marty's words.

She described how Hurricane Ivan had rolled over the island, taking the roof off the island's small archive building, scattering documents far and wide, and how Gil Doubtwater had orchestrated the collecting and drying of the documents at the Windward Inn on the island. Finally, she told him of her startling discovery of the old newspaper clipping and her feeling that the deaths of Claire Whitehall and Blythe Whitehall were somehow linked.

Jack set his plate aside and leaned his forearms on the table. As he spoke, he gazed out the window at the river. "It's fascinating how the past sometimes reaches forward into the present, like a ghost trying to be heard. The case of Blythe Whitehall haunts me to this day. When you called today, it brought fresh hope that my feelings about the case, all those years ago, were right—that Mrs. Whitehall was murdered." He turned and studied Brie. "Have you had a chance to look through the case file?" he asked.

"I've read some of it, but I just got the file today. I'd really like to hear your thoughts on why the case went cold."

Jack Le Beau reached for the envelope, took the old case file out and laid it on the table. He opened the file and leafed through it, pausing here and there to read something. But Brie could see that these actions were just a means of collecting his thoughts—that all the details of the Blythe Whitehall case were still emblazoned in his memory.

He closed the file and leaned back in his chair to tell the story. "Blythe Whitehall's body was found in the sea. The coroner on the island at that time—Ezra Appleton—declared the cause of death as drowning. She'd been in the water for a week or more before the body surfaced, but no one had reported her missing. Funny, you'd think someone would have noticed, but then again, the family's summer cottage was up on the cliffs on an isolated part of the island. And Mrs. Whitehall was staying there by herself."

"The newspaper I saw mentioned a rest cure," Brie said.

"Yes. Apparently she'd been battling depression, or at least that's what her husband said when questioned. She was an actress—her stage name was Blythe Danes. The husband said she'd been passed over for a couple of key roles in New York. He thought at the time that had led to her depression. We interviewed her shrink, who corroborated the husband's story."

"So suicide was not outside the realm of possibility," Brie said.

"That's right," Jack said.

"But you didn't believe it was a suicide."

"Nope. Never did."

"Why?" Brie asked, and the word hung in the air like a disembodied ghost.

"I never thought it fit the mold. There was no note. And the odd way the body was attired . . . Just a slip and one stocking. Like maybe she was getting dressed to meet someone and never finished."

"Huh," Brie said and gazed toward the river, thinking she might have come to the very same conclusion Jack had.

After a few moments she turned back to him. "Didn't it seem odd that she would have gone to the island by herself if she was depressed?"

"Back then, I don't think it was uncommon for wealthy women to do just that. Look at Anne Morrow Lindberg's story and that wonderful book—*Gift from the Sea*—that resulted from the summer she spent by herself beside the ocean. My Annie loved that book. Used to reread it every year."

"I suppose women of that economic status had nannies or governesses," Brie said.

"That's right. And back then, it wasn't uncommon for such a woman to leave her children to go on holiday."

"From what I saw in the case file, it looks like you interviewed most of the residents on Apparition Island that summer."

"We did," Jack admitted. "But to little avail."

"I read in the file that some islanders claimed to have seen a suspicious man get off the ferry around the time Blythe Whitehall would have disappeared."

"That's right, and those testimonies led to the theory that Harrison Whitehall had hired someone to kill his wife. A possibility we thought most plausible and one that we pursued tenaciously. But we were never able to find a shred of evidence to suggest a hired killing. In fact, the deeper we dug, the more it appeared that Whitehall had loved his wife devotedly." Jack shook his head. "Who knows, maybe the islanders who made those claims about the mystery man on the ferry were just trying to put us off the scent."

"But why would they do that?" Brie asked.

"To protect their own—other islanders. You have to remember, Brie, that not that long ago—certainly more recently than 1958—folks on the outer islands still referred to leaving the island for the mainland as 'going to America.'"

Brie shook her head in amazement. "I know. The captain on the *Maine Wind* has told me the same thing. Talk about separatists. But to protect a murderer . . ."

"I'm not saying they did, mind you, but there's a tendency among islanders to close ranks. And they don't much like the police poking into their business. Now my partner, Tom Stratton, who worked the case with me. He believed to his dying day that the husband was behind it. And evidence or not, I never could dissuade him." Jack fixed his eyes on Brie. "And now this recent development—the death of another Whitehall. What do you make of that, Detective?"

Brie told him about the arrest of James Levy for breaking into Claire's camp on the island, about the restraining order, the marks on Claire's neck, and his history of attacking another woman in the same manner.

"When we searched her apartment in Portsmouth, we found a window broken and assume Levy broke in there to try and learn where Claire had gone. Lieutenant Fenton and Detective Marty Dupuis will be questioning him about that break-in today or tomorrow." Brie took a drink of her tea. "So, you see, we thought we had our killer. But the autopsy revealed that Claire died not by strangulation, but from injuries sustained by a fall from a high place, and so the death ruling is 'undetermined.' Without more evidence—for instance, someone who saw Levy with Claire that morning, heading for those cliffs—it will be hard to get a conviction. But Lieutenant Fenton still thinks Levy is our man."

"And what about you, Brie?"

"I don't like coincidences. Claire Whitehall is found floating off the same island where fifty-some years ago her grandmother died mysteriously in the same manner. I have to believe there is a connection."

"So, what we need is a motive," Jack said.

"Possibly the fear that Claire Whitehall would bring something to light. Something long hidden and nearly forgotten."

Jack nodded. "The very fact that she was an investigative reporter could have been a threat, and that information would have traveled around the island like wildfire," he said.

"And she was there digging into the history of some of the families on the island, under the guise of writing an article about the lobster wars. In fact, she interviewed several of the families that have been involved in those feuds for decades and . . ."

Brie stopped, suddenly having a thought, wondering if one of the families Claire had interviewed about the lobster wars might somehow have been involved in the death in 1958. She thought back on the lobstermen she herself had interviewed—Logan Lancaster, Gus "Buzz" Beloit, and Paul Herrington—men whose fathers and maybe grandfathers had been involved in the same feuds. She was suddenly struck by the strength of generational ties on these islands, and for some reason, that thought sent a chill through her. If feuds were maintained for generations over lobstering territories, then certainly other kinds of grudges could be held as well.

She told Jack what she was thinking. "Even if the two issues—the death of Blythe Whitehall in 1958 and the lobster wars—are totally unrelated, here was an investigative reporter digging into the past; talking to families; possibly talking to Ezra Appleton, the old coroner, or the island historian . . ." Brie paused and pulled out her small notebook and leafed through till she found the name. "Belle Westgate, that's the island historian."

"So if we posit the theory that Blythe Whitehall was murdered in 1958, do you believe there is a second killer?" Jack asked.

"It seems unlikely that a person who killed in 1958 would still be physically capable of doing so today, assuming he or she were still alive. Plus, the side of the island with those high cliffs is quite remote and accessible only by foot. And while Claire was a petite person, she was young and strong. I have to believe she would have put up a fight. So, even if the killer had been very young in 1958, say sixteen, and of course it's more likely the perpetrator was older, but for argument's sake, let's say he was sixteen. Today, that person would be seventy-two years old. Now say the perp was thirty-five when Blythe Whitehall was killed . . ."

Jack filled in the blank. "He'd be ninety-one today."

"But all that said, let's list the possibilities. Do you have another sheet of paper, Jack?"

He pulled one out and picked up his pen, and Brie started to enumerate the possibilities.

"One—Blythe Danes Whitehall committed suicide as a result of her depression.

"Two—she was murdered, and the original killer is dead.

"Three—the original killer is still alive, and he or she murdered Claire Whitehall.

"Four—there is a second killer, the person who murdered Claire Whitehall, but this person is somehow connected to Blythe Whitehall's murderer from 1958.

"And five—the situation is a coincidence, and James Levy killed Claire Whitehall. Personally, I reject the possibility that Claire's death was an accident or a suicide."

Brie remembered she hadn't told Jack about the diary. She took it out of the envelope and showed it to him. "The entries were written in the summer of 1958 while Blythe was staying on the island."

Jack shook his head in disbelief. He reached over and took the diary from Brie. "This might have held key information that would have helped in the case."

"I believe something in there raised questions for Claire Whitehall about her grandmother's death. And that something lit a fire in her that led to her traveling to Apparition Island to look for answers—to do what she does best—investigate."

Jack handed the diary back, and Brie turned the book in her hands, feeling the thick leather, thinking about the past. "Did you search the Whitehalls' cottage on Apparition Island after the death?"

"We did, but by the time the autopsy results came through and we obtained a warrant, the husband had already come to Maine and gone to the cottage. I suspect he found the diary and took it with him. Possibly to protect his wife's privacy."

"Interesting," Brie said. "I haven't read the diary yet, but the last entry is dated a week or so before Mrs. Whitehall's body was found. So we know she had the diary with her on the island, and we can assume that last entry was written very near her death."

"I'll be curious to know what you find in there," Jack said.

Brie slid the diary back into the evidence envelope. "I plan to read through it tonight, so I'll let you know if I find any clues that might give us a direction."

"And if you don't?"

"Either way, I need to go back to the island. I want to talk to Ezra Appleton. Not only was he the coroner in 1958, but he's old enough to remember Blythe Whitehall—to remember that summer. And I want to hike up to the cliffs on the far side of the island. See the lay of the land. The hurricane passed over the island a few hours after we recovered Claire Whitehall's body from the ocean, so I have little hope of finding any evidence that might relate to her fall."

"Still, it's always valuable to visit the last place the victim was known to have been," Jack said.

"I agree." Brie stared out at the river for a few moments. "It's hard to imagine what would be worth killing for, all these years later."

"It doesn't make much sense," Jack said. "But then, murder seldom does. As detectives, we're rationalists, Brie. But murder, even with a motive, is never rational."

Brie nodded, recognizing the wisdom of Jack's words. Angus lifted his big head off the floor and laid it across her leg. She was surprised at the weight of it. She stroked his head, and he rolled his eyes up and studied her contentedly, as if this were the perfect arrangement.

"Angus, you're quite a presence," she said.

"He keeps the loneliness at bay," Jack said.

"I can believe that." Just then Brie thought of something. "Jack, can you tell me where I can catch the ferry to Apparition Island?"

"Best place to catch it is New Harbor. From there the crossing is no more than an hour." Jack went and got a map and showed her where to go. "Follow Route One east and take the turn for Damariscotta. It's just a few miles from Wiscasset here." He ran his finger down the map. "Follow One-thirty south through Pemaquid to New Harbor. Take a left on Thirty-two. You'll see the ferry dock."

"Thanks, Jack. This has been really nice, and it's such a pleasure meeting you. I'm glad I got to talk to you about both the Whitehall cases. But I should probably be heading back to my motel. I've got some reading to do, and it's already been a long day."

Brie stood up, and Angus, with some effort, raised himself from the floor. He and Jack walked her to the door.

"Keep me posted," Jack said. "Let me know if there's anything I can do to help. And you be careful, Brie. I don't like the feel of this case."

"I will be, Jack, and I'll keep you apprised. I know you have as much interest in this case as I do."

Jack gave Brie a warm handshake, and Angus lifted a giant paw off the floor and plopped it into her hand as well, which tickled Brie no end. She said "Good night" and headed out the door and down the walk to John's truck.

Chapter 17

Brie made her way back through the village and turned onto Route 1, heading west. She was feeling the effects of an extremely long day but was still bent on reading the Blythe Whitehall diary. Every detective bone in her body required that she do so. She stopped at a gas station on the outskirts of the village and went in to get a cup of coffee. The woman at the counter told her the dark roast was a new pot, and Brie opted for a large cup of that and bought a candy bar to go with it. "Coffee likes chocolate," she told the clerk, who smiled at that.

She got back on the road and in a few minutes came in view of the Wiscasset Motor Lodge and slowed the truck to a near stop to make the turn onto the gravel driveway. She parked the truck, grabbed her room key off the console, and headed inside.

She set her car keys, room key, phone, and the evidence envelope on the built-in desk against the wall. The room felt a bit warm, so she slid open the window to let in the cool evening air. She went to her duffel on the bed, pulled out a pair of knit pajama bottoms and a tee shirt, and headed for the shower, snagging her shampoo and conditioner off the sink on the way in. She hoped the shower and the coffee would restore her enough that she could get through the diary.

The hot water brought her back to life, and she lingered a few minutes longer than normal, sudsing up her hair twice and scrubbing away the long day of travel. She climbed out of the shower, dried off, put on her PJs, and headed out to the sink to comb her hair. There was a hairdryer on the wall, and she debated about using it but decided just to work her hair back into a braid and let it dry overnight. When she was done, she reached for the hairdryer and did her bangs. Under the heat, they morphed from dark strings to a pale blonde fringe that fell just below her eyebrows and framed her blue eyes.

Brie had just taken out the diary and climbed onto the bed to start reading when her phone rang. She hopped up and grabbed it from the desk. It was Dent Fenton.

"Hi, Lieutenant. There must be news."

"Yes. We located William Whitehall's cell number and have just reached him and his wife. They were on vacation. They're leaving for Maine immediately to identify and claim Claire's body."

Brie was silent for a moment, imagining their grief.

"I mentioned the diary, and William confirmed that Blythe Whitehall was indeed Claire's grandmother, but he knew nothing about Claire having the diary. Mr. Whitehall said that when they moved out of their large home in Boston, Claire had helped them go through things to give away. He said she came across a trunk of her grandmother's things in the attic and asked if she could take it home and go through it. He told me that Claire had always been curious about her grandmother Whitehall—that she seemed to feel a connection to her even though they obviously had never met. He also said that he had only the vaguest recollection of his mother, Blythe, and that he was only five years old when she died on that godforsaken island."

"Were those his words? 'Godforsaken island'?" Brie asked.

"That's right. And the thought that the same island had now claimed his daughter was more than he could bear."

"I don't think it was the island that claimed her," Brie said.

"That may be, but until we know more, this is an 'undetermined death,' and that's all we can tell the parents. They knew nothing about why she had gone to the island, so apparently she hadn't shared that information with them."

"I can see why she wouldn't have," Brie said. "I was just sitting down to read the diary."

"It's getting late, Brie. Can't that wait till tomorrow?"

"It can't, Dent. I need to know what's in here. And I need to go back to the island tomorrow and talk to Ezra Appleton, the coroner from the Blythe Whitehall case."

"It's rather amazing that he's still alive."

"He's probably about Jack Le Beau's age now, and as I told Jack, he might have some important recollections of that summer and of Blythe Whitehall."

"It's worth following up on, Brie. How is Jack, by the way?"

"He's doing all right," Brie said. "What a wonderful man he seems to be. He's intensely interested in the Claire Whitehall case, as you might imagine."

"I'm not surprised. No matter how old and cold a case gets, men like Jack never really let it go."

"He offered to help. Don't know if there's any call, but what do you think?"

"I think it would be really good for him. I know he's been lonely since Annie died. But I wouldn't want to see him in harm's way."

"Of course not," Brie said.

"Keep me posted, Brie. I'll let Marty know you're going back to the island tomorrow."

"Thanks, Dent."

They ended the call.

Brie was about to set the phone down when she remembered she needed to call John. She brought up his number and put through the call.

He answered on the third ring. "Brie, I was just going to call you and see what's going on."

"Sorry, John. Believe it or not, I've been tied up with the case ever since I left you. Marty and I had to go to Portsmouth to pick up the warrant and search Claire Whitehall's place, and I just got back from meeting with the detective who worked the Blythe Whitehall case back in 1958."

"He's still alive?"

"Yes. He's a really nice old fellow. Name's Jack Le Beau. He lives here in Wiscasset."

She told him about finding the diary at Claire's residence and feeling sure now that Claire had gone to Apparition Island to look into her grandmother's death.

"I know the *Maine Wind* sails tomorrow, but I need to go back to the island. The coroner who did the autopsy on Blythe Whitehall still lives on Apparition Island, and I need to interview him. I'm hoping he'll recall the case and maybe also have some recollections of Blythe Whitehall from that summer."

"It's so long ago," John said.

"Yes, but as the coroner on the case, he had a special connection to the victim, and so he may remember something about her time on the island that summer."

"Well, I had a feeling you might be tied up, so I spoke to Ed Browning, and he said he'd be happy to fill in for you."

"That's great, John. It takes the pressure off."

"This is just a two-night trip with that group of Girl Scouts. They boarded this evening, and we'll be back at the dock the day after tomorrow. So where are you staying?" he asked.

"The Wiscasset Motor Lodge. It's a nice place."

"I know where that is," John said. "You taking the ferry tomorrow?"

"Yes, from New Harbor. Besides the coroner, Ezra Appleton, I need to talk to a few other folks out there."

"Well, be safe, Brie."

"Thanks for the use of your truck, John."

"No problem. See you in a couple days. Miss you."

"Miss you, too."

They ended the call, and Brie picked up her coffee and drank some of it. She closed the window, climbed onto the bed, and folded her legs Indian style. Then she opened the diary and stepped back into the life of Blythe Whitehall in 1958.

The first entry was written aboard the ferry on June 15, the day Blythe was journeying to the island, and the handwriting reflected the motion of the sea.

> *The sea is in a mood today. I wonder which of my moods it reflects, for I feel many things as the boat takes me farther and farther from my normal reality. I feel excitement and anticipation and freedom. I feel selfish and afraid and already a bit lonely. But my ghostly island calls to me, an Apparition that will not be ignored. I wonder what will be revealed this summer? I wonder what awaits? I feel strong to have made this decision.*

Brie stopped, reflecting on the words. The entry touched her, and she already felt a bit haunted by the presence of Blythe Whitehall. That was all Mrs. Whitehall had penned that first day. Brie turned the page and read on.

As she progressed through the chronicling of the early days, Brie began to see why Blythe Whitehall had retreated to the island, and she began to flesh out the woman who had penned the diary—the mother, the wife, the actress, the frightened human being looking for her place in life. The diary revealed the true life of Blythe Whitehall through a series of haunting questions she had posited within its pages.

> *Am I neglecting my children? Will my career fade? Does my husband love me? Do I love my husband? Will my children know me, being raised by someone else? Why am I so afraid?*

Like most mothers, she worried about her children and her place in their lives. She wrote:

> *My children are being raised by a nanny. I am losing these precious years with them, and for what? I feel the need to be here by myself, but the selfishness of the decision weighs on me. What must my son think?*

Brie gleaned from the diary that Blythe Whitehall had become an actress of some note and that she worried about her career fading as she aged. She wrote:

> *The stage is cruel to actresses far more than actors. There's always some young thing, breathless and wide-eyed, waiting in the wings to take one's place. Will there be a place for me there as my beauty fades? Is my talent great enough to make up for that loss?*

The diary revealed how different the world had been for women in 1958. The old leather-bound volume was like a portal back to a time that Brie thought little about—to a world where women were repressed and marginalized. A world where few opportunities existed for a woman like Blythe, who was obviously smart and creative, and who longed for the independence that such women have always sought.

Brie reflected on how many taboos, how many glass ceilings had been shattered over the past fifty-plus years to make this a better place for her generation of women. She stopped reading, feeling as if she were looking through a lens that had just brought the world into sharp focus, revealing how many things women in the present take for granted, and how hard the generations of women before her had worked to make this a country of opportunity and equality for her. She reminded herself to talk more to her mother and her grandmother about what the world had been like for them.

Brie read on, and as she did, Blythe Whitehall's longings for self-actualization seemed to become the theme of the diary. She reflected on her husband's wealth, on what a privileged life she had, and more than once, she wondered why she couldn't be more satisfied—more grateful, why she was so restless, and why she always felt she had something to prove. She wrote:

> *It is hard to live with someone who is powerful; who wields wealth and power as easily as I might wield a pair of gardening shears. Seeing Harrison's reach over things makes me want to prove myself all the more; makes me want to strike out. I can do more than appear in the occasional play or head up the garden society. I know I can.*

Brie kept reading, struggling to keep her eyes open. As she progressed further into the diary, there was more and more reason to stay awake, and she couldn't help thinking about the fact that diaries, by their very nature, are meant to remain private. She wondered, did the people who wrote them believe they would live forever? Did they not have any concerns that they might die and that the diary might be found and read? She wondered if Blythe Whitehall had ever stopped to contemplate that question.

Brie had found something in the diary that changed everything. She got up and set the book on the desk. She had to get to sleep or she'd never be up in time to catch the ferry in the morning. And she had to catch that ferry. She felt a pressing need to get back to Apparition Island. It was like a strong hand pushing her forward toward something both urgent and menacing. The ghosts of the past had been whispering up to this point, but suddenly they were like banshees, wailing to be heard. She suspected Claire Whitehall had heard their cries as well when she had read the diary—that she had gone to the island to answer their call—gone to uncover the real reason her grandmother had died.

Chapter 18

Brie was up early the following morning. She dressed and called Jack Le Beau to see if she could leave the diary at his place for safekeeping before she headed for the ferry. He said that was fine, and she told him she'd be there within the hour.

She had rolled up her small day pack and put it in her duffel when she left the ship. She got it out and put the case file in the pack to take with her on the ferry. There was something she wanted to look for in the file on the way to the island, and she also wanted the file with her when she talked to Ezra Appleton, in case there was anything in it he might need to reference.

She packed her other things, checked the room, and headed out the door to the truck. She locked her stuff inside and went to the office to turn in her key and grab a quick breakfast. The breakfast room was just off the office. Brie got a cup of coffee and ladled out a bowl of steaming oatmeal. There were warm boiled eggs, and she took two of those as well. She sat down and focused on her breakfast, pleased with the hearty fare she knew would stay with her for the next few hours. She polished off her breakfast within fifteen minutes, refilled her coffee, and left the motor lodge.

Jack's house was just a ten minute drive, and the traffic moving her direction was light, so before she knew it, she was pulling up in front of his place. She ran the diary up to the door. Jack was waiting and hurried her on her way so she'd have time to make the ferry.

It was a quarter of eight as Brie left Wiscasset and crossed the bridge over the Sheepscot River. Thoughts and questions about the case jockeyed for position in her mind. The cold case involving Blythe Whitehall's death had moved to the forefront, and Brie had been a detective for long enough to know there had to be a very good reason for that. She believed Claire Whitehall's death of a few days ago had its roots in that distant past. Like Siamese twins, these two cases somehow shared a life, and Brie knew it was up to her to keep both cases alive until she could get to the heart of what linked them.

It was a half hour drive to New Harbor, where she would catch the ferry for Apparition Island, so Brie let her mind slip into neutral. At the sign for Routes 129 and 130, she turned right and followed the road south. Almost immediately she descended into picturesque Damariscotta, where she rolled down Main Street—not yet awake—and out the other end of the village. The rolling terrain held surprises over every crest of hill. Vibrant patches of color and small valleys cloaked in fog. Air and sky held all the clarity of a crisp fall morning. Brie drew in a deep breath, as if she could inhale the beauty of the morning and hold it inside against some inevitable ugliness she was bound to encounter.

Hard as she tried, she could not keep her mind from revisiting the diary she had read the night before. It had revealed a secret, partway through Blythe's first month on the island—the mention of a man, referred to only as "he," except for once. Only one time had Blythe slipped and called him Douglas. *Just a small slip, but a huge clue,* Brie thought.

The fact that Blythe Whitehall might have had a relationship with this man changed everything. The cold case now had something that had been missing for over fifty years—a suspect who had lived on the island. And the fact of him brought more weight to the theory that either Blythe's husband or some mysterious hired killer had been involved in her death.

The presence of a lover on the island would have provided a strong motive for her murder, as well as a reason for her husband to remove the diary and keep it hidden.

Brie was still considering these possibilities as she entered New Harbor. She set her thoughts aside and followed the signs for the ferry. She parked the truck and went into the small building to collect her ticket. The ferry wasn't boarding for a little while, so she sauntered along one of the village roads, happy for the chance to stretch her legs and get a little exercise.

She made sure she was back in plenty of time and stopped by the truck. She took her gun and badge out of the lock box under the passenger seat where she had stashed them when she left the motor lodge, clipped the shield and holster onto her waistband, and holstered her gun. Then she pulled her windbreaker and ball cap out of the truck and put them on. She zipped up the jacket, and it covered both the gun and the badge, so at least on the trip out she could remain incognito.

Almost as an afterthought, she grabbed her small toiletries bag out of the duffel along with a change of underwear, a clean shirt, and her pajama pants. She had no plan to stay on the island, but best to be prepared. During an investigation, plans can change quickly. John kept some bottled water behind the seat, and she tossed a bottle in her day pack, locked the truck, and headed down to board the ferry.

There was a fresh breeze from the southeast. In sailors' parlance, a fresh breeze clocks in at 17 – 21 knots and is ideal wind for sailing. But Brie wanted to spend the time aboard looking through the cold case file some more, so she opted for a seat on a bench inside the ferry's cabin where she'd be out of the wind. They cast off their lines right at nine o'clock and got underway.

The powerful engine churned out a loud, low, vibrating rumble that was no hindrance to thinking but made communication difficult. That was fine with Brie since she wanted to remain to herself on the trip over. The woman seated behind her had eyed her expectantly when she boarded, possibly hoping to strike up a shouted conversation. Brie nipped that in the bud by unzipping her jacket. The woman's eyes had immediately traveled to the badge on her belt and the gun, which was just visible under Brie's windbreaker. She had looked away when she realized Brie was a cop. Brie smiled to herself. *Nothing makes the public more nervous than the close proximity of a police officer. Unless, of course, they're in trouble.*

The sea had a chop to it, and the ferry yawed a bit as it pushed out into Muscongus Bay. Brie's mind rolled back to the first entry she had read in Blythe Whitehall's diary: "The sea is in a mood today. I wonder which of my moods it reflects." She mulled on the fact that here she was, half a century later, sailing on a ferry to the same island with those same words running through her mind. And she again felt haunted by the shadow of this woman—by the hopes and dreams of a once vibrant Blythe Whitehall, whose death had lain so long unresolved.

The crossing was expected to take about fifty minutes. Brie unzipped her day pack and pulled out the large manila envelope that contained the cold case file. She took out the file, set it on her lap, and started to leaf through the pages, stopping here and there to read a part of an interview or a note that Jack Le Beau had attached to one of the pages. She was looking for someone Jack might have interviewed with a first name of Douglas. Along the way it occurred to her that Douglas could also be a last name, and so she began to pay attention to both first and last names of the interviewees. But she got to the end of the case file without finding anything, which was troubling considering how many people Jack and his partner had interviewed on the island in 1958.

All of a sudden she wondered if Douglas was just a code name that Blythe Whitehall had given the man to protect his identity should anyone read her journal. That thought thoroughly depressed Brie because, were that the case, her chances of finding Blythe's mystery man were just about nil. *One step forward, two steps back,* she thought. *Why do investigations always feel that way?*

The sound of the ferry's engine suddenly changed, and Brie looked up from her file. Through the window she could see they were fast approaching the island. She checked her watch. It was 9:45. She had been so engrossed in the details of the case file that she hadn't realized the crossing to the island was nearly over.

The deck hands had gone fore and aft on the starboard side to ready the docking lines. Seeing them there made Brie homesick for her job aboard the *Maine Wind* and for John, even though they'd only been apart for a day. Although her police work had only required her to leave her duties aboard the *Maine Wind* twice since May, still she felt guilty about it. She wasn't one to shirk her duties, but she'd never expected to become connected with the Maine State Police when she had taken the crew position aboard the *Maine Wind* in May.

The gangway was down now, and Brie stuffed the envelope with the case file back into her pack, zipped her jacket, and headed forward to disembark. The captain was there, and she thanked him for the trip before stepping down the gangway. She had bought a round trip fare, so she had a little over six hours to finish her business on the island. The last ferry back to the mainland would leave the island at 4:15.

She wondered if she should have planned to stay overnight, but at this point she saw no real need for that. She had three things she needed to accomplish. Interview Ezra Appleton, the elderly coroner from the Blythe Whitehall case; revisit the camp where Claire had been staying to see if she could find the pocket recorder that had been mentioned by one of the lobstermen Claire had interviewed; and if there was time, hike up to the cliffs from which Claire was thought to have fallen.

Brie saw that the small deli and café next to the ferry dock had its "Open" sign prominently displayed on an upper window facing the dock. She thought the proprietor might know where on the island Ezra Appleton lived, so she headed up the hill and over to the stairs that led to the Ferry Good Deli—a name Brie added to her list of whimsical place names she'd encountered since being in Maine. A bell jingled over the door as she opened it, and a short, stout woman turned and greeted her as she entered.

"Are you here for a box lunch?" the woman asked, and Brie noticed her name tag said "Sally."

"Actually, no," Brie said. "I'm just looking for information."

Sally nodded, but Brie saw her gaze wander to the half-made sandwiches on her board.

"It will only take a second," Brie reassured her. "I'm just looking for Ezra Appleton's house."

"Doc Appleton?" the woman said. "Well, you couldn't be closer. He's just up the hill here a bit. Take the first road to the left and his is the second house."

Brie thanked her and, not wanting to leave empty-handed, she pointed to one of the molasses cookies in the case. "I'll take one of those, please. They look delicious."

Sally took one out and slipped it into a small wax paper bag just the right size for the cookie. Brie paid and thanked her, slipped the cookie into an outside pocket on her day pack, and left the deli.

Chapter 19

Brie headed up the hill to find Ezra Appleton's abode. His house was along the same road as Logan Lancaster's—one of the lobstermen she had interviewed about Claire Whitehall.

A white picket fence with a gate framed Doc Appleton's small Cape. Brie opened the gate and walked up the flagstone path to his door. She hadn't known he was the island doctor, but of course it made sense that the coroner would have been a doctor, even though back in the day, not all of them were.

There was a knocker in the center of the door, and she rapped it three times and waited. No answer. After a respectable amount of time, considering Ezra Appleton's age, she knocked again. Still no answer. Feeling concerned, she stepped off the front stoop and looked in the window to the right of the door. Everything seemed in order—no sign of a problem—so she headed back down the path, thinking maybe he was visiting someone on the island.

She needed to go back to the Westburgs' place to have another look around the camp where Claire had been staying. She decided to do that and then stop back here afterward to see if she could catch Doc Appleton then. She'd made the trip to the island expressly to talk to him, so she hoped she wouldn't strike out and miss him. She chided herself for not calling him first—for just assuming he'd be at home.

She headed down the main street of the village to pick up the road that led south to the Westburgs' property. Edie Hanover was sweeping the porch in front of the general store, and

Brie waved to her as she walked by. She followed the road out of the village. Although only two days had passed since she'd been here, more autumn color had popped out. The sumac was now a brilliant red, and here and there a maple was beginning to flame out in a near fluorescent orange.

Brie picked up her pace, conscious that she had a limited amount of time on the island and a number of things to accomplish. She took the trail that branched off toward the Westburgs' and soon heard the whine of a power tool in the distance. When she got to their property, she headed straight for the barn to check in with Walter. He nodded when he saw her enter but wasn't sending out a very friendly vibe. Brie imagined life with Muriel had been hell since the investigation into Claire's death began. She told him she needed to visit the camp again, and he produced the key from his pocket, where she guessed it had taken up residence to keep Muriel out of the camp.

Brie didn't linger but headed along the wooded path to the camp. When it came into view, she cut across the woodland grass that formed a kind of front yard for the camp and entered the porch. She inserted the key in the door, stepped inside, and stood there looking around. Then she went straight to the bedroom where Claire had slept. Nothing had been touched, and she began her search there for the pocket recorder Claire had supposedly used in her interviews. Aside from the interviews themselves, Brie hoped, if she could find the recorder, that it might reveal some of Claire's thoughts about her reasons for being on the island where her grandmother had died.

When she came up empty-handed in the bedroom, she moved on to the rest of the cabin and searched methodically in every possible place the recorder could be—cabinets, furniture cushions, bookcases. Nothing. She resigned herself to the fact that it just wasn't here. She left by the front door, locking it behind her, headed across the yard and picked up the trail. She was oh-for-two so far—no Ezra Appleton and no recorder. She suddenly felt a little down, wondering if she was entirely on the wrong track—if in fact Dent Fenton was right and James Levy was the killer. But then she heard the shush of the wind through the pine and the distant melodic sound of the wind chime on Claire's front porch, and she took it as a sign that things would work out, that maybe Claire Whitehall was somehow still there, just beyond sight, pushing her in a direction that might hold the solution—that might finish the investigation the reporter had started.

"Sheese, you're getting more like Ariel every day," Brie said to herself.

She thought about her friend and how nice it would be to see her again when she got back to Minnesota.

Walking at a brisk pace, she made the outskirts of the village in just under fifteen minutes and headed north through the village to where Ezra Appleton lived. At his house she opened the picket gate and walked up to the door. This time the knocker produced a result, and within a minute or so, the door opened and a slender, bald man in horn-rimmed glasses stood before her. He appeared frail, but his eyes were still bright with intelligence. Brie placed him at right around Jack Le Beau's age, which was eighty-six.

Brie introduced herself and told him about her connection with the Maine State Police.

"Please come in, Detective," he said. "I've been expecting a visit from the police." He showed Brie into the living room and over to a pair of comfortable armchairs at the far end of the room that faced out a large cottage pane window toward the ocean.

"So, you must know about the death of Claire Whitehall if you've been expecting us," Brie said.

"Yes, well, I knew that a young woman's body had been found in the ocean. And yesterday Gil Doubtwater visited me and told me it was the body of Claire Whitehall. He also told me about the newspaper clipping you found up at the inn. He was most troubled that the names of the two women were the same, and what that might mean. He knows I've lived here on the island my whole adult life, and he wanted to know if I had been involved with the Blythe Whitehall case all those decades ago."

Brie nodded, waiting for him to finish.

"So you see, I've been expecting a visit from the Maine State Police." He gestured toward the chairs. "Please sit down, Detective. I just made some tea. Would you like some?"

"I would. Thank you, Dr. Appleton. Can I help you?"

"No, no. I'll just go bring it from the kitchen. And please feel free to call me Ezra."

He left the room to get the tea, and Brie pulled out her small notebook and jotted down a few of questions she wanted to remember to ask. Ezra was back in a couple of minutes and set the tea tray on a large ottoman in front of the chairs. He poured out two cups of tea and handed one to Brie. She took a sip or two and then set her cup and saucer on the table between them.

"I'm sure you know by now that I was the coroner who did the autopsy on Mrs. Whitehall," Doc Appleton said.

"Yes, I've looked through the case file and have talked with Detective Le Beau about his recollections of the case."

"I didn't know that Jack was still alive," Appleton said. "That's good to hear. He worked so tirelessly on Mrs. Whitehall's case, but in spite of his best efforts, the case went cold—was never solved."

"How well do you recall the case, Doctor?"

"It's a long time ago—over fifty years—but I recall it well, I believe. There was so much mystery and speculation surrounding the death, and of course Mrs. Whitehall was the wife of a wealthy man and also a well-known actress. While it wouldn't be much by today's standards, we had a bit of a media circus here that fall. Reporters coming to the island, police, and Mr. Whitehall, along with a private investigator he had hired. I guess he didn't trust the police to solve the crime."

"And as it turns out, they didn't," Brie said.

"No one did," the doctor said. "It seems all the money in the world couldn't uncover the truth."

"We know now that Claire Whitehall was the granddaughter of Blythe Whitehall."

"Remarkable," the doctor said.

"We also know that Ms. Whitehall visited police headquarters and viewed the cold case file on her grandmother's case, so she would have known that you performed the autopsy in 1958. Did she come here to visit you, Ezra? To ask you questions?"

Ezra hesitated for just a moment before answering. "Yes, she did."

"And what was she looking for, Doctor? I'm assuming she already knew the cause of death was drowning, since she had seen the case file."

"That's correct."

Brie waited, but Ezra didn't answer her first question. She noted that getting at the information was beginning to feel somewhat like extracting a tooth. She reiterated, "So I'm assuming she was looking for something else from you. Am I right? Maybe some historical context, since you would have been an adult when her grandmother was here that summer so long ago."

"I told her what I remembered of that summer and of her grandmother. But as the coroner, it would never be my job to speculate on the case beyond giving the details of the autopsy. And no matter how old the case, I would feel bound by those protocols."

"So, what that means is that you were not about to give Claire Whitehall any information, even if you'd had any. Am I right?"

"Yes." It came out almost as a whisper. "I didn't think it was good for her to be digging up the past."

"Even if the past held unanswered questions?"

Ezra Appleton sat silently, and his gaze shifted from Brie to the window and the ocean beyond it.

Brie decided to shift gears. "When we searched Claire Whitehall's premises in Portsmouth, we discovered a diary that had belonged to Blythe Whitehall. The diary was written the summer of 1958, when she was here on the island—the summer that she died."

"How remarkable," Ezra said.

Brie noted it was the second time he had used the word "remarkable." But even though the doctor apparently found the information "remarkable," he did not seem inclined to engage with it in any demonstrative way.

She pressed on. "Somehow the diary came into the possession of Claire Whitehall. Now as it turns out, Ms. Whitehall was an independent investigative reporter by profession. Did you know that, Doctor?"

"Not specifically, but she just mentioned she was a writer by trade."

"I believe the diary was the catalyst for Ms. Whitehall coming out here under the guise of researching an article on lobster wars."

"Are you suggesting that her death might be related to that diary? That it could relate to her poking into her grandmother's time here so long ago? Are you suggesting that her death was not an accident, as the autopsy suggests?" He seemed incredulous.

"I believe it's a possibility," Brie said. "Tell me, Doctor, how do you happen to know that Claire Whitehall's manner of death was ruled 'undetermined' and therefore that her death could have been an accident, among other possibilities?"

Ezra Appleton seemed flustered by the directness of her question. He glanced at her almost shyly. "When Gil Doubtwater came by to tell me about the remarkable turn of events with the two names, I called a contact of mine at the Maine State Police to see if I could find out what the cause of death had been. Call it an old coroner's curiosity," he said. "The autopsy had already been completed and the death verdict recorded. Her injuries were consistent with a fall from a high place, so I assumed that it had been an accident."

"Pardon me for saying so, Doctor, but that seems like an odd assumption. A verdict of 'undetermined death' would leave the door open for several possibilities. An accident, yes, but also the possibility of suicide, and of course you would have to agree, homicide."

Ezra Appleton seemed deeply unsettled by what Brie had just said, and his gaze slid away from her.

Brie could see that he was off balance and possibly questioning both his actions and conclusions, so the time seemed ripe to ask her next set of questions. But the old doctor appeared so drawn that she paused a moment. "Can I refresh your tea?" she asked.

"Yes, thank you, Detective. All of this is quite shocking, you know."

"I can understand that," Brie said.

They drank their tea in silence for a few minutes before she moved on to the question she most hoped he would have an answer to. When she saw him begin to relax a bit, she went back to the question on her mind.

"Ezra, in her diary Mrs. Whitehall—Blythe Whitehall—mentioned a man named Douglas—a man she seemed to have been in contact with here on the island that summer in 1958. I know it's a long time ago, but do you recall anyone by that name who lived here during that time?"

The doctor appeared to hesitate. "There could have been a number of men on the island at that time with the name Douglas," he said and then fell silent.

Brie studied him. "But I get the feeling that you are thinking of one in particular. Am I right, Dr. Appleton?"

He sighed. "You're very perceptive, Detective."

Brie smiled, and she could feel that break the ice. "It's a big part of my job, Ezra."

"Yes, of course it would be. But as you must know, not all detectives are created equal."

Ezra set his cup down. There was another sigh, and Brie thought possibly it marked the release of something long held inside—a weight, long carried, that was finally about to be put down.

"It was a tragic business," he began. "I believe they were truly star-crossed lovers."

"Blythe Whitehall and . . ."

"Douglas Lancaster," Ezra said, again almost in a whisper.

"Was he any relation to Logan Lancaster here on the island?" Brie asked.

"Yes, Douglas would have been Logan's grandfather."

Brie felt a chill travel down her spine as she thought back momentarily on the first lobsterman she had interviewed—Logan Lancaster, or "Log" as his buddy had called him.

"Go on," she said to Ezra. "How did they meet? Do you recall?"

The doctor chuckled. "An island is a small place. One thing is for certain; people are bound to meet. I suspect they were both lonely, and they found each other the way people do. You see, Douglas' wife Abigail had died about a year before Blythe came to the island."

"How did she die? Do you recall?"

"Oh, it was most certainly cancer. But lots of folks back in those days just got sick and died. Especially in remote places.

Today, of course, we would discover that it was cancer, and whether survivable or not, at least we would know."

"Did Douglas and Abigail have any children?" Brie asked.

"There were two children. The girl was just about a year old when Abigail died and the boy, maybe three or four."

"So Blythe Whitehall and Douglas Lancaster became lovers that summer in1958. Is that correct?"

"Understand, Detective, I only came to surmise what had happened between them in bits and pieces over the period of a year or more after Mrs. Whitehall's death."

Brie waited for him to continue.

"A couple of months after Blythe died, Douglas came to see me. Said he wasn't sleeping. He asked if I could give him something."

"And did you?"

"Yes, I gave him tranquilizers. I figured he was depressed about his wife Abigail and, given enough time, it would pass. But as the island murmurings about Blythe's and Douglas' affair became louder and more persistent, I began to realize that his condition was somehow connected to Blythe Whitehall. I should have taken more notice when he sent the children away, because it was just two weeks after they left the island that his lobsterboat was found at sea with no one aboard."

"You believe he committed suicide."

"I'm sure of it," he said.

"Do you believe Douglas Lancaster could have killed Blythe Whitehall, Doctor?"

He hesitated for a long moment. "Yes, I do," he finally said. "But what would lead *you* to think that, Detective, if I might ask?"

"It was the last entry in Blythe's diary, written about a week before her body was found in the sea. She wrote that she had decided to return to her husband and her life, much as she knew Douglas and his children needed her. It was the only time in the diary that she used his name." Brie paused and studied the doctor. "But I'm curious, Ezra. How and when did you come to the conclusion that Douglas Lancaster could have killed Blythe Whitehall?"

"There was never any outright admission, just a collection of small things over time. Call it a gut sense. You know, it isn't only detectives that experience that curious phenomenon. Coroners and medical examiners—well, we're detectives too. Just in a different way."

"I would never argue with that," Brie said. "But go on."

"When Douglas first came to me, he seemed a haunted man. And, of course, he had good reason. His wife had died, followed a year later by Blythe Whitehall's death and the subsequent investigation. But as time wore on, he behaved more and more like a guilty man, and I began to suspect that he was haunted by what he had done."

"Can you say a little more about what you remember of his behavior during that time?"

"As the weeks wore on after Mrs. Whitehall's death, Douglas seemed, well . . . he seemed to almost be in hiding."

"Curious you should say that, because while nearly everyone on the island at that time seems to have been interviewed during the investigation, there's no record in the case file that either Jack Le Beau or his partner ever interviewed anyone by the name of Douglas here on the island.

"So you felt his behavior was unusual, Doctor. Possibly guilty."

"And then suddenly he was gone, too. Just two or three months after Blythe's drowning."

"Why did you not bring your suspicions to Detective Le Beau? As the coroner, you were functioning as an officer of the law. How could you not bring those suspicions to the police?"

"To what end?" Doc Appleton asked. "Everyone involved was dead. And there was no proof of any of it. Just murmurings that grew louder as the years passed. And there were Douglas and Abigail's children to be considered. They'd lost both their parents. Did they really need to grow up with that knowledge of their father? The knowledge that he might have been a murderer? Sometimes it's best to just let the dead rest."

"But you knew that Jack Le Beau never stopped looking for answers in this case. And you also knew that Blythe Whitehall's husband Harrison was suspected of the murder of his wife. Did that not trouble you?"

"He was never arrested," the doctor said. "I never would have allowed an innocent man to go to jail without bringing forward my suspicions about the case."

Brie thought she recognized, in the decisions Ezra Appleton had made, the strong tendency of islanders to protect their own. She had encountered the same phenomenon while investigating the case of Amanda Whitcomb, the artist who had gone missing on Sentinel Island.

"Has it occurred to you that Claire Whitehall might not have died this past week if the truth had ever been known about Douglas Lancaster?" Brie paused to let the question sink in. "Yes, Blythe Whitehall died a long time ago, but the past has a way of reaching forward into the present. And Claire Whitehall? She had not even been born, yet *her* fate also lay entangled in that web of secrets spun so long ago."

Ezra Appleton looked shocked by what she had just suggested, and what little color remained in his face drained away.

"You see, Doctor, there is a malignant nature to secrets. They fester; the infection spreads, and the effects can be felt years later."

Ezra shook his head slowly, and Brie saw tears well up in his eyes.

"Sometimes we do what we think is right and it goes terribly wrong. Has that never happened to you, Detective?"

His words hit home, and Brie sat silently thinking about the guilt she had grappled with over the past year and a half. The guilt of knowing that her partner Phil had died and that she might have saved him by doing something, anything, differently. Survivor's guilt. Whatever split-second decisions she had made, they had been wrong, and she would forever have to live with the psychological consequences of her choices.

After a few moments of charged silence in which the only sound was the ticking of the old mantel clock above the fireplace, Brie decided to move on. There were several other topics related to the deaths that she wanted to cover: what Ezra Appleton recalled about the condition of Blythe Whitehall's body; what had happened to Douglas Lancaster's children; and questions about Logan Lancaster, who currently lived on the island. She decided to start with the first topic.

"Doctor Appleton, I'd like to ask you what you recall about the condition of Blythe Whitehall's body when you did the autopsy. Specifically, if there were any marks on the body or signs that she may have struggled or been attacked."

"I thought I might be asked about that, so I pulled the file on her case from my records. If you'll wait just a minute, I'll go to my study and get it."

"Of course."

Ezra rose and shuffled out of the room, and Brie sat looking out at the ocean, thinking about what she had learned in the past hour and what implications that information might have in the death of Claire Whitehall. She took a drink of her tea, and in a few minutes Ezra returned with the coroner's report on Blythe Whitehall.

He lowered himself carefully into his chair and turned to face her. "I don't see any mention in the report of there being any marks on Mrs. Whitehall's body. If there had been any, I certainly would have noted it. But that said, you must remember that she had been in the ocean for a few days, and the body was quite bloated. Mrs. Whitehall had water in her lungs. The cause of death was obvious—she had drowned."

He adjusted himself in his chair and Brie thought that he must be getting tired, but then he continued.

"You have to understand, Detective, back in those days modern forensic science was just becoming a glimmer on the horizon. In this day and age, with such a case, the medical examiner would dry the body to look for any defensive wounds or any signs of assault. But there was no such technology here that long ago. Blythe Whitehall's husband, Harrison Whitehall, arrived the same day that her body was found. So there was pressure on us to release the body. Once the cause of death had been determined, he had his wife's body shipped back to Boston."

"So the manner of death could not be determined."

"That's correct. Certain evidence suggested suicide, but the police were investigating her death as a potential homicide."

Brie heard the echo of Joe Wolf's words when he had called her with the death verdict on Claire Whitehall two days earlier. It didn't matter, though. Death 'undetermined' or not, Brie was going to get to the bottom of this. The more resistance a case offered, the more she made it her mission to crack it open. After all, any locked door can withstand only so much pressure—can offer only so much resistance.

She moved on to her next set of questions. "Ezra, you mentioned that Douglas Lancaster had two children who were very young in 1958 and that he sent them away a few weeks before he died."

"That's right."

"Do you know where they were sent?"

"I have to assume Douglas sent them to relatives, but I never knew to whom they went or where. As I said, he had become unusually secretive in those final weeks."

"Do you recall the children's names, by chance?"

Ezra sat quietly for a minute, reflecting. Suddenly he brightened. "The little boy was named Duncan, after his grandfather, I believe. He was a cute little fellow. I can still remember Douglas carrying him on his shoulders." A shadow of sadness clouded the doctor's face at the memory.

He sat a little longer, trying to recover the girl's name, but could not. "She was little more than an infant when they left the island," he said. "You'll have to locate her birth certificate."

"Would there be any birth records on the island?"

"Copies maybe, but after what happened to the archive building during the hurricane, it may be easier just to go to the county seat and get them."

"Where would that be?" Brie asked.

"We're part of Lincoln County," Ezra said. "The county seat is Wiscasset."

She remembered passing the Lincoln County courthouse on Route 1. "Perfect," she said. "I stayed in Wiscasset last night and am returning on the ferry today. I'll go tomorrow and see what I can learn about Douglas Lancaster's children.

"Did Douglas' son Duncan ever return to the island?"

"He never did. For many years the house sat empty, falling into disrepair. As it turned out, though, it was still owned by the Lancasters, and ten years ago Logan came to the island with his bride, moved into the house, and managed to reclaim his grandfather's lobstering territory."

"How well do you know Logan Lancaster?" Brie asked.

"Not well, but we are neighbors. He lives just up the road here, so we talk from time to time."

"Has he ever asked you about his grandfather's time here?"

"Funny you should ask, because Logan has lived here for ten years, but just recently he has asked me if I remembered his grandfather, Douglas."

"Huh. That's interesting," Brie said, wondering what Claire Whitehall might have asked Logan while interviewing him. She must have pushed some kind of a button that got him wondering about his family lineage.

Brie thought back on the one interview she'd had with Logan Lancaster, trying to remember what he had said. Suddenly the words came back to her: "I got the feelin' she was fishin' for something other than lobster." It hadn't meant a lot to Brie at the time because she had yet to stumble on the newspaper story about the death of Claire's grandmother in 1958.

Brie turned back to Ezra. "And what did you tell Logan about his grandfather when he asked?"

"Just that I had known his grandfather Douglas and also his father Duncan when he was a very young boy."

"And did he ask anything about the name Blythe Whitehall?"

"Not in particular," Ezra said.

"What does that mean, Doctor?"

"He asked if the name Whitehall meant anything to me."

Brie wondered if the doctor would ever have gotten around to telling her that bit of information if she hadn't asked.

"And how did you respond?"

"I'm afraid I hedged on the question a bit. I just mentioned that I'd met a young woman named Whitehall who was on the island working on an article. I saw no point in casting the shadow of the past across young Logan's life."

"And what do you think now, Dr. Appleton—now that Claire is dead?"

"Frankly, I don't know what to think, Detective."

Brie knew what to think, and Logan Lancaster had just gone to the top of her suspect list.

She studied Ezra for a moment. "Is it not possible, Doctor, that Logan Lancaster could have been as invested in protecting his grandfather's reputation as Claire Whitehall was in uncovering the cause of her grandmother's death?"

Ezra suddenly looked tired as death. "Logan is no killer. I know that."

"That may be, Dr. Appleton, but there is no way you can know such a thing for sure. The possibility is quite strong that another killer lurks on this island." She hadn't forgotten about the arrest of James Levy, nor had she totally eliminated him as a possibility, but her gut told her that somehow the key to both of the Whitehall deaths lay hidden right here on Apparition Island.

"Well, maybe it's best you talk to Logan," Ezra said. "Personally, I have faith that he'd never have hurt Miss Whitehall."

"I plan to call on him next," Brie said. "One final thing, Doctor. Can you tell me anything about the house the Whitehalls owned here? Does it still stand? And if so, do you know who owns it now?"

"Ah, it was a grand summer cottage—worthy of the best vantage on the island, which it had." Ezra's eyes shifted to the ocean beyond the window.

"After the Second World War, when the economy started to boom, many of the wealthy of New York and Boston came to Maine and built expansive summer cottages. Mostly on the mainland in places like Mount Desert Island and Kennebunkport. But some chose the more remote island life—ones who wanted the quintessential Maine experience. I'd say those folks were the true 'rusticators,' although most of the wealthy summer folk would have been referred to as such.

"As I recall, the Whitehalls began building here around 1951, and it took a couple of years before the house was completed. It created quite a buzz, of course, having that kind of wealth become part of our island community. Harrison and Blythe came every summer until the last couple of years. I believe only Blythe came those last two summers. And after she died, the family never came again. The property has remained in the Whitehall family, but the house, once so grand and beautiful, now shows the neglect of all the decades that have passed. And the road that was built to access the cottage has grown over to a large extent. It's really quite sad."

"It's odd the family never sold the property, don't you think?"

"I always thought that maybe one day when the ghosts of all the sadness surrounding that ill-fated summer were laid to rest—maybe then the family would return. But now that Blythe's granddaughter has died here, well, I doubt that will ever happen," Ezra said.

"If it's any help, I believe there's a key to the estate at the town hall. The town manager from a number of years back was a friend of mine and told me the family had left the key with him in case access to the property was ever needed."

"I take it we're not talking about Gil Doubtwater, the current town manager."

"No, this was before his time. It was when Joseph Fields was town manager. Joseph has since passed away."

Brie wrote the name in her notebook with a notation "town manager—deceased."

Just then she thought of something. "Ezra, when I asked Gil Doubtwater who Claire might have talked to about the history of families on the island, he said he'd directed her to Belle Westgate, the island historian. I know Ms. Westgate is currently off island, but could you tell me how old she is?"

"Well, she's one of our senior citizens here. Not quite as senior as I am," Ezra joked, but he must have caught a hint of impatience in Brie because he stopped midstream and said, "Belle is in her early seventies."

Brie did the math and realized Belle would have been around eighteen years old back in 1958. Certainly at an age where she would have been very curious about a presence like

Blythe Whitehall, and possibly that awareness would have extended to include whomever Blythe was involved with that summer. Brie did not remember seeing Belle Westgate's name among those Jack and his partner had interviewed that summer. At the time Belle would have been around college age.

"Do you happen to recall if Belle Westgate left the island to go to college?" Brie asked Ezra.

"Why, yes she did. I knew her parents well."

"And was she in college that fall, do you recall? The fall of 1958?"

"As a matter of fact, she was. I remember her parents were happy she was off the island when all the ugliness unfolded."

"That's valuable information, Doctor. I believe Claire Whitehall may have interviewed Belle about her recollections of that summer, as well as using her as a source of information on the island's history. But I've taken up enough of your time. You've given me an answer to a major puzzle in the case—the identity of the 'Douglas' I found in Blythe Whitehall's diary. And that information may be invaluable in the case. So thank you for that."

Brie decided it was best to accentuate the positive, much as she felt Ezra Appleton had not done as he should have back in 1958. If at any point he had shared what came to light on the island about the love affair between Douglas and Blythe . . . There was no way to say for sure, but maybe Claire Whitehall would be alive today. It was the Butterfly Effect, after all—change one small thing and it changes everything.

She put her notebook away, and Ezra Appleton rose stiffly from his chair. "I'll show you out, Detective, and then I think it's time for my nap." He stooped slightly as he shuffled toward the door, and Brie felt bad she had stayed so long. A part of her regretted the things she'd had to say to him. Getting old is hard enough without having to second guess what one did fifty years ago.

She shook his hand at the door. "I know you did what you thought was best at the time, Ezra. Try to put the rest of this out of your mind."

He brightened a bit. "Thank you, Detective Beaumont. That's most kind of you."

Brie stepped out the door, and he closed it behind her. She walked back down to the road. The sun was warm on her face, and the wind brought the smell of the sea with it. After so much talk of death, she basked in those life-affirming sensations. She drank them in, tasting their sweetness as only one who has taken a draught of something bitter can.

Chapter 20

Brie stood on the road in front of Ezra Appleton's house and debated what to do next. She checked her watch. It was just after one o'clock—too early for Logan Lancaster to be in from his day of lobstering. But maybe his wife might offer a different perspective on things. It was often helpful to interview the spouse of a suspect separately, and Logan's house was just up the road from the doctor's.

But before she headed up there, she needed to call Lieutenant Fenton. She hadn't talked to him since she'd read the diary, so she wanted to bring him up to speed on the whole Douglas Lancaster connection to the cold case, and also see if the interrogation of James Levy at headquarters had revealed anything.

Fenton answered on the second ring. "Hello, Brie. Did you get to the island? Were you able to speak with Ezra Appleton?"

"Yes and yes," Brie said. She told Dent about finding the name of Douglas in the diary and about the whole story that had unfolded as a result.

"Damn, Jack Le Beau would have given his eyeteeth to have had that information back in 1958," Dent said.

"Ezra claimed that by the time he knew the whole story—connected all the pieces—both Blythe and Douglas Lancaster were dead. There was a strong tone of 'let the dead rest' in his thinking. Maybe it's all that time spent as a coroner. I don't know."

"Damn," Dent Fenton said again. "Jack Le Beau will blow a gasket when he learns there was information held back."

"Better let me break it to him, Dent. He seems to like me."

"Okay, Ms. Charming. You work your magic on him. You know what else is strange?" Dent said. "The husband must have found that diary and taken it back to Boston when he came to claim his wife's body. Wouldn't he have read it? Wouldn't he have wanted to know what his wife's last thoughts were? Wouldn't he have seen mention of this Douglas guy in there and raised holy hell?"

"Hard to say, Dent. Maybe it was more important to him to protect his wife's reputation and his children. You know, I've heard only good things about Harrison Whitehall. Apparently he was a stand-up guy and a devoted husband. Maybe he was a true gentleman—you know, protect the wife at all costs. And, while he was a suspect, he was never arrested, so no reason to reveal the diary. And there's another way to look at it, too. The fact that his wife had a lover on the island back in 1958 might have cast more suspicion on him. It certainly would have given him a strong motive for murder."

"So maybe he was protecting himself as much as his wife."

"Maybe," Brie said.

"So what now?" Fenton asked.

Brie told him about Logan Lancaster, Douglas' grandson. "Apparently Claire Whitehall interviewed him enough that he visited old Ezra with some questions about his forebears."

"Huh. So she shook the family tree to see what might fall out," Dent said.

"Maybe," Brie responded. "I'm planning to go to his place next—see if I can talk to his wife, get her perspective. I'll interview Logan Lancaster when he gets in off his boat for the day."

"What's your gut telling you, Brie?"

"It's telling me Logan Lancaster may have decided that the family bones needed to stay buried."

"In that case, watch yourself."

"Don't worry. I've got my trusty Glock by my side."

"Good."

"So what's happening on the James Levy front?" Brie asked.

"He's lawyered up, so we won't be getting much out of him. But he's admitted to the break-in at Claire Whitehall's camp on the island there, and I just heard from the Portsmouth PD that they picked up two of his prints near the broken window at her apartment. They're planning to charge him with the break-in when we're done with him. So he's in a world of hurt. But lawyer or not, he claims vehemently that he had nothing to do with Claire's death."

"Interesting," Brie said. "On another front, I'd like to track down some information on Douglas Lancaster's children who were sent away from the island back in 1958, just a couple of weeks before Lancaster disappeared from his lobsterboat. Another 'undetermined' death to add to the growing collection, but Ezra Appleton had treated him for depression that long ago summer and believes his death was a suicide. In fact, he believes Douglas Lancaster killed Blythe Whitehall and then himself. He referred to them as star-crossed lovers."

"Wow," was all Fenton could say.

"Anyway, I thought if it's okay with you, I could send Jack Le Beau to the county seat—which is right in Wiscasset where he lives—to see if he could find anything on Douglas Lancaster's children—a boy born in approximately 1955 and a girl born in fifty-six or fifty-seven. She'd be in her late fifties. He'd be early sixties."

"I'm fine with that idea, Brie."

"First, though, I want to interview Logan Lancaster. One of those children, Duncan, became his father. So he may be able to answer all the questions about where he and the sister are now."

"Well, you're on the trail of something. Don't know if it will lead where you're hoping or not," Dent said.

"We just need to find justice for this young woman whose only mistake was in hoping to know her grandmother better."

They ended the call, and Brie carried on up the road to the Lancaster house. She made her way across the yard and knocked on the back door. In a couple of minutes a woman opened the door. Brie placed her in her early thirties. She had very dark, curly shoulder-length hair and the kind of perceptive eyes that assessed a situation quickly.

"Mrs. Lancaster?"

"Yes?" she said, curiosity coloring her inflection.

"I'm Detective Brie Beaumont. I spoke to your husband Logan the day before yesterday."

"Oh, yes. He told me about that poor young woman who drowned."

"Claire Whitehall."

"Yes."

"Had you met her, Mrs. Lancaster?"

"Just briefly. I stayed out of it when she visited because she seemed to be focused on interviewing my husband." She hesitated. "Logan isn't in off the water yet."

"I understand," Brie said. "But there may be a few questions you could answer, if you wouldn't mind."

"I can try. Would you like to step in?"

"Thank you," Brie said. She followed the woman down the hall and into a large living room. Brie looked around. The term "cottage industry" could have been coined based on this room alone. In among the regular furniture, a business was in full swing. The center of the room was consumed by a large table covered with pieces of fabric, patterns, and partially stitched quilts. Two very large sewing machines sat on tables under the front and side windows where the light was really good.

"Looks like this is more than a hobby," Brie said.

"Yes, it's my work. I sell my quilts here in Maine, but also to people all over the map via the internet. It's an amazing world, isn't it?"

"It sure is."

Mrs. Lancaster led Brie over to two chairs in the back corner of the room.

"I was just down the road talking to Doc Appleton," Brie said. "Since I was so close by, I thought I might as well stop by and talk to you, Mrs. Lancaster."

"You can call me Ally. Mrs. Lancaster makes me feel kind of old."

"All right then, Ally." Brie took out her small notebook and pen.

"Do you know if Claire Whitehall came to visit your husband just that one time?"

"No, she actually talked to him several times over the weeks she was here."

"I assume you know she was a writer working on an article on lobster wars."

"That's what Logan said. I was surprised when she came back for extra interviews. It just seems to me there wouldn't be that much to say about it—the lobster wars, I mean."

"Why is that?" Brie asked.

"Oh, I don't know. The whole thing about there still being a war between Logan and Buzz Beloit is kind of an island joke. Don't get me wrong; Buzz can be a mean guy at times, but I can't see him doing anything really over the top."

Brie thought about her one encounter with Henry "Buzz" Beloit. She remembered him glaring at her and blowing cigarette smoke in her face. *A real charmer.*

Ally was talking again. "Most of the territory infractions out on the water are accidental. You know—somebody's trap floats across the line into the other guy's territory. You hear a lot of stories about retribution, but really, most of the guys just try to work it out. You know, buy the guy a case of beer and watch your boundary lines more carefully.

"What I couldn't understand was that the more Claire Whitehall interviewed Logan, the more troubled and, well, almost somber he became."

That piqued Brie's interest, but she let Ally keep talking.

"One evening after she had been here talking to Logan, he seemed unusually upset. I asked him if he was afraid that the article she was writing might reignite the tension between him and Buzz Beloit."

"And what did he say?" Brie asked.

"He got really angry and told me I should stay out of it. Thing is, that's just not like Logan. He never talks to me that way. He's an easygoing guy."

"Did Logan ever mention to you that Claire's grandmother had stayed on the island many years ago?"

"No . . ." Ally's voice trailed off. "That's interesting."

Brie heard the mounting curiosity. "In fact, it's quite possible that Logan's grandfather Douglas knew Claire's grandmother."

"Knew in what way?" Ally asked.

Brie ignored that question for the time being. "We believe Claire's reason for being here on the island was to gather information on her grandmother's death in 1958."

"Oh my God, her grandmother died here too?"

"As a matter of fact, yes."

"No wonder Logan was upset. You see, he knows the story of his grandfather's death—that it was thought to be a suicide. That's why Logan's father would never come back here as an adult."

"So Logan's father remained on the mainland."

"That's right. He was raised by an uncle who had a lobstering territory near Spruce Head. Logan's father eventually took that over," Ally said.

"And does he still live in Spruce Head?" Brie asked, doing the geographical math—realizing that Logan's father could easily have gotten out here by ferry or on his own boat, and that he too might have had a motive to murder Claire. The same one Logan could have had—keeping the family bones buried.

"He's still there," Ally said. "Still lobstering."

"What is the father's name?" Brie asked. She'd already learned the name from Ezra Appleton, but it never hurt to double check.

"His name is Duncan," Ally said.

"Doc Appleton told me he had a sister. She would be Logan's aunt. Do you know her name?"

"No. Logan never knew her. For that matter, neither did his father. Duncan and the sister were separated as very young children—sent to different relatives to be raised. I don't know her name. I don't think Logan does either, but you could ask him."

Ally glanced around the room, and Brie could see that she needed to get back to her work.

"Just a few more questions, Ally. Going back to the day of the hurricane, did Logan go out on his boat that day—pull his pots?"

"He did, but he was back in earlier than normal—by just a little past noon. He wanted to make sure everything was secure around the house."

"So, he was at home here for the rest of the afternoon?"

"I guess," Ally said. "I was gone for a few hours that afternoon. I took two of my quilts down to the village to the gift shop. A friend of mine owns the shop, and she sells my work. With the hurricane coming there was no foot traffic in the village—no tourists—so she closed the shop, and we sat and had coffee and visited for most of the afternoon."

"And did you happen to see Claire Whitehall that afternoon?"

"I don't think so. Wait, yes I did. We were walking down to the village."

"You and Logan?"

"Yes. He needed to get some more screws—he was covering some of the windows with plywood. So he carried the quilts for me. When we got to the outskirts of the village, Claire was heading up the road with a backpack on. I said hello to her and asked where she was headed. She said she was hiking up to the bluffs on the far side of the island. I told her it might not be the best day to go up there with the hurricane moving in."

"And what did she say?"

"She said she wanted to see the waves driving in—exploding off the cliffs. That it would be spectacular. She seemed determined, so I left it alone."

"And you and Logan continued on to the village?"

"Claire wanted to know how to pick up the trail. I guess she hadn't been up there. I was eager to get to my friend's shop, so I took the quilts from Logan and left."

"And he continued talking to Claire—telling her how to pick up the trail?"

"That's right," Ally said.

Brie made a note to ask Logan if that was all they had talked about.

"And Logan was here when you got home?"

"Yes. He was boarding up the windows."

"And did everything seem normal?"

Ally studied her for a minute, possibly beginning to catch the drift of the questions. "Actually, nothing seemed normal that afternoon. We were in the path of a hurricane. No one knew for sure what would happen. Logan was quiet—I could tell he was nervous about the storm."

Brie wondered if that was all he was nervous about.

"So, that was the last time you saw Claire Whitehall?"

"That's right," Ally said. "But when I got to the village, Paul Herrington was looking for her."

"Go on," Brie said.

"Claire and Paul had become an item over the month she'd been on the island. Everyone here pretty much knew about them."

"Did you tell him where Claire had gone?"

"Yes, and the last I knew he had headed off in that direction."

"Huh," said Brie. "That's a very helpful bit of information. I'll follow up on that." Maybe it was the truth or simply Ally's way of diverting suspicion from her husband. Either way, Brie planned to check it out.

"Well, thanks for your time, Mrs. Lancaster. I may still have a couple questions for Logan. If so, I'll stop by later." She tried to be nonchalant about it since she didn't want Ally sounding the alarm. But there was no way of stopping that—Ally was bound to tell Logan that she had been there asking questions.

Ally Lancaster didn't know it, but something she had just revealed cast further suspicion on her husband. When Brie had interviewed him on Saturday—the day after Claire's body was recovered from the sea—Lancaster had said he hadn't talked to Claire for a week to a week and a half. Yet, according to his wife, she and Logan would have been among the last people to see Claire Whitehall on the day she died.

Ally showed Brie to the door, and Brie walked back down toward the road. She paused there and flipped through her notebook to the notes she had written at her first interview with Lancaster. There it was: "last saw C. W. 1 – 2 weeks ago." If Logan had his guard up when she came back, she would know why. The lie he had told certainly focused further suspicion on him.

But she was equally interested in the tidbit about Paul Herrington possibly following Claire up to the cliffs. He hadn't mentioned that when she'd interviewed him on Saturday. In fact, he had claimed he'd looked everywhere for her that day and couldn't find her.

Brie had been planning on hiking up to those cliffs, but now it seemed more pressing to find Paul Herrington and question him. The fact that he'd been seen heading after Claire the day she hiked up to the cliffs definitely cast suspicion on him. Maybe they'd had a fight. Maybe he'd pressed her to stay on the island with him. Maybe things escalated after they got to the cliffs. Many murders between spouses and lovers are not premeditated. They are crimes of passion—crimes of the moment. She headed south through the village toward Paul Herrington's house.

Chapter 21

A crisp breeze carrying the tang of autumn swooped through the village as Brie headed toward Paul Herrington's house. The wind showed no selectivity, but scooped up fallen leaves and bits of debris left by the hurricane and capriciously sent them forth to their next resting place. Sometimes Brie felt as if humans were flung about just as inconsequentially by the whims of some great and uncaring universal force. The thoughts of a cop can sometimes lean toward darkness, even despair. Brie was used to fighting the stalwart battle to stay out in front of the shadows, so she put those thoughts out of her mind.

As a homicide detective, she always felt the weight of responsibility heavy upon her—the need to procure justice for the victims and, in whatever way possible, to finish their unfinished business. This particular case had an interesting circular nature to it and was, in some ways, one of the most unusual and challenging cases Brie had worked on. It had started in the present with the recovery of Claire Whitehall's body from the sea, and then, through the most unexpected of twists, had looped back to a decades-old cold case. There Brie had picked up the threads that could possibly be woven into a solution in the present-day case.

The arc of time and the relationship between the two victims made it tempting to look only at motives that would somehow connect the two deaths. But she cautioned herself to be open to the whole spectrum of motives that existed here. While she didn't like coincidence nor the idea that Claire's death might be unrelated to her grandmother's, Brie knew she had to be cautious about eliminating suspects who didn't fit into the Claire Whitehall—Blythe Whitehall arc of history. With that in mind, she reviewed all the facts and motives carefully as she made her way to Paul Herrington's house that sat on the shore south of the village.

The first motive belonged to James Levy. He was a dangerous stalker, willing to break into Claire's home in Portsmouth, New Hampshire, and into her cabin here on the island to try and gain access to her. He had choked a former girlfriend and done the same to Claire here during a confrontation at the camp she was renting. He could claim innocence till the cows came home, but Brie was a realist. She knew he was still the most likely suspect, if in fact Claire had been murdered.

Then there was Paul Herrington, who had been Claire's lover here on the island. The bit of information she'd just received from Ally Lancaster was damning. He had been told where Claire was going the day of her death, and according to Ally, he had been seen heading after her toward the trail up to the cliffs. Damning—no two ways about it. And even though he had seemed a likeable and trustworthy fellow when Brie had interviewed him, as a cop, she had seen too many lovers' quarrels escalate into something deadly. And the environment up there had to be dangerous. What if he had pushed her or grabbed her and she had tried to break free? It was conceivable that she could have fallen by accident, but that he was in some way culpable.

All she knew was that he had denied seeing Claire the day she died—had said he had looked everywhere for her. Why? Someone was lying—either Ally Lancaster or Paul Herrington. The reason for Ally's lying was obvious; she wanted to divert suspicion away from her husband Logan. But the reason for Herrington lying was far more troubling. It meant he was somehow in the soup and was feeling the heat.

Finally there were the Lancasters. Two generations of Lancasters who could have been determined to keep the ugly truth of the death of both Blythe Whitehall and that of Douglas Lancaster buried in the past. Ezra Appleton had come to believe decades ago that Douglas had killed Blythe and then had committed suicide. He was a doctor, and therefore Brie put stock in his assessment of the events gone by. On top of that, Brie had the diary. She had read the final entry that Blythe had made—possibly the day of her death. She recalled the gist of the passage now.

> *It is with a heavy but resolute heart that I have decided to return to my husband; to my children; to my life in Boston, even though I know how desperately Douglas loves me; how desperately he needs a mother for his children. And I love him too. Everything in me that is wild and free loves him.*

Those last words had caught at Brie's heart. When she had read them, she'd thought about John and what it would have been like had she found him too late. But the real significance of that last diary entry was that Blythe had resolved to return to her life in Boston, and that choice had most certainly given Douglas Lancaster a motive to kill her.

Brie thought about Blythe's decision to return and take up her life with courage and resolve. She knew firsthand how hard it was to make decisions to change one's life and carry through with them. *She never got the chance to redeem herself,* Brie thought.

She had stopped walking and stood looking out at the harbor. The lobsterboats there stood stiffly into the wind, their mooring lines taut. She remembered Ezra's words: "Star-crossed lovers." The weight of all that history—of all that sadness suddenly engulfed her, and she didn't even try to stem the flow of tears. *Life is relentless in the complications it presents, and it's painful and often heartbreaking.*

Something about the depth of this case—the depth of the history involved—was working on Brie, making her think about the connectedness of past and present. It had been a long time since she'd let the tears flow, and she knew it was a good thing. For much of the past year and a half she had simply felt numb, but over the past few months, she kept coming back to the idea of connectedness—the idea that maybe Phil's death was part of an important continuum. That it wasn't something random. These were the thoughts that were slowly making her whole again—that were slowly freeing her from the shackles of post-traumatic stress and survivor's guilt. These were the thoughts that gave her hope.

Brie took a tissue from her pocket and dried her eyes. *Good grief,* she thought. *You need to pull yourself together.* But then she smiled to herself, knowing that, in fact, she was. Slowly but surely, she was pulling herself together. She turned and continued along the road to Paul Herrington's place with a newfound lightness in her step.

She pulled out her phone, knowing she needed to talk to Jack Le Beau. She wanted to see if he was game for driving down to Spruce Head to do some checking on Logan's father, Duncan Lancaster. Jack answered on the second ring.

"Hello, Brie. This is a pleasant surprise. Did you get to the ferry on time?"

"Hi, Jack. Yes, I'm on the island and have had a couple of interesting interviews so far."

She told him about what she'd found in the diary and also about the history of Blythe Whitehall and Douglas Lancaster that Ezra Appleton had sketched out. She tried to soften the blow as much as possible, but the very air around her felt suffused with Jack's anger.

Finally he spoke. More than anything, it was disbelief she heard.

"How could he not bring his suppositions to the police—to me? He knows I worked that case tirelessly for many years. In my gut I always knew it was a homicide."

"I know, Jack. It's a bitter pill to swallow." She paused for a moment, giving him time to process what he was feeling.

After a few moments she went on. "The one positive outcome is that this information may help us find Claire Whitehall's killer, because like you with the Blythe Whitehall case, my gut is telling me Claire was murdered." Brie paused but he didn't say anything, so she continued. "I could use your help to run down some information."

His response was immediate. "Sure. What can I do?"

"I believe the new findings in the case provide motives for the two remaining generations of Lancasters in the Claire Whitehall death. Logan Lancaster lives on the island here. He's Douglas Lancaster's grandson. And Duncan Lancaster is Logan's father, and the son of Douglas Lancaster. To my way of thinking, either one of them might want the family history to stay interred. After all, who wants it known that your father or grandfather was a murderer? It's a secret that was buried over fifty years ago, and I can imagine the desire to keep it that way might be very strong."

"I think you're right," Jack said. "So how can I help?"

"Duncan Lancaster lives in Spruce Head. He was sent to live with an uncle there in 1958, at the age of three, shortly before his father Douglas committed suicide. He never returned to the island.

"I'm wondering if you can take a drive down to Spruce Head and do a little digging? See where Duncan Lancaster was on Friday—the day the hurricane rolled in—the day Claire Whitehall died. See if you can establish that he was in Spruce Head that afternoon. I'm also curious to know if Claire Whitehall contacted him or maybe even interviewed him."

"I'll see what I can find out on both those fronts," Jack said.

"Douglas Lancaster also had a daughter who was sent to another relative back in 1958. Apparently she and her brother were never reunited. I'm wondering if you can check the records at the courthouse in Wiscasset. See if you can find her birth certificate—get a name on her, as well as anything on her current whereabouts."

"So, do a little detective work," Jack said jokingly.

"You've got it," Brie said. She kicked a stone to the side of the road as she walked along. "You're still okay to drive, right, Jack?"

"Still good to go," he said. "Believe me, if I start losing my marbles, I'll know it's time to stop. Until then, they'll have to pry the keys from my cold dead hands."

Brie smiled to herself. "Good to know, Jack."

"I'll pack up Angus and we'll head down to Spruce Head and ask around."

"Does Angus like the car?" Brie asked.

"More than anything in the world," Jack said. "I've got a Highlander. Took the middle seats out. That's Angus' space."

Brie pictured the big furry giant enjoying his car travels.

"I'm going to interview Logan Lancaster when he gets in from his boat—shake the family tree a little more, see what falls out. Let's touch base tonight and you can tell me what you've found out on your end."

"You got it, Brie."

"Thanks, Jack, and give Angus a pat for me."

"Will do."

They ended the call.

By the time she hung up from Jack, she was standing at the foot of the driveway leading up to Paul Herrington's house. When she got close to the house, she could see him through the kitchen window, working at the sink. He spotted her and a moment later she saw the back door open, and he came down the steps toward her, wiping his hands on a kitchen towel. He smiled at her, but his handsome face looked drawn.

"Hello, Detective."

"Good afternoon, Mr. Herrington."

He must have caught something in the tone of her voice because his expression instantly shifted to one more removed and guarded. He was no dummy. He certainly knew she would have been pursuing the investigation since they had last met. The change in his expression suggested there was something he was hiding.

"If you have a few minutes, I'd like to ask you a couple more questions about Claire Whitehall."

"Sure," Herrington said, but he crossed his arms on his chest—body language that told Brie he was not completely open to the subject.

Brie took out her small notebook and pen and leafed through the notebook.

"You told me at our interview on Saturday that you had not seen Claire on Friday—the day of the hurricane. The day she died."

"Yes," was all Herrington said.

"Do you still stand by that testimony, Mr. Herrington?"

Paul Herrington lowered his head, and Brie saw his eyes slide to the left. She could see he was making a decision about something. She guessed it was about whether to come clean or perpetuate the lie.

Finally he looked up. "All right, I did see her that day—Friday."

"So why did you lie about it?" Brie asked.

"I don't know." His eyes slid past her to the sea beyond.

"I think you do know, Mr. Herrington. I think it's because you followed Claire that day—Friday—and I think you argued with her. She had told Logan Lancaster and his wife that she was going up to the cliffs. I believe you followed her up there.

Maybe the two of you argued. Maybe things got out of hand. All I know is you've lied to me twice, so even though you appeared deeply moved by the news of Claire's death, I'm not inclined to believe much of what you've said."

Maybe Claire Whitehall had seen this chink in his knightly armor and decided she didn't like it. Most women Brie had ever met had no time for guys that lied. And most guys she'd ever met seemed to have a problem with honesty. So far, John appeared to be a rare exception to that rule.

Finally Paul Herrington's eyes moved back to her, and he let out a sigh of resignation. "I did follow her out of the village that day, and I caught up with her. But she wasn't going to the cliffs. She was going up to an old abandoned house near there."

Brie's ears perked up at that. *Claire must have been headed for the Whitehall estate.* She thought back to what Ezra had told her about the house, but she also noted that Herrington's testimony conflicted with what Ally Lancaster had told her—that Claire had asked for directions to the cliffs. Only one could be the truth—someone was lying.

"So you must have known about her grandmother's tragic connection to the island."

"Not until that moment," Herrington said. "When I first caught up with her, she said she was going to the cliffs. I told her that was crazy—that there was a hurricane coming. But she was determined, so I said I'd go with her." Herrington paused and shook his head, like maybe he couldn't believe his own story. "She said she wanted to go alone, but I insisted. We were at an impasse. It was then that she told me she was going to the house—the house that had belonged to her grandparents, and she told me the whole tragic story of her grandmother's death. She said she'd kept it secret because if word had gotten out about who she was, it would have made it harder for her to find the truth."

Brie thought about that for a second. *Had Claire somehow discovered the truth about her grandmother's death? Had she somehow reached the same conclusion that Brie had—namely that Blythe Whitehall had been murdered in 1958? If so, had that knowledge put her in grave danger?*

"You must have felt hurt that she hadn't confided in you," Brie said.

Herrington shrugged. "I don't know. Maybe in her line of work you have to be tight-lipped. Anyway, she said the cat was out of the bag, so it didn't matter."

"Did you ask what she meant by that?"

"Sure. She said that there were people on the island who knew exactly what she was doing here, and probably more."

Brie thought about the words, "and probably more." Their implication was chilling. It meant that someone on the island may have had a strong desire to silence Claire; to put a stop to what she could make public—to what she might write about her grandmother's cold case.

"Did she say who those people were?"

"No, by then she was getting antsy to be on her way. She said she needed to go up to the house by herself. She was strong willed. I knew I had to let her go."

"Mr. Herrington, did Claire ever tell you that she believed her grandmother had been murdered?"

His head came up with a jerk. "God, no. Is that what really happened all those years ago?"

Brie started to answer but then changed her mind and proceeded to the next question. "Do you know if she had been up to the old estate before last Friday?"

"I have no idea, but she mentioned she had a key so she could go inside. Maybe that's why she wanted to be alone. You know—commune with the spirits, so to speak."

Brie thought about that, and it made sense to her. But she wondered where Claire had gotten the key. Ezra Appleton had told her there used to be a key to the property at the town hall. Had she gone there and gotten the key from Gil Doubtwater? But Doubtwater claimed he'd never met her. So had she brought the key with her?

Brie studied Herrington for a few moments, wondering how much of what he had just told her was the truth. Once someone withholds information, or outright lies, there's simply no way to know what to believe and not to believe.

"So why didn't you tell me all of this when I first interviewed you?" Brie asked.

"I don't know. Honestly, I was in shock after seeing that god-awful picture of her on your phone. I guess I panicked. I figured I might have been the last person to see her alive. I know there's no reason for you to believe anything I say at this point."

"Well, *honestly*, as you put it, you're absolutely right about that."

Herrington shoved his hands in his pockets and looked up at the sky. His face was etched with emotion—disgust, sadness, helplessness. Brie wondered if guilt also lurked somewhere there below the surface. She put her notebook back in her pocket.

"That's all for now, Mr. Herrington."

He lowered his head and looked at her—in fact, seemed to look right through her. He turned without a word and walked back to the house.

Chapter 22

Brie headed back toward the village, thinking about her interview with Herrington. He was becoming more and more of an enigma to her. Nothing about his testimony so far compelled her to cross him off the suspect list.

She checked her watch. It was just after two-twenty. Logan Lancaster should be in from his boat by now, but she knew lobstermen usually eat when they come in off the water, so she decided to give it a little more time before heading back to his place to question him.

The thought of food brought an uncomfortable rumble from her stomach, as if a storm were brewing down there. She realized she was starving—she hadn't eaten anything since seven o'clock that morning. She fished the molasses cookie out of her pack and demolished it.

"Nice appetizer," she said to herself. "Now for some real food." She picked up her pace, anticipating what the Ferry Good Deli might have on its bill of fare.

As she made her way through the village toward the ferry dock and the deli, she thought about the other lobsterman she had interviewed—Henry "Buzz" Beloit. The mean-faced guy who'd blown smoke in her face. She wondered if he was seriously in the running as a suspect. Her gut told her no. But why? She thought about it for a few moments. The fact was that once she had discovered Claire Whitehall's real reason for being on the island, the idea of a lobsterman killing her over a story that was nothing more than a smokescreen seemed remote.

As facts about the Whitehall history had come to light, the focus of the case had shifted to people who were somehow related to that history or, in Paul Herrington's and James Levy's case, to Claire personally. Buzz Beloit sat outside of that circle, and so for now, Brie saw no reason to pursue further investigation of him.

The road ran down a short hill toward the ferry dock, and the Ferry Good Deli came into view. Brie headed toward it and climbed the wood stairs to the outside deck. She opened the door and stepped inside. The smell of hot soup simmering away reactivated the thunder down under in her stomach.

Sally smiled at her. "Back for a meal?" she asked.

"You betcha," Brie said, slipping in a little Minnesota speak. "What's in the soup kettle today?"

"We've got two—clam chowder and tomato bisque," Sally said.

Brie studied the board overhead that had the menu chalked on it. "I think I'll have a tuna melt and the clam chowder."

"We just have one size bowl." Sally held one up. "Not too big; not too small."

"That's perfect," Brie said. "And I'll have a Coke with it." She headed over to a table by the windows to wait. The only other soul in the place was a lobsterman—recognizable by his rubber boots and ravenous appetite. He had two large sandwiches on his plate, a bowl of soup, two bags of chips and a large drink.

Brie sat down and stared out at the harbor while she waited for her food. She pulled out her small notebook and looked at the notes she'd written while talking to Ally Lancaster. By the time she had jotted down a couple questions she wanted to ask Logan Lancaster, Sally was setting her food down on the table. Brie put the notebook back in her pocket and focused on her meal. The hot soup and sandwich hit the spot. There was a bite in the air today—an omen of winter lurking just down the pike. She lingered over her food for a few extra minutes. It seemed unlikely that she'd be taking the afternoon ferry back to the mainland. She still had a number of things to attend to on the island. She was glad she'd packed what she needed for overnight.

She finished off her soup and sandwich, complimented Sally on the food, and headed out the door. In a fortuitous turn of events, she saw Gil Doubtwater heading toward the deli. He was walking with Edie Hanover, carrying a large box of groceries that Brie assumed was being delivered to Sally at the deli.

"Mr. Doubtwater, I wonder if I could talk to you for a minute," Brie said as she approached.

Gil handed the box to Edie, and she continued down the hill to the deli.

"I didn't expect to see you back on the island so soon, Detective," Gil said. "Any new developments in the case?" he asked. "I have to tell you I'm still haunted by that newspaper article that came to light up at the inn day before yesterday."

"Yes, it certainly has caused us to look at things from a different angle," Brie said. "But I'm not at liberty to say much about the case at this point."

"No, of course not." Doubtwater shook his head gravely.

"I interviewed Ezra Appleton this morning. He did the autopsy on Mrs. Whitehall back in 1958."

"Is that right?" Gil said, shaking his head again.

"He mentioned that years ago a key to the Whitehall cottage was left with the town manager, in case entry to the property was ever necessary."

"If that's the case, it would be in the safe at the town hall," Doubtwater said.

"And Claire never came to ask for that key?"

"Not that I know of. And the town hall was closed while I was on vacation, so there's no way she could have gotten it then. If it's in the safe, she would have had to see me to get it."

Brie thought for a minute. Claire had gotten a key from somewhere, and it hadn't been from her father, since he'd had no idea she was coming here to the island. The only other logical explanation was that Claire had found a key to the house in the trunk of her grandmother's effects where she had found the diary.

She turned back to Doubtwater. "I may stop down there later—see if the key is still in the safe. We may need to access the old Whitehall property."

"That's fine, Detective."

"I'll let you go. It looks like you were on your way into the deli for lunch."

"Yes, it's a good day for hot soup, don't you think?"

"I just finished some. It was delicious," Brie said.

She and Doubtwater parted ways, and she headed up the road toward the Windward Inn to procure a room for the night.

The road dead-ended at the top of the hill behind the inn. Brie crossed the small parking area and entered at the back door as she had on her two previous visits. She waited for a couple of minutes at the reception desk and finally rang the small bell on the desk.

Almost immediately, Mary, of the voluminous red hair, came through the door behind the desk. She seemed flustered to see her, which didn't surprise Brie. After all, she'd come bearing photos of a dead woman on her first visit. The woman lowered her eyes and adjusted a stack of flyers on the top of the desk, obviously waiting for Brie to drop the next bomb.

"I need a room for the night," Brie said.

Mary looked surprised and relieved all at once. "Of course," she said.

"Just a basic room with a double or queen bed will be fine," Brie said.

"I'll give you a nice room on the second floor with a view of the sea. It has a queen bed and bath with tub and shower."

"That will be perfect," Brie said.

She handed over her credit card, and Mary ran it and then handed her the key and one of the flyers with a small diagram of the rooms. She circled one of the small squares to show Brie where her room was and directed her to the stairs a short way down the hall.

Brie headed up the stairs and found her room. She unlocked the door and stepped inside. She dropped her daypack on the bed and walked over to the window. There was a wonderful view of the sea out beyond the harbor. So wonderful that Brie drew in a deep breath and let it out slowly. She'd learned over the past four months that nothing calmed her like the sea. She felt a small ache in her chest—the desire to be back out there with the *Maine Wind* and John.

She turned from the window and went back to the bed and emptied everything out of her pack except for the bottle of water and a small pack of tissues. After she interviewed Logan Lancaster, she planned to hike up to the cliffs where it was thought Claire had fallen to her death. It sounded like the trail was long and rough—no point packing any extra weight. After using the bathroom, she slung her pack over her shoulder and headed out the door.

She followed the road down the hill and headed back in the direction of Logan Lancaster's house.

As she passed the ferry dock, she looked down and saw the ferry was just arriving. She suddenly had a thought and changed course for the dock. She waited patiently at the bottom of the hill until the few passengers had disembarked and the supplies had been offloaded. She made her way down the gangway and waited at the helm for the captain to return.

When he came forward, she introduced herself and showed him her Maine State Police ID.

He nodded. "You were aboard this morning. Sailing back with us?"

"Not till tomorrow," Brie said.

She took out her phone and showed him the picture of Claire Whitehall. "Captain, this woman had been staying here on Apparition Island for the past month or so. Do you recognize her?"

The ferry captain looked distressed, as Brie had expected.

"Ayah," he said. "She was a real pretty gal. Heard what happened. A shame, it is."

"She was here for over a month, Captain. Do you recall if she ever took the ferry back and forth to the mainland during that time?"

The captain stroked his full reddish beard. "She ferried back and forth a couple times, as I recall. Couldn't say when exactly, but I remember seeing her aboard."

"And do you recall if she always returned the same day?"

"I think there was one time she didn't," the captain said. "I think it was a day or two before she returned to the island."

"Thank you, Captain. That may be helpful. I'll let you go. I know you have a schedule to keep."

Brie made her way up the gangway and walked up the hill. At the top she pulled her small notebook out of her pocket and made a couple of notes. Then she tucked the notebook back away and walked up the road to the Lancaster house.

Chapter 23

As Brie turned off the road and approached the house, she saw Logan Lancaster out back moving a stack of lobster traps. She didn't want to surprise him, so she called his name.

"Mr. Lancaster?"

At the sound of her voice, he turned so suddenly he dropped the large metal cage. He jumped back just before it hit the ground so it wouldn't land on his foot.

"I'm sorry if I startled you," Brie said.

"You didn't. Just being clumsy."

It was a lie. Brie knew startled when she saw it. Lancaster tried for a smile, but that just made him look more nervous.

"Do you have a couple of minutes, Mr. Lancaster? I'd like to ask you a few more questions about Claire Whitehall."

Lancaster glanced over his shoulder toward the house as if he didn't want his wife to see what was going on. "I guess."

Brie had noticed an old picnic table off to the side of the house out of earshot. She nodded toward it. "Mind if we sit over there?"

"I guess not," Lancaster said noncommittally.

They walked over to the table and sat down. Brie sat directly across from him so she could look him in the eye. She took out her notebook and flipped back to the notes from her first interview with him.

"Mr. Lancaster, you stated at our first interview the day before yesterday that you hadn't talked to Claire Whitehall for a week to a week and a half."

"That's right," he said, stepping unknowingly into Brie's trap.

"Is it? Are you sure? Because I interviewed your wife Ally today, and she said that the two of you ran into Claire on the way into the village on Friday—the day of the hurricane. The day Claire Whitehall died."

"Wait a minute." Lancaster held up his big hands in a stop gesture and tried to backpedal. But like a lobster trap, there was no exit from the snare Brie had set.

"Why did you lie, Mr. Lancaster?"

"I didn't. I mean, I thought you meant when was the last time she come up here with that recorder, askin' me questions."

"Nice try, Mr. Lancaster, but I think we both know I'm not going to believe that."

He looked to left and right like he wanted to bolt.

"The truth is, Logan, that you were one of the very last people to ever see Claire Whitehall alive. Isn't that right?"

He shrugged and crossed his brawny arms over his chest. "Dunno," he said.

"You knew she was headed up to the cliffs that day—in fact, you gave her directions to the trail. Isn't that right?"

Lancaster didn't answer but kept his arms firmly locked across his chest—body language that said he had nothing more to contribute.

That didn't stop Brie. "Did you follow her, Logan? Were you tired of her poking into your family business, asking questions about your grandfather? Questions you didn't want to think about. Questions that raised the specter of suicide and maybe even murder. Questions that cast a terrible shadow over your family name."

Lancaster's eyes darkened like storm clouds, but he held his silence.

"Did you follow her up to the cliffs that day? Did you see your opportunity to make all the bad press about your family go away? Did you push Claire Whitehall off that cliff—push her to her death?"

The big hands came down on the table like a thunderclap.

"NO!" he bellowed like a wounded beast.

The word rang with fear but something else. A kind of enraged nobility, Brie thought. She also thought it must be a terrible thing to have to defend the honor of a family member—a forebear who may have committed a heinous crime.

"Look, I never laid a hand on her," Lancaster said and crossed his arms on his chest again. "But to have all this stuff about my grandfather dredged up when Lancasters have finally come back to the island after two generations—it's a bitter pill to swallow. That's what my dad said."

"Your dad—that would be Duncan Lancaster?"

Logan nodded.

"And he said it was a bitter pill to swallow?"

"That's right."

"When did he say that?"

"Claire Whitehall asked for his name and about where he lived. I knew she was going to go looking for him, so I called to warn him. That's when he said it was a bitter pill and all that."

"So, do you know if Claire ever went to see him?"

"Dunno. Didn't hear." Logan stared off into space as he said it.

Brie wondered if that was why Claire had taken the ferry to the mainland. The ferry captain said she had traveled back and forth a couple of times.

"What do you think Claire Whitehall was looking for from you, Logan?"

Lancaster sat there thinking, and Brie waited patiently. After a while his expression softened.

"I think maybe she wanted to lay the past to rest. She said something funny one day . . . something like, 'There's no rest for a soul without the truth.'" Lancaster lowered his arms from his chest. "I guess I can understand what she meant."

"Do you think she was referring to her grandmother or herself when she said that?" Brie asked.

"Huh . . . Dunno. I thought the grandmother, but I guess she coulda been talkin' about herself, now's you mention it."

Being an investigative reporter, Claire Whitehall was used to tenaciously pursuing the truth. Something about the case suddenly moved into sharper focus for Brie. She had thought that Claire's interest was solely about finding the truth and letting it be known, thereby claiming some kind of justice for her grandmother, or at least giving closure to a case that had remained an enigma for fifty-plus years.

But each and every time truth is revealed, whether by a reporter or a detective, there is also a kind of respite for the soul of that truth seeker. Nor does that person ever rest easy when the truth evades him. Brie thought about Jack Le Beau and the Blythe Whitehall case, which had gone cold despite his best efforts. That lack of closure can rob a cop of his peace of mind, and Brie suspected it was much the same for an investigative reporter. In such careers, truth is like water—essential to survival.

But along with that hard-won truth, there is always pain for those on the periphery of a crime. In each and every case there is collateral damage. Children left destitute by swindling, or worse, murderous parents. Parents left heartbroken by the choices of a misguided or mentally ill child. Truth and the ensuing justice are not necessarily kind. Lady Justice holds her sword, and there are those, both bad and good, who suffer at the hands of the blind maiden.

Brie studied Logan Lancaster. *Instigator or collateral damage*? she wondered. He appeared miserable, but she could only guess at why that was.

"Just one more question, Mr. Lancaster. Your father had a sister—she'd be your aunt—who was also sent away from the island back in 1958. Are you or your father in touch with her, or do either of you know anything about her or her whereabouts?"

Lancaster shook his head. "Nope. Never knew her. Somewhere along the line, I heard she'd grown up in Belfast, Maine. It's quite a ways from Spruce Head, you know—where my dad grew up. Maybe it just wasn't practical getting 'em together. Her and my dad, I mean, when they was kids."

Brie nodded. She knew one thing from her time here. The Mainers were big on frugality and practicality.

"Well, Mr. Lancaster. I think that's all for now." She started to get up and then thought of something. "Can you tell me where I pick up the trail to the cliffs?" she said, sitting back down.

"Sure," Logan said. It came out "shu-ah." "I'll draw it for you."

Brie flipped to an empty page in her notebook and handed it to him along with her pen.

He placed his big, beefy hand on the notebook and started to draw a diagram with his left hand. Brie noticed he wore a gold signet ring engraved with a coat of arms on his right hand. The engraving seemed vaguely familiar, but she couldn't think why.

"Interesting ring," Brie said.

"It's our family crest," Logan said. "It was my grandfather's ring. Story goes that when my father was sent from the island as a little boy, my grandfather sent the ring along to be kept till he was grown. My father gave it to me on my twenty-first birthday."

Lancaster finished drawing the map and showed it to her. "You go back down to the village and head up the road toward the lighthouse. About halfway up you'll see a fork, and a grassy trail leads off to the north. Follow that. It will take you into the forest. The trail gets rougher and steeper from there on."

He handed the notebook back to her. "Trail might be blocked by downfalls since the hurricane. You might not get through."

"Maybe not, but I'll give it a try."

Brie put the notebook in her pocket, extricated herself from the seat of the picnic table, and took her leave of Logan Lancaster. When she got down to the road, she turned to look back. He was standing there watching her, feet spread, arms across his chest, his expression unreadable. A gust of wind swooped down from the north, and Brie felt its chill. But there was something else here—something sensed rather than felt. She knew it well—it was danger.

Chapter 24

Brie followed Logan Lancaster's directions, and where the road branched off to the village, she headed up the hill toward the lighthouse. She watched for the trailhead that Lancaster said would fork off to the north, partway up the hill. About halfway up, the trail branched, and Brie took the northbound fork, hoping this was the right way. Within five minutes the trail narrowed and entered a dense spruce forest just as Logan had said it would.

This was no groomed hiking trail. Sharp rocks like large jagged teeth broke the soil, and ankle-twisting gullies rutted the uphill grade. Brie liked the woods, but today the forest felt claustrophobic. The steep terrain and thick spruce blocked the wind. A deer fly had taken a liking to her long blonde braid, and it circled her in an ever-shrinking orbit, lining up for its final approach. Brie took off her ball cap and swatted unsuccessfully at the large fly. She stopped and wound her braid into a bun, stuffed it under her cap, turned up the collar on her jacket to protect her neck, and proceeded on up the trail.

Logan Lancaster had been right in his prediction of deadfalls. The force that was Hurricane Ivan had combed through the forest, snapping or uprooting trees and dropping them like so many loose hairs. Every hundred yards or so, Brie was forced to leave the trail and make her way around another felled tree. It was getting tiresome, and she tried to pass the time by thinking about the case.

She thought about what Claire Whitehall had said to Logan Lancaster. *Without the truth, there's no rest for a soul.*

Haunting words in a case where the echoes of the distant past were still audible. They had called Claire to the island—called her to her death.

Brie also thought about the Whitehall and Lancaster children left motherless or fatherless all those years ago. When the brushstrokes of fate had painted Douglas and Blythe into this island landscape so many years ago, that same designing fate had cut those children free of their moorings and set them adrift.

As she continued up the trail, the thought of those children opened some floodgate in Brie's mind, and she was soon caught in a current of thought, a river of unwanted reflections. Some were snapshots from her own life; others were more universal. Things people long to fix but can't. Things left unsaid, undone. Outcomes hoped for but never realized. Unrequited longings, desires. Those things that haunt us—the apparitions that lurk behind the veil of our regrets.

Since her life had fallen apart a year and a half ago, Brie had been drawn over and over to the brink of that river whose undertow was so strong, she knew she could easily drown if she stayed in too long—if she let it wear her down.

She stopped for a minute and drew in a breath and tried to focus on the whisperings of nature around her. She listened for the wind through the pine—a sound that always soothed her—but the trees had gone silent.

Suddenly all her spidey senses were tingling. She turned and surveyed the terrain below her. There was no way for anyone to covertly follow—the trail was too narrow and tortuous, and it was covered with loose rocks. Even so, Brie drew her gun and held it two-fisted, pointed toward the ground. She waited, statue-still, feeling vulnerable. She glanced to right and left, scanning for cover, and moved as silently as possible off the trail toward a clump of dense spruce. Stepping into the shadowy thicket, she stood stock-still and waited. Since being shot, unreadable situations like this one had become more frequent. Post-traumatic stress plays mind games, makes the victim doubt himself—second guess himself when he shouldn't. For a cop, that can be deadly dangerous. Brie was second-guessing herself now. *Maybe it's my imagination.* She smiled cynically. Or maybe some unearthly apparition had swum past her in the ethers—some presence that felt welcome on an island whose legends favored ghostly manifestations.

After a few minutes she holstered her gun and made her way back to the trail. She had to keep going but did so with a heightened sense of awareness. One thing had not been imagined—the violent death of Claire Whitehall. That meant someone was responsible—the perpetrator—a being stone cold and dangerous as hell.

Brie was in shape and set a good pace despite the rigors of the climb and roughness of the trail. Still, it took her over an hour to reach the far side of the island. Finally the spruce began to thin, and after one final uphill scramble over bare granite slippery as a dolphin's back, she stood on the bluffs that marked the eastern boundary of the island. The view was breathtaking, and before she even ventured near the edge of the cliffs, she knew they had to be a couple hundred feet high.

As expected, Ivan with its Force 12 winds and torrential rains had scoured the area. It was as if some great atmospheric cleaning crew had descended on the bluffs. Only patches of moss and lichen—flora designed by nature to withstand the most inhospitable of environments—clung to the smooth gray granite.

In the wake of the hurricane, Brie had not expected to find any clues, any explanations of the fate that had befallen Claire Whitehall. Even so, she had needed to visit this spot since it was thought to be the only place on the island from which Claire could have fallen to her death and also the last place she was thought to have been alive. So Brie walked the area of the bluff, first moving to the cliff's precipice and looking over. The height was dizzying. Great black-backed gulls and northern gannets soared on the air currents as the sea ran in and licked the base of the cliffs far below. A body falling from here would plunge directly into the ocean, and Brie knew no one could survive such a drop.

She looked southeast and noted thunderheads massing on the horizon. The sea had a slow oily roll to it—the kind that preceded a storm. She figured by tonight or tomorrow the island was in for another blow—although nothing more than a meteorological speed bump compared to what they'd survived last week with the passing of Ivan.

Brie walked away from the precipice and stood on the dome of gray granite. To her right, or north, reaching above the treetops, she saw the roofline of what once might have been a grand summer cottage but now somehow put her in mind of the House of Usher. The tattered roof was pocked with missing shingles, the window trim showed rot, and paint peeled from the wooden exterior, leaving weathered gray wounds.

Brie wondered if this could be the old Whitehall estate, and she moved toward the tree line to the north to see if she could find a trail that might lead to the house. At the edge of the forest she patrolled up and down, looking for any sign of a trail, and made a couple of aborted forays into the spruce only to return unsuccessful. Finally, nearer the edge of the bluff, she stepped past a screen of spruce and saw a narrow track. She followed it for fifty yards or so, but the going was rough and the mosquitoes were starting to swarm. What's more, she was feeling the first cloying fingers of exhaustion. She'd had little sleep last night and had arisen quite early to catch the ferry to the island.

She studied the roofline of the house again and then looked at her watch. It was past five-thirty. The descent down the trail could be even slower than the ascent had been, which meant she might not get back to the inn till after seven o'clock. She made a decision to investigate the house the following day. Ezra Appleton had told her there had been a road up there from the village when the house was built. Even though it might be overgrown, it would probably provide a better route to the house than this, assuming what she was seeing was the old Whitehall cottage.

She turned and headed back toward the bluffs, watching her footing along the trail. She'd only gone about ten yards or so when she thought she caught the glint of something on the ground to the left of the trail. She squatted down and in a small round hollow almost completely covered by spruce needles, she found a brass key. Brie pulled a latex glove from her pocket, slipped it on, and picked the key up by the very end of the shaft. It was heavy, and the brass finish had been dulled by time. It looked like the key to the front door of a house.

Could this be the key to the Whitehall house? She turned it in her hand, wondering how it had gotten here. Had Claire dropped it as a way to leave a sign that she had been here? If that were the case, she would have been coming from the house along this trail, and she would not have been alone.

Brie stood up and pulled off the glove on her right hand so it formed a little pouch for the key and tucked the glove into her pocket. She made her way back to the open bluffs and started down the trail toward the other side of the island. The air hung dead still, and except for the whine of mosquitoes that swarmed around her head, the forest spread out quiet as a graveyard. The descent on a rough trail is far more treacherous than the ascent, and the potential for a twisted or sprained ankle is only one loose rock or hidden tree root away. Brie emptied her mind of all consideration of the case and focused on getting down the trail in one piece. If her suspicions about Claire's fate were correct, she could only imagine the terror that must have gripped the woman's heart before she went off that cliff to her death.

Chapter 25

By the time Brie made her way down the trail and back to the hill overlooking Ghost Cove, the sun was already making a rapid retreat toward the western horizon of ocean. Now on level ground, she picked up her pace, eager to reach the village, the inn, and a hot shower.

Ten minutes later and just past seven o'clock, she stepped in the back door of the inn. She checked the small placard outside the dining room to see how late dinner was served and was pleased to see that the dining room was open until eight o'clock. She hurried along the hallway and, tired as she was, mounted the steps to her room two at a time.

She fished the room key out of her pocket as she approached the door. Inside, she locked the door, dropped her pack on the bed, stripped off her hat and jacket, and set her holster and gun on the dresser. She headed into the bathroom, turned on the hot water, peeled off her clothes, and stepped in the shower. The hot water cascaded over her head and shoulders like a healing balm, soothing itchy mosquito bites and loosening muscles tensed by the nearly three hours of strenuous climbing getting to and from the far side of the island. She washed her hair, soaped up, and fifteen minutes later stepped from the shower feeling reborn. She combed out her hair and worked it into a braid and pulled on her clothes. She only had one change of underwear and was saving them for tomorrow, but she did put on a clean, long-sleeved tee shirt.

She took out her cell phone and climbed on the bed, where she sat with legs crossed Indian-style and brought up Jack Le

Beau's number. She wanted to call him before it got any later to see what he had found out at the courthouse in Wiscasset and also down in Spruce Head where Duncan Lancaster lived.

He answered on the third ring. "Hello, Brie."

"Hi, Jack. Are you safely home from Spruce Head?"

"Yes indeedy," he chirped and she was surprised by the lightness in his tone. He had to be tired after the day he'd put in, but then Brie realized that being part of an investigation again would have breathed new life into Jack, or any retired detective for that matter.

"I'm not interrupting your dinner, am I?"

"Nope. Angus and I grabbed a burger on the way home."

"Any success in Wiscasset with the birth records?"

"Easy as pie. I found the marriage license for Douglas and Abigail Lancaster and birth certificates for their two children—a son named Duncan George, now living in Spruce Head as we know, and a daughter named Mary Edna Lancaster, just a year and a half younger than her brother. I also found the death certificate for Douglas Lancaster. Cause of death was drowning and manner of death 'undetermined.'"

Brie was mulling over the name of the daughter. 'Mary' had been the most common girl's name of that generation. There was one Mary she knew of on the island, who worked here at the hotel, but she was far too young to have been Douglas' daughter.

"So we know the son has lived in Spruce Head all his life, where he was raised by his uncle. Any idea where the daughter grew up or her current whereabouts?"

"No. There's no record of her until she obtained a Maine driver's license at the age of eighteen. Her address at that time was in Belfast, Maine. I contacted the current residents at the address on the license, but that's nearly forty years ago and the property has changed hands. Tomorrow I plan to do a search of the property records to see if I can find out the name of the family the daughter grew up with. They must have been relatives of Douglas Lancaster, since the son was sent to be raised by his uncle."

"It would certainly make sense," Brie said. "I interviewed Duncan's son, Logan, here on the island, again today, and he said he'd heard the sister grew up in Belfast. But apparently once the children were separated back in 1958, they were lost to each other for all intents and purposes."

"Kinda sad, isn't it?" Jack said.

"I'll say."

"I'm also going to check the DMV for surrounding states —see if maybe she moved out of Maine."

"Good idea, Jack."

"I would have done more digging today, but I wanted to get down to Spruce Head—see if I could locate Duncan Lancaster."

"So you found him?"

"Yes. But I didn't like what I found."

"Why's that?"

"Lot of anger there. Now that doesn't necessarily mean anything—lots of folks are angry. But lots of folks aren't potential suspects in a murder."

"Go on," Brie said.

"Once I established that he was the son of Douglas Lancaster and had left Apparition Island as a young child, shortly before his father's death, I questioned him about his whereabouts on the day of the hurricane—the day Claire Whitehall died. He flew into a rage at the mention of her name. Called her 'the goddamn reporter that was trying to ruin his son's life.' Railed on about her visiting Logan out on Apparition Island and raising all kinds of troubling questions about the past."

"Huh. Did you ask if he had met Claire Whitehall?"

"Yup. Said she tried to set a meeting with him but he refused to talk to her. Said she had the gall to show up at his house trying to ask him questions about his father. He told her to never come on his property again."

"Do you think he threatened her?"

"I asked him that point blank. He said no, but his body language said something else."

"Huh," Brie said again.

"I didn't leave it at that. I talked to other lobstermen in the village. The guy whose territory abuts Lancaster's said he saw him out there early on Friday, pulling his pots. But that guy said he came in off the water by ten that morning to work on his house. No one else could say for sure they saw him on the water that day. His wife works in Rockland—didn't get home till five o'clock that day. She said he was at home when she arrived."

"Lots of wiggle room there, especially if he has a fast lobsterboat," Brie said.

"He could have made it out to the island, killed Claire Whitehall, and made it back to Spruce Head by five o'clock."

"Problem is, he'd have to have had a crystal ball, since Claire didn't make the decision to head up to the cliffs till around noon. What's more, there's some evidence that she was actually going up to the old Whitehall estate."

"How about at your end, Brie? Have you turned up anything else out there?" She told him about finding the brass key next to the trail up near the cliffs and what she thought it might imply. "It's possible Claire dropped it on purpose to leave a clue that she'd been there."

"So you're saying someone else was with her and that someone was her killer."

"I think it's a good possibility," Brie said. "I suppose she could have dropped the key by accident, but considering she plummeted to her death a short while later, I think it's unlikely."

Brie checked her watch. It was approaching seven-thirty. If she hoped to eat tonight, she'd have to wrap up the call in the next ten minutes or so. She continued with the rest of what she wanted to tell Jack.

"I also have testimony that both Paul Herrington, Claire's lover, and Logan Lancaster encountered Claire Whitehall the afternoon she died as she was leaving the village headed either for the Whitehall estate or the cliffs. Either of them could have followed her and pushed her to her death."

"So you need something that will narrow it down to one of them," Jack said.

"Right, and that's the problem. There's something here, Jack. I feel like it's staring me in the face, but I can't see it. Like one of those Waldo puzzles where the answer is hiding in plain sight."

"I know the feeling, Brie. You need to step back. Empty your mind—get a good night's sleep. You sure couldn't have gotten much last night."

Brie yawned, feeling exhaustion closing in. "No, I didn't."

"Listen, sometimes the harder you push, the greater the resistance the case seems to offer."

"For every action there's an equal and opposite reaction," Brie said. "Newton's third law of motion."

"Sounds right to me," Jack said, "but I don't know much about physics."

"It's all about equal and opposing forces," Brie said.

"You mean like good and evil? Now you're talking about every detective's realm."

"I'll take your advice, Jack. Let go of it—just get a good night's sleep."

"That a girl," Jack said.

"I sure wish I could locate this pocket recorder of Claire's that people have mentioned. Apparently she used it in her interviews, but where is it?"

"You think it might hold a clue to what happened?" Jack asked.

"I do," said Brie.

"Oh, I almost forgot. I talked to Lieutenant Fenton today. He was trying to reach you—said you weren't answering your phone."

Brie glanced at her phone and saw she had a message waiting. "Yeah, I lost reception when I hiked up to the far side of the island. I was in a dead zone for over three hours. Was it anything important?"

"Just wanted to let you know that the final decision will come down by the end of the day tomorrow on the arrest of James Levy in the Claire Whitehall death."

Brie was silent.

"You don't think he did it, do you?"

"Look, Jack, there's no doubt he's a dangerous guy. I mean, he choked a former girlfriend and also Claire Whitehall. What's more, he broke into her apartment in Portsmouth, and Marty and I arrested him right here on the island in Claire's camp after a second break-in. But like I told Marty, if Levy killed her, what would he be doing in her camp the next day? Don't you think he would have headed for the hills?"

"Good point, Brie. You don't have to convince me. I was always a follow-your-gut kind of detective. You work the evidence; you figure out who has motive, means, and opportunity, but beyond that is the uncharted territory of gut instinct."

"Thanks, Jack. It's good to hear that from you. Listen, I'd better wrap it up if I'm going to get in on dinner here at the inn before they close."

"Go. Have a nice meal, and sleep. Maybe things will come clear in the morning."

"I hope so. Thanks, Jack. Goodnight." Brie set the phone on the dresser, grabbed some money out of her pack, and headed down to the dining room.

She sat by the window. The sun, a giant saffron disk, was just slipping into the sea. It was so beautiful she drew in an involuntary breath and let it out. She opened the menu and went straight to the seafood listing. When the waitress arrived, she ordered the halibut, pan sautéed in butter and herbs. It came with fingerling potatoes and a salad. Brie decided against coffee and instead ordered a glass of pinot grigio that she thought would be wonderful with the fish. There was only one other couple in the dining room, so the food came out quickly. She was hungry—it had been six hours and a very long hike since lunch at the Ferry Good Deli. But she was equally exhausted, so she ate slowly and sipped her wine. The sun melted into the ocean like a great wafer of butter spreading its essence across the water in undulating ripples of gold. Brie felt the wine begin to work, easing knots in her mind and body, releasing her from the trials of a long day.

Chapter 26

By the time Brie left the dining room and headed back upstairs to her room, it was almost nine o'clock. The room was dark, and she turned on a small lamp on the table next to the bed. In the yellow glow cast by the light, she pulled her pajamas out of the backpack and headed into the bathroom to put them on and brush her teeth. When she came out, she went to the dresser for her phone and brought up John's number. The call went directly to his voice mail. She was too tired to think of anything clever to say, so her message was brief.

"Hi, John. Miss you and the guys and the *Maine Wind*. Case still unresolved. I'll call you tomorrow."

Brie put the phone down and did some stretches to work out the kinks. She always slept better when she took a few minutes to stretch before bed. She kept thinking about the suspects in the Claire Whitehall case, and finally she pulled the small notebook out of her jacket pocket and jotted down a list of names. "Maybe if I put you all down here, I can stop thinking about you," she said to herself. She looked at the list, feeling exasperated. At the top and currently under arrest was James Levy, the stalker who had broken into Claire's apartment. Next was Paul Herrington—Claire's lover on the island, who for whatever reason kept lying to Brie about a variety of things. Third on the list she had written Logan Lancaster. As the grandson of Douglas Lancaster, he was tied by blood to the original crime which Claire Whitehall had been investigating —the death of Blythe Whitehall in 1958. Finally Brie had put down Duncan Lancaster. He was Logan's father and had the same motive as Logan for killing Claire—keeping the family history buried. At the bottom of the list under the four names, Brie put a question mark. She looked at it for a moment, thinking, wondering if there was anyone else that should be on the list.

She closed the notebook, set it on the dresser, and cracked open the windows that faced the ocean to let in the cool night air and the hypnotic sound of the sea. Then she walked over, turned out the lamp, and crawled into bed. She lay there for a few minutes, listening to the night sounds outside. The list of suspects rolled through her mind like a persistent surf, wearing her down. But after a few minutes the names started to evaporate one by one like a troublesome fog, and she took shelter in sleep.

A lone hurricane flag whips wildly in the killer wind. Clouds heavy and black as iron boil overhead. Brie stands alone on the bluffs, facing the approaching maelstrom. At her feet the body of Blythe Whitehall lies ravaged by death. Droplets of scarlet red begin to fall from the flag like rain. Brie holds out her hands to catch them and sees the drops are not dye from the flag, but blood. She looks at the body again, but now it is Claire Whitehall who lies there, lovely even in death. In the vicious wind, the hurricane flag rips violently from the pole and covers Claire's body like a shroud. A pitch black shadow engulfs Brie and she turns. A hand, just a hand, but big as a shovel and strong as fear itself pushes her toward the edge of the cliff. She fights against it but knows she is powerless and death lies but a few yards behind her. On the hand a gold ring emblazoned with a coat of arms is slowly turning black as a cancer. Helpless to change her fate, she plummets into the void.

Brie woke with a jolt from the dream. Her heart was racing. She fumbled in the dark for the small lamp and turned it on and sat there thinking about the nightmare. After a few minutes, she got out of bed and went to the bathroom for a glass of water. Only then did she hear the rain coming down hard outside the window. She closed the two windows and stood for a minute looking out at the pitch black night. A brilliant spear of electricity shot straight down into the sea, laying a ghostly, momentary snapshot before her, and from her high vantage point Brie saw the dark waters of the ocean spread out as if they ran on forever. She turned from the window just as the thunderclap shook the old walls of the Windward Inn.

She picked up her small notebook and pen from the dresser and climbed back into bed. She wrote some notes about the images in the dream—the flag, the hand, the ring, the two bodies—figuring she wouldn't remember them in the morning. It was then she realized the nightmare hadn't affected her in the usual way—hadn't had the shattering effect that had accompanied such dreams over the past year and a half. Since being shot—since her battles with PTSD had begun—she would wake from these nightmares covered with sweat, short of breath, and often nauseated. But tonight had been different, and she took it as a sign she might be making progress.

She set the notebook and pen on the small table, turned off the lamp, and snuggled back under the soft quilt. Having written down the dream, she found it easier to release those images from her mind. The rain assaulted the windows in waves and Brie listened to the sound, thinking about the *Maine Wind* and the sound the rain always made on the deck above where she slept, and somehow that familiar and fond memory lulled her back to sleep.

Chapter 27

Brie woke the following morning with a clear head and a plan. After breakfast she would hike up to the old Whitehall estate. Finding the key on the path the day before had led her to believe that Claire Whitehall had indeed gone to her grandparents' estate the day of the hurricane. What had happened after that was unknown, but she felt there was a strong possibility Claire had gone from the house along the narrow trail Brie had seen yesterday that led to the bluffs. But was she alone, or had someone been with her? That was the question. Brie knew that either Paul Herrington or Logan Lancaster could have followed Claire.

And what had happened to her daypack and her recorder? Might they still be at the house? If so, might they provide a clue to what had transpired in the final hours of Claire Whitehall's life?

Brie pulled her legs out from under the quilt and sat on the edge of the bed for a few moments. She needed to call Dent Fenton and see which way the DA was leaning with regards to the arrest of James Levy. Her guess was they were probably going to charge Levy with the murder of Claire Whitehall. Be that as it may, she still felt the answer might lie here on the island, and there were a few more stones she had yet to turn over.

As for James Levy, she knew one thing. Except in rare cases, stalkers do not usually kill the object of their obsession. It would be counterproductive for them. Except for a few truly homicidal cases, the majority of stalkers just want access to their object.

Brie headed for the bathroom to wash up. The pine floor was chilly, and she grabbed a pair of socks out of her pack and pulled them on. The island was completely blanketed with fog, and she had no view whatsoever from her windows. But the rain had stopped, and she figured as the morning wore on, the wind would come up and sweep away the fog. She washed her face and brushed her teeth and dressed in jeans, a long-sleeved white tee shirt, and her hiking boots. She grabbed her watch and key off the dresser and headed downstairs for breakfast.

Even though there was no view, she sat by the window in the dining room. Being up against the wall somehow felt comforting and a bit more private. When the waitress came, she ordered black coffee and glanced over the menu. When the woman came back with water and coffee, Brie put in her order for a ham and cheese omelet, whole grain toast, and a fruit cup.

She checked her watch—it was just after eight o'clock. After breakfast she would put in that call to Dent Fenton. Then she needed to locate Gil Doubtwater and find out if there was indeed a key to the Whitehall cottage in the safe at the town hall, and if there was, she needed to see if it matched the key she had found on the trail up near the cliffs yesterday.

With no view out the window next to her, Brie's thoughts turned inward. The ring she had seen on Logan Lancaster's hand when she'd interviewed him yesterday had seemed familiar. Why? And the same ring had shown up in her nightmare last night when the hand had pushed her over the cliff. She felt a chill run through her as she remembered the dream. The obvious interpretation of it was that Logan Lancaster had killed Claire. He had been one of the last people to see her alive, and he had motive and opportunity. But so did Paul Herrington, and Brie's gut was telling her there was still a missing piece. That was why she was eager to go up to the old Whitehall place. Maybe it held the answer.

The waitress came back with her food, and Brie asked her to put the breakfast on her room tab. She took a sip of her coffee, which was strong but very good, and dug into the omelet. But her mind was so preoccupied with the case, she barely noticed how delicious the food was.

She remembered Jack Le Beau's advice yesterday about not pushing too hard—about taking a step back, giving things a chance to be revealed. But time was running short, and Brie had never been one to sit back and wait for a case to solve itself or for the answer to be mystically revealed.

Chapter 28

After finishing breakfast, Brie went up to her room to get her jacket and daypack and clip on her gun holster. She put through a call to Dent Fenton, but it went immediately to his voicemail. She left a message that it was nothing urgent—she was just curious about which way the wind was blowing with the James Levy situation. Grabbing her daypack, she headed out of the inn and down into the village to find Gil Doubtwater.

Fog still clung to the island, giving the buildings an otherworldly feel. She'd seen the town hall the last time she'd been through the village. It was down toward the end of the main street, cattycorner from the general store. When she walked in, Gil Doubtwater was sitting behind a large wooden desk typing on his computer. The clock on the wall over his head read eight forty-five. As soon as he saw her, he stood up.

"Hello, Detective. What can I do for you this morning?"

"Hello, Mr. Doubtwater. I'd like to check and see if that key is in the safe—the key to the old Whitehall place."

"After we talked about it yesterday, I looked for it, and there is a key in the safe."

He got up and headed into the back room and over to a large olive-green safe that stood in the corner. He opened the safe and took out a manila envelope that he handed to Brie. The words "Whitehall cottage" were written on the front in ink.

Brie pulled out a latex glove and put it on. She took the key she had found on the trail from her jacket pocket and placed it on the table that stood next to the safe. Then she opened the envelope and slid out the key that was inside. It looked identical to the one she had found—same shape, size, and patina.

Doubtwater looked confused and surprised all at once. "Where did you find the other key?" he asked.

"I'm not at liberty to say right now."

He sunk his hands in his pockets and rocked back and forth on his feet.

Brie picked up the two keys and laid them one on top of the other. They were a perfect match. The key she had found on the trail was still wrapped in a latex glove, and she put it back in her pocket. She slid the other key back into the envelope and took it into evidence, tucking it inside her pack. They walked back to the front room, and Gil Doubtwater seemed at a loss for words.

Brie asked if he could give her directions up to the old Whitehall estate. "I've been told there was an old road that was originally built to access the property."

"The road is quite overgrown. It hasn't been used in years, but you can still find it. You should be able to follow it up to the old Whitehall cottage without losing your way. Would you like me to accompany you?"

"Oh, that's not necessary," Brie said. "I'm sure I'll find the way just fine if you give me a couple of directions." The last thing she wanted was someone tagging along with her. She needed to investigate the Whitehall cottage without any distractions—see if she could divine from the surroundings there what might have happened to Claire in the final hours of her life.

"Well, you follow the north road out of the village—the one where Doc Appleton lives—and about a quarter of a mile along you'll see another road branch off to the northeast. It's just a grassy track, but you'll recognize it. A little ways along there you'll pass an old barn that's seen better days. Just keep going. The road winds a bit as it climbs toward the north side of the island. At a good pace you should get up there in thirty-five to forty minutes. And you have the key, so access to the house will be no problem."

"Thank you for your help, Mr. Doubtwater. I'll let you get back to your work."

"I hope you get to the bottom of this, Detective. Miss Whitehall was a lovely young woman and one with a history here on our island. We all would want the truth about what happened to her discovered."

"I'm sure that's the case, Mr. Doubtwater. Rest assured that we're doing all we can to solve the case."

Doubtwater nodded, and Brie headed for the front door of the town hall. When she glanced back he was still standing there, hands in his pockets, rocking to and fro, his expression unreadable.

Brie headed back through the village toward the north road. She was eager to get up to the Whitehall place and see what she could find there. With luck she'd make it up to the house by nine-thirty and have all the time she needed to investigate.

A leaden sky brooded over the village like a bad dream as she swung past the ferry dock and up the north road. She passed Logan Lancaster's house and saw no sign of anyone. Logan would be out pulling his pots, and his wife would be busy at one of her quilting machines. Brie passed the Foster house where one of the lobstermen lived that she'd interviewed early in the case. She carried on up the north road, watching for the grassy road Gil Doubtwater had told her would branch off.

Another few minutes along, the road swung inland, and just beyond that Brie saw the fork she was looking for and headed up it. The grassy track meandered past a small orchard, and there was the old barn Gil had mentioned, literally leaning toward extinction. But even Hurricane Ivan had failed to have its way with the sturdy old structure. Brie skirted the weathered gray goliath which somehow seemed a metaphor for all the adversity that is faced down in a lifetime and all the courage that is required to do so.

Past the orchard and the barn, an old hard-packed road headed upland. The roadbed had once been gravel and remnants of that surface still survived, but the spruce had invaded and rainfall had carved deep rivulets down into the once-solid surface. Nature has a way of undoing all human endeavor, and that determination was apparent here. Brie hiked upward, sidestepping trees that had established themselves, and soon the spruce forest closed in around her almost claustrophobically.

What little wind existed on the shore of the island today could not penetrate this inland forest, and a ghostly fog suffocated the landscape. Cocooned as she was by her surroundings, Brie's thoughts turned inward and she mulled on the case. She wondered how Jack Le Beau was doing on the mainland tracking down the whereabouts of Douglas Lancaster's second child. And she wondered whether James Levy, now in custody, would be charged in Claire's death. She thought about her two suspects here on the island—Logan Lancaster and Paul Herrington. Might her visit to the Whitehall estate reveal something—some clue that would implicate one or the other of them? Finally she thought again about the ring that Logan Lancaster wore, emblazoned with the crest of his ancestors. The ring that had been on the hand in her nightmare—the hand that had pushed her over the edge of the cliff.

Chapter 29

Jack Le Beau drove the winding coastal road toward Belfast, Maine. Route 1 was completely fogbound this morning and white-knuckle treacherous with its many hills and curves.

He had arisen quite early, packed up Angus in the Highlander, and headed out. Belfast was the government seat for Waldo County and where he needed to go to track down the history of property ownership for the address he was investigating in Belfast.

He parked in front of the Waldo County courthouse and went directly to the Registry of Deeds to search for who had owned the property at 25 Sea Street in the 1960s and '70s. It was the address he had found on Mary Lancaster's Maine state driver's license that had been issued in 1974. He wanted to find out who had owned the property at that time. Hopefully the history within the deed would give him the name of the family who had taken in Mary Lancaster as an infant and raised her. Jack's other hope was that someone in the family still lived in Belfast. He thought there was a good chance of it since Mainers tended to stay put a lot.

Twenty minutes later he was headed out of the courthouse with the information he needed, thanks to a jolly, amply-bosomed woman named Maggie who had flirted with him just enough to make him feel alive again. She had helped him not only discover who had owned the property on Sea Street in the 1970s, but through the wonders of the computer age, had also tracked down an address for the man here in Belfast. His name was Tom Lewis.

As Jack approached the Highlander, Angus lumbered up from the car floor and stuck his big head out the window. Jack pulled a dog biscuit out of an inner jacket pocket and gave it to his big friend. Angus drooled just enough to make a mess of the lower part of the car window.

Jack climbed in. "One more step, fella, and then we'll go down to the water so you can have a swim."

He followed Maggie's directions through Belfast and located the address on the outskirts of town. He pulled up in front of a modest house at 84 Oak Street and lowered the windows enough that Angus would have plenty of air. "I'll be back in a jiffy, big boy." He patted the Newfie's head, climbed out of the car, walked up to the door and rang the bell. As he waited for an answer, he pulled his ID out of his pocket, and just as he did so, an older man opened the front door. He was a short fellow with piercing blue eyes and a friendly aura.

"Tom Lewis?" Jack said.

"Yes?"

"I'm retired detective Jack Le Beau of the Maine State Police. I wonder if I could ask you a few questions." He showed Lewis his ID.

"About what?" Lewis said. There was no antagonism in his voice but rather a strong inflection of curiosity.

"A couple of things," Jack said. "First off, I'm wondering if you are related in any way to a Mary Edna Lancaster."

"Is something wrong?" Lewis' voice rang with concern.

"No, just a few questions."

"Well, come in then, Detective." He held the door open and Jack stepped inside. Tom Lewis showed him into a modestly furnished living room to the right of the hallway.

"Mary was the daughter of my wife's cousin. His name was Douglas Lancaster. She came to live with us as an infant. Douglas had lost his wife shortly after Mary was born. He couldn't care for the children—there was a boy too—a couple of years older as I recall. Don't know offhand what all the problems were, but he asked my wife if she would take the baby girl till he got himself straightened around. We agreed to do it, and it was nice to have a little one around—especially for Beth. We hadn't been able to have children. Then just a month after the baby came here, Douglas went missing from his lobsterboat. There was talk of suicide back then—I guess he had been depressed, but I don't think they ever knew for sure how he died. Just that he drowned."

When Tom Lewis started talking, Jack had taken out his small notebook and begun jotting down notes.

"I notice the name on Mary's Maine driver's license was Lancaster. Does that mean you never adopted her?"

Lewis looked down at his feet like he was ashamed. "We raised her just like our own daughter, but we never got around to adopting her."

"Might I ask why?" Jack felt somehow troubled by the revelation though he tried not to show it.

"The young boy had gone to be raised by Douglas' brother down in Spruce Head. He had a lot more money than us, and I guess we always thought he might want to reunite the children."

"Didn't you ever worry about how never being adopted might affect this young girl you were raising?"

"We loved her and gave her all we could. She knew that."

Even though Lewis hadn't exactly answered the question, Jack let it go and moved to his questions about Mary Lancaster's current whereabouts.

"According to Maine's DMV records, Mary's driver's license expired when she was thirty-four years old and was never renewed. Can you tell me where she lives now?"

"A-yah," Lewis said. "She met a guy when she was thirty. He come 'from away'—Vermont—and she ended up moving there. That was back in, oh, maybe eighty-six or so."

Jack could see that Tom Lewis liked chronology and planned to relate Mary Lancaster's history in proper order.

"Is she still living in Vermont?" Jack asked, hoping to speed up the process.

"Nooo. She finally married that guy, but I knew it wouldn't last and it didn't. She moved back to Maine 'bout five years ago. Lives out on one of the islands."

Jack's ears perked up at that, but before he could pose his next question, Tom Lewis was talking again.

"When my Beth died a few years back and I went through her things, I found a stack of letters that her cousin Douglas had written to her in the months before his death back in 1958 or thereabouts. I thought Mary might like to have them, so I sent them out to her on the island."

"Did you read them?" Jack asked.

"No." Lewis shook his head. "Didn't think it was my business to. But I thought since Mary never knew her father that she might like to have them."

Jack was feeling increasingly alarmed by this narrative. "Weren't you worried about what might have been in the letters?"

"She's a grown woman—I didn't think about it, I guess."

"Which island is Mary living on, Mr. Lewis?" But Jack figured he already knew what the answer would be.

"Well, she went back to the island where she was born—Apparition Island. Kind of a creepy name, if you ask me. Don't know as I'd wanna live there." He said it "they-ah"—Yankee-style.

"Have you visited Mary out on the island?" Jack asked.

"No, but she visits here two or three times a year."

"Can you give me her address on the island?"

Lewis nodded. "I got it in the kitchen. I'll go fetch it."

"And do you happen to have an address for her ex-husband in Vermont?"

Tom Lewis looked like he wanted to spit, and his blue eyes suddenly went hard as granite. "I'd like to take his head off for hurting our Mary. I've got the address though," he said grudgingly. He went to the kitchen and came back a couple minutes later with the information.

Jack looked at the husband's name—Jacob Hanover. The name didn't ring any bells, but he felt an urgency to reach Brie and let her know that the other Lancaster child was on the island. He checked his watch. It was nine-twenty.

"Well, thank you, Mr. Lewis—Tom. You've been very helpful."

"Mary's not in any trouble, is she?"

"No. We just want to ask her some questions relating to a case we're working on."

Lewis nodded but looked worried nonetheless.

"And let me extend my condolences on the death of your wife," Jack said. "I lost my wife a year ago, and it's a terrible thing to get through."

"Thank you, Detective," Lewis said.

The blue eyes softened, and Jack saw the loneliness there and the fear he himself knew so well—it was the fear of an uncertain world—a world turned upside down, a world where the one left behind slowly slips away, having lost his mooring in life.

Jack left the Lewis house and walked to his car on the other side of the street. Angus was at the window waiting for him, and Jack handed in another biscuit to the big fella. He pulled out his phone and called Brie, but the call went directly to her voicemail. He left her a message about Mary Lancaster living on the island as well as the married name he'd gotten from Tom Lewis. He wished he could have reached her. Something about this new development troubled him. He put through a call to Dent Fenton at the Maine State Police.

When Lieutenant Fenton answered, Jack filled him in on what he'd discovered. "I know Brie is very capable—that she can take care of herself. Still . . ."

"I'm with you, Jack. We need to reach her. I'll get a call through to someone of authority on the island. There should be a town manager out there."

"Thanks, Dent. It may just be smoke . . ."

"Yeah, but smoke can lead to fire. I'm on it, Jack. Thanks for the heads up."

Jack Le Beau climbed into the car and turned over the engine, and Angus thumped him with a giant black paw.

"I'm worried about Brie, fella."

At the mention of her name, Angus sat up straight, suddenly alert, and let out a baritone "woof."

"You can't be a cop as long as she has, though, without facing down danger. Right, boy?"

Angus looked Jack straight in the eye like he could read his mind.

Jack sat for a minute, deciding if there was anything else he could do, but he knew the situation was in Dent Fenton's hands now. The tide was high. Jack worked his way down to the water, looking for a spot where Angus could have a swim.

Chapter 30

Brie had been following the road upward for nearly thirty minutes when suddenly, like phantoms rising from the mist, the chimneys and gables of the old Whitehall cottage suddenly rose out of the forest to the northeast. She felt a chill of anticipation at seeing them and increased her pace. The wind was picking up as she climbed higher, and the forest had suddenly come alive with sounds—creaks and moans from skeletons of trees that had long since given up the ghost. And now the haunting calls of gulls, carried to her on the wind, told Brie she was close to the coastline.

Thunderheads massed themselves to the northeast, and as she climbed higher, the cloud deck seemed to be descending ominously, and it was rumbling like a beast, even though Brie saw no lightning. Just ahead a large boulder loomed out of the ground next to the old road. She took off her daypack, pulled out her water bottle, and leaned against the boulder for a drink. The dream she'd had the night before still troubled her. She took out her small notebook and flipped through, looking for the list of elements that had appeared in the nightmare. On the way to the dream she came to the list of suspects she'd written down the night before. Suddenly a single word popped into her mind, and it was lit up like a neon sign. The word was "Lists." Brie thought that was strange, but she'd been a detective long enough to know it meant something. *The neon was kind of a sign,* she thought, smiling.

She reflected on the single word "lists" now emblazoned in her mind and looked down at the list of suspects in her notebook, but nothing seemed to jump out. She put her water bottle back in the pack and continued up the old road, waiting for something to click—waiting for the aha moment. She was close to the Whitehall cottage now, and her curiosity about that made it hard for her to focus on the flashing neon sign in her mind.

She still had the notebook in her hand, and she flipped to the list of elements from her dream the night before. She ran her eye down the list, and when she got to the word "ring," the answer hit her hard like a piece of loose rigging. She suddenly knew why Logan's ring had seemed familiar. It wasn't the ring, but the crest on the ring that had triggered a sense of *déjà vu*. And now she knew where she'd seen that family crest.

The first day she had come on the island seeking the identity of the woman they'd found in the ocean, she had gone into the general store and talked to Edie Hanover. Now she distinctly recalled that when she had followed her into the storeroom that day, she had seen several grocery lists written on pieces of tablet paper. She had been looking at the sheets upside down, but now she remembered there had been a small coat-of-arms in the top corner of the paper, and it was the same coat-of-arms that was on the ring Logan Lancaster wore. Hence the word "Lists" in neon. Her subconscious mind was trying to give her the answer. She thought about the name of Douglas Lancaster's daughter that Jack Le Beau had found in the birth records—Mary Edna Lancaster, born in 1956—the daughter who had been sent away from the island as an infant back in 1958. The age was a fit, and Edie could be a nickname for Mary Edna. Could Edie Hanover be the missing Lancaster—Mary Edna Lancaster?

But did this discovery change anything? Brie stood rooted to the spot where she'd stopped in the middle of the road when the answer had dawned on her. The other Lancaster child, the daughter, had been here on the island all along. At some point she'd obviously returned to the place of her birth to live. Nothing incriminating there. And when Brie first came on the island, she certainly wasn't looking for Lancasters. She was only seeking Claire Whitehall's identity. So what she'd seen in the general store that day had meant nothing. And for her part, Edie Hanover had no way of knowing Brie was looking for the offspring of Douglas Lancaster.

What seemed really strange, though—in fact almost unbelievable—was that Logan's aunt was living right there in the village, and he didn't know who she was. Granted, she and her brother had been separated when she was an infant and never reunited, but surely she knew Logan was her nephew. Or maybe she didn't. Or maybe at this point in her life she didn't want to be part of the family. After all, she had her own family somewhere. In fact, Jack Le Beau had gone to Belfast today to see if he could locate the family who had raised her. She pulled out her phone, wondering if he had found anything out, but there was no reception this far out of the village. She put her phone away and decided to go on to the Whitehall cottage, knowing she was almost there.

There was no doubt that Edie Hanover should be on the suspect list, and when she was done up here, Brie planned to head back down to the village and interview her. After all, Edie, as one of the Lancaster children, shared the same motive as her brother and her nephew—the desire to keep the family history buried—to keep Claire Whitehall from resurrecting the ghosts of the past and from bringing to light the truth about her grandmother's murder.

Brie put her notebook back in her pocket, satisfied that a key piece of information had just come to light. Right now, though, she needed to see what the old Whitehall cottage might reveal. She hoped Claire's pocket recorder might still be found—might still contribute some crucial piece of evidence linked to the cause of her death. Because, while Brie had an array of suspects with motive, means, and opportunity, she was missing that all important element in any murder case—proof.

She headed up the road again with increased vigor. The darkening sky rumbled a warning, and Brie looked up, as if it might be meant for her personally. Her gut told her she was closing the gap on the killer.

Unbeknownst to Brie, down in the village twenty minutes earlier, Edie Hanover had turned the sign on her store window to "Closed," placed her shotgun in the bottom of her delivery wagon under two boxes of produce, and headed north out of the village.

Chapter 31

Brie continued her trek up the old road which serpentined now as the terrain got steeper. The bluffs she had visited the day before, where Claire was thought to have fallen to her death, lay on the east side of the island. The Whitehall cottage was north of there along the same part of the island where cliffs rose high and steep.

As she climbed, she kept thinking about Edie Hanover, and snatches of that first conversation came back to her. It was Edie who had identified Claire from the picture on Brie's phone of the dead woman. Brie thought back on the dialogue.

"It's Claire Whitehall," Edie had said. Brie remembered now that Edie had paused and then said, "Not the kind of name you'd easily forget."

Brie had asked why that was and Edie had responded, "It's got kind of a grand sound to it, don't you think?"

Brie had agreed with that because, after all, the name did somehow conjure up thoughts of wealth and position. But now Brie realized there was an entirely different reason why that name would have been hard for Edie to forget. Not because it had a grand sound to it, but because the name Whitehall was woven into the very fabric of Edie's life and how that life had unraveled when she was no more than an infant.

As a detective, Brie was aware of the nuances of language and how a thing said may carry an entirely different implication when the full story comes to light. Knowing now who Edie Hanover was cast a different light on that conversation. A conversation that had seemed as innocuous as a sunny day now carried the shadow of something hidden, and in Brie's mind, Edie Hanover moved up the suspect list past Paul Herrington and even James Levy. She thought about the dream again—that ring with the crest of the House of Lancaster. In her mind only Lancasters topped the list of suspects now. But which one of them? She needed proof.

Brie rounded the last bend in the road, and the old Whitehall estate spread out before her. The once-grand summer cottage now waged a hopeless war against the encroaching forest. The stately roofline sagged, and moss and lichen pocked the shingles. The gutters resembled hanging gardens, so much vegetation had taken root there. It was sad, really, because the house had such symmetry and appeal Brie had to assume the design of it had been the work of a fine architect.

But the massive wrought iron fence that surrounded the estate still stood tall and straight, guarding the memory of brighter, happier days. The gate stood open, and Brie passed through it and walked up the drive to the front door, which stood directly in the center of the house. A beautiful gabled window overhung the open porch outside the front door. Decorative railings and a small built-in bench gave the porch a welcoming feel, and with the window jutting out overhead, a visitor would be sheltered from rain.

Before taking the key out of her pocket, Brie tried the door and found it unlocked. "That's troubling," she said to herself. She thought it unlikely that Claire would have intentionally left the door unlocked. Brie stepped inside and closed the door. A two-story central hallway that could have accommodated a good-sized schooner and masts ran all the way through the house. At the back of the hall, light poured in through French doors and windows, giving a breathtaking view of the ocean beyond. The effect was magical. Brie guessed the presence of the sea had been as important an element to the architect as design of rooms or décor.

A curved freestanding stairway of beautiful wood rose to the second floor, leaving the hallway below it open. Brie walked past the stairway to the back of the hall and gazed out the windows. The house sat on a granite bluff where no trees obscured the view of the sea beyond.

She walked into the library on her left. It was not a huge room, which added to its coziness and appeal. Every inch of wall was lined with books, but again the back wall of the room was given over to windows that let in the sea. The room had a fireplace for cold Maine nights, and the heavy leather furniture was partially draped with sheets.

She walked through an archway into the living room, which ran back toward the front of the house where she had entered. There was a large grouping of furniture—looking ghostly under its sheets—around the fireplace. A once-brilliant-colored Oriental rug had faded from the assault of too much light and dust over too many years, but the house still whispered of glorious summers spent here by a family of means. Sheltered as it was by the forest to the east, the dwelling had withstood Hurricane Ivan that had swept in from the southeast.

At the far end of the living room she walked through a small passageway with a tall window to seaside and a built-in window seat—as cozy a spot as one could ever imagine. The other end of the small passageway opened into a music room with a curving arc of windows at the back. A beautiful grand piano in the center of the room was situated so the person playing could look toward the sea beyond. A gold gilt pedal harp sat off to one side in front of a lovely little tapestry bench.

The sheet had been pulled off the grand piano and lay on the floor like a deflated ghost. The top of the piano had been raised, and sheet music for Beethoven's "Moonlight Sonata" stood open on the music rack. Brie wondered if Claire had sat here and played the sonata, trying to capture some feel for those glorious bygone days.

Brie had not played the piano in many years, but the "Moonlight Sonata" was particularly dear to her heart with its minor key and sad, brooding melody. She remembered sitting at the old upright piano in their living room—the piano that had belonged to her grandmother—and playing the sonata over and over as if she could play all the grief from her heart that summer her father had died—the summer of her twentieth year.

She stepped between the bench and the keyboard, sat down at the piano, and began to play the haunting melody that had become so much a part of her that tragic summer. And as her fingers plied the keys and the melancholy strains filled the room, she felt the presence of her father very strongly. It wasn't the first time she'd had the experience since being in Maine, and she had decided it must somehow be part of the healing process she was going through. She guessed it made sense in a way—after all, Maine was where her father had grown up—where she had spent happy summers as a child at her grandparents' house.

The room suddenly grew dark, and through the windows beyond Brie saw thunderheads massing—part of a weather system working its way up the coast, the same system that had dumped down rain the night before. She stood up and made her way back through the living room and walked through the dining room and kitchen that lay on the other side of the hall. Other than the sheet being removed from the piano and the top raised, there was no sign of Claire's having been here—no backpack, no recorder.

Brie headed up the stairs to the second floor, and as she came out in the upper hallway, the wind buffeted the house. To the right of the stairs at the front of the house was a moderately-sized bedroom. She stepped in and looked around, peeking under the sheets that covered the furniture. The room was set up as a nursery with a baby crib, a changing table and a rocking chair.

The wind shook the house again, and Brie heard its old boards creak as if a ghost patrolled the halls. She looked over the railing to the first floor. She hadn't locked the door when she entered and thought about going down to do so, but she didn't plan to be here much longer, and anyway, no one but Gil Doubtwater knew she was coming up here this morning.

She walked down the hall and entered the master bedroom, and it was like stepping through a portal in time. No sheets covered the furniture here, and Brie felt the hair rise on the back of her neck. It was as if Blythe Whitehall still sat at the lovely Art Deco dressing table, staring into the mirror, now gone cloudy with the passage of years, trying to work out who she was and what she wanted from her life. Brie was a woman of the twenty-first century, but in that moment she felt connected to Blythe Whitehall and her long-ago struggle to find happiness.

A magnificent canopy bed filled the center of the room, and a once-vibrant quilt of red and gold silk, Chinese in design, had grown pale—muted by time. Brie wondered if Douglas Lancaster had made love to Blythe Whitehall here in this room on this elegant bed. Of course he would have. She was here alone that summer, and the house was so secluded—the perfect lovers' hideaway. A chill ran through her. So secluded—the perfect place for murder. Even all these years later, the room still felt alive with memories, haunted with emotions—passion, pain, love, loss.

Brie walked around the room, looking carefully to see if Claire's daypack or voice recorder were anywhere in evidence, but she found nothing. An air of sadness brooded over the room, and she moved toward the French doors that opened onto a covered balcony. She tried the door handle. It turned and the door swung open easily, as if the ghosts that haunted this place came and went by it regularly. Brie stepped onto the balcony, walked across and stood with her hands on the railing.

Vines had grown up and entwined the balusters along the front of the balcony. The second story vantage offered a spectacular view of the sea, and she could smell the coming storm.

The sky had grown black as chimney soot, and low, continuous thunder rumbled in the still air. She wondered how long the storm would last, knowing she was marooned here until it passed. As she stood there breathing in the salt air, thinking momentarily about the *Maine Wind,* the first large raindrops hit her hands. She stepped back under the roof of the house that covered the balcony as the rain came down like a heavy gray curtain.

When it started to really blow, she turned and retreated back into the bedroom. As she passed through the doors, something caught her eye. To her left, an ornate wood plant stand was tucked behind heavy curtains that could be drawn across the bank of French windows and doors. There was something on the table. She walked over to it. It was a small silver digital recorder—Claire's recorder. Brie pulled her latex glove from her pocket, put it on, and picked up the device. She owned a similar voice recorder, and after playing with the buttons for a few seconds, she knew the batteries were dead, which meant it might well have been turned on when Claire left it here. *She must have been recording her impressions of the room,* Brie thought. But why had she left it behind? Brie felt that tingle in the blood detectives get when evidence comes to light. If something had happened here at the house the day Claire died, the recorder might very well hold a clue to what had unfolded.

She took a small evidence envelope from her pack, placed the recorder inside, and tucked the envelope back into her pack. Then she did another thorough search of the room to be sure she hadn't missed Claire's daypack. Rain pelted the French windows. Over the decades the glazing had grown brittle as old bones, and the panes rattled in their wooden frames. The wind whispered and moaned down the chimney like a disembodied spirit as Brie moved about the bedroom. She found no daypack and was left wondering what had happened that Claire would leave her recorder behind, still turned on. Her only guess was that something had distracted her, and Claire had left the room and obviously not returned.

Brie exited the master bedroom and walked around the gallery that overlooked the lower hall to the bedrooms on the opposite side. As she entered the room directly across from the master bedroom, she immediately saw that something was wrong. Near the doorway, pieces of a broken vase were scattered across the floor, and she could see where the vase had hit the door frame and damaged the woodwork. She set her pack down outside the room, pulled out a pair of booties, and gloved up, and walked across the room to where a table was overturned. The lamp that had sat on it lay smashed on the floor. She squatted down and ran a finger over a large broken shard of the china lamp. No dust had collected there. It was clear to her that some kind of violent confrontation had taken place here quite recently, which might answer why Claire's recorder had been left running. Now Brie was even more curious to see what was on that recorder and whether it might provide a clue as to what had happened here and who had been involved.

But a scene was shaping up in her detective mind, and based on many previous crime scenes, she thought she had a sense of what might have unfolded here. She walked back to the doorway and looked out into the hall. She guessed Claire had been in the master bedroom, possibly recording her impressions of the room where her grandmother had slept. Something had drawn her attention away—maybe a sound, maybe a sense that someone was in the house—and she had gone out into the hall. Maybe she saw someone in the hall downstairs, and maybe that someone had seen her as well.

With no exit down the stairway, Claire had retreated to this room and possibly grabbed the vase in hopes of defending herself. A struggle of some kind had ensued.

Whatever else had unfolded here, one thing was known; Claire had ended up dead after a fall from the cliffs east of here. So it was Brie's guess that whoever the killer was, Claire had been taken hostage, very likely at gunpoint, and then marched to the cliffs near where Brie had found the key yesterday. Her only hope now was that Claire's recorder had picked up the voice of the perpetrator as that person took Claire down the stairs and out of the house. If so, Brie would have the proof she needed to make an arrest.

The trail of evidence put Claire here in the house the day she had died and later on placed her near the cliffs, where she had managed to secretly drop the key to the Whitehall cottage. Brie knew she was closing in on the truth. She started a careful search of the room and almost immediately discovered Claire's backpack tucked behind the open door—probably hidden there moments before the perp entered the room. *She was leaving signs she'd been here*, Brie thought, which told her that in the few moments she'd had to do so, Claire had assessed the situation and known she was in dire peril. It was clear she had thrown the vase. Had she also gone for the perp's gun? It would be a gutsy move, but Brie sensed Claire Whitehall had not been short on courage.

If she had engaged the killer, Claire could have been driven back into the table, where the lamp fell and broke. Brie walked over to that spot, squatted down, and cast her eyes across the floor again to make sure she hadn't missed any crucial bit of evidence, but she saw nothing. She stood up. The rain had stopped its assault on the windows. She left the room, pulled off her booties and gloves, and stuffed them in her pack that sat outside the door on the hallway floor. She slung the pack on her back and did a quick search of the remaining bedrooms, but there was no sign that Claire had been in any of them. With the break in the rain, she needed to get back down to the village. She needed to see what was on Claire's voice recorder, and it was time to track down Edie Hanover—the missing variable in the Lancaster equation.

She walked down the curving stairs, carrying Claire Whitehall's daypack, and headed for the front door. She stepped out onto the small porch and turned to lock the door. The key was still wrapped in the latex glove to preserve any fingerprints, and she inserted it into the lock and shot the deadbolt. She turned and jerked backwards into the door. Edie Hanover stood no more than six feet away with a shotgun pointed at her heart.

Chapter 32

Edie edged forward, shotgun to her shoulder. "Take out your gun, nice and easy," she said.

Brie might have found the phraseology humorous if she hadn't been looking down the barrel of a shotgun. She reached under her jacket and removed her Glock from its holster.

"Toss it over here," Edie said. "And the key too. You won't be needing either of them. We're going for a little walk."

Brie did as ordered, and Edie pocketed the key and picked up the Glock and hurled it into the undergrowth behind her. Brie spotted a can of gasoline over near the trunk of a large cedar tree, and it didn't take a rocket scientist to know what Edie planned to do with it. Brie's mind flashed to the beautiful piano in the music room where she'd sat a little while ago, and the thought of that wonderful room and the rest of this fine old cottage burning made her heart ache. But it was clear to her now that Edie Hanover—aka Mary Edna Lancaster—would not rest until every trace of the Whitehall family was wiped from the island.

"Why are you doing this, Edie, or should I call you Mary?"

A brief flash of surprise crossed Edie's face.

"Why did you kill Claire?" Brie was pretty sure she knew the answers, but she wanted to get Edie talking if she could. She knew Edie had one of two things planned for her, and she also knew it was much easier for a hostage to take evasive action if the perpetrator is distracted in any way. As a cop, Brie knew that talking causes a person to be less focused physically.

"If you know my name, you must also know about the history between my father and Blythe Whitehall."

She paused a moment, but Brie said nothing, which seemed to frustrate her. "Let's get moving." With the barrel of the shotgun, Edie motioned toward the forest east of the house.

As they approached the edge of the forest, Brie noticed a narrow trail that angled off into the spruce, and her internal compass told her the trail ran toward the high bluffs where she had been yesterday. Her mind was working feverishly on escape, and she tried to get Edie talking again.

"Your father and Blythe Whitehall were a long time ago. Has all this really been worth it? You've ruined your life."

"My life was ruined long ago, by the death of both my parents. First my mother died of cancer when I was an infant, and then my father killed himself because he couldn't have that woman—Blythe Whitehall. I've read the letters."

Brie had no idea what letters she was talking about but decided to ask. "What letters do you mean?"

"Letters my father sent to his cousin—the woman who raised me—back in 1958. He admitted everything in them. Guess he didn't want to go to his grave without confessing. My cousin that raised me died not too long ago, and my father—I mean her husband—found the letters and saw they had been written by Douglas Lancaster, my real father. So he sent them to me."

Brie assumed Edie's adoptive father had not read the letters or he never would have sent them to her. She reflected momentarily on the stupid things people do, but knew she needed to keep Edie talking—keep her somehow off balance.

"So the truth is, your father was a murderer. He murdered Blythe Whitehall when she told him she was going back to her family in Boston."

"Shut up and keep moving," Edie said.

They had hiked in silence for a few minutes when Edie ordered her to stop and drop the two daypacks—hers and the one of Claire's she had recovered in the house. Edie tossed them into the undergrowth. She obviously planned to retrieve them when she returned to the cottage.

Brie knew she had to reopen the dialogue with Edie.

"But weren't you sent to relatives? Didn't they raise you like their own child? Didn't they love you?" Brie waited for an answer, but Edie had gone silent, and Brie guessed she'd hit on the truth.

"They never adopted me. Means they never really wanted me."

"I doubt that's true, Edie." But Brie was thinking about the letters again and wondering why the man who had raised her would be so careless about sending her something so hurtful. "Anyway, it seems like you have a pretty nice life out here on the island."

"Had," Edie said bitterly. "Until Claire Whitehall arrived. I came out here for a fresh start. I should've known it wouldn't work. It never does for me. She just couldn't let the past be—had to keep digging around out here till she uncovered . . ." Edie's voice drifted off, and Brie cast a furtive glance back over her shoulder.

"And what if the truth about your father had come out after all these years? Was it worth throwing your life away?"

"You don't know anything about it, so you need to shut up, or I'll kill you right here."

Brie wondered if Edie's birth father had somehow grown into a figure of mythic status for her—a situation not uncommon for children who have never known a birth parent. Maybe Edie had taken on the job of protecting the father she never knew. And even though she had learned the truth about his actions from the letters she had mentioned, it didn't seem to matter to her, possibly because she had long ago constructed her own narrative—a narrative that Claire Whitehall had threatened to destroy.

Brie knew that mental instability can run in families, and she decided Edie had inherited hers from her father, Douglas Lancaster. She also knew she had to come up with a plan—it was clear where they were headed. She guessed Edie had decided to shove her off the same cliffs that Claire had fallen from, and since they'd been on the trail for a quite a while, she knew time was running short.

At that moment an idea popped into her head. She was thinking of a move she'd learned in martial arts called a flat fall. If she did it adeptly, it might take Edie by surprise and cause her to trip and fall. Brie knew it was risky—the shotgun could discharge and depending on its trajectory, she could be killed. But she had to do something. She could see the edge of the forest approaching fast, and once out on the granite shelf, she'd have little chance for evasive action.

In the few seconds she had, Brie centered herself by taking a couple of deep breaths, and when the moment came, she suddenly fell flat to the ground, landing on her forearms. Exactly what she had hoped would unfold did. Edie, caught unawares, tripped over her body, and as she stumbled and hit the ground hard, the gun came out of her hands. Brie was up in a flash and went for the shotgun.

Edie was momentarily dazed by the fall, but then the adrenaline kicked in. She scrambled to her feet and, letting out a war cry, charged Brie, hitting her headlong and knocking her flat. The gun discharged, shattering the stillness of the forest. With life and death on the line, they grappled for possession, all four hands on the shotgun, twisting and pulling in a violent battle for control of the weapon.

They wrestled, locked in mortal combat for what felt like minutes, though Brie knew it was only seconds. Edie was strong and surprisingly agile, but Brie had youth, athleticism, and training on her side. When Edie tried to head butt her, Brie dodged, and with one monumental surge of will, rolled Edie over. Before the other woman could react, Brie put a knee hard into her chest and wrenched the shotgun with every ounce of strength she could muster, breaking Edie's hold on the weapon.

Brie was up like a shot and, stepping back, held the gun on Edie.

"Get up," she ordered. "Slowly."

Edie climbed to her feet, eyes fixed like a bird of prey on Brie.

"Now, walk." Brie motioned toward the trail that led back to the house.

Edie started to turn and then bolted the other way, running flat out toward the edge of the forest that opened onto the high bluffs.

Brie raced after her. "Stop," she shouted, but up ahead Edie had already cleared the forest. Brie fired a warning shot into the air, and Edie stopped and turned as Brie came out of the forest onto the bare granite. They were just yards from the precipice.

"Stop right there," Brie said, but now Edie was backing toward the edge of the cliff.

Brie made a decision. She set the shotgun on the ground to level the playing field—see if she could talk Edie Hanover down. She held up her hands and said in a calm voice, "It doesn't have to end this way, Edie. You can come back down to the village with me." But it wasn't working—Edie just kept on slowly backing up, and Brie saw something in her eyes—a look of determination coupled with surrender. She'd seen it before in the eyes of those who decided to jump. It was the look of one who had given up.

Edie was so close to the edge now that Brie knew if she were to dive for her, she might go over the cliff as well. Brie had no feeling one way or the other for Edie Hanover. In her cop emotions, Edie was a killer who needed to be brought to justice. Even so, a sense of helplessness and regret gripped her as Edie took that last step backwards. Brie saw surprise flash across her face in that split second, but no fear. She ran to the edge and saw the body hit the water. She watched for any movement, any sign of life, as Edie Hanover floated face up. But there was none.

The seas were running in from the southeast, but the tide was starting to turn. Brie knew she had to get to a spot with phone reception and call the Coast Guard, or the body would be carried out. She walked back and picked up the shotgun and headed along the trail toward the house. It would be faster to make her way down to the village by the old road, and anyway, she needed to retrieve the daypacks, the gasoline, and her gun if she could find it.

Chapter 33

Brie hiked back to the Whitehall cottage as fast as the trail would allow. Along the way she retrieved the two daypacks from the undergrowth where Edie had thrown them. When she got to the cottage, she walked to the exact spot she'd stood when Edie had flung her gun toward the edge of the forest. As it had unfolded, Brie had watched the arc of her arm and the trajectory on which the gun had flown. She now walked on a bead in that direction and began to search the ground a short ways into the forest.

Thunderheads rumbled overhead, threatening to drop the next deluge, but Brie kept her focus on the ground and within ten minutes was able to locate her gun. She holstered it and rushed back to grab the packs and gas can. She stuffed Claire's daypack into her own, flipped the pack onto her back, picked up the gas can, and started down the old road.

The key to the cottage was gone. It had been pocketed by Edie and now floated with her body in the ocean. But Brie had searched the house and removed what evidence she'd found there, which eliminated any need to reenter the premises.

She carried her phone in her right hand, and every few minutes along the road she checked for reception. Finally she got near enough to the village that she could place the call to Dent Fenton at the Maine State Police. As briefly as possible, she sketched out what had happened and told him to send the Coast Guard to the northeast side of the island where Edie Hanover had gone into the sea.

Next she called John and told him the case was wrapping up—that she had a few final things to do on the island but would be taking the afternoon ferry back to New Harbor. She knew the *Maine Wind* would be boarding passengers tomorrow evening for the next cruise, but she hoped they could grab some time together this evening. John said they were just getting ready to dock, but he'd call her later and make a plan.

Once down in the village, Brie went to find Gil Doubtwater. He was still at his desk in the town hall office. She told him what had unfolded, and Gil opened his mouth in fishlike fashion and didn't close it for the longest time. She asked if he would accompany her to the general store so she could make sure that Edie's apartment above the store was locked until someone from the Maine State Police could get out here with a search warrant. The letters Edie had mentioned were proof of motive, and they needed to be found and taken into evidence. According to her, they also contained a confession that would close the Blythe Whitehall case.

She and Gil headed for the general store and located the key to Edie's apartment in a drawer under her cash register. They went upstairs and locked things up, and Brie asked Gil to keep the key at the town hall until the police arrived with a warrant.

Brie walked up the hill to the Windward Inn and headed up to her room to pack her few belongings. She washed up, worked her hair into a neat braid, and wet down her bangs so she could get them to cooperate. She put on her jacket, grabbed her pack, and went downstairs to check out of the inn. She had an hour to kill before the ferry docked, so she headed for the deli. She'd worked up quite an appetite, and a bowl of steaming chowder sounded like a perfect fit for the cold, rainy afternoon.

When Brie walked in the door, Sally started to say, "Hi, hon," but then reconsidered and "Hon" turned into a clearing of the throat followed by, "Hi, Officer. How's your day going?"

Brie couldn't tell her it was a pretty good day since she'd avoided being shot or pushed off a cliff. So she settled for, "It's going okay."

"What can I get you?"

"I'll have a bowl of your amazing clam chowder," Brie said.

"Well, isn't that nice of you?" Sally beamed. "You just sit on down and I'll bring it out to you."

"Thanks," Brie said. She was the only one in the deli. She went to a table by the window and sat down, and it felt good to rest. She slipped out of her jacket, sat back and closed her eyes, and let her mind slide into neutral. What a crazy turn of events, she thought. She wondered what Jack Le Beau would think when she told him what had unfolded.

"Here you go," Sally said with such kindness in her voice Brie wondered if she could tell it had been a tough day for the detective. She set down the soup, which came with a warm, fragrant piece of garlic toast.

"Thank you. That looks delicious."

Sally also set down a steaming mug of coffee. "On the house," she said, nodding toward the coffee. "Looks like you could use some."

"Thank you," Brie said. "That's very kind, and now that you mention it, I could use some."

Sally beamed and walked back behind the counter. Brie lingered over the soup and coffee, and the world felt like a civilized place again.

In a little while she saw the ferry glide like a phantom out of a mist of rain a ways out to sea, and in a few more minutes the captain sounded the horn to alert the dock of his approach. Sally had topped off Brie's cup of coffee twice, and Brie took a final swallow and left Sally a hefty tip on the table to thank her for her kindness.

The rain was coming down again, and she took her cap out of her pack and pulled it on. She said goodbye to Sally, zipped up her jacket, and once out the door, made a dash down to the ferry dock. At the foot of the gangway, she handed over her ticket and went aboard. She headed to the back of the cabin, knowing the seas would be rough today, and in the aft of the vessel she'd feel the pitch and yaw a little less. She settled onto one of the wooden benches on the starboard side for the ride back to the mainland and checked her phone to be sure she had reception. She felt a little deflated that John hadn't called her back, but he was probably busy. The day's heavy dose of adrenaline was beginning to fade away, leaving a kind of raw exhaustion. In spite of the coffee she had drunk, she put her head against the side of the cabin and went to sleep.

Chapter 34

The ferry was rolling pretty good when Brie woke up thirty-five minutes later. She looked out the window and saw they were taking spray over the bow. Throughout the season she'd become so acclimated to changing sea conditions that it took a lot to make her seasick.

The drone of the engine was loud enough that it would have been hard to carry on a conversation. No chance of that, though, since she was one of only two passengers aboard—the other one being a man who sat on the port side of the ferry, amidships. Brie pulled a sweater out of her pack, tucked it under her head and went back to sleep.

The ferry's horn signaled their approach to the dock and jolted Brie from her slumber. She stuffed her sweater back in her pack and watched as the captain maneuvered the ferry up to the dock, and the crew got the hefty docking lines over the bollards and put the gangway in place.

Brie made her way forward, thanked the captain, and disembarked. As she headed off the dock, she thought about how the past two days felt more like two weeks. She pulled out her phone and put through a call to Marty Dupuis to see if he might be anywhere nearby so she could transfer the evidence she'd collected to him. She knew the *Maine Wind* was boarding passengers for the next cruise tomorrow, so she wanted to get back up the coast as soon as possible. Marty picked up on the second ring. He was about to head home to Bangor, and they agreed to rendezvous at the intersection of Routes 1 and 32 so she could sign over Claire Whitehall's daypack and voice recorder to him. They ended the call, and Brie stuffed her phone back in her pocket.

When she came in view of the pickup truck, she saw John leaning back against the hood, arms crossed, smiling at her.

"How did you get here?" Brie called out, feeling her heartbeat pick up at the sight of him.

They hugged each other and shared a quick kiss. "After we talked, I decided to head down here and surprise you, so Scott drove me down."

"He probably wants to be sure I get back to the ship and start pulling my weight."

John smiled. "Tomorrow's soon enough to worry about that. Right now, how about I take you to dinner?"

"Great," Brie said.

"What do you feel like?"

"Lobstah," Brie said in her best Maine speak.

"How about Waterman's?" John asked.

"Yes!" Brie pumped a fist. "My favorite. I love that place."

"Good." He kissed her on the forehead. "Hop in," he said, opening the passenger side door of the truck for her.

"Just one thing we have to do first. I have to rendezvous with Marty and hand over some evidence. I just spoke with him. He's in Augusta and was just getting ready to head back toward Bangor. We agreed to meet up at the intersection of Routes One and Thirty-two."

"We're headed back up that way anyhow," John said. "It's around a half hour's drive for Marty and about the same for us."

He started the truck, pulled out of the parking lot, and headed north on Route 32. As they drove, Brie filled him in on what had unfolded out on Apparition Island, and she could see from the concerned glances he gave her that he didn't like what he was hearing. He was slowly adjusting to his new reality of being in a relationship with someone who, because of her line of work, often faced danger.

When they got to the intersection of US Route 1, they found a safe spot to pull off the road and wait for Marty. He arrived ten minutes later, and Brie got out of the truck to talk to him. She signed over the evidence and filled him in briefly on what had unfolded. Marty told Brie that James Levy would be cleared for the murder of Claire Whitehall, but he would be charged in the break-in at the Westburgs' camp, where Claire had stayed on Apparition Island. Before he headed out, Marty stopped over and said hi to John. They had met following a previous case Brie had worked on, and she had seen right away that Marty took to John.

After Marty pulled away, John turned to Brie. "Well, it's just us now."

"Good," Brie said. "Just the way I like it."

"How about that lobstah?"

"What are we waiting for?"

John pulled out onto Route 1 and headed east. About twenty minutes later they passed through Thomaston, and just beyond the town he took a right onto 131, jogged east toward South Thomaston, and headed down 73 toward Spruce Head. The wind had driven off the clouds, leaving in their place a perfect Maine evening.

"This'll be our last trip to Waterman's for the season," John said. "They close next week."

Brie turned and studied him for a moment. "There's always next year," she said softly.

He took his eyes off the road just long enough to look into hers, and she could see that those few words had given him hope that there would be a John and Brie come next summer.

Waterman's Beach Lobster had as picturesque a setting as any lobster stand could ask for. It stood next to a meadow right by the sea, and the picnic tables on the shore looked out over

Muscle Ridge Channel. Brie and John got in line to wait their turn, and John opened two beers from a small cooler he'd brought with him. Waterman's didn't sell alcohol, but they were fine with patrons bringing their own. When their turn came, they both ordered the twin lobster dinner, which meant four lobsters between them, corn on the cob and coleslaw. For dessert they chose Waterman's homemade pie and ice cream. John went for the rhubarb, and Brie ordered the blueberry.

John paid and they stepped away from the window. "We'll work all this off tomorrow loading the ship," John said.

"If not sooner." Brie gave him a sly smile.

"I'll drink to sooner," John said. They clinked their beer bottles and wandered down and found a table by the shore. The picnic tables had checkered cloths and jars of flowers and candles that had been lit since the evening was wearing on. They sat and waited for their order and talked more about the case.

Brie filled John in on the history of Edie Hanover's life as well as the mission Claire Whitehall had been on to find the truth.

"She was trying to discover what ever happened to her grandmother," Brie said. "A case gone cold; a family mystery never solved. She was an investigative reporter; I can see how drawn to it she would have been."

"And juxtaposed, this other woman—Edie Hanover—trying to protect the father she never knew. Tragic, isn't it?" John said.

"Tragic on a grand scale," Brie responded. "A case spanning three generations that devastated two families."

"The ghosts of our pasts—they haunt us, don't they?"

"Sometimes beyond all reasoning," Brie said.

Later as they finished their meal, the sun sank down in the western sky, and as it did so, cast its last blush of color on the mirror of the sea. John and Brie walked reluctantly back to the truck. The night had turned cool, and Brie pulled the sweater out of her pack and put it on. John backed the truck around, and they headed along the coast toward Camden. They didn't talk much on the trip back. The beauty of the evening was enough for them.

Darkness had overtaken the harbor by the time they parked in the village and made their way back to the ship. They headed down the gangway. John went first, and when he got aboard, he turned and, just for the fun of it, lifted Brie by the waist onto the deck, and just for the fun of it, she let him. They took a turn or two around the deck of the *Maine Wind*, making sure everything was shipshape.

"I gave the crew the night off, so we've got the ship to ourselves tonight."

"Ahh." Brie smiled enigmatically. "In that case, I'm suddenly feeling the need to retire. Shall we go below, Captain?"

"I believe that would be the right course to plot."

Epilogue

By studying the tidal flow and direction the seas were running, the Coast Guard was able to recover Edie Hanover's body.

James Levy was cleared by the Maine State Police in the murder of Claire Whitehall and arrested for the break-in at Claire's camp on Apparition Island. Charges against him are pending in Portsmouth, New Hampshire, for the break-in at Claire Whitehall's apartment.

The daypack that Brie found at the Whitehall cottage contained Claire's missing cell phone and also a notebook with all the research Claire had done on her grandmother's case from 1958.

Claire Whitehall's voice recorder, also found at the house, had captured the confrontation between Claire and Edie Hanover when Claire was taken hostage. Claire was clearly heard saying in a loud voice, "Why are you doing this, Edie? Why are you taking me hostage?"

Edie's chilling response was also heard clearly. "Because I'm going to kill you."

Later in September, Brie interviewed Belle Westgate, the island historian, and found that Claire had spent a fair amount of time with her and received Belle's impressions of what had happened that summer so long ago, including her memory of both Blythe Danes and Douglas Lancaster. Apparently Mrs.

Westgate had recounted for Claire the stories she had heard as a teen about the two of them being ill-fated lovers.

In searching Edie Hanover's premises after her death, the Maine State Police discovered the letters that Douglas Lancaster had sent to his cousin Beth. Written in the fall of 1958, they revealed the unraveling of his mind as well as the unburdening of his heart. In them he confessed to the murder of Blythe Danes Whitehall. The cold case that had haunted Detective Jack Le Beau for 57 years was finally closed.

Brie went to visit Jack Le Beau and Angus on a beautiful fall day when the *Maine Wind* was in port, and she brought food from the Sea Basket and doggy treats for Angus. They sat in Jack's back yard as leaves drifted down around them from a fiery maple tree. Angus lay next to Brie, his giant head on her knee, and she stroked his head as she and Jack talked. Jack told her about his visit with Tom Lewis, who had raised Edie, and that he didn't believe Lewis would ever have sent those letters to Edie had he known their content—letters that became the catalyst of all that happened in their aftermath.

Brie admitted she had mixed feelings about leaving letters and diaries behind after one dies.

"I know they can have historical significance for famous people and sentimental value for the rest, but generally I think those things should go to the grave with a person. If Blythe Whitehall's husband had destroyed that diary in 1958, it never would have fallen into the hands of Claire Whitehall. And if Douglas Lancaster's cousin had destroyed those letters, Edie never would have known the terrible truth of her father's guilt."

"Makes you wonder if fate is just a cruel master we can't escape."

"I used to think so, Jack, until quite recently, actually. But lately I'm developing a more quantum view of existence."

Jack smiled. "Like I told you before, Brie, I'm not up on my physics."

"It just means there are lots of possibilities out there for how things can unfold. Nothing's dialed in. And after this summer, I'm becoming less of a fatalist and more of a believer in the wonders of possibility."

"I'm glad to hear that, Brie." He patted her arm in a grandfatherly way. "I've talked to Dent Fenton, and I know you went through a rough patch back there in Minneapolis."

The sun dipped lower and rested in the top of that fiery maple, creating quite a show. Brie and Jack sat and soaked in the beauty of the dying season, and as she stroked Angus, she reflected quietly on all the wonderful people she had come to know here—all the reasons she had to make this her new home. And she thought about the fact that her father had left Maine as a young man and that she had come back here now. It felt like the closing of a circle—like the next chapter in her new life of possibility.

2000 – 2013

In memory of Angus, our beloved Newfoundland dog
—our best dog ever.

Acknowledgements

Many thanks to my wonderful crew of support people who read, edit, typeset, and help create a fantastic-looking book: Chris Valen, fellow mystery author, friend and colleague at Conquill Press; Jennifer Adkins; Jeanette Brown; Linda Boulanger at Tell Tale Book Covers; Nina Pauls at eBook Prep; and of course, my husband, Craig. Thanks also to the Maine State Police for help with details—any inaccuracies are entirely my fault or the result of this being a work of fiction. Special thanks to Minnesota author Steve Thayer for reading *Apparition Island* and offering a comment for the book jacket. Also, many thanks to Pat Frovarp and Gary Schulze at Once Upon a Crime in Minneapolis, Minnesota, for their tireless work promoting all of us Minnesota mystery authors. Finally, thank you to all the bookstores in Maine and greater New England, the Midwest, and around the US who are faithful supporters of my work, and special thanks to my fans who send me such kind words that keep me motivated.

Glossary of Sailing Terms

Aft: Toward the back of the boat.

Abeam: At right angles to the boat.

Alee: Helm's alee or hard alee is the command for tacking or coming about.

Amidships: In the middle of the boat.

Athwartships: In a direction at right angles to the fore-and-aft line of the vessel.

Ballantine: To coil a halyard into three overlapping piles. The finished pile of line looks like a 3-leaf clover. Ballantining keeps the line from fouling as the sail is doused or lowered.

Batten down the hatches: Secure a ship's hatch-tarpaulins, especially when rough weather is expected.

Beam reach: Also "reach." To sail across the wind, or with the wind abeam.

Bearing: The angle from the boat to an object.

Beating: Sailing close-hauled, or as close to the wind as is efficient.

Belaying pin: A wood pin used onboard ship to secure a line fastened around it.

Berth: A fixed bed or bunk on a ship, train, or other means of transport. Also, a ship's allotted place at a wharf or dock.

Bollard: A thick, low post, usually of iron or steel, mounted on a wharf or the like, to which mooring lines from vessels are attached.

Boom: The spar that extends and supports the foot of the sail.

Bow: The most forward part of the boat.

Bowsprit: Permanent spar attached to the bow, to which jib-stays and forestays are fastened.

Close-hauled: Sailing as close to the wind as is efficient; also beating or on the wind.

Come about: Also "tack." To bring the boat across the wind to a new heading.

Companionway: A set of steps leading from a ship's deck down to a cabin or lower deck.

Davits: Outboard rigging for raising and lowering the ship's yawl boat or dory.

Dory: A small multipurpose craft usually propelled by pulling (using oars) or sailing.

Downwind: Away from the direction from which the wind blows.

Foremast: On a schooner, the mast closer to the bow.

Foresail: The sail that is rigged on the foremast.

Furl: To roll or fold up and secure neatly, as a sail against a spar or a flag against its staff

Gaff: The spar that supports the top edge of a four-sided sail.

Gaff-rigged: A boat with four-sided sails rigged to gaffs.

Galley: A boat's kitchen.

Grabrail: A handrail running along the edge of the deckhouse or cabin top.

Gunwale (pronounced *gunnel*): A boat's rail at the edge of the deck.

Hatch: An opening in a deck, covered by a hatch cover.

Halyard: A line that hoists a sail and keeps it up.

Head: A boat's bathroom.

Heading: The course, or direction the boat is pointing.

Heaving line: A line thrown outboard to another vessel or to a person in the water.

Heel: The tilt or laying over of a boat caused by wind.

Helm: The tiller or steering wheel.

Hurricane hole: An area for safe anchorage, with good protection from the wind on as many sides as possible.

Jib: A sail carried on the headstay or forestay.

Jibe: To change tacks by heading off, or turning away from the wind, until the sails swing across the boat.

Knot: One nautical mile per hour.

Lace-lines: Also reefing lines. Used to secure a sail to the bowsprit or boom.

Lazarette: A small hold, usually in the stern, for stores and gear.

Lee deck: The side of the ship away from the wind.

Lee of the island: The side of the island sheltered from the wind.

Leeward: Away from the direction of the wind. Pronounced *lu-ard.*

Longboat: The longest boat carried by a sailing ship.

Luff: When a sailing vessel is steered far enough toward the direction of the wind, or the sheet controlling a sail is eased so far past optimal trim that airflow over the surfaces of the sail is disrupted and the sail begins to "flap" or "luff."

Make off or Make fast: To secure a line to a belaying pin or cleat.

Mainmast: Mast farthest aft on a schooner. Carries the mainsail.

Mainsail: The sail attached to the largest mast on the boat.

Mainsheet: The line that controls the mainsail.

Mayday: An international radio distress signal used by ships and aircraft.

Middle watch: 0000 – 0400, or 12:00 – 4:00 a.m.

Outboard: On, toward, or near the outside, especially of a ship.

Painter: The bow line on a dinghy.

Pan-Pan: Three calls of pan-pan in radiotelephone communications is used to signify that there is an urgency on board a boat, ship, aircraft, or other vehicle but that, for the time being at least, there is no immediate danger to anyone's life or to the vessel itself. This is referred to as a state of urgency.

Peak halyard: Raises the end of the gaff farthest from the mast.

PFDs: Personal flotation devices.

Pitch: Movement of the vessel on the athwartships axis, causing the bow and stern to rise and fall alternately.

Port: The left side of the ship when facing forward.

Port tack: Sailing to windward with the wind coming over the port side of the boat.

Quarter: The side of the boat near the stern.

Ratlines: System of tarred rungs used to climb to the top of the mast.

Reef: A part of a sail that is rolled and tied down to reduce the area exposed to the wind. Verb: to shorten (sail) by tying in one or more reefs.

Rode: The anchor line.

Running: Sailing with the wind astern.

Running rigging: The term for the rigging of a sailing vessel that is used for raising, lowering, and controlling the sails, as opposed to the standing rigging, which supports the mast and other spars.

Saloon: The main cabin on a ship.

Scandalize the forepeak: On a gaff-rigged vessel, lowering the peak of the sail to slow the vessel.

Schooner: A boat with two or more masts: the foremast or forewardmost mast is shorter that the mainmast.

Scuppers: Holes in the rail or gunwale that allow water drain-age.

Sea-kindly: A vessel's ability to move comfortably, or without undue strain, in rough seas.

Sea-worthy: A vessel able to survive heavy weather.

Sennit: Braided small stuff or cordage of many varieties. Used for everything from lanyards to chafing gear.

Sole: A cabin or cockpit floor.

Spindrift: The spray of salt water blown along the surface of the sea in heavy winds.

GLOSSARY

Starboard: The right side of the ship when facing forward.

Starboard tack: Sailing to windward with the wind coming over the starboard side of the boat.

Staysail: A small headsail set between the jib and the foremast.

Stem: The forward edge of the bow.

Stern: The aftmost part of the hull.

Storm jib: a small heavy jib for use in a high wind.

Thwarts: The seats in a dory or dinghy.

Upwind: Toward the wind.

Windlass: Winch used to raise a ship's anchor

Windward: Upwind.

Yaw: A side-to-side movement of the bow of the ship, usually in heavy seas.

Yawl boat: A small, powerful motorized boat used to push a motorless vessel.

Visit Jenifer LeClair's website at:

www.windjammermysteries.com